LAST CHANCE COWBOYS
THE
DRIFTER

ANNA SCHMIDT

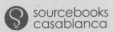

sourcebooks
casablanca

Published by Sourcebooks Casablanca, an imprint of Sourcebooks, Inc.
P.O. Box 4410, Naperville, Illinois 60567-4410
(630) 961-3900
Fax: (630) 961-2168
www.sourcebooks.com

Printed and bound in Canada.
MBP 10 9 8 7 6 5 4 3 2 1

For my father, who loved a good Western

first—in the distance, grazing on open land. There had to be a ranch somewhere around—maybe two or three smaller places. Plenty enough work to be had for a drifter who knew his way around a herd.

∽

Maria Porterfield had had almost no sleep and the last thing she needed was a confrontation with the ranch foreman. But like it or not, Roger Turnbull was striding toward her, and every muscle in his body told her he was not happy.

"Cyrus Cardwell said you went to the bank asking for a loan, Maria."

She took another sip of her coffee and gazed out at the horizon that marked the boundaries of the Clear Springs Ranch. "And just why would Mr. Cardwell be discussing my family's personal business with you, Roger?" Behind him, she saw a trio of hired hands who worked for her family pretending not to listen. She acknowledged them with a wave, which made Roger wheel around to face them.

"Go check on the horses," he ordered. "I'll be along directly."

When the men pushed themselves from the corral fence and sauntered away, Roger turned back to Maria. "I am trying to do my job."

"I fail to understand how the financial affairs of this ranch are part of your job."

"Maybe that was true before your father died and your brother took off, instead of staying and running this place like a man should. But things are different now. What do you expect?"

the instruction was not necessary. The brown-and-white collie, her fur matted with dirt and debris, had an instinct for knowing what Chet might need, especially now that the two of them had traveled halfway across the country with pretty much just each other for company. In a lot of ways, Chet felt as if he and the dog had melded into a single being. Cracker picked her way over the rutted path that ran parallel to the fence—a fence that appeared to stretch on all the way to the horizon.

Nope. No free range here.

He rode along the fence, studying the land on the other side. Now that he was level with the grass, he saw that it too was stunted and parched, but that was to be expected, given the heat and obvious lack of rain. At least here there was grass—not like the barren landscape he'd left behind in Texas. On the Tipton side of the barbed-wire barrier, he spotted some skeleton remains of steers left to rot, their bones bleached by the sun. Cracker saw them too and pressed her nose between the strands of wire, then let out a yelp.

"This way, Crack," Chet said as he turned his horse away from the fencing. By contrast, the land where he was riding showed signs of new growth in spite of the drought. Of course, he also had not seen any cattle on this side of the fence. But he figured that if the fence marked a boundary for the Tipton Brothers Company, then outside the fence must be land owned by some independent rancher or farmer—land that Tipton's owners had not yet swallowed up. Chet crossed a running creek and climbed back up to higher ground. As he followed the mesa, he spotted another herd—much smaller than the

The scene below looked about as close to paradise as he ever thought he'd see in this part of the country.

Maybe it was one of those mirages he'd heard about. From what he'd always figured, Arizona Territory was desert and rock with cactus plants tall as any man providing the only hints of green…and the only relief from the unrelenting sun that scorched the land from morning to evening. But here the white light of the noonday sun made the land stretch out flat, and the mountains in the distance jutted up from a purplish-blue haze. Beyond the river, he saw what looked like hundreds—no, more like thousands of cattle grazing. The herd stretched out for miles, and that could mean the work he needed to shore up his savings and eventually get him to California—not to mention the chance of a decent meal.

And if he couldn't find a likely ranch before sundown, the area below the mesa looked like it might be as good a place as any to set up camp. For one thing, he could bathe in the river that had more flow than any he'd seen in a while. It would feel mighty good to wash off the layers of dust and sweaty grime that clung to his clothes and skin. Cracker could take a bath as well and cool off some. But as he zigzagged his way along the terraces that led down to the valley and to what, from above, had seemed to be open land in all directions, he realized that the way to the river was blocked. Barbed-wire fencing stretched on as far as the eye could see with signs warning that the land was property of the Tipton Brothers Cattle and Land Company and there was to be No Trespassing.

"Come along, Cracker," he murmured, although

One

CHET HUNTER TUGGED ON HIS HORSE'S REINS AS HE paused on a flat mesa and studied the terrain below. His dog, Cracker, glanced up at him. Their journey had already taken them hundreds of miles from Florida, traveling across territory that was a far cry from the tropics they'd left behind. He eased a speck of the never-ending dust from his eye with the knuckles of one hand and surveyed his surroundings.

Below was a river, a cluster of trees—most likely cottonwoods—some scrubby mesquite, and miles of open grassland as far as he could see. The river was low, but that was the only clear evidence of the drought that had followed him from West Texas and into the semi-arid landscape of New Mexico and Arizona. For days, he'd picked his way through open range that had been overgrazed until the grass he'd been told could grow as high as seven feet was little more than stubble. He'd crossed dried-up creek beds and rivers with waters that barely reached his boot tips.

"I expect you to trust that I know what I'm doing."

Roger removed his hat and looked down at her with a glint in his eyes that told her he was about to try to sweet-talk her into seeing things his way. If she lived to be a hundred, she would never understand why men thought women couldn't see straight through such tactics.

"Now, Maria, everybody here knows that you are as good as any man when it comes to certain things, but—"

"My father taught me and my brother everything we needed to know to take over the running of this ranch, Roger. Jess isn't here, so it falls to me."

"But I am here, and with all you've got to worry about, taking care of your mama and sister and young Trey, letting me run the business end of things is exactly what your pa—"

She took a step closer to him, her chin jutted out in anger. "Do not presume to think you know what my father would want, Roger. You've made it clear you know nothing about him. He would *not* want to sell out to the Tiptons—as you have repeatedly urged me to do since the day he died."

Roger's eyes narrowed. "Well, if you keep borrowing money you can't repay, you won't have to sell, Maria. You'll lose this place for sure and not have a dime to show for it."

The fact that he had a point just infuriated her more. A big part of what kept her awake at night was worrying that she might make a mistake. Asking for a loan from the bank was just one example. "We need that money to see us through until we take the herd to market," she said.

"Face facts, Maria. The men haven't been paid in a couple of weeks, and I haven't taken anything for the last month."

"They have food and a roof over their heads, and are free to move on and seek work elsewhere—as are you," she blustered. "I understand the Tipton brothers are hiring."

The minute the words left her mouth, she knew she had gone too far. Roger Turnbull was a good man—a man her father had trusted. On top of that, she was well aware that he had feelings for her. She might not return those feelings, but she had certainly relied on Roger a good deal since her father's death. Perhaps too much. "Roger, I didn't mean—"

He slowly put on his hat and stepped away. "Guess if that's the way you feel, then I'm wasting my time staying. I'll be out of your hair in an hour." He turned and walked away.

"Roger, no." Panic filled her chest as she watched him just keep on walking. But she knew from experience that trying to argue further would do no good when his pride was stung. Maria turned away, frustrated. Now she was really in trouble. She was short of money and short of help. Maybe asking for the bank loan hadn't been a mistake, but losing Roger—and any of the hands who might defect with him—surely was.

She took a deep breath and let her eyes roam over the land—her family's land that stretched as far as she could see and beyond. She needed to get away from her own crushing worries for a time; she needed to ride.

She slapped her father's battered hat over her long braid and whistled for his favorite horse, Macho. Once the animal was saddled, she mounted and rode slowly out of the yard. But when she reached open land, she urged Macho to a full gallop, relishing the hot, dry air that stroked her face and the wild freedom of knowing that she could ride like this for an hour or more and still be on Porterfield land.

Roger, his cronies, even her own brother might desert her and her family, but with or without them, she would find a way.

❧

The sun was low on the horizon and streaking the sky with purples and oranges by the time Chet spotted a small house, a few rough but well-maintained outbuildings, and a thin stream of smoke from a cooking fire rising up toward the sky. The house—built in the Spanish style—was a low, rambling single-story structure with a tiled roof, adobe walls, and trees shading the courtyard that marked the entrance. In addition to the cluster of outbuildings, he noticed some fenced pastures. But this was fencing that was intended to divide the land into areas for dedicated use. It was fencing intended to keep animals in, not people out. He saw several dozen beef cattle grazing in the largest area and a smaller group of dairy cows in another. Beyond the house, he could see trees and a stream that was probably an offshoot of the river he'd seen on the Tipton property.

He watched as a couple of men rode slowly up the dirt road and on past the house, where they dismounted and unsaddled their horses before turning them loose in the corral. If he had to guess, these men were coming off the trail, where they'd probably spent twelve to fifteen hours circling the herd along with hands from other small ranches. Others would take the night shift. Suddenly, a third horse and rider galloped into the yard, stopping near the house. The rider slid down from the saddle and tossed the reins to a kid, then walked determinedly across the courtyard, headed for the house. He figured the rider was a woman by the way she moved and her size, although she was dressed like a man—trousers tucked into boots, a vest worn over a long-sleeved shirt, and a hat. She disappeared inside the house. Chet waited to see what might happen next, and a few minutes later, he heard the clang of a bell and several men emerged from a bunkhouse and ambled across the yard.

"Chow time," he said, and Cracker started down the almost nonexistent trail. Chet gave a whistle and the dog returned. "Not for us," Chet corrected. "Not yet." He leaned one elbow on the horn of his saddle and kept watching the activity below. He was dead tired and the thought of a home-cooked meal and maybe a chance to wash up had him staring so hard that his vision blurred, and once again he wondered if maybe the whole business was nothing more than some mirage. But he had heard the clang of the dinner bell, he saw the men making their way over to the court-yard, and he could practically *smell* the stew a short, squat woman was serving up. He was down to his last tin of beans—which he had saved for times when there were no jackrabbits or friendly prospectors. He needed a bath, a decent meal, and work—work that paid.

He'd left Florida in a hurry, but he'd been pretty sure that he could make it to Texas in time to hire on as an extra hand for the calving and branding season. Only, by the time he reached West Texas, he'd had to face facts. No one was hiring. The grasslands there were barren and the cattle that hadn't been moved farther west were scrawny and underfed. So he had pushed on. Somebody had told him about a big cattle company in Arizona that might be hiring—clearly the Tipton Brothers—so he'd kept on riding. Tomorrow he would see if he could find their offices. Based on the fencing and No Trespassing signs, he doubted the men who owned Tipton Brothers would be the sympathetic sort. But work was work, and given a chance, Chet could outwork the best cowhand anywhere.

Cracker barked, ran in a circle around Chet and his horse, and barked again. "Okay, Crack, let's go see if those folks will give us supper and maybe let us camp out in their barn for the night. If nothing else, they'll be able to give us directions." Chet straightened in the saddle and clicked his tongue to urge the horse forward.

&

"Rider coming, Miss Maria."

Maria stepped into the courtyard and followed ten-year-old Javier's pointing finger to the eastern horizon, where a lone rider sat motionless at the top of a rise before he slowly started down the trail, a mangy-looking dog leading the way. After the day she'd had, the last thing she needed was more trouble. But the man was taking his time, which could be a good thing. If he'd been riding hard, she would have steeled herself for yet another bit of bad news—and frankly, she had had about all the bad news she could take. She shaded her eyes even though her back was to the setting sun. The dog was probably a good sign. A man up to no good was unlikely to travel with a dog.

Just another cowboy, she decided. Probably from Texas, no doubt looking for work or a handout—maybe both. "Fix him a plate, Juanita, and send Javier to give him the food, give the dog a bone, and take his horse to the corral while he eats."

"You can't be feeding them all, Maria," the house-keeper who had worked for their family from the day Maria's parents arrived in the territory huffed. "Word will get out and you'll—"

"You know that Papa would never turn any of them away—not as long as he had something to share." This man was hardly the first to come to the Clear Springs Ranch, and he would not be the last. Times were hard, especially for those men who had worked the herds in Texas.

"Well, your papa is not here, *mi hija*, and—you'll not like me saying it—with that no-good brother of yours taking off for the city just when he's most needed and leaving you to try to run this place on your own…"

Maria kept her eyes on the rider, all the while trying to figure out why this one seemed different. She heard Juanita's tirade, agreed with some of it, and dismissed the rest. Certainly her brother, Jess, had stunned them all when he'd left for a life in the city after their father's death just six months earlier, but so far they had managed. "I'm hardly alone, Juanita."

"Oh, forgive me. I forgot that you have your mother, who has not been right in the head since your papa died. And then there's Master Trey, who always has his nose stuck in some book and doesn't know the first thing about running a ranch. And let's not forget Miss Amanda, who from the day she turned sixteen can't seem to pass a looking glass without stopping to stare at herself for…"

Maria smiled at the housekeeper, who was like a second mother to them all. "Yes, and besides Mama and my sister and at least one brother, there's you and Eduardo and—"

Juanita threw up her hands in a gesture of surrender. "Then we are going to need more stew if you insist on feedin' every stray that comes by. Rico," she shouted to her elder son who was leaning on the corral talking to two cowhands just back from riding the herd. "Make yourself useful for once and help me in the kitchen."

Maria turned her attention back to the rider, who was close enough now for her to see his features. He was tall in spite of the fact that his shoulders slumped with weariness. He—and the horse and dog—was covered in dust. His clothing was stained with sweat. He wore a soft-crowned, wide-brimmed hat different from the stiffer Stetsons preferred by Roger and the other hands. His hair skimmed the collar of his shirt—or what would have been the collar had the shirt had one. He wore dark trousers, chaps, and boots without spurs. His horse was a mare, larger than the quarter horses most ranch hands rode. The way the dog pranced around them made Maria smile. It was as if the dog refused to be defeated no matter how hungry or tired it might be. But as the rider came closer, the thing that caught her attention above anything else was that this cowboy did not have the traditional rope and lariat so common to men who worked cattle. This cowboy had a whip—coiled like a large snake—around the horn of his saddle.

Horse and rider ambled up to the filigreed iron fence leading into the courtyard. The man kept his eyes, which were shaded by the brim of his hat, on her. He did not appear to be in a hurry—or maybe the approach was calculated to keep her from running away. Did he think she was some skittish colt in need of taming? That was certainly how Roger and probably at least half the hands still working the ranch saw her. And it was certainly the way the other ranchers at the association meeting had treated her.

"Evening, ma'am." He removed his hat and ran his fingers through his hair to push it back from his face. His hair was thick and straight and black as her father's favorite quarter horse. His face was mostly covered by stubble, and his exposed forearms were brown like leather, the same as most men who worked outdoors for long hours…but there was a difference. There was a golden cast to his tanned complexion that made her think of sunshine. He was definitely not from this part of the country, and for the first time since Juanita's son had spotted him, Maria had doubts. Perhaps he had friends waiting. Gangs were not uncommon in the territory. And if word had spread that Roger had left… There hadn't been trouble in a while, but these were desperate times.

"Evenin'," she replied as she met his gaze and offered the knuckles of one hand for the dog to sniff. She was glad to see Juanita's husband, Eduardo, coming across the yard, and she knew Juanita was probably positioned just inside the kitchen door, her hand fairly twitching to grab the Parker twin-barrel shotgun they kept nearby. "Can I help you?"

"Well, yes, ma'am. I'm hoping you and the mister can spare a bite to eat for me and my horse and ol' Cracker there." He nodded toward the dog. "I could also use directions to the Tipton Brothers Cattle and Land Company."

All Maria's senses went on instant alert. Was this a trick? Was Roger testing her? Had he sent this man?

"You work for Tipton Brothers, amigo?" Eduardo scowled up at the stranger.

"Not yet. I'm just looking for work and heard they might be hiring." He gave Eduardo his full attention, apparently trying to decide if Juanita's husband was the owner of the ranch. "Truth is, I'd just as soon work on a spread like this one."

He spoke softly with a definite drawing out of his words—from the South if she had to guess. Could be another Texan, but his accent was different from the Texas men she'd met. This man's voice lacked the roughness. There was a gentleness to him—and yet by the look of him, he could handle himself in a fight. "We aren't hiring at the moment," she said. "Eduardo can show you where to rest your horse, and Javier will bring you out some supper and something for your dog."

"I'm most grateful, ma'am. Thank you." He replaced his hat as he turned his horse to follow Eduardo.

"Where are you from?" Maria asked, unable to contain her curiosity a minute longer.

"Florida, ma'am."

Eduardo let out a long, low whistle. "You are a long way from home, amigo."

Maria stood rooted to the spot as the two men started across the yard. Florida? Did the man know the first thing about herding and branding and such—even if she were of a mind to hire him? And what the devil was he doing so far from home?

As she headed into the kitchen, Juanita released the shotgun's dual hammers and put the weapon back in the corner before going to the stove to dish up a bowl of stew. "I suppose you want me to give him some biscuits and a slice of that apple pie as well?"

"That would be nice."

"Do you plan on letting him stay? You're short-handed now, I know, but even so…"

Maria was aware of Ricardo, now seated at the table chopping onions and listening intently to whatever she might say so he could carry the news back to the other hands. "I don't know, Nita. Like I said before, I'm not doing anything that Papa wouldn't do by feeding him."

"You are not your father, Maria."

"Have Javier take the man his food, all right?" Maria sat down in the nearest chair and rested her elbows on her knees. What would her father do? Would he give the man work? Probably. But she knew nothing about him.

You get a sense of people, Maria, her father had once told her. *You need to listen to that and act accordingly*.

She closed her eyes and thought about the man… and realized there had been no introductions. He had assumed she was married—that business about "you and the mister." She had liked the way he spoke—his voice deep, a little hoarse, probably from the dust of his journey, and yet soft-spoken in a way that let her know he was feeling his way and not taking anything for granted. She had also been impressed with the way he had shown respect to Eduardo. Roger would have dismissed the older man as not worth his time. This man was nothing like Roger. She was sure of that.

"Juanita?"

Juanita paused at the kitchen door, her weathered hands still cradling the bowl of stew, on top of which she'd stacked a biscuit and a saucer with a slab of pie. She looked back, one eyebrow arched.

"Now that Roger and… There's room in the bunkhouse. Have Javier tell the man he can stay the night but needs to be on his way at first light."

Juanita shooed Javier out of the way and started walking toward the bunkhouse carrying the steaming bowl. "I'll tell him," she announced. "Somebody needs to get a good, long look at this drifter." But by the way she trudged along, shaking her head the entire time, Maria had no doubt that the housekeeper had already made up her mind.

Maria glanced at Ricardo, who was watching his mother as well. "Well, Papa *would* have let him stay," she said defensively.

"Yes, Miss Maria." Ricardo returned to chopping onions, keeping whatever he might be thinking to himself, as usual.

Two

It came as no surprise to Chet that none of the other men talked to him as he sat on a rough wooden *banco* outside the bunkhouse eating his supper. A couple of them nodded as they finished their meal and passed him on their way into the bunkhouse. One of them held out his hand for Cracker to sniff, then scratched the dog's ears. Two of the men spoke Spanish to Eduardo and his son, Javier, who had taken Chet's mare to the corral, ruffling the boy's hair as they passed by. He wondered if it would surprise the men to know that he understood almost every word, even though they spoke a different version of the language than the men he'd worked with—men who had come to Florida from islands in the Caribbean while these men were from just across the border in Mexico. Chet smiled as he shoveled another spoon filled with a thick beef stew into his mouth and savored the wonderful mix of flavors that were a far cry from the canned beans and charred jackrabbit he'd existed on for weeks. At his feet, Cracker gnawed the marrow from a soup bone.

"Something funny, Cracker?"

A barrel-chested, bearded man who spoke English with a drawl that left no doubt he was from Texas ambled toward him. At first Chet thought the man was referring to his dog, but then he understood that the cowhand must have heard him tell the lady of the house he'd come from Florida. It was common among ranch hands to bestow nicknames on the new guys—Cookie and Red were fairly common. It was a mark of acceptance. But the way this man drew out the word told Chet that it was intended as a slur.

He set his plate on the bench and stood up, wiping a palm on his trousers before he extended it. "Name's Chet Hunter," he said.

The man ignored his outstretched hand and took a seat on the bench, setting Chet's unfinished supper on the floor. "From Florida, right?"

"That's right."

The man snorted and leaned against the bunkhouse wall. He folded his brawny arms across his chest and lowered the brim of his hat to cover his eyes.

Chet sat on the step and picked up his plate. "You got a name?" he asked.

"Yep."

Chet waited and, when he was sure the man did not intend to share any further information, added, "Good to know." He sopped up the last of the stew with the heel of bread, wolfed down the apple concoction, and then took the bowl, plate, tin cup of coffee, and spoon and headed for the house.

"Where do you think you're going?"

"To return these dishes and thank the lady of the

house for letting me stay the night." He glanced back. "That suit you?"

The cowboy grumbled something.

Chet kept walking past Eduardo and his friends. "I'll sleep in the barn with my horse," he said in Spanish. "Okay?" he added in English.

"*Sí*, amigo," Eduardo answered, exchanging a nervous look with his stunned friends.

"And the lady's name?" Chet nodded toward the house. "I want to thank her."

"Miss Maria," Eduardo replied. "I mean, Miss Porterfield."

That stopped Chet in his tracks. "She's not...I mean, there's no man who..."

"Senor Porterfield died a few months ago," Eduardo replied, removing his hat as a sign of his respect.

"Miss Porterfield's father?"

"*Sí*."

Having figured out that Eduardo was not the owner of the ranch, Chet had hoped by showing appreciation and respect for their supper and kindness, he might risk asking to speak to the man of the house about work. But a woman? "I could maybe speak to the foreman," he said, without realizing he had spoken aloud.

"Senor Turnbull left this morning—he quit."

"Yeah, him and Miss Maria got into it," the man from the bunkhouse said as he wandered over to join the conversation. "I expect he'll be back. He knows where his bread is buttered and with Jess gone..."

Chet glanced at Eduardo. "Her brother," Eduardo explained.

The woman who had brought Chet his supper

stalked across the yard. "You men are worse than a bunch of old hens gossiping this way. And you, Bunker, are worse than the rest put together," she told the big man. "Seems to me the lot of you have got evening chores that need tendin', so I would suggest you be gettin' to it."

Chet saw how quickly the men scattered, and it dawned on him that he probably needed to get on this woman's good side if he was going to have any chance of staying on for work. He handed her the dishes. "That was the best stew I've—"

"And there's no need for you to go trying to cozy up to anybody on this ranch. You can stay the night, but at dawn, if you know what's good for you, you'll be on your way."

"Yes, ma'am."

"Don't know what that girl was thinkin'," she mumbled to herself in Spanish. "Taking in strangers with all she's…" The rest was lost as she entered the courtyard.

∽

Once again, Maria could not seem to settle down for the night. "You're just overtired," her mother would have said with a knowing smile. Of course, that was when her mother had taken notice of anything her four children might be doing. These days Constance Porterfield was like a child herself. She either stayed curled in her bed for hours at a time or wandered through the house, her dressing gown hanging from her bony shoulders and skimming the tile floors.

Was that a voice? And had it come from inside or outside the house?

Maria sat up in bed, her senses on full alert. Her younger sister, Amanda, slept on the bed next to hers. A beam of weak light found its way under the closed door from Trey's room across the hall. No doubt her brother was reading. For the first several years of his young life, Trey had been ill and often confined to his room. In spite of that, he always seemed to look at adversity as a challenge to be overcome. Unable to run and play or learn the activities most children of ranchers were taught practically from the day they started to walk, Trey had focused his time on reading and drawing. Even though his health had improved over the last year or so, he still was rarely without a book or his sketch pad.

There it was again. Outside.

Perhaps it was the wind. All indicators were that there would be rain before dawn. She left her bed and curled onto the seat next to the window that overlooked the courtyard and the outbuildings beyond. The bunkhouse was dark, but there was a thin stream of light coming from the barn.

The drifter.

Eduardo had reported that the man had elected to sleep in the barn rather than the bunkhouse—something about not wanting to disturb the others if he decided to leave after just a couple hours sleep. She hadn't even gotten his name—just that he came from Florida. That seemed impossible. Florida was hundreds—maybe even thousands—of miles away. Of course, these days people seemed to think nothing of taking off for someplace they'd never been before and knew nothing about. Seemed downright foolish to her. On the other hand, knowing the man came from someplace so different explained a lot about the way he dressed and his accent and mannerisms. But it did not explain what he was doing so far from home.

He'd mentioned the Tipton Brothers Company, but how would he have heard of that all the way back in Florida? And even if he had, wasn't this an awfully long way to come for a job? These were all questions that she had overheard Juanita asking Eduardo. Obviously Juanita had decided the stranger was someone in need of watching. She'd even instructed Eduardo to make up some excuse for sleeping in the barn as well—with his pistol at the ready.

And of course, Eduardo had complied. It was the rare occasion when he dared to go against his wife's orders. So maybe Eduardo had left the lamp burning. But other than the light and the wind rustling through the cluster of paloverde trees that sheltered the courtyard, there was no sign of movement that Maria could see. The night riders would be out watching the herd grazing nearby while the others slept. With some of the problems she and the other small ranchers had experienced lately, they had agreed to keep their combined herd closer to one of their ranches. That way if trouble came, the night riders could sound the alarm and help would be close at hand. She'd followed that advice, but still she had an uneasy feeling.

"What are you doing up?" Amanda asked, her voice raspy with sleep.

"I thought I heard something." Maria moved back to her bed.

"Mama?"

Maria had been so engrossed in wondering if the stranger might be up to something that she hadn't thought about her mother. Constance Porterfield not only wandered through the rooms of the sprawling house during the day, but lately she had also developed the disturbing habit of wandering out into the night. The night before Roger quit, Constance Porterfield had been found in the family cemetery sound asleep, leaning against the marker for her husband's grave. "I hadn't thought of that," she admitted and once again shoved her bare feet into her slippers.

"I'll go," Amanda said wearily, padding barefoot across the room and leaving the door open as she went down the hall to their parents' bedroom. After only a moment, she was back. "Sleeping soundly," she reported. "And yes, I checked to be sure."

"It's probably just the wind and the storm coming," Maria said. "Let's get some sleep." Casting one last glance at the light from the barn, she returned to her bed and pulled the covers over her.

"What did you think of the drifter?" Amanda asked.

"I didn't. Now go to sleep."

"I did." Amanda giggled. "He's really good-looking. Don't you think? I mean, he's so nice and tall, and that hair and those eyes."

At sixteen, Amanda had taken to looking at every available male as a potential candidate for courtship. Exactly when her younger sister might have had the opportunity to observe the drifter's eyes was a mystery to Maria—one that promised to add to her trouble getting any sleep.

"What about his eyes?"

"They sparkle. Especially when he smiles."

"And just when did you have the occasion to observe his sparkling eyes and smile?"

There was a long silence.

"Amanda?"

"I was in the barn when he came over from the bunkhouse, all right? That's not exactly a crime, is it?"

"It depends. What did he do?"

"Oh, he was ever so polite—even a little shy. He took off his hat, introduced himself, and begged my pardon for startling me, and…"

"You know his name?"

"Chester Hunter, but he said he goes by Chet. I mean, is that not the most perfect name for him? Chet—strong but friendly-like."

Maria was well aware that she should have been reminding her sister of the dangers of becoming overly friendly with hired help—not that this Chet was, but still. On the other hand, she wanted to hear more. "And what did you do?"

"Introduced myself, of course. 'I am Amanda Porterfield,' I said, and then I told him he could call me *Manda*."

Maria could not help but laugh. "No one calls you that."

"Well, I think I might just insist that all of you do. It suits me. Amanda is far too formal." She pushed herself higher onto her pillows—a sure sign she was settling in for a long talk. "He asked me about you."

Outside the open window, the wind had picked up. A horse whinnied, and Maria heard the murmur of men's voices. As much as she wanted to pursue

Amanda's last comment, she chose instead to shush her sister and hurry back to the window. Eduardo and the drifter—Chet—were standing outside the barn. By their posture, Maria was sure they also had heard something amiss.

And then there was no more need to guess what that might be. The distant thunder of thousands of hooves told Maria exactly what had happened. Something or someone had spooked the cattle, and they were stampeding. Although the closest grazing fields were still some distance from the complex, there was no mistaking that sound. She could hear the night riders firing shots in the air to try to contain the herd. At the same time, the rest of the men came running from the bunkhouse. Their loyalty touched her, especially in light of the fact that they had not been paid in weeks and most of them had just come in off the trail and would need to be back out there in just a few hours. But she was even more impressed when she saw that the drifter did not hesitate to saddle his horse and take off after the others, his dog racing to keep up.

"Now what?" Amanda demanded. She seemed very close to tears. "Roger Turnbull is gone, and there's no one to take charge and Papa…" She burst into sobs.

Maria sat on her sister's bed and held her. "The men know what to do. It will be all right. Shhh."

"But this ranch was everything to Papa and now…"

"It's a stampede. We've been through them before, and this one is no different. Now pull yourself together, and go check on Mama and Trey while I get dressed." She was already reaching for her riding pants and pulling them on, stuffing her nightgown into them like an oversized shirt. "Toss me my boots," she said as Amanda headed for the hallway where Trey was just emerging from his room, a puzzled smile on his face.

"What's going on?"

"It's a stampede, dummy," Amanda barked as she flung Maria's boots across the room and hurried down the hall. "Put down that book for once and make yourself useful."

Maria shook her head as, from long-standing habit, she shook out each boot before tugging it on just in case a scorpion or some other critter had decided to take a nap. Amanda had always treated Trey as if he were the healthiest member of the family and more of a laggard than someone who had been seriously ill for much of his young life. Certain that Amanda would watch over Trey and their mother, she ran to the kitchen.

"And just where do you think you're going, young lady?" Juanita demanded, already at the stove preparing the coffee the men would need once they had things under control.

"To do what I can to help. Where's my blasted hat?"

"Do not use that language in my kitchen, Maria Porterfield. You may think you're one of the hired hands, but you are not. Do you understand me?"

"Yes, ma'am. Where is my hat?"

"I hid it." Her words were delivered with infuriating nonchalance.

"Why would you do that?"

"Because I had to think fast, and it was the only way I thought I might be able to stop you from going off half-cocked and getting yourself trampled to death." Juanita handed her a cold biscuit and a cup for the tea already steeping in a pot on the kitchen table. "There are experienced hands out there, so you just need to sit yourself down. We'll wait together for our boys to return. It'll be daylight soon enough."

Reluctantly seeing the wisdom in Juanita's words even if she was itching to get out there to help, Maria sat. And waited.

A few hours later, they heard the creaking wheels of the chuck wagon outside the kitchen door. Eduardo entered the kitchen, and both women straightened. "Well?" Juanita demanded.

"They got the herd turned in on itself. It slowed them down, but…"

"Any idea how many we lost?" Maria asked, resigned to the fact that in a stampede, the weaker and smaller animals were in as much danger of being trampled as any fence might be.

"We'll know more once it gets light out."

"What started it?"

"Aw, Miss Maria, you know it could have been anything. A cowhand striking a match is enough sometimes, and the herd was already restless with the coming storm and all."

"I suppose." She glanced outside, where the sky roiled with storm clouds but as of yet, not a drop of rain had fallen. "You don't think it might have been deliberate?" There had been more than one occasion when a rancher's refusal to sell to Tipton Brothers had been followed by a fire or a stampede or a tainted water supply just when the owners seemed most vulnerable. Maria didn't want to say aloud what she was thinking, but the fact was that for all his good qualities,

Roger had a temper, and he did not like being crossed. Might this be a warning he'd decided to send her to prove that he was right? "Eduardo, did any of the men say they saw—"

Eduardo shrugged. "Like I said, Miss Maria, there's no way of knowing for sure what started things going." He turned to his wife. "The boys said they would stay out there rounding up the strays and making sure the rest of the herd is all right. I just came back to get Javier and the wagon. They'll be needing breakfast," he added.

Juanita nodded and began packing food that her husband then loaded onto the wagon he'd brought to the kitchen door. Then she wrapped towels around the handles of two large coffee pots and handed them to him. "This should hold them until you get the fire going," she said.

Eduardo leaned in and kissed her cheek. "I'll send Rico back to help with the milking," he promised.

"Amanda, Trey, and I can handle that," Maria assured him. "Just let the men know how much I appreciate their quick action. That as much as anything probably saved everybody some loss."

"It was that Florida fella that made the difference. The night riders were having a devil of a time getting things calmed down. If it hadn't been for him…" He just shook his head, then flicked the reins to set the team in motion. "You shoulda seen the way he snapped that whip of his."

"Seems like that drifter might be good for something after all," Juanita said as she waved good-bye, then turned back to the kitchen.

Maria was surprised that Juanita would even consider this sudden change of heart. Most of the time,
once she made up her mind about a person, it took a
lot more than something like this to get her to switch
opinions. "Maybe I should offer him a job after all."

"Don't go getting all carried away, *mi hija.* My
guess is that Roger Turnbull and those others will be
back here wantin' their old jobs back once they see
that working for Tipton Brothers is no barn dance.
And then where will you be? You were the one all
worried about making the payroll."

Juanita was right, of course. On the other hand, if
Roger and the others did not return and if the drifter
was as good as Eduardo said, wouldn't she be foolish
to let him go?

❧

The rain started around six that morning, and it was
what Maria's father would have labeled a "right smart
gully washer," soaking the ground and filling the creek
in what seemed like no time at all. It was still coming
down when the men who'd been out the longest finally
came back to grab a couple hours' sleep. "Based on the
tally we did a couple of days ago, there's only three
more missing, Miss Maria," Bunker reported. He had
been on the night shift when the stampede started, and
now he stood under the overhang outside the kitchen
door, rainwater running off his hat and his beard soaked.
"I have to give the fella from Florida his due. He was
something to see the way he cracked that whip of his
and turned the herd." He stroked his beard, and his eyes
softened. "Sorry now that I was so hard on him earlier."

"Where is Mr. Hunter? I'd like to thank him."

"He took off once we'd calmed the herd and made the best count we could. Didn't say nothing—just waved his hat and started riding west like the very devil was after him."

Maria did not want to admit how disappointed she was. She'd spent some time thinking about him while she and Trey had milked the dairy cows, waiting for the men to return and report the damage. She'd thought about the way he'd spoken to her and Eduardo when he'd first arrived and about how he'd been credited with making a difference when it came to stopping the stampede...and mostly about how Amanda had described his eyes. *They sparkle.* She was more than a little annoyed at herself for wishing she could get a look at those eyes.

❧

Chet had gotten next to no sleep, and his eyes were bleary, making it hard to focus. He could see that it was raining in the distance—probably at the Porterfield ranch, but he was miles from there and the sky was clear. The dust that the wind was whipping up kept him from seeing more than a foot in front of his horse's nose, and the fact was that the missing cows were almost the same color as the landscape. According to Bunker's best guess, a steer and two calves were still missing. Bunker and the other hands seemed willing to accept the losses as normal, apparently satisfied that they had rounded up most of the herd and the damage was not too great. But Chet didn't like leaving even one animal behind. Not knowing their fate ate at him.

Cracker scouted ahead, then ran back, tail wagging. She knew the drill but not the territory, and she was being extra cautious. After an hour with no luck, Chet turned away from the river and the terrain changed from parched grassland to barren dry rock formations that jutted up out of the land as if they'd exploded. Chet thought he heard something, and Cracker turned and sniffed the air to their left.

There it was again. The bleating cry told Chet it was one of the calves, and he gently kneed his horse's sides, at the same time signaling Cracker to approach with caution. They wound their way around an out-cropping of jagged rocks and there stood the calf, none the worse for his adventure but obviously scared and confused. Chet loosed his rope from the back of his saddle and dismounted.

"Hey there, young man," he said, keeping his voice low and soft and forming his noose as he approached. The calf backed away and let out another loud bleat for help. "Your mama's probably back at the ranch by now. How 'bout we go find her?" He swung the rope once and let it fall right over the calf's head and neck. The calf startled and turned to run, but Cracker was right there. Chet hung on, planting his boot heels in the dirt. "Whoa there, my little friend."

It took less than five minutes for him to gain control of the calf and mount up again to continue the search. He doubted that the steer would go along as easily… if he even found it.

Another hour, then two. The sun had reached its peak, and Chet drained the last of his water. He hadn't bothered to refill it before turning away from the river.

In fact, he'd not filled it last night before turning in, distracted by the way the day had gone. He'd been more concentrated on brushing down his horse and ridding Cracker of the dust and dirt of their journey. Then he'd washed up and put on a clean shirt, thinking all the time about how he might best approach Maria Porterfield, who seemed—in spite of her gender and the fact that she couldn't be more than twenty, if that—to be in charge of the ranch.

He had to figure out the right way to speak to her so she might offer him a job. From the minute he'd stumbled across the fenced land of the Tipton Brothers Company, he'd begun to have his doubts about working for that outfit. He tended to be a live-and-let-live kind of guy. Judging by all that barbed wire, those who ran Tipton Brothers liked being in control. There would be a lot of rules and probably not much pay. Men who owned big companies like that could be pretty tightfisted when it came to sharing the profits. If he could work at a smaller spread like the Porterfield ranch, it would probably be a better fit.

Eduardo had come to the barn while Chet was washing up. Chet hadn't been fooled for one minute when the Mexican babbled on about needing to stay out there for the night. Something about a coyote coming after the chickens. Truth was that he was glad for the company. Eduardo seemed inclined to talk, and that suited Chet just fine. It had been Eduardo who had advised him to wait until morning before trying to talk to "Miss Maria."

"She's been having a pretty hard time of it these last few months. My Juanita says she hasn't even grieved properly for her papa."

Over the course of the evening, he'd learned all about Mr. Porterfield's tragic death, the fact that the eldest son had taken his inheritance out in cash and headed east, and the details of how the ranch's foreman had just that morning quit and left with three of the ranch's most experienced hands. What he hadn't been able to get Eduardo to talk about was the women of the house—especially the fair-haired beauty the men called *Miss Maria* in a tone that bordered on reverence. As he rode on, searching for the other missing animals, he realized that as much as he wanted to find out what had happened to those strays, he wanted more than anything to return them to *Miss Maria*. He wondered if that might even make her smile. She struck him as someone who did not smile nearly enough.

≪∽≫

It was late afternoon when Maria saw Roger Turnbull's mustang gallop into the courtyard. He slid from the saddle and ran toward her as if he had just discovered that the house was on fire and he was needed to rescue its occupants.

"Maria, are you all right? Is everyone all right?"

It occurred to Maria that there had been a time before her father died that he would never have been so familiar—Miss Maria, yes. Just Maria? Certainly not.

As she had feared, the rain had come and gone and done about as much good as someone spitting on a patch of dirt and hoping grass would grow. The ground was so hard packed that the rain had simply run off the surface. But at least when she'd gone to wash clothes, she'd been thankful to see that the stream that ran through their property had risen some. She continued to hang clothes on the line that stretched across the yard while she spoke to Roger around a wooden clothespin she held between her teeth—a clothespin that would bear the mark of those teeth. The minute she had seen him galloping up to the gate, she had bitten down hard.

"We are fine."

Roger tipped his hat back and surveyed the area. "How many did we lose?"

His proprietary tone was her breaking point. "We? We! You left yesterday if you recall, taking three of my men with you. Why do you care how many of the herd I lost?"

"Now, Maria, just calm down. I am here now and..."

Just then Maria became aware of a ruckus near the corral. "Well, will you look at that?" she heard Bunker bellow, followed by whistles and cheers from the other men.

"Who the devil is that?" Roger growled as he watched the drifter ride up to the corral leading a calf and a steer with another smaller calf draped across the saddle in front of him.

Maria slowly removed the clothespin from her mouth. With her eyes riveted on Chet Hunter as he and the other men carried the wounded calf out of the heat and into the barn, she started walking away from Roger.

"Maria? Who is that?" he demanded as he caught up to her, matching her stride for stride.

She smiled and said, "That is our new foreman."

Three

Roger let out a derisive laugh. "That cowboy? How do you know him?"

"I don't, but as you can see, he appears to have already earned the respect of the men. Where the others were satisfied with a loss of three animals—as you would have been, as you taught them to be—he did not give up. So in answer to your question about how many we lost, the answer is apparently not one single animal." Maria turned and strode away.

By the time she reached the barn, she heard Bunker saying, "I have to hand it to you, Florida, you did one fine job saving this little guy."

"Thank you for that, but could we get one thing straight? My name is either Chet or Hunter."

The circle of men froze. No one—not even Turnbull—crossed Bunker. But then Bunker let out a laugh and clapped the drifter on the back. "Got it," he said. "Tell you what. How about you teach me and the other boys here a little something about the way you use that whip, and we'll count you as one of us?"

Someone spotted Maria and nudged Bunker, and

the men fell silent as they whipped off their hats in a gesture of respect. Maria was well aware that while their deference was partly because she was their boss, more likely it was born of habit. Hired help had a long and unbreakable tradition of showing special respect for their boss's female family members. They might court the daughter of a neighboring rancher, but she knew that not a man among them would think of showing that kind of interest in either her or Amanda. *No man except Roger*, she thought. But then Roger did not consider himself one of the men. She walked directly to the drifter and looked up at him.

"Mr. Hunter, I would like to thank you. You certainly did not need to go out of your way to find these strays, but I am truly grateful that you did."

"You're welcome, ma'am."

He ducked his head, and with all the shadows in the barn, she could not see if Amanda's assessment of his eyes was correct. "I wonder if I might speak to you after you've finished here," she added.

"I expect these men know a good deal more than I do about how to save this little guy, ma'am." With his hat, he gestured toward the doors and waited for her to lead the way. The problem was that Roger was between them and the door, observing every move she made—as usual. So she turned in the opposite direction, moving deeper into the shadows. The drifter hesitated, then followed her, and thankfully the rest of the men turned their attention back to the injured calf, discussing treatments and whether or not the little guy would make it.

"I believe you mentioned that you are looking for work, Mr. Hunter?"

He was still holding his hat, and he cocked his head to one side as he looked down at her. "You don't call the others Mister. Why me?"

Rattled by his sudden switch in topic, Maria felt her cheeks flush and was glad for the protection of the shadows. From the corner of her eye, she saw that Roger had moved closer and was now standing on the edge of the circle of men, pretending to give his advice on the calf, but Maria was not fooled. She decided to ignore the stranger's question and get to the point.

"I would like to offer you the position of foreman for the Clear Springs Ranch, Mister…Chet."

"You're offering me work?"

"I am offering you the position of *foreman*."

He leaned against a stall and crossed his arms over his chest. "And if I say I don't want to be your foreman, what then?"

"Why would you turn me down?"

The late afternoon sun was coming in through gaps in the rafters, and the light settled on his face. He grinned, and the way that smile relaxed his features made her look away. Amanda was right—sparkling eyes or not, this was one good-looking cowboy.

"Because, Miss Porterfield, I don't want to be the boss of these men. Besides, they know what they need to do. They are all good at their jobs from what I've seen."

"But they need direction."

He uncrossed his arms and ran a hand through his thick hair. "Well now, from what I've been hearing, miss, that would be your job. You are in charge since your father died, right?" He glanced back toward the men—toward Roger. "On the other hand, maybe that guy has realized his mistake in leaving. Looks to me like he's gotten right back into that saddle."

He had a point. Roger was ordering the men around, raising his voice when they didn't react with the speed he expected. "Excuse me a moment, Chet." She headed back to where Roger stood over the calf. The other hands had scattered to do his bidding. "Exactly what do you think you're doing, Mr. Turnbull?"

"Taking charge. Looks to me like somebody needs to." This last he aimed directly at Chet.

"I am in charge," she said quietly. Behind her, she heard Chet clear his throat and had the oddest feeling that he was offering his support—or perhaps his admiration. Either way, that gave her the strength she needed to stand her ground. In spite of her uncertainty about how she was going to keep this place that had been her father's legacy from going bankrupt, like so many other small neighboring ranches already had, she would not back down.

Roger cupped her cheek, and behind her she heard the drifter take a step in their direction. "Just go, Roger," she said, lowering her voice so the others would not hear. Then she stepped away from him, breaking the contact. "You made your choice. Now please just go," she repeated and walked past him and out into the yard. She hoped that neither man was aware that her knees were shaking so badly that walking was a new adventure.

❧

She was quite a woman, this Maria Porterfield, Chet thought as he watched her walk across the yard and resume the task of hanging the wash. First she had stood up to him and then the guy who seemed to think his job as foreman carried with it certain side benefits when it came to his former boss's daughter. Now that the boss's daughter was in charge, that probably didn't sit well with a man like Turnbull. From what Chet had observed, this was a man who was used to having his way.

Turnbull was watching *him* now, sizing him up. Neither man moved. Neither man blinked. It was a contest to see who would speak first. As far as Chet was concerned, it was not worth his time to play this game. He was tired and hungry. He jammed his hat in place and walked past Turnbull, nodding once before continuing on his way. Once he reached the yard, he wondered if he ought not to just keep on walking.

His horse's reins were looped over the corral fence and Cracker was waiting, as always, for him to make a decision about what they would do next. That dog was the closest thing he had to a best friend, someone he could talk to and trust. Whatever decision he made, he had to do right by her. He had pretty much decided that whether he stayed or went, Cracker deserved her dinner and the horse could use a good brushing. He led the animal to one side of the stable. Some time later, he was just finishing the grooming when he turned to find Maria clutching a bundle of laundry she'd evidently collected from the clothesline. The setting sun was behind him, and he knew she was having trouble seeing him clearly.

"Something you need, ma'am?"

"I believe I offered you a position. I need your decision."

He swallowed, taking his time, hoping he wasn't about to make a big mistake. "I'll take the work—as a hand, not as your foreman."

"I don't understand why you wouldn't want to take a position that will pay more."

He thought about everything that Eduardo had told him the night before. "It's not my place to offer you advice, miss, but seems to me that Mr. Turnbull wants to come back. Don't you think it might work out better for you having him here than over working for the Tiptons?"

Her eyes narrowed as she studied him. "Mr. Turnbull is none of your business. The question is will you stay on."

He shrugged. "For a while."

"I need people I can depend on, Chet."

"Yes, ma'am."

She scowled up at him. "Does that mean I can trust you to be here when we need you?"

He allowed himself the pleasure of looking her over for a long moment. "Can't say, ma'am. Only you can decide if you trust me or not. It means I'll work hard for as long as I'm here." He realized he was wearing his hat and snatched it off his head. "I do thank you for the chance to work, Miss Porterfield. I won't let you down."

She studied him for a long moment, squinting up into his eyes as if trying to decide whether or not to believe him. Then she brushed past him on her way back to the house. "We'll see about that," she muttered.

❧

Amanda was waiting just inside the kitchen door when Maria finally made it to the house after what seemed like the longest walk in her life.

"They sparkle, don't they?" Amanda demanded. "Did I not tell you?" She sighed dramatically.

Juanita stood behind Trey, cutting the boy's hair while he, as usual, read a book. The housekeeper's snort said what she was thinking more clearly than any words: Maria's asking the cowboy to stay on might just have been a huge mistake. Amanda was an innocent when it came to men, and when their father had been alive, she had had little choice but to live by his strict rules of decorum. But now that he was dead and their mother was incapable of getting dressed by herself, the role of disciplinarian fell to Maria…along with everything else.

Trey was no problem. In fact, if anything, she worried about his social ineptitude, and it occurred to her that a soft-spoken sort like Chet Hunter might be a good influence on her younger brother. But it was equally clear that Amanda was in danger of thinking she was in love with the drifter.

"Is he staying? Nita said you were going to hire him."

"What I said, *chica*, is that your sister was going to let her temper get the best of her once Roger Turnbull showed up and started throwing his weight around like he'd never left." Juanita stared at Maria, raising one quizzical eyebrow. "Well? *Que, no?*"

Even Trey lowered his book as they all waited for Maria to admit the housekeeper was right—as usual.

"Mr. Hunter has agreed to stay on."

Amanda let out a squeal of delight while Juanita

turned away with a shake of her head and Trey went back to his book. "Well, we are shorthanded," Maria reminded Juanita defensively.

"You're the *jefe*," Juanita said, brushing the hair clippings from Trey's neck and shoulders.

And of course that was the problem. The last thing Maria wanted was to be the boss. What she really wanted was to be her father's daughter and see his eyes light up again with love and pride. What she really wanted was to sit with her mother late at night, sharing her dreams of a husband and family and hearing her mother assure her that someday...

"Well, the boss has had a long day," she said. "I'm going to lie down." She started up the two steps that led to the wing where their bedrooms were and hesitated. "Is Mama all right?"

"She hasn't left her room all day. Hasn't eaten anything either." Juanita sounded more worried than usual. "She'll eat for you, Maria."

Maria retraced her steps and waited while Juanita filled a plate and set it on a tray along with a pot of hot tea, a porcelain cup and saucer, a linen napkin, and a setting of Constance's good silver.

"Don't forget the bud vase," Amanda said as she plucked a single yellow and orange painted daisy from the bouquet on the kitchen table and stuck it in a crystal vase she grabbed from a shelf.

"Tell her we love her," Trey added.

Maria could not seem to swallow around the lump that had filled her throat. Sometimes she got so caught up in the expansion of her responsibilities that she forgot that she was not alone. Jess might have left, but

Amanda and Trey were still there, and their grief was no less than hers—different perhaps, but no less. Surely if they all worked together, they could bring their mother back to the world of the living.

She walked to the end of the hall and tapped on the door. "Mama?"

No response.

Balancing the tray in one hand, she turned the handle and pushed the door open. The room was dark, but she could see her mother sitting at the open window, the curtains billowing around her like a veil.

"Is your father back, Maria?"

"No, Mama. You should eat something."

"I'll wait for him."

This was the hardest part. Maria did not know what to do. Should she go along with her mother's fantasies or be brutally honest in her attempts to make her mother face reality? She didn't know. What would her father do? She didn't know.

"I think you should eat something. Nita says you haven't eaten all day."

"I was busy." She patted the space beside her on the chaise. "Come, sit with me and tell me about your day, Maria. We may as well wait together."

With the back of one hand, Maria brushed away a single tear that had escaped as she set down the tray. She poured her mother a cup of tea and handed it to her. "He would want you to eat," she said.

Her mother smiled and sipped the tea. "Oh, Maria, men always have to find a way to be in control. The secret is to let them believe that they are."

"Yes, Mama," she said. Maria sat down and

wrapped her arm around her mother's thin shoulders as together they looked out the window at the deserted yard below.

◦◦◦

Judging by the way the men included him in their conversation as they all sat outside the bunkhouse after supper, Chet was pretty sure he'd been given the stamp of approval.

"Hunt," Bunker muttered and nodded his head. The rest of the men glanced his way uneasily.

"Pardon?" Chet asked.

"Hunt—that'll be what we call you. It's your name, ain't it?"

"Hunter," Chet corrected.

Bunker shrugged. "Hunt—Hunter. It suits because you finished the hunt for the strays. Brought 'em back."

Chet heard the others murmur the nickname, trying it out, squinting at him to see if it fit, then nodding and grinning.

He glanced back at Bunker. "Well, it'll sure keep the distinction between me and my dog," he said.

"Cracker," Bunker announced to the others as if they didn't already know the border collie's name. "So we've got Hunt here and his trusty dog Cracker." Bunker stroked Cracker's neck. "And now that we've tended to that bit of business, I'm hitting the hay." He stood up, yawned loudly, and headed inside. Just before entering, he turned back. "Hunt!"

"That's me," Chet replied.

"You don't snore, do you?"

"Haven't had any complaints before."

"Good. Your bunk's right under mine, and I'm a light sleeper."

The others did not even attempt to disguise their snickers. A couple of men laughed out loud as they dumped the last of their coffee onto the dry ground and followed Bunker inside.

An hour later, Chet understood the men's humor. Above him, Bunker snored like a steam engine at full throttle. The others seemed to have grown used to the noise, but although Chet was exhausted, he could not get to sleep. His mind was cluttered with unfinished business. He'd agreed to stay on, but once he'd turned down the foreman's position, there had been no discussion of wages. A woman trying to run a ranch under the best of circumstances could be tricky. This woman—this slip of a girl—trying to run a ranch on the very border of a company determined to buy up as much land as possible could be a total disaster. According to the gossip he'd gotten during supper, Tipton Brothers had already bought up several other small ranches in the area. Those who refused to sell had been driven out by the combination of the ongoing drought and Tipton undercutting the going beef prices.

Nope, from where he sat, Maria Porterfield didn't stand a chance, and if that was the case, there was no reason for him to stay on. Maybe tomorrow he would go see her and let her know that it wasn't going to work out…

Between one thought and the other, exhaustion finally claimed him.

He was dreaming about her just before someone shook him awake. But his dream had had nothing to do with conducting business. In his dream, they had been dancing, and she had been wearing a lavender gown.

"Hunt? Wake up."

It was pitch-black outside. Eduardo was leaning over him, whispering as if he didn't want to wake anyone else.

"What's—"

"Shhh. Miss Maria needs your help."

Chet sat on the side of his bunk and reached for his boots. He shook first one and then the other and heard something scuttle across the floor. He saw a critter the size of the palmetto bug that might have been in his boot if this was Florida. But this was Arizona. Still, critters were critters. "What's going on?"

"The senora is missing. Miss Maria has gone out looking for her, but my wife Juanita is worried, so she sent me to look." Nothing about Eduardo's message made sense, but he followed the bow-legged Mexican out into the yard anyway. "I do not see so well in the dark anymore," Eduardo continued in a more normal tone as he led the way to the corral.

"Miss Porterfield's mother took a horse?" Chet asked.

Eduardo shrugged. "I don't think so. Usually she can be found in the cemetery." He gestured to a fenced area set some distance from the house. "But Miss Maria and I looked there already."

"Where is she now?"

"She went inside to change into her riding clothes. She told me to keep looking, but then I thought about the way you found those strays and…"

Cracker, who had reluctantly risen from her place on the floor next to Chet's cot and followed them out, perked up. The dog was uncanny when it came to sensing adventure.

"This woman is not a stray, Eduardo. How would I begin to know…" He glanced up at the sound of a door closing, then saw Maria striding toward them. She was dressed in canvas trousers, a shirt a couple of sizes too big for her, and boots.

"Did you find her?" This was directed to Eduardo. "Really, Mr. Hunter, you need not concern yourself with this. I—"

"I asked him to help," Eduardo admitted.

"Why? He doesn't even know Mama."

Chet cleared his throat. "Uh, folks, maybe we could settle my being here or not later. If Mrs. Porterfield is out there somewhere…"

"Let's go," Maria said and started for the corral.

"Have you checked down by the stream?" Chet asked, suddenly aware of the sound of moving water nearby. "I mean, how far could she have gotten?"

"You don't know my mother when she sets her mind on something," Maria replied. But then she paused and glanced toward the place in the darkness where the stream ran closest to the house. "Earlier she mentioned the picnic…" she whispered and took off at a run.

Chet didn't pause to ask questions but set out after her, surprised at how fast she could move. By the time they reached the bank of the water, he was breathing hard and she was stalking up and down, calling for her mother as if she'd just taken a leisurely stroll down to the water's edge.

"Mama?"

A branch cracked under Chet's boot, and Maria held up her hand, signaling him to stay where he was. Then he watched as she pulled off her boots and started to slowly wade into the water, looking downstream.

"Mama?" she said again, a child calling her parent.

He peered beyond her, knowing she had spotted something—someone. He caught a glimpse of white in the shadows and let his eyes adjust to the darkness until he'd located the older woman standing in the water farther downstream. He moved along the bank, taking care not to startle her as Maria moved forward with more difficulty over the slippery rocks that lined the shallows.

When he was nearly opposite Mrs. Porterfield, he saw a wide-brimmed man's hat on a fallen tree that jutted out over the water. It was the hat Maria had been wearing earlier, but Maria had not brought the hat—her mother had. Acting purely on instinct, he picked it up, attracting the woman's attention as he did. He froze. But instead of bolting as he had feared she might, she smiled and stretched out her hand to him. "The water is lovely, my darling."

He flicked a glance upstream to where Maria had stopped. She nodded and motioned him forward.

Mrs. Porterfield laughed—giggled really. "Don't be such a scaredy-cat, Isaac. The water is not even up to your knees. Come on. If you had let me teach you to swim when I taught the children…"

Not knowing what else to do, he jammed the hat onto his head and walked into the water.

"You're wearing your good boots," she chastised as he waded toward her. "Juanita will not be pleased."

She shook her finger at him, but he took some comfort in the fact that she was still smiling.

He caught hold of her hand. "And you are shivering," he said. "Why don't we go back to the house and Juanita can make you some tea?" Keeping hold of her hand, he moved slowly. To his surprise, she stepped closer to him and rested her head on his shoulder.

"Hot chocolate," she whispered. "With cinnamon. I know it's for special occasions but…"

He wrapped his arm around her back and lifted her from the water. Her nightgown was soaked and the sheer volume of fabric—not to mention the fact that his boots were half-filled with water—threatened to throw him off balance, but he made it to shore without mishap.

Now what?

He set the elder Porterfield woman on a flat rock while he pulled off his boots and dumped the water, all the while looking for Maria. Where was she? He scanned the creek, but there was no sign of her. Then he heard footsteps.

"Mama?" she called as if she had just arrived on the scene. "Oh, Mama, Eduardo has been looking for you." Sure enough, Eduardo stepped forward.

"I'm sure it's nothing, senora," he said, taking both her hands in his as he led her back toward the house. "You know how my Juanita can be…" Chet did not bother to listen to the rest of whatever tale he was telling. He pulled his boots back on and stood up. He handed Maria the hat. "I saw this on the bank."

"She thought you were my father," she said softly as she turned the hat around and around in her hands.

"This is his hat. She must have taken it from the hook in the kitchen, thinking he would want it. On the day before he died, they came here—just the two of them—at midnight for a picnic. They did that sometimes. They were so very much in love." This last was whispered, and he knew that if he could see her features, there would be tears. "Thank you," she managed and started the walk back to the house.

This time he caught up to her and fished out a cotton neckerchief worn thin from years of use and repeated washings. He'd stuffed it in his pocket earlier—a precaution against a repeat of last night's stampede and the need to protect his mouth and nose from the dust of rounding up the herd. He passed it to her. She dabbed at her eyes before handing it back to him.

"She misses him. It hasn't been that long since…"

To his shock, she suddenly broke into heart-rending sobs—sobs that shook her small frame until he feared she might actually collapse.

"Come over here," he instructed, guiding her to the nearest resting spot—a wobbly bench outside the barn. He gave her the kerchief again and then pumped the well to fill a dipper and brought it to her. "Take a sip," he said.

She grasped the dipper with both hands and gulped down the water, then spit half of it back up as a sob welled again.

"Easy there," he said and realized he was talking to her as if she were a colt he was trying to gentle. She took a steadier sip, then handed it back. "Is that better?" he asked.

She nodded and then stood and ran her hands down

the sides of her trousers to dry them. Sniffing back her tears, she stuck out her hand. "Thank you again, Mr. Hunter. I promise you that your job does not normally include rescuing members of my family."

He set aside the dipper and accepted her handshake. "The men have decided to call me Hunt. If you usually call them by their nicknames—Bunker and Rico and the rest—I thought maybe you ought to drop the Mister in favor of just Hunt."

She straightened to her full height—a good eight inches less than his six feet—and in spite of the shadows, he knew she was staring up at him. "Since I was a child, I have called the men by their given names. Rico is Ricardo. Juanita and Eduardo gave him my father's middle name. And Bunker is Seymour and—"

"Got it," Chet said, barely able to contain his smile upon learning Bunker's given name. "Well, then, I'm Chet—and what should I call you?"

She brushed past him. "Miss Maria will do nicely," she said as she headed back to the house without the slightest sign that only minutes earlier she had been close to a breakdown.

Four

MARIA WAS SURPRISED TO REALIZE THAT SHE HAD SLEPT late. When she woke, Amanda's bed was empty, the covers tossed aside and her nightgown wadded into a ball near her pillow. From outside, she heard Juanita barking out orders to Trey.

"I thought maybe the new hand was going to—" Trey protested.

"Well, you thought wrong," Juanita interrupted. "The new hand has other things to do, and now that you're feeling so good, young man, it's past the time that you start doing your part around here."

As Maria dressed quickly, she saw Chet walk out of the barn. He said something to Juanita and nodded toward Trey. Juanita threw up her hands and headed back across the yard toward the house. Maria lingered near the window, watching her brother and Chet walk back to the barn. Chet said something that made Trey laugh. The dog danced around both of them, nipping at Trey's heels, herding him along.

There was something about this cowhand from Florida, Maria thought as she dressed and made up both her bed and her sister's. It was something that both disturbed Maria and made her curious to know more about him. Was Florida really his home, or had he always drifted from place to place? Somehow that idea gave her more comfort than thinking he had traveled so far and perhaps left loved ones behind. After all, if he had made a habit of staying awhile and then moving on—if he was the restless sort—she could accept that. More than one of the hands her father had hired had stayed for a time and then vanished overnight. Her father had taught her to take such comings and goings in stride.

"Just have to figure nobody's here for the long haul except us," he'd told her. "And maybe Bunker," he'd added with a grin.

Chet Hunter also was not the first good-looking ranch hand to work for them. Roger Turnbull had turned more than a few female heads—including hers, once—at the picnics and dances that her parents and the neighboring ranches used as an excuse to visit. Roger was a man who took a good deal of pride in his looks. He chose his clothing carefully and kept his mustache precisely trimmed. Of course, she had been Amanda's age when Roger first came to work at the ranch—young and impressionable with no idea what her future might hold.

Amanda.

Maria drew in a deep breath. She needed to keep an eye on that. With her father gone and her mother incapable of mothering an idealistic girl, that task fell to her. *Or perhaps Nita.* She let out her breath on a whisper of hope. None of the Porterfield siblings had ever dared cross Juanita.

"Did you get things settled with Turnbull?" Juanita asked as soon as Maria entered the kitchen.

"I doubt he thinks anything is settled," she replied, pouring herself a cup of coffee. "But he quit as foreman, and if he thinks he can simply come riding back in here and—"

"That's exactly what he thinks," Juanita interrupted. "And you'd be wise not to forget that." She slammed a large lump of bread dough onto the wooden table and began kneading it, running her flat palms over the dough from front to back, then folding it over and repeating the process in time with her measured words. "If I were you, I would be talking to some of your pa's friends, getting their advice about hiring a new foreman."

"The new man will be foreman."

"The new man turned you down."

"He'll change his mind."

"That cowhand will be gone before the month's out, if you want my opinion. He's got that look about him."

"What look?"

Juanita shrugged. "Hunted…wounded…something that makes a man like him want to keep movin'."

Maria laughed. "You've barely shared half a dozen words with the man."

"When you get to be as old as I am, *mi hija*, you get a sense of things—of people. Mark my words, this man has something he's carrying around with him like an open sore."

Maria shook her head. Juanita was known for usually looking at the darker side of any situation. She said it helped prepare her for when the worst happened.

"Well, I do have a worry about the new man," she admitted. "And it has to do with Amanda."

"Wondered when it might strike you that she's gone all moon-eyed over this cowhand the same way you lost any good sense you had the first time Roger Turnbull showed up here."

So, Juanita had been thinking along the same lines as Maria. "Well then, will you help?"

"Help? How are you expectin' me to do anything?"

"She won't listen to me. In fact, if I try to say anything, she'll just dig in her heels. But you could—"

"I got enough to do around here without being you children's *mama*."

Maria stepped behind the older woman and wrapped her arms around Juanita's shoulders as she rested her cheek against the housekeeper's broad, solid back. "You're the only mother we've got right now," she said softly.

Juanita's hands stilled, buried in the soft dough. She heaved a long sigh. "She's going to come back to us, Maria. You just need to give her some time to work it all out in her head that he's gone for good."

"And in the meantime?"

Juanita chuckled. "In the meantime, I'll look out for your sister. You just keep your own distance from that drifter. Don't let the fact that he was able to round up those strays turn your head." She wagged her finger at Maria. "I'm warnin' you, Maria. That man's got trouble doggin' him, and the last thing we need around here is somebody else's misery."

"I know," Maria said softly.

"Knowin' and doin' is two different things."

"Just say you'll help me keep Amanda away from him."

Juanita cracked a half smile. "Oh, that can be arranged. I'll keep that *chica* so busy, the only thing she'll have on her mind is what time she can get clear of me and get some sleep." As if to prove her point, she went to the kitchen door and bellowed, "Amanda, I need help in here now. This bread is not gonna bake itself."

"Baking is Maria's—" Amanda complained as she strolled into the kitchen.

"Do not cross me, young lady. Maria's got her hands full trying to do your daddy's job. Now put on this apron and pay attention. You're so set on finding yourself a man to settle down with, high time you learned how to cook and bake."

Satisfied that Nita had Amanda in hand, Maria headed out to the yard—and ran straight into Roger Turnbull. He slapped his hat against his thigh to remove some of the dust from the ride he'd just taken from town—or, more likely, the Tipton place.

"Maria, we need to talk."

"We are talking."

"Privately. Can we go for a walk?" He glanced back toward the barn. Chet Hunter was showing Trey how to pitch hay to feed the dairy herd.

"If you wish to talk business, then…"

Roger scowled at her and then visibly calmed himself by taking a deep breath. "Maria, stop pretending that all there is between us is a job."

"Or more precisely, the abandonment of a job," she snapped. "Thanks to you, I am three men short, and I need to rework the schedule to cover that without driving more hands away by overworking them."

"I thought the new guy could handle the work of ten men with one hand tied behind his back," Roger muttered sarcastically.

"The new guy is unproven, and I have no way of knowing how long he will stay, so I am not counting on that. Now if you will excuse me."

He let her get a couple steps closer to the small outbuilding that housed her father's office before he said softly, "Isaac had plans for us, Maria. He hoped you and me would—"

She wheeled around. "Do not dare to invoke the name of my father in your attempt to wheedle your way back into my good graces or my life. And when was my father ever *Isaac* to you?"

He held up both hands in a gesture of surrender. "Sorry. That was unfair, but honest to Pete, woman, you make it hard for a guy to own up to making a mistake." His smile was calculated to win her forgiveness, and she had to admit that perhaps she wasn't being fair.

"Stop tryin' to flirt with me, Roger Turnbull." She couldn't help smiling though. Nor could she help thinking that this was a man she knew—had known for years, while Chet Hunter was...

Once again, she glanced back toward the barn. The drifter was nowhere in sight. He must have moved on to some other chore. Juanita was right. He would no doubt move on for good sooner rather than later. She turned back to Roger. "All right. I admit it. I could use your help."

He grinned and offered her his arm as they walked the rest of the way to her father's office. "I'll move my stuff back into the anteroom tonight."

❦

"You'd best watch your back, Hunt." Most of the other men were already sleeping when Bunker rolled over on his upper bunk and whispered the words in the dark.

"Go to sleep," Chet said. After being up half the night before and working all day, he was wiped out. It would be dawn before he knew it. At least he'd come up with a solution for Bunker's snoring. He'd picked up a glob of candle wax from a fat candle he'd seen resting on a shelf in the barn, rolled it between his thumb and forefinger to soften it, and divided it in half. He was just about to use them as earplugs when Bunker started in talking.

"You'd be smart to listen to me." Bunker was now leaning over the edge of his bunk, his whisper filled with urgency.

Chet rolled onto his back and stared at the dip the large man made in the straw mattress above him. "Listenin'."

"Okay." Bunker lowered his voice again. "Turnbull has charmed his way back into Miss Maria's good graces and that, my friend, is not good news for you."

"Because?"

"What, are you stupid or something? Turnbull thinks you've got eyes on Miss Maria. More to the point, he thinks she might have eyes on you. Turnbull don't like competition—not in his work and not with his woman."

The idea that Turnbull felt any claim to Maria irritated Chet. On the other hand, why should he care? He was just passing through. The best thing that could happen would be for him to stay clear of any personal involvement with the Porterfields. "I'm not a threat to Turnbull," he muttered.

"Not your decision," Bunker hissed. "Just watch yourself."

"Thanks for the warning," Chet said and rolled onto his side, facing away from Bunker. But the big man wasn't through talking.

"The boys and me will do what we can," he promised. "Just don't let yourself get in a situation where you and Turnbull are alone."

"Got it."

"And keep your distance from Miss Maria."

"Okay. Can we get some sleep now? It'll be sunup before we know it."

"Yeah. Sleep." Not fifteen seconds later, the air was filled with Bunker's snoring.

"Glad somebody's going to get some rest," Chet grumbled as he pressed the wax into his ears.

He'd finally managed to dose off when someone started shaking him. He must have overslept. "Hunt!"

"Right here." He rolled to a sitting position and reached for his boots. Through the small bunkhouse window, he saw that it was still pitch-black outside. "What time is it?"

Eduardo was standing by his bunk. "It's the senora," he whispered.

"What?" Chet remembered the earplugs and pulled them out.

"The senora is back at the stream, and Miss Maria can't get her to listen to reason and…"

Chet followed the man from the bunkhouse. "This habit she has of taking these midnight strolls must have happened before I got here," he said, unable to disguise his annoyance. "Who got her back to the house then?"

"Senor Turnbull, but—"

"Then go wake up Turnbull. I've got to relieve Happy in another couple of hours, and it'll take me near to an hour just to reach the herd. That leaves me less than—"

"Turnbull is already down there with Miss Maria, but Senora Porterfield knows him. Miss Maria sent me to get you."

They were making their way toward the water. "So she recognized Turnbull. What's the problem?"

Eduardo frowned. "The senora does not like him and is not pleased that he and Miss Maria are there together."

"Wait until your father hears about this, young lady." Mrs. Porterfield was standing on the shore shaking her finger at her daughter. "Sneaking around with this no-good... And you." She wheeled around to face Turnbull. "You may think you have my husband wrapped around your little finger, but when he finds out..."

Chet stepped into the clearing. "Is there a problem?" he asked, his eyes on Maria, who motioned him toward her mother, keeping one hand on Turnbull's arm to restrain him from interfering—as he seemed inclined to do.

"Of course there's a problem, Isaac. It's after midnight, and I came here and found these two—"

"Mother, Roger and I came to find you," Maria protested.

"Mrs. Porterfield..." Roger took a step toward her.

"You keep your distance, young man," the older woman warned. "Isaac, do something. You have spoiled this child rotten, and I frankly wash my hands of the entire matter."

And with that, she stalked up the path that led back to the house with Eduardo at her side. Maria watched them go and then let out a breath she seemed to have been holding. "Well, at least now she'll sleep," she said wearily. "Thank you, Chet, for your help. It would appear that Mother continues to believe that you are my father and that calms her."

Roger snorted. "You call that calm? She nearly took my head off." He focused on Chet for the first time. "You can go now."

Chet ignored him and turned his attention to Maria. "Will she be okay? Because I'm scheduled to take the early shift out on the range and—"

Maria placed her hand on his bare forearm. "She'll be fine now. I really appreciate that you... That she..." Tears glistened in her eyes.

Roger stepped forward and wrapped his arm around her, dismissing Chet with a scowl that needed no words. "Come, Maria, you're overwrought. Tomorrow, I'll send for the doctor, and he can advise us on the best way to handle your—"

Maria pulled free of him and glared up at the man. "Don't you dare finish that sentence, Roger Turnbull. That woman is my mother—not some wild horse in need of 'handling.' She needs time, is all, and patience, and if you are unwilling..."

As Chet made his way back to the bunkhouse, he couldn't help but smile. Despite whatever Roger Turnbull

hoped, it was pretty clear to him that Maria Porterfield—
and her mother—could take care of themselves.

༄

Weeks passed without any more late-night calls to
rescue Mrs. Porterfield. Chet settled into the routine
of the ranch, taking his turn keeping watch on the
herd, handling chores, and when he was off for a
night, he spent the hours between supper and bedtime
with the other cowhands in the bunkhouse playing
cards or sitting outside trying to catch a breeze. Talk
now had turned to the ongoing drought and just
when the rains might come—if they would come.
Every night before turning in, Bunker drew a large
X through the date on the calendar and announced,
"Maybe tomorrow, gents."

But the cloudless sky and the relentless heat gave
no sign of relief. Other than that little rain they'd had
the morning after the herd was spooked, every day had
been the same. They were more than halfway through
June, and according to Bunker and the others, none of
them could recall a season when the rain came so late.

Riding the range was solitary work. Sure there
were other men around—maybe a dozen or more.
But with a herd the size of the combined stock of four
ranches, even a dozen men were spread too far apart to
do more than communicate with a whistle, a shout, a
wave of a hat, or in the case of an emergency, a gunshot fired in the air. Chet had learned to use the long
hours spent alone in the saddle in ways that passed the
time without jeopardizing the work. Sometimes he
worked out little songs in his head—silly little ditties

about his surroundings or a calf who refused to go along with the herd. Sometimes he thought about the people he'd left behind in Florida—friends he missed, family he might never see again. Sometimes he wrote letters to his sister, Kate—his only close family—who lived with their aunt and uncle. Often he carried on a conversation with Cracker, and all the while he kept watch, his senses on alert for some sound, scent, or movement that seemed misplaced.

He chose to ride his own horse when he could but was equally at home on any one of the ranch's quarter horses. Usually he left the reins slack, looped around the horn of his saddle, his hands free to write his letter or lines of a song or devour an apple or piece of jerky he'd brought along. Chet didn't smoke or chew tobacco—never could understand the attraction of either one. Besides he was saving his money—what little there was of it. He had plans. They were little more than dreams now, but some day...

Cracker let out a short bark and sniffed the air to the east. Chet pocketed his paper and stub of a pencil and shifted in the saddle to watch the horizon behind him. As he did, he scanned the herd—saw the other hands going about their business, saw a whisper of smoke rising from the cook wagon Eduardo had set up in a grove of trees near the river—and decided to wait and see what was coming before raising a false alarm. He watched a puff of dust blossom and then settle as the lone rider became fully visible. Instantly he knew the rider was Maria. How he knew that he couldn't say, but he had the oddest sensation of pleasure at the sight of her. He shook off that feeling. He'd gotten himself mixed up with a woman before. It was the main reason he'd left Florida. "Leave the ladies to someone else, Hunter," he muttered, but Cracker continued to stand at attention, tail wagging and eyes riveted on Maria's horse.

Chet couldn't seem to help himself, and he too watched as Maria rode up to the cook wagon, slid off her horse, and spoke with Eduardo for several minutes. He saw her scan the range, then remount and head toward the cowboy positioned closest to the cook wagon. Rico raised his hat in greeting as Maria reined up beside him. He and Chet had teamed up—one on either side of this section of the herd, Chet riding the Tipton fence line while Rico took the other side. Other pairs of cowboys from the other ranches had taken up similar positions until the entire area was patrolled. At this point, the stock from several smaller ranches was mixed in together, but Chet knew that by week's end, they would need to start the process of separating out the Porterfield stock that still needed branding.

He watched the exchange of conversation between Rico and Maria, although he could hear nothing. They spoke for several minutes. Apparently she was able to get more conversation out of the young man than any hand—even Bunker—could spark when the men were all together in the bunkhouse. Rico was a couple years younger than the next youngest hand, and Chet remembered how that felt. He expected that the others had played some nasty tricks on the kid when he first joined their ranks, in spite of the fact that he was the son of the Porterfields' housekeeper. And from what he'd observed of the young man, he doubted Rico had seen the humor in those tricks—or realized that they were the men's way of saying he was accepted as one of them.

Still, even though Chet could not hear the conversation, there were signs that Maria had a talent for drawing the boy out—even making him laugh. After a while, she turned her horse's head and rode on, waving to Rico as she left.

He realized that she was coming toward him, slowly weaving her way through the herd as she came. The closer she got, the more nervous Chet was. What was she doing out here? Where was Turnbull? As Bunker had reported, the foreman had once again taken up residence—not in the bunkhouse but in an anteroom just off the kitchen of the main house. Aside from Bunker's warning to stay clear of the man, there had been gossip in the bunkhouse that Turnbull considered Maria his woman…although from the little Chet had seen of the two of them together, that feeling was pretty much one-sided. It was pretty clear to him that Maria was the kind of woman who did not see herself as property. He'd also noticed that she seemed pretty good at handling herself, so it was nothing that Chet needed to get mixed up in. But he also figured that staying on Turnbull's good side was just common sense if a man wanted to keep on working at the Clear Springs Ranch.

But shouldn't it be Turnbull out here checking on things, getting reports, and giving orders? Why was Maria out here without him? Why was she out here at all?

Cracker ran a few steps forward, then returned and

looked up at Chet. "Yeah, I see her." Should he ride over and meet her? Should he wait? Cracker took matters in hand by running to meet the approaching horse—a black quarter horse that the men had told him had been her father's—and then racing back to Chet, tail wagging. "He's not your type," Chet muttered. He pointed down at Cracker. "Dog." And then at the horse coming their way. "Horse. Figure it out."

He felt the heat of embarrassment rise on the back of his neck when he saw Maria smile as she came alongside him. No doubt she had heard him talking to his dog.

"Hello, Chet. Cracker."

"Miss Maria." Chet touched two fingers to the brim of his hat. "You're a long way from home," he added before he could censor himself.

She laughed. "This is home." She swept her hand to encompass the range as far as they could see. She sat back in her saddle—as comfortable as any man—and took in her surroundings. And as she did, Chet took the opportunity to study her. He'd acknowledged her beauty that first day he'd ridden up to the adobe house, but now that he knew her, he could see a calmness and contentment that held no trace of arrogance or vanity. A half smile curved the corners of her mouth—full lips that a man had to practically drag his eyes away from to tamp down thoughts of how it might be to hold her, kiss her...

"I spoke with the other ranchers, and we've decided that tomorrow, we'll need to move the herd to higher ground," she said without looking at him. She continued to stare out over the land and speak more to herself than to him. "Roger says it's too soon, but Papa always believed…" Her voice trailed off.

"You want to make sure the land doesn't get over-grazed, that it has a chance to recover some."

She looked at him. "Exactly. Papa always said that we have to learn the lessons nature gives us, and after what happened in Texas… Well, the same thing could happen here as well. Roger says—"

"Begging your pardon, Miss Maria, but it seems to me that your father taught you well. I'd be inclined to stick with his advice if I were you—and the advice of your neighbors."

She squinted at him as if trying to figure him out. "You don't like Roger, do you?"

"I don't know the man well enough to form an opinion. What I'm saying is that your father knew this land better than any man currently working your ranch. For that reason alone, I would think first about what he might say or do."

"Roger does not like you."

"Well, now that's a shame since he doesn't know me any better than I know him, and by some people's judgment, I'm a pretty likeable guy." He grinned at her, wanting to lighten the mood and move away from any further discussion of Turnbull.

She laughed. It bubbled up from someplace deep inside her as if it had been kept under control far too long. "Not exactly the self-deprecating type, are you?"

"Here's the thing, Miss Maria—if I knew what that fifty-cent word meant, I just might have to agree with you. But since I don't know whether you've insulted me or paid me a compliment, I'll just keep quiet." He was teasing her and acting like they'd known each other for some time. He thought she might take offense, but she didn't. In fact she smiled at him.

"Fair enough." She took up her reins and turned the horse toward the camp, but just before she rode off, she looked back at him and added, "The fact is, Chet Hunter, *I* like you. I'm not sure I can trust you to stick around for as long as I'm going to need help, but I like you."

"Now that's a straight-up compliment," he replied and tipped his hat to her again.

She turned fully in the saddle to look back at him, any trace of lightheartedness gone. "Yes, it is. Don't disappoint me, Chet. I've had about all the disappointment I can handle for a while."

He watched her knee her horse and ride fast toward the cook wagon where Chet could see the night riders finishing their food before taking up their posts to relieve the day shift overseeing the herd. She'd asked him not to disappoint her. But in the end, he knew he would because she would want him to stay…and if he was going to realize his dream, he would have to go.

What had she been thinking? *I like you?* That sounded like something her sixteen-year-old sister might blurt out. She was a grown woman and the head of this family now. These men worked for her. *That* man worked for her. "Oh, Papa, this is so much harder than you made it seem," she muttered as, instead of stopping, she waved to the men around the chuck wagon and turned her horse for home.

Her mother and Juanita were sitting in the court-yard when she arrived as the sun set, the shadows of dusk settling in. Trey was there as well, sketching them. Amanda was no doubt in her room, where she spent every spare minute trying new styles for her long strawberry-blond hair or experimenting with the rouge and powders she wasn't supposed to wear. Maria waved as she rode past the house to the corral. She was pulling off Macho's saddle when she saw Roger come striding out of the barn toward her.

"Where were you?" he demanded.

"I went out to check the herd." She certainly did not owe him an explanation, so why was she giving him one? "I wanted to let Ricardo and the others know we've decided that it's best to move to higher ground. The north slopes will provide more relief from the heat and better grazing until we get rain." She swung the saddle around and rested it on the fence, then faced Roger. "It's the right decision, Roger. Grass in that area is already patchy. Besides, moving them north gets them farther away from the Tipton boundary."

"You could have told them all that here at the ranch."

"I like being out there. It makes me feel…I don't know, like maybe I can do this."

"You're the boss," Roger muttered without looking at her.

"For now, yes I am, and I am doing the best I can, Roger."

"I just don't get why you think you have to do it alone."

"I don't. I'm not. This was a group decision made

at the cattlemen's association meeting the other day. Besides, in addition to our good neighbors, I have Nita and Eduardo and you and—"

"The drifter?"

"I was going to say the men."

"But you seem to want his opinion over the others."

She was incredulous at the assumptions he was making without the slimmest bit of proof. "Roger, stop this. Chet Hunter is no threat to you. He has proven himself to be a good worker, and right now, we need good workers. We are shorthanded," she reminded him.

"I came back," he fumed.

"That you did, but where were you this morning?"

"I had to go into town—some unfinished business. I'm back to stay, Maria."

"But the men who left with you are not. We are still short of a full group, and there's the rest of the branding to be done, and then we have to move the herd to market—" She stopped. She understood that Roger needed a gesture, some assurance that she trusted him and had accepted him back into the fold. Recalling what Chet had said about it maybe being better to have Roger on her ranch instead of working for the Tiptons, she pulled off her riding gloves and placed her hand on his forearm. "Roger, don't fight me on this. I need you."

"And Hunter?"

She sighed. Experience had taught her that Roger was a jealous man, perceiving every new man as a potential threat. "The men have accepted him. Why can't you?"

"Maybe it's because I know that any man who is that far from home with no sign of having a plan is a man with something to hide. He's trouble, Maria, and even your father would have doubts about such a man."

He was right. For all his generosity and kindness to men like Chet, by now her father would have expected to know a good deal more, and he certainly never would have offered a complete stranger the foreman's job. Nor would he have allowed such a man to witness firsthand his wife's fragile state, as Chet already had twice. But something about this particular drifter told Maria that whatever his past, whatever his secret might be, it had nothing to do with his ability to do the job. "He's a good hand, Roger, and right now, I can't afford to let that pass."

"Suit yourself, Maria. Just be prepared to wake up one morning and find him long gone, and maybe your best horse with him." He started to walk away but stopped, not looking back at her. "I need to know, Maria. Who's in charge?"

She knew what he was asking. She also knew that it would be a mistake to choose. "I am. Tomorrow we move the herd."

Five

"TURNBULL'S HAD ANOTHER RUN-IN WITH MISS Maria—best stay clear," Bunker warned all the men that evening. "You especially, Hunt. That man is a powder keg sitting next to a campfire if you ask me. Real strange the way he keeps taking off for town, and the way he just hightailed it out of here that morning a couple weeks ago and then came crawling back."

"Got no plans to be in his company unless it can't be helped. You gonna deal those cards or sit there shuffling them till they give you the hand you need?"

"Just keep on acting like you don't understand a fair warning, Hunt. You don't know this man and you do not want to cross him." Bunker started doling out the cards. A few of the other men—including Rico—nodded.

"Got no reason to know him or cross him. On the other hand, if he's got some bone to pick with me, I expect sooner or later, we're gonna need to have a conversation." Chet discarded a couple of cards and waited for Bunker to replace them. "What is it you think he wants?"

"He wants you gone," Happy muttered, pushing three matchsticks into the pile in the center of the table.

Chet smiled as he waited for the rest of the group to place their bets or fold and then laid out his hand—three tens. "Then he's got nothin' to worry about."

"You figuring on leavin' us already?" Bunker thundered, slamming his cards on the table as Chet collected his matchsticks.

"Didn't say nothin' about when."

"Miss Maria's not goin' to like that," a small, bow-legged man called Joker said, shaking his head as he stood up and stretched. "She's not goin' to like that one little bit."

Chet noticed that all the men agreed, and yet at the same time he realized they all understood. Life as a ranch hand was like that. A man stayed awhile—a good long while if he was lucky—but most moved on eventually. These men would not blame Chet. Still, he felt he owed them an explanation. "I'm heading for California," he said. "Hope to buy a little place there and settle down. From what I hear, it's a lot like Florida. I might grow me some oranges and strawberries and…"

As he shared his hope for the future, around the table, he saw the men nod. They understood a dream like his. At one time or another, every one of them had probably had the same dream. No doubt one or two of them still hoped the day might come when they'd have that place of their own.

⁓

After weeks of riding the range, it hadn't taken long for Chet to form an opinion of the Tipton Brothers outfit. With their land surrounding the smaller ranches—at least the ones they hadn't been able to buy—it was not unusual for him to pass one of their hands working the other side of the fence. Now, as he passed close to the fence separating the properties, he acknowledged the other man's presence with a nod. The Tipton man scowled at him and then turned his horse and galloped off. Half an hour later, he was back with another man who looked as if he'd just as soon shoot a man as look at him.

"You there," the second man shouted, and Chet turned in the saddle to look back at him. "You're riding awfully close to private property, cowboy." The Tipton man came alongside him now with only the fence between them.

"Well now, the way I see it, you and your friend there are riding just a close to this private property," Chet replied.

"A smart aleck," the larger man sneered.

"Nope. Just making an observation."

"Well, here's an ob-ser-VA-tion for you, cowboy: Stay well away from this boundary, got it?"

"Or?"

"Or you might just find yourself in trouble." He tipped his hat back and spit as he scanned the territory surrounding them. "Yup, could take days for somebody to find a man in trouble out here—ain't that the truth, Shorty?"

"Be a gol-darned shame," Shorty replied, but he was grinning up at his partner.

"Is that why you rode off like something was chasing you to get your friend here, Shorty?" Chet saw the man go for his pistol, but he was quicker, having wrapped his hand around the butt of his whip and released it from the saddle horn. The crack of the whip startled the men and their horses. The horses bucked against their reins, and once the men let the reins go slack, the horses took off with their riders flailing wildly as they tried to regain control. "Nice talkin' to you," Chet called out, and he couldn't help but grin as he watched the Tipton men ride away.

That night, when he relayed the story in the bunkhouse, the other men did not laugh as he would have expected. They just kept playing cards, glancing nervously at each other. As usual, it was Bunker who finally spoke up. "You got a death wish, Hunt? 'Cause unless you do, you'd best watch yourself out there. Those boys mean what they say. You don't want to be stirring them up none."

Chet frowned as he studied his cards. "You're sayin' this was nothing new?"

There were snorts of disbelief from the other men. "You cannot be that dumb," Joker said. "Tipton's men would not think twice about shooting you and claiming you was trying to steal their stock."

"And what happens if they steal from Miss Maria or her neighbors?"

Once again the room went absolutely still.

"It wouldn't be the first time," Rico muttered as he discarded a single card.

"Back before Miss Maria's father died?" Chet asked, tossing Rico another card.

"And since," the older hand said. "She don't know it though."

"Is it a good idea to keep such information from her?" Chet asked.

Joker shrugged. "There's a lot that Miss Maria and her family don't know." He paused and glanced around, then leaned in as if about to share a secret. "Thing is, there's a lot more going on here than most know for sure. You're a stranger here, and maybe you can get closer to the whole mess without raising suspicion, the way I can't. Look, we've been keeping our traps closed because of—"

Bunker cleared his throat loudly, interrupting whatever Joker had been about to say just as Turnbull walked in.

"Because of what, Joker?" the foreman asked in a voice that was far too quiet to be friendly.

Joker gave him a nervous grin, immediately pulling back. He almost looked scared. "Because we didn't want her getting upset after losin' her pa and all, ain't that right, boss?"

"That's exactly right." Turnbull focused his attention on Chet. "Got any more questions?"

"Not right now."

"Good." Turnbull pulled a three-legged stool up to the table. "How about dealing me in then?"

The next morning, as they got ready to ride out for their shift, Chet noticed Joker was missing.

"He left," Bunker said.

"On his own?"

"Stay out of it, Hunt," Bunker advised. He jerked his head toward the house. Turnbull was talking to Maria—or rather, she was talking to him, gesturing toward the corral before planting her hands on her hips and apparently waiting for Turnbull to speak. Instead the foreman shrugged and strode toward them.

"Mount up and get going," he bellowed as he snatched the reins for his horse from Eduardo's hands, mounted the animal, and dug in his spurs, sending the horse galloping off toward town while the rest of the men headed in the opposite direction.

"Chet!"

All the men turned to glance back at Maria. Chet waved them on before turning back toward the house. "Something you need, Miss Maria?" he asked.

She shot a look at the dust Turnbull was leaving in his wake and then looked back at Chet. "What happened with Joker?" she asked. It was a question that Chet was fairly certain she had just asked Turnbull. He didn't like being put on the spot, and he definitely didn't want any part of saying something that might make Turnbull more determined than ever to have him gone.

So he shrugged and, not wanting to meet her gaze, stared at a point on the horizon where he could see the other men winding their way along the trail. "You know how it is, Miss Maria. A man gets an itch to move on and then up and goes without a word."

"Did something happen with Roger?" she pressed.

"Maybe that's a talk you'd best have with Turnbull."

"I did. Now I'm having that conversation with you. I just learned that yet another of my hands has left the ranch. I'm not sure what's going on here, but I do know that we can't handle getting stock to market unless we have the men to drive them. Now for the last time, Chet, what happened to Joker—because that man was devoted to my father and would never have left unless—"

"Begging your pardon, Miss Maria, but Joker might not be as devoted to you as he was to your pa."

She bristled. Chet couldn't help thinking that if she had a porcupine's quills, they would be splayed out, ready to take on all challengers. He fought back a smile at the thought. It wouldn't do for her to think he might be smiling at her expense.

She narrowed her eyes, studying him closely. "Are you suggesting that these men are leaving the ranch because of me?"

"No. I'm just speculatin' about Joker, but I do know one thing, Miss Maria."

"And what is that?"

"I know it's a fact that you're shorthanded and yet you're keeping me here jawin' instead of letting me go out there where I'm needed."

She bit her lower lip and stared out over the land that surrounded them. "I just want to know what happened."

"And what good would that do you? Joker has gone. What does it matter why?"

She opened and closed her mouth a couple of times, starting to say something, then rejecting each idea. "Oh, go do your job," she finally said with a dismissive wave of her hand. She turned away from him, but he saw that her fists were clinched. Chet figured that was about as close as she would ever come to admitting that he'd been right—that whatever had driven Joker away didn't much matter now that he was gone.

"Miss Maria?"

She looked back at him.

"The men are bound to wonder why Turnbull rode off toward town again without really giving us any direction."

"I am wondering the same thing." Once again, she glanced down the road. Then she seemed to gather herself. "Move the herd to higher ground. Also, the Tipton fencing needs checking," she said. "We've lost half a dozen calves in the last few weeks."

So she knew more than the others gave her credit for. "And if we find holes?"

"Close them up."

"But…"

"I don't care if that's Tipton property. The rest of us have the right to protect our property, and since we have repeatedly asked them nicely to patrol the fences they insisted on installing, and they have not, then I will take matters into my own hands. Repair the fences before we lose any more unbranded calves."

"We could brand the stock," he suggested.

"Don't treat me like some novice, Chet. Branding was to finish up weeks ago as you well know, but with all the setbacks—Papa's death, the men leaving, and now Joker gone—we need to reconsider our schedule. Joker is the best iron man this side of the Mississippi and losing him is like losing two men. I aim to get to the bottom of this and, with any luck at all, get him to come back. So we will check the fencing, close the holes, and brand the stock in that order, understood?"

"Yes, ma'am." This time he made no attempt at smothering the grin. He tipped his hat to her. "Be seein' you in a few weeks then." The amount of work spread over miles of territory meant the men would camp out on the range rather than returning to the bunkhouse each night.

"You'll be seeing me and my younger brother, Trey, by tomorrow," she replied. She must have noticed the way Chet couldn't keep his jaw from dropping in surprise because it was her turn to smile. "We're shorthanded, remember?" She walked into the courtyard. "Trey Porterfield," Chet heard her shout. "Stop whatever you're doing and get down here now."

Shorthanded without a doubt, but if she thought she and that boy could make up for a man like Joker… well, she was not as smart as Chet had thought.

❧

"I'm not asking you to make ranching your life's work, Trey," Maria said. "It's just that we all have to pitch in. Papa always said you were ready. Maybe Mama didn't agree, but if Papa thought you were well enough to start doing your part, that's good enough for me. We're coming up on our busiest time and—"

"I'll go," Amanda volunteered. "Anything to escape this," she added as she held up her hands covered in soapy water.

Juanita handed Amanda a scrub brush and motioned to the shirt draped over the washboard. "Just keep working that stain, *mi hija*. You got no business out there alone with a bunch of cowboys. A body shudders to think what might come of that."

Maria wiped a scattering of soap bubbles from her

sister's cheek. "I need someone to watch Mama," she said, "and we won't be gone long."

"You're going?" Amanda looked back at Juanita. "How come she can go and you don't say a word?"

"She isn't likely to throw herself at that good-looking drifter, and more to the point, she is the boss. I got no way of stopping her, but you, little one, are another story."

"Can I take my sketchbook?" Trey asked, interrupting the women.

"Yes, as long as I don't see you drawing in it when you're supposed to be keeping watch or doing some other chore."

Sensing that he was dealing from a position of power, Trey pressed on, "And my books?"

"One book. Now go change and meet me at the corral in fifteen minutes."

"We're going now?"

Maria sighed. "No, I thought we would wait for the next lunar eclipse," she said, giving vent to her frustration. "Yes, now, Trey—so go."

When he had headed down the hall, she turned back to Amanda. "Now remember Mama—"

"You don't have to order everybody around, Maria. We are all aware that you're in charge. Nita and I can take care of Mama. You just take care of Trey." And with that, she wiped her hands on her apron and hurried down the hall to her brother's room.

The kitchen was silent for a long moment, and then Juanita started scrubbing the stain herself. "Those two might bicker and scratch like a couple of wild dogs, but I never saw a brother and sister closer than they are."

"Not like Jess and me?"

Juanita snorted. "You lost Jess when he realized your papa took more pride in you and what you could do when it came to ranching. That hurt him as it would any boy. And he blamed you."

"What could I have done?"

"Nothing, but he couldn't take it out on his pa, so he took it out on you. That night he left? His parting words to Eduardo and me were 'We'll just see how good she is at running things.'"

"But he never wanted this life."

"Not necessarily. Truth is that he could just never figure out where he fit into the scheme of things."

Maria stared out the window, fighting the tears that these days were never far from the surface. "Do you think he'll ever come home again?"

"Jess? More than likely. When he goes through that money and realizes life out there is nothing like the life he had here. Question you need to be asking yourself is what you'll do when that day comes."

Maria pushed herself off the kitchen stool. "That'll hold. For now, I've got to get the horses saddled."

෴

Bunker was the first to notice the two riders approaching from the east. "Holy…" He stood up in his stirrups as if that might give him a better view. "That woman is crazy as they come, bringing that tenderfoot out here. What's she thinking?"

Chet looked up from his work and saw Maria riding toward them. There was something about her that made him just want to stop whatever he was doing and watch her—something that made him think he would never get enough of looking at her.

"Why, Bunker, I heard her say she wanted to be sure that boy was trained by the best," one of the younger cowboys said. "That'd be you, wouldn't it? Ain't that what you keep telling us?"

"Shut up, Slim," Bunker growled. He edged his horse closer to the place where Chet was closing a large hole in the Tipton fence, twisting the wires together, his shirt soaked through with sweat. "You know about this, Hunt?"

"She said something about being shorthanded and seemed real upset about Joker leaving."

"Joker didn't leave," Bunker muttered. "At least not on his own." He glanced around as if to assure himself that none of the others were listening. Sure enough, Slim and a couple of the other hands had gone back to watching the herd. "You get my meaning, Hunt?" Bunker asked.

"You're saying he had help."

"I'm saying he was forced out by Turnbull. I'm saying that if he's even still breathing, he is miles from here by now."

Chet's hands stilled as he gripped the pliers hard. He'd had little doubt that Joker had left because of the encounter with Turnbull, but what Bunker was suggesting was something far more sinister. "You think Turnbull..."

"You been here long enough to know Joker ain't afraid of nothing, man or beast, and he sure ain't afraid of that dandy Turnbull. Course, accidents do happen, and just maybe later last night when we was all sleeping..."

"You're imagining things. Joker and his horse and

all his stuff was gone this morning. He left, Bunker. Men do it all the time."

Bunker shrugged. "Maybe so. But I'm recalling that Turnbull came storming into the bunkhouse before sunup bellowing about how we was a bunch of no-good layabouts and how we better get used to the idea that we'd be working short again. How did he know Joker was gone when none of us knew? And unless Miss Maria has taken to ordering bed checks..." He glanced back at the approaching riders.

Chet went back to work. "She wants to get him to come back," he said, jerking his head toward Maria. "Joker. Says he's the best iron man around."

"Is or was?"

"Is," Chet said firmly and stood up to survey his work. He had reset the fence post and tightened the strands of barbed wire. Taking off his hat and swiping the back of one hand across his forehead, he watched Maria and her brother riding toward them. The kid was nervous—it was plain as day in the way he kept looking around and talking nonstop to his sister. Maria had her eyes fixed on the fence that ran along the border of her property. When she saw Chet standing next to it, she raised her hand in greeting and then kicked her horse into a gallop to cover the distance between them.

"Any trouble?" she asked.

"It's pretty much a matter of just resetting the posts and twisting the wires together again," Chet replied, a little insulted that she seemed to be questioning his ability to handle such a simple job.

"I meant with the Tipton men."

"Not a sign of 'em, Miss Maria," Bunker assured

her. "Those boys will look for any way out of work they can find. Bunch of no-good layabouts, they are."

Chet wondered if Maria knew the whole truth about the Tipton brothers and their attempts to cause problems for her and the other small ranchers. He doubted it. It seemed pretty obvious to him from things he'd heard Bunker and the other cowhands say that they saw it as their job to protect "the little lady," as they were fond of calling her. Now Bunker turned his attention to Trey. "Well, young fella, you ready to round up some strays and get set to finish the branding?"

Trey glanced at his sister, his eyes wide with pleading. Chet expected that all that chatter he'd been doing as they rode was about begging her to let him go back home.

"It's not as hard as it looks once you get the hang of it," he told the boy.

"That's right," Maria said. "If I can do it—a mere girl—it should be easy for you."

"You can do anything," Trey murmured.

"Tell you what, how about you stick with me for today?" Chet said, wondering even as he said the words why on earth he was making such an offer. Taking care of young-uns was woman's work—a thought he could see from Bunker's smirk that he and the other men would surely echo.

"Thank you, Chet. Trey can start with fence mending and ease into the rest."

Chet whistled for Cracker and the dog took one more bite of something she'd found in the tall grass before ambling over and waiting for Chet to mount his horse. "Come on, Trey. This is the easy part.

We're just going to keep riding along the fence, looking for places where it's down. When we find that
place, we fix it and then move on, okay?"

"Yes, sir."

"No need to be so formal. I'm Hunt to the other
men."

"Boy needs his own name," Bunker announced.

"My name is Trey."

"Naw. That's your name for your sister and the
others. Out here we're gonna call you…"

They all waited as Bunker scratched his beard and
pondered the possibilities. Once or twice, he started
to say something but shook it off. Then he grinned.
"Snap," he said. "On account of you being no more than
a young whippersnapper. I'll let the others know." And
without waiting for Trey to either agree or not, Bunker
took off riding through the clusters of grazing cattle.

"Snap," Trey repeated softly as if trying it on for
size. Then he settled his hat more firmly on his thick
hair, leaned forward to rest his hands on his saddle
horn, and said, "Ready when you are, Hunt."

Chet touched the brim of his hat as he looked at
Maria. "We'll get started then, Miss Maria," he said.

Trey repeated the motion. "Miss Maria," he said
softly, and he was smiling at her.

She let them get maybe twenty yards away before
calling out, "You be careful, Trey."

Trey sighed and did not acknowledge the warning.
"She thinks I'm a baby," he muttered.

"But it sure must be real nice to have somebody—
more than one—who cares about you," Chet replied,
and he spurred his horse into a trot.

Six

MARIA WAS BONE TIRED. THE TEMPERATURES HAD soared well past one hundred degrees over the last few days, by Bunker's reckoning. The nights brought little relief, and sleeping on the hard ground did not help, even though she and Trey had the luxury of a tent and more than enough blankets to pad their bedrolls. But nine days of hours in the saddle, eating the dust that dogged them every step, followed by meals taken while seated on the ground or a fallen log and nights spent on that hard earth mattress had taken their toll. The men seemed used to this life, but why wouldn't they be? Almost to a man, they had spent years following this routine. And she wasn't about to complain—not when Trey had endured the same.

That first day after he'd ridden off with Chet, he had returned to camp full of stories he could not wait to tell her and even a few sketches he had made. He had also returned sunburned anywhere his skin had been exposed—even his face, in spite of his hat. When she tried to rub some salve on the worst areas, he had brushed her away.

"Hunt says he was burned worse than this one time back in Florida when he lost his hat—burned right on his scalp," he added. "And Bunker says once my skin tans like leather, then it'll be all right. He says it's all those years I had to be in bed and stay inside." His eyes were bright with excitement each day when he returned to camp and told her all that he had seen that day. "I never really looked at it all before, you know? The sky was like a painting. Hunt says that in Florida…"

He went on and on, and every other sentence seemed to begin with two words: "Hunt says." She was surprised to hear that "Hunt" talked so much. Whenever she was around, she had the feeling that he only spoke when necessary. On the other hand, though she took her meals with the men, she had purposely avoided any direct contact with Chet, especially once Roger joined them on the trail. She saw no sense in aggravating an already touchy situation. But one night when she saw Chet head down to the stream after supper, she decided to follow him. She told herself that her intention was to thank him for taking such good care of Trey, but the truth was Trey's stories had raised her curiosity…and she found herself longing to spend time with him.

"Good evening, Miss Maria," he said, not turning at her approach. "Was there something you were needing?" He tossed a small stick into the water and watched it drift downstream, then gave his dog permission to retrieve it and did the same thing again. The water level was lower than ever, and over the last week the association had lost more than a dozen steers to the drought, but the dog seemed to enjoy the game.

"I came to thank you for the time you've taken with Trey. It can't be easy."

"Snap's a quick learner. No trouble at all." He tossed another stick.

"What are you doing?" she asked, moving closer so she too could watch the stick's journey. She realized that Cracker stayed put until Chet gave a signal, but she also realized that this was more than a game.

"Checking the water flow."

"Not much flow there," she said. "With this drought—"

"Are you so sure it's all drought?"

She stepped closer and nearly lost her footing. His hand was tight but gentle as he caught her. "Easy there, ma'am," he said.

She told herself that it was her imagination that he held on to her a little longer than was necessary. And yet the way his gaze locked in on her…

"Clearly you think it is more than the drought." Her voice was surprisingly husky. "Perhaps you should discuss your thoughts with Roger." To her surprise, this brought a smile and a chuckle as he discarded the other sticks he was holding and bent to rinse his hands in the water.

"I see he's back. The others were beginning to wonder."

"He had business in town." The fact that Roger had been away so long with no explanation before showing up had rankled her. She needed to get to the bottom of why he kept riding off like that. Later—after she'd solved the other dozen or so problems demanding her attention. "And you did not wonder?" she asked Chet now.

He shrugged. "Truth is, I didn't much care one way or the other. We were getting work done. Now if Joker had been the one come riding into camp the other night, that might have been a different story—cause for celebration."

She was surprised by his brazenness. After all, technically speaking, Roger was his boss. "I see your opinion of my foreman has not changed. May I remind you that you could have had the job?"

"And would I have still had the job once you and Turnbull patched up things between the two of you?"

"Yes. I do not go back on my word."

"Another lesson you learned from your pa?"

"That's right. And you, Chet? What lessons did you learn from your father?"

He looked out toward the setting sun, watching the orange globe on the horizon as if it held the answer to her question. "Those lessons were more about what a man shouldn't do."

"I don't understand."

"He left us when I was eight—me, my sister, my ma. One day he was there and then he wasn't. A little like Joker."

"You're changing the subject."

"I'm asking if you've been able to learn anything more about Joker leaving."

"In other words, did I talk to Roger?" she challenged.

"That would be one course of action. Another would be to go back to the ranch and town and see what you could learn. Now that your foreman's here—and appears to be planning to stay awhile—I'm not sure why you think you need to be here."

She was not used to the hired men speaking to her with such directness, and she certainly was not used to them studying her so openly. Chet had left his hat on the ground and his eyes—those sparkling eyes—were probing hers, seeking answers. "Trey…"

"Trey is doing far better than you or any of us hands would have thought. The boy's a natural. Question is why are *you* here, Maria?"

She did not miss the fact that he had dropped the "Miss" from her name. And she could not ignore the fact that the first answer that sprang to mind—one she forced herself to swallow without speaking—was *because you are.*

"I should get back," she said, aware that the sun had slipped below the horizon and the shadows were closing in on them like a cloak. "Thank you again for helping Trey adjust, for everything you've been doing. It's…been a big help."

"Maria?"

There it was again—that familiarity she should never permit. She paused but did not turn to face him.

"Talk to Turnbull about the creek. Even with the drought, this stream is not running the way similar streams appear to be running on the other side of Tipton's fence."

"All right. I'll mention it." She took a few more steps, and then she added, "And if you are certain that Trey is adjusting and will be all right, perhaps I should get back to help Amanda and Juanita."

"And find out what happened to Joker?"

"Yes, that too. Good night, Chet."

"Night, Miss Maria."

So as she had expected, the times he had called her by her given name were no more than slips of the tongue. Why was it that instead of the relief she should have felt at learning he was not going to take advantage, all she felt was disappointment?

Roger was sitting outside her tent, talking to Trey when she returned to the campsite. He continued talking but watched her. Trey had always gotten along well with Roger, and Maria could not help wondering if spending time with Chet might change that.

"You were gone for some time," Roger said as soon as Maria reached the tent.

Before Maria could answer, Trey interrupted. "I was telling Roger how Hunt and me had been working the fence and how many places we found posts pulled out and the wire gone all slack," Trey reported. "We fixed them all but Hunt says—"

"Hunter seems to have a lot of opinions," Roger interrupted, his eyes still on Maria.

"He's always watching for stuff," Trey went on as if Roger had not cut him off. "Just yesterday my horse was headed straight toward a rattler. I didn't see it but Hunt did, and he cracked that whip of his and clean cut that snake near in half. Hunt told me that…"

Maria watched Roger's face work as he tried hard to contain his irritation at Trey's chatter. "Trey, I need to speak with Roger for a minute. Could you go help Eduardo finish cleaning up?"

"Sure thing." He strode confidently past the men gathered around the campfire, calling out to them and getting greeted in return.

"Your brother appears to have taken to life on the trail," Roger said.

"Yes, the men have taken him into their circle as if he were one of their own. I'm so pleased with the progress he's made that I've decided to return to the ranch tomorrow."

"Not alone." It was a commandment.

"And why not alone? I'll be on Porterfield land the entire way. Besides, it's not as if we can spare anyone to travel with me there and then back again. We've already lost valuable time, and we need to do our share here, Roger. We can't expect the men from the other ranches to do more because we're shorthanded."

"Maybe if the drifter wasn't taking his own sweet time checking the fence line, he might be able to do some actual work. Seems to me Trey could handle the fencing job and free up Hunter to do his part with the branding."

"I asked him to stay with Trey. I really don't want Trey working alone, especially not where he might run into some of those ruffians who work for Tipton. The man is simply following orders."

"Is he now? Or is he trying to worm his way into your good graces?"

"To what purpose?"

"Just take my word for it, Maria—I've done some checking, and he is not what he seems to be. But since you refuse to believe me and my instincts and instead choose to rely on those of this total stranger..."

"Oh for heaven's sake, Roger. Will you please just stop this? Chet Hunter works for us both. By every measure I can think of, since coming here he has shown he is loyal and dedicated. One day he may move on, but as long as he is here, I have no doubt—"

"Based on what?"

"Based on the fact that he's suggested I talk to you about the possibility that the water here is running lower and slower than it is just over the fence on Tipton property. To my way of thinking, that is a hand looking out for his boss's property."

"Are you suggesting that I am not?"

"I am suggesting that you work with Chet instead of trying to find ways to drive him away. And speaking of that, while you were attending this mysterious business you had in town, I assume you stopped in at the saloon at least once."

"And what if I did?"

"I'm just wondering what the talk was about Joker. Surely someone must have heard something."

"Will you stop worrying about Joker, Maria? The man up and left." The men around the campfire had stopped their own conversation in order to listen to his suddenly raised voice.

Noticing this, as well as Chet coming back to the campsite, Maria took hold of Roger's arm and turned him away from the others. "Lower your voice please. And stop fighting me, Roger. I thought we both wanted the same thing—to save Clear Springs Ranch."

Her touch had calmed Roger, and he covered her hand with his. "Of course we do. I just wish you would allow me to take some of the responsibility you carry on those beautiful shoulders. I can manage the ranch while you do what comes naturally to women."

"And that would be?"

"Caring for your mother and siblings. And I think your idea of returning to the ranch is exactly the right one. I will choose one of the less experienced men to accompany you."

"I have a better idea. Assign one of the men to take over Eduardo's duties, so he can ride back with me. It will be a nice surprise for Juanita."

"Splendid idea."

"And in the meantime, talk to Chet and find out what he's seen regarding the water supply."

"Of course." The man was all smiles now that he thought he had gotten his way. "I'll make all the arrangements. You should get some rest. Even with an early start, you'll still have another night under the stars before you can sleep in a real bed again." He caressed her cheek and frowned when she stepped away and he caught her looking at something—or rather someone—over his shoulder.

"Ah, Chet," Maria said, "I was just telling Roger about your concerns regarding the water. Why don't I say good night and leave you to talk?"

Both men watched as Maria returned to her tent and closed the flap. Roger spoke first.

"You've got a way of sticking your nose in where it don't belong, Hunter."

"Just doing my job."

"Meaning I'm not?"

Roger had turned on him and was standing close enough that Chet could feel the man's breath on his face. "Can't say since I'm not real sure what your job is. But if I was the one trying to make sure Miss Maria and her family didn't lose their place, I'd be wondering how come the water on that side of the fence is running slow but free, while over here it seems to come in fits and starts."

He'd gone too far and he knew it when Turnbull reared back and took a swing at him. The fact that Chet saw the punch coming and ducked only infuriated the man more. The fact that Cracker had seen someone attacking his master and decided to take matters into her own teeth only complicated things.

"Crack!" Chet ordered, and the dog let go of Turnbull's pants leg and took up a position next to Chet.

"Get your gear and be gone by morning," Turnbull roared. When he noticed the other men inching toward them, smelling a fight the way they could smell a thunderstorm coming, he turned on them. "And that goes for any man here who thinks he knows more about running this herd and this ranch than I do."

The flap to Maria's tent snapped back, and she emerged—her hair streaming down her back, her eyes narrowed in fury. "What the devil is going on out here?" The question was directed at Turnbull. "Well?" she demanded when Turnbull did not answer her in the split second that passed.

"Now, Miss Maria, don't go getting all—"

"He just sent Hunt packing," Bunker reported.

"Oh no, he did not," Maria said. "You must have misunderstood, isn't that right, Roger? I mean, think about it, Seymour—we're already shorthanded, so why would Mr. Turnbull—"

"It was my doing, ma'am," Chet said. "I made a comment I shouldn't have, and the boss rightly took offense. Then my dog got into it and…" He turned to the foreman. "I'd like to apologize." He offered Turnbull a handshake.

All the men froze, waiting to see what would happen, half of them no doubt expecting Turnbull to take another swing at him. But instead, the foreman spit on his own palm and then clasped Chet's hand, squeezing with such force that Chet was pretty sure he'd have some bruised if not broken fingers.

"Better," Maria said. "Now could we all get some sleep please? And, Mr. Turnbull, tomorrow you and Chet should ride out and have a look at that water flow farther upstream."

"Yes, ma'am," Chet said.

"Maria?" Roger's voice was gentle—the voice of a sweetheart pleading with his lady.

Maria ignored him, and as Roger brushed past Chet, this time he was the one to murmur, "Watch your back, Hunter."

Once Turnbull reached the makeshift corral that held the horses, the other men moved closer to Chet. "I warned you," Bunker muttered as he and the others went back to their bedrolls laid out around the campfire.

❧

The rain started just after midnight. Maria was awakened by the plop of large raindrops on the canvas of the tent. She lay very still, willing each plop to bring more and more until there was a true downpour. When it happened, she grinned, then laughed out loud and shook Trey. "Wake up," she said. "It's finally raining."

From outside the tent, she heard first grumbles and then shouts of pure joy as the men came awake and realized that they and their belongings were soaked. Trey sat up and rubbed his eyes with his knuckles. Then, as he became aware of the sounds of the rain and the men's shouts, he grinned. "Can I go?" he asked.

"We both will," Maria said, tossing him his boots before pulling on hers. She lifted the flap and followed Trey outside. In seconds, they were both drenched, and she had to laugh when she saw Happy, Bunker, and Slim dancing around what had been the campfire. Even Roger was smiling, and when he saw her, he came to her at once and bowed. "May I have this dance, Miss Maria?"

Deciding it was time to put aside her irritation with Roger and his jealousy, she took hold of his hand as they joined the cowboys circling the fire pit. She looked for Chet and saw him standing off to the side, his face turned up to the sky and the balm of the falling rain.

"Come on, Trey," she called and broke the circle to grasp her brother's hand. Trey pulled Chet into the circle as well.

"And promenade," Bunker shouted and began weaving his way along the circle, nodding to each man he passed until he reached Maria. "And swing your partner," he bellowed as he practically lifted Maria off her feet and swung her around. She basked in the swirl of faces spinning past and laughed. "Put me down, Seymour," she ordered, but she wasn't serious.

The truth was that she could have stayed that way all night—her face pelted with rain, the air already beginning to cool, and the promise of new growth on the range something she could practically taste.

Bunker set her on her feet and instructed the others to bow to their partners as he was bowing to her, his grizzly beard sopping wet. As she promenaded with Bunker down the line, she felt a lightness and joy that she had not known in months. The rain and the cadence the men kept to substitute for music made her feel as if just maybe everything would be all right after all. These men were like family, and together they would find their way.

"Change partners," Bunker shouted and spun her away and straight into the arms of Chet Hunter.

All at once, the world went still.

He held her as if she were something fragile and precious, and yet she could feel the warmth of his hand spanning her waist and see the silhouette of his rock-solid muscles beneath the soaked fabric of his shirt. He locked his gaze on her face—and as he guided her through the dance, she found that she could not look away. No, it was more like she did not *want* to look away.

Then a flash of lightning lit the night sky, spooking the horses, and as suddenly as the celebration had begun, it was over. The men ran to calm the horses, leaving her standing next to the dead campfire. But before he left her, Chet leaned in close and said, "Best find cover, Miss Maria. Looks like this might be some storm." He hooked an errant curl behind her ear. "Go," he said, and his voice was husky—intimate.

She did not move, not even when he glanced back at her. She thought she saw the hint of a smile cross his lips, but then he was lost in the blackness of the night. As she hurried back to the tent she shared with Trey, she tried to remind herself that the moment they had just shared was nothing more than a mutual celebration. Would he be any different when he saw her? Of course not. Chet Hunter was a good and kind man—who worked for her, who had made it clear that in time he would be moving on.

She was the one who was going to feel awkward when she saw him next. She was the one acting like a love-struck girl experiencing her first real crush. She was the one who could not seem to think about anything except how his arm had felt when he danced with her and how those lips had quirked into that half smile…and how very much she wondered what it might be like to kiss the handsome drifter.

&

Morning came too soon. An hour before first light, with the rain still falling, the men were roused. "Rustlers." The word spread quickly as they saddled up and rode off into the darkness. The herd was restless, a sure indication that something was up. Chet and the others communicated with hand signals and now and then a low birdcall—a trick they had learned from Indians. He had to give it to Turnbull—the man knew how to put the men in position quickly and quietly.

The rustlers were trying to cut the unbranded calves away from their mothers and the rest of the herd. They were working the area close to the fence. The day before, Chet had seen one place along the Tipton property where the post had been loosened but put back in its hole, and the wire had been cut but strung to seem as if it were tight. He'd been about to repair the gap in the fencing when the call went out for everyone to head in. He'd planned to finish the job today.

Now Chet would be willing to bet that the post and wire had both been rolled back to provide an opening for the rustlers to use. The plan was probably to spirit the calves through the hole, where more Tipton men waited, and then move on to another part of the herd. Who knew how many calves they'd already taken? They really didn't even have to check if the calf had been branded. Truth of the matter was that the Clear Springs mark was close enough to what the Tiptons now used that changing it would be easy.

Turnbull came alongside him and pointed in the direction of the Tipton boundary. Chet nodded and turned his horse away from the herd as he worked his way slowly along the fence. The rustlers would know that there would be night riders watching the herd. They also no doubt knew they were shorthanded. Word would have spread quickly about Joker leaving and that the others who had left with Turnbull had not returned. It occurred to him that one or more of the rustlers might have worked for the Porterfields before joining up with Tipton. *Not Joker*, he thought.

A calf bleated, and Chet signaled Cracker to stay put as he eased his rifle from its holster. Sure enough, through the curtain of steady rainfall, he could just make out two men tugging the calf toward the hole. The little guy was resisting with all its might, not wanting to be separated from its ma. Chet waited, watching as one of the men pushed back the post and wire to make a wider opening.

"Going somewhere, boys?" he asked, leveling the gun at them.

They dropped the rope tied round the calf's neck and took off running. Chet slid off his saddle, eased off the noose, and patted the calf on its rump. "Go find your ma," he said softly and watched as Cracker herded the little guy back into the thick of the herd. In the distance, he heard shouting and knew that Turnbull and the others had surprised the rest of the gang. He saw three riders headed for the fence and a couple more on foot, chased by Rico and another hand. The rustlers fired their guns, and the cowboys from Clear Springs and the other ranches had to abandon the chase to keep the herd from stampeding, giving the rustlers the time they needed to make a clean getaway. Chet moved his horse into position to help calm the herd and saw that Cracker was already hard at work keeping the stock from scattering.

The whole thing was over before what would have been sunrise. "How many?" Maria asked as she and Trey waited with Eduardo for the men to return and get their breakfast.

"Can't tell yet," Turnbull said. "But they won't be back, so you and Eduardo can head on back to the ranch as planned."

Chet watched Maria as she stared out at the herd and then let her gaze drift to the endless span of barbed wire that ran like a scar across the land. "You're sure they were Tipton's men?"

"We don't know that, Maria."

"But it's a pretty good bet," Bunker muttered.

Turnbull shot him a warning look.

"Okay, let's get the herd moved to higher ground today, as far away from that fence as you can move them."

"That means crossing Turkey Creek, and that thing will be running deep and fast with this rain," Turnbull told her.

"Just do whatever you have to do to get as far away from Tipton's land as possible and get me a full count of how many are missing. Trey, you ride with Mr. Turnbull until I get back."

"But…" Trey glanced at Chet and then back at his sister. It was clear that she was in no mood for a debate. "All right," he grumbled. "When you coming back?"

"I'm not sure. I want to check on Mama, and I have some business in town to attend to. Could be a couple of weeks." Chet saw her eyes soften as she brushed her younger brother's wet hair away from his cheeks. "Soon as I can," she added. "I promise."

Eduardo clanged a bell, signaling breakfast was ready. Chet and the others grabbed a soggy, cold biscuit and some hardtack and filled their tin cups with coffee. They ate standing up, ready to head out to relieve the night riders even though their own sleep had been interrupted to deal with the rustlers. As he rode off with the other men, Chet saw Maria and Eduardo ride off in the opposite direction, back toward the ranch. He couldn't help but think he was going to miss her…and the days ahead would be a little longer without her around.

Seven

MARIA WAS DETERMINED TO PUT A STOP TO THE RAIDS on the herd—not that she could prove the brothers had any involvement, but there was no denying that since her father's death, more stock had gone missing than ever before. It was as if once her father died, the Clear Springs ranch became a target, and in the months since her father's passing, whoever was behind the raids and other mischief had become more brazen. They would never have dared such tactics when her father ran the ranch. She doubted they would have been so bold if Jess had been the one in charge. No, because she was a woman, they thought they could do as they pleased.

She had tried several things—hiring extra men when she could afford them, having the regular cowhands drive the herd to grazing land as far as possible from Tipton land—but these days she couldn't afford the payroll for the regulars and good grazing land was harder to find. She didn't know how she was going to stop them, but if she and the other small ranchers didn't do something, they would lose their ranches for sure. In her case, the rustlers were not only stealing unbranded calves but also steers that carried the Clear Springs brand because it was easily altered to match the Tipton brand. Chet's suspicions about the water flow might be a place to start. She would talk to a couple of the neighboring ranchers and then go see Marshal Tucker.

"You thinking about going to town and stirring up trouble, Maria?" Eduardo asked later that evening as the two of them sat next to the campfire he'd built. They were eating their supper of cold tortillas filled with black beans and salsa.

She started to deny it, but understood that the man who knew her at least as well as her father had would not be fooled. "I'm not the one who has stirred up anything," she replied. "If the Tipton brothers would keep their men under control and leave us alone, there wouldn't be any trouble."

"Maybe." Eduardo scraped the bottom of a tin of beans with his fingers and licked them clean. "But Marshal Tucker can't help you. He's just a town marshal. It's the federal government that's in charge of things out here."

"Well, then I'll go see Colonel Ashwood at the fort. Ever since Papa worked out that deal for us to supply cheese, eggs, and beef to the fort, he's been most friendly."

Eduardo made no comment.

"I mean, what am I supposed to do? Just let the Tiptons march in and take over like they did with the Buchanans and the Kellers?"

"Now you know as well as I do that both those families came West for the wrong reasons and neither

one was cut out for the life here. Keller's wife hightailed it back East almost before he could get a house
built, and Buchanan knew about as much about
handling a herd as young Trey does."

"Trey was sick and has some catching up to do."

"He's also fourteen and learning—not a grown-up
man like Buchanan." Eduardo flung the dregs of his
coffee on the ground and stood up to stretch.

"So what do you think I should do? What do you
think Papa would do?" she asked softly.

Eduardo was quiet for so long that she thought
maybe he hadn't heard her. Then he squatted down
and picked up a stick to stir the fire. "I think you've
got a hired manager, Maria, and dealing with the
Tiptons is his job. Let him do it. As for your pa? He's
not here. If he was, he could take care of things, but
you aren't him. Like it or not, you'll not get very far
going up against men like Jasper and Buck Tipton,
and you'll not like me saying this, but the other ranchers aren't all that likely to listen to you either—you
being a *mujer* and all. You want my advice? Let *Senor*
Turnbull handle the Tiptons."

She knew he was right. And yet the truth was she
didn't entirely trust Roger to take care of the matter.
After all, he had urged her to sell out and had even left
to go work for the land company. Of course, he had
explained all that the day he'd followed her out to her
father's office.

"Maria, you have this way of making me do the
darnedest things," he'd said. "I swear, honey, you can
drive a smart man to stupid."

"Like running off to work for Tipton?" she'd asked.

He'd smiled sheepishly and put his arms loosely around her waist. "Exactly. I was mad, and I did the one thing I thought would make you see what you might be losing if I left."

"It didn't work." She had firmly but gently pushed him away and turned back to her father's desk.

"No. I see that now. Take me back, Maria. Let's put things back the way they used to be between us. I promise you won't regret it."

And because she saw no other option and she truly wanted to believe in Roger's loyalty to her family, she had agreed. "No more talk of me selling out?" she had asked.

"Nope. I learned that lesson, honey." He had taken a step closer, but she had stopped his embrace by sticking out her hand and shaking his as firmly as any man would have—as firmly as her father would have—to seal their bargain.

Yet in spite of that, she still had doubts. Her relationship with Roger confused her now that she had stepped into the position of running the ranch. The truth was that sometimes it was so nice to lay down that burden of responsibility. On the other hand, there had been a time when she, like pretty much everyone else, had thought she and Roger would marry. If she wanted to marry at all, he was certainly the most likely candidate. But lately she realized she had begun to question Roger's intentions—for her and the ranch. She'd never really been in a position to observe him at work, and what she had seen over the last several weeks disturbed her. His hair-trigger temper was a problem. She certainly did not recall him ever acting the way he did with her when her father was alive. The way he'd gone storming off that day after she'd refused to even consider selling out was typical. He'd come back of course, and he'd kept his word about saying no more about her selling out, but things were not the same between them. He still did as he pleased without consulting her.

"Do you trust Roger?" she asked Eduardo.

"He's good at his job," he replied.

"That's not an answer. Do you trust him to do what's best for us?"

Eduardo shrugged. "Do we have a choice?" He laid out his bedroll and settled in for the night. "You take first watch," he said, passing her his rifle. "Wake me in an hour and I'll take watch till morning."

"You need sleep too."

Eduardo grinned. "I'll have plenty of sleep tomorrow as we ride. You see, I long ago learned the fine art of dozing on my horse." He winked at her and then turned his back to the campfire and let out a sigh of pure exhaustion.

Maria sat staring at the fire, oblivious to the way the hot coals only added to the heat that had built throughout the day in spite of the rain the night before. Her tin coffee cup was cradled in her hands. The coffee was cold now, but she paid no mind to it. She thought about what Eduardo had said about having no choice but to trust Roger. *We do have a choice,* she decided. *I can trust myself.* By the time she woke Eduardo, she knew exactly what she was going to do once they got back to the ranch.

But the following evening, as they rode up to the

ranch house, Amanda came running to meet them. "Thank heavens," she shouted. "You have to do something, Maria."

"Is Mama—"

"Mama is fine, or as fine as she ever gets these days. It's me that's going crazy. Nita has me working from sunup to sundown. And even when I'm not working, there is nothing to do. I even miss Trey."

Maria smiled as she dismounted and tied the reins of her horse in a half hitch knot around the corral fence. "Well, I have to go into town tomorrow. Would you like to come with me? We could do some shopping and—"

Amanda threw herself into Maria's arms. "Thank you. Thank you. Thank you."

Arm in arm, the sisters walked into the courtyard, where their mother was sitting, her eyes closed, her face lifted to the setting sun.

"Hello, Mama." Maria kissed her mother's cheek.

"Ah, Maria, did you have a nice ride?" She touched Maria's hand.

"Yes, Mama." She glanced at Amanda, wondering if perhaps at last their mother realized that Maria had been away.

"That young man wasn't with you, was he?"

"What young man, Mama?"

"That Roger. Your father tells me the two of you—"

"Mama, I was out with the herd. We're late with the branding and need everyone working."

Her mother frowned. "I forgot. Trey was with you?"

"That's right. He's doing a wonderful job, Mama. The men have all taken to him like he's one of them."

"Branding time?"

"Yes, Mama."

She smiled. "Then comes market time and that means party time. We need to start planning. Once the herd is taken to market and the men and your father return…"

"I don't know, Mama. Maybe this year we should—"

"I'll help you write letters to the other wives, Mama," Amanda said before Maria could say more. "Maria and I are going into town tomorrow, and she's going to see the other ranchers, so it's the perfect time to get them to take your letter home to their wives. We could have them come for lunch one day and plan the whole thing just like always." She looked pleadingly up at Maria. "Isn't that right, Maria?"

Maria ignored her. "A party is a lot of work, Mama, and you haven't been feeling well. Maybe just for this year the other ranchers' wives could—"

"They'll all pitch in and do their parts, of course, but the party has always been here, Maria. What would your father think if he learned we were not hosting this year's celebration?" She stood up and walked with surprising vigor into the house. "Well, come along, Amanda. Let's get started on those letters. Perhaps we can speed things along by suggesting assignments—after all, everyone pretty much does the same thing every year. Of course…" She began ticking off a list of tasks, matching them with the person she thought best capable of delivering.

Among the names she gave were the Kellers and Buchanans. Both families had been gone since at least a year before Isaac Porterfield died. It was hard for Maria not to envy her mother's fantasy world—life had been so much simpler then.

◈

The town of Whitman Falls was small but bustling. In spite of the fact that the railroad had bypassed the town, it was still the thriving place it had been when Maria was a child coming into town with her parents. Of course there were telltale signs that all was not as it had once been—a couple of empty storefronts, open businesses where the owners had given up trying to fight the dust, and more than the usual number of men sitting outside the saloon whittling on a stick or just staring out at the street.

When Maria and Amanda pulled their wagon up to the general mercantile store, Eliza McNew was sweeping the boardwalk—a useless task since it would be covered in more gritty dirt not half an hour after she finished. It was pretty obvious that the rain they had celebrated out in the valley had not reached town.

"Good morning, Eliza," Maria called as she set the brake on the buckboard and climbed down.

"Mornin'," Eliza replied, leaning on her broom. "Another perfect day in Whitman Falls," she added as she squinted up at the cloudless sky.

"You could sure use some not so perfect days," Maria replied. Amanda hugged Eliza before rushing into the store.

"Where's the fire?" Eliza asked, nodding toward the door.

Maria sighed. "Mama wants to have a party, and of

course Amanda is all for that since she assumes it means new clothes and such."

"Constance is better then?"

"Not really."

Eliza wrapped her arm around Maria's shoulders as they walked into the store. "Anything I can do?" Eliza and Maria's mother were lifelong friends, having grown up together, gone through school together, and attended each other at weddings, births, and most recently the funeral of Isaac Porterfield.

"Keep coming to visit when you can, I guess. That's all anybody outside the family can do."

"Maybe the party is a good idea. It might just bring her back to us," Eliza said as she and Maria entered the cool shade of the store.

"It's the perfect idea," Amanda announced, already standing before the store's full-length mirror, draping herself in a beautiful satin damask fabric she'd unwound from its bolt. Three more bolts of fabric were stacked on the glass-topped counter next to her. "Lavender has never been my color." She sighed. "But it's perfect for you, Maria."

Maria held up her hands to stop her sister's advance. "I have to meet with the association, and I want to speak with Marshal Tucker. After that, I have an appointment with Mr. Cardwell at the bank," she reminded Amanda. "Wait for me here, and we'll have lunch at the hotel before we start back. I won't be long."

"Take your time, and don't forget to hand out the letters for the wives. Eliza and I have so much to do—pick out fabrics and patterns for dresses for you, Mama, and me…" She glanced around and focused on a Stetson displayed behind the counter. "Maybe a new hat for Trey to celebrate that he's one of the hands now?"

"Maybe. Let's not spend us the rest of the way into bankruptcy," Maria said, glancing at Eliza, who nodded, signaling that she would keep Amanda's shopping spree under control. Reassured, Maria left the store, nodding to two men on their way into the store who had stepped aside to allow her to pass as they tipped their hats.

The meeting with her father's fellow ranchers went about the way Eduardo had predicted. They listened politely to her impassioned call for the need to take a united stand against the Tipton outfit. Then they thanked her for coming and turned back to their conversation about the drought and whether or not moving their stock to higher ground where there was more shade and cooler temperatures would be enough. It was as if she were invisible. After the meeting finally broke up, she saw Marshal Tucker and called out to him. He might not have jurisdiction outside of town, but maybe he would have some ideas about how she might go about finding out what happened to Oscar.

"Well, hello, Maria." He removed his hat, exposing his thinning gray hair to the hot sun. "How's your mama doing?"

"About the same," Maria replied. "I hope everyone in your family is well." She was anxious to dispose of the small talk and get down to business.

"Fit as fiddles," he said. "Was there something you needed?"

She told him about her concern for Joker's welfare.

He listened politely—as the men from the neighboring ranches had—and then he gazed out toward the edge of town. "You see, Maria, times are hard, and when hard times come, it's not all that unusual for a man to just decide the grass might be greener down the road somewhere. The truth of the matter is that unless you have some proof that this man has met with—"

"You mean some crime has to be committed before you can help me find him?"

"I mean you need proof, and the truth is that he may not want to be found."

"Well, if you can't help me find my hired hand, then what are you going to do about the rustlers who raided the herd the other night? They were taking the stock right onto Tipton land and…" He listened patiently while she ran through the list of events she had tallied and chalked up to the Tiptons.

"You know that's not my jurisdiction, and even if you go to the fort…do you have proof, Maria? Are you sure that the barn burning that forced the Kellers out was more than just a case of no rain and dry wood?"

"Well…"

The lawman was taking the points she had tried to make and ticking them off one by one, and the fact of the matter was that he was right. She had no proof.

"I can't do anything about Joker, Maria, and as for the rustlers, if you bring me hard evidence that can lead to an arrest, I'll take it to the right people in the militia myself." He put his hat back in place and looked at her with eyes full of pity. "Ah, there goes Clyde Cardwell. Didn't you have a meeting?"

Once again, she had been dismissed.

At the bank Clyde Cardwell greeted her with a wide smile and the clasp of her hand between both of his. "Maria, I do believe you get prettier every day," he said. He released her hand and used his handkerchief to dust off the seat of the chair across from his. "Now what can I do for you, little lady?"

The fact that he insisted on speaking to her as if she were ten and had stopped by for the free piece of stick peppermint that the bank handed out to the children of their customers made Maria grind her teeth as she smiled back at him and settled herself in the wooden chair. "I still need that loan, Mr. Cardwell. You said you would look into it and give me your answer by this week," she reminded him.

His whiskered jowls drooped as the smile disappeared. "Well now, Maria, we've already talked about this. Times are hard and—"

"Which is why I need the loan. I will repay it in full as soon as we get the herd to market."

"You are aware that beef prices are down? When the market gets flooded with product…"

"I understand the market, Mr. Cardwell. The Tipton concern has ruined that for everyone—including themselves, although with their huge resources and inventory, they hardly feel the pinch."

His bushy eyebrows shot up as he gazed at her. Then he grinned as if he'd solved a puzzle. He shook his finger at her. "Roger Turnbull told you to make that point, didn't he?"

Maria squeezed her gloved fingers into a fist. She had worn her Sunday best, right down to a bonnet and her good shoes for this meeting. That had definitely been a waste of time and energy. She might as well have shown up dressed for a roundup for all the respect the banker was giving her. But she needed this money in the short-term, so she decided that in spite of how it galled her to do so, she needed to change her approach. "Would you rather deal with Mr. Turnbull on my behalf?" she asked, fighting to make her tone sweet. "Because I assure you, if that will make a difference, I can arrange for him to be here in the next couple of days. It's just that Papa always said what a fair and understanding man you were. His respect for you knew no bounds." For good measure, she pulled the lace handkerchief Juanita always made sure was in her purse and dabbed at the corner of her eye. Sometimes a woman had a few more weapons at her disposal than a man did—and Maria was not above using a few fake tears if it meant she was going to get what she needed to save the ranch.

Flustered, Clyde Cardwell pushed himself away from his desk. "Now, now, Maria." He poured a little water into a crystal glass and handed it to her. She remembered that whenever her father met with the banker, that crystal glass was filled with whiskey. She wondered what Clyde Cardwell would think if she asked him if she might have something stronger than water.

"Dry those pretty eyes of yours. I never said no. I just wanted you to understand the circumstances."

Maria kept her eyes lowered as she sipped the water. "You'll give me the loan then?"

"I think we can manage half of what you requested," he replied as he returned to his chair.

She looked up at him then, her eyes dry. "Three-quarters," she bargained.

The banker stared at her for a long moment. "All right, but the terms include repayment in full on…" He flipped ahead in the calendar on his desk and tapped a date in October that would fall just after they had taken their stock to market. "In full, Maria, understood?"

"Yes, sir. Thank you." She extended her hand the way her father would have when sealing a business deal. Cardwell stared at it as if not sure what she was doing and then shook it firmly.

"In full with interest, Maria."

"I understand."

Clyde walked her out into the bank's main area, where he instructed a teller about preparing the paperwork and transferring the funds. "I'll have the papers ready for you to sign this afternoon. Shall I send them to the ranch?"

"No. My sister and I plan to have lunch at the hotel. I can sign them after that."

"Then I'll look forward to seeing you later, Miss Porterfield."

Maria understood that the formality was in part for the benefit of the teller, but she couldn't help thinking that just maybe it was also a mark of the banker's respect.

Back on the street, Maria felt as if a bale of hay had been lifted from her shoulders. With the money she'd borrowed, she'd be able to keep up with bills until they could get the herd to market. She wondered what Clyde Cardwell would have said if he'd known Amanda was at McNew's Mercantile planning a party. Her brow furrowed as she stepped into the street, determined to keep her younger sister in check. They could have a party, but it would not be one of the lavish affairs their parents had given for a variety of holidays or other special occasions in the past. It would not be the ball she knew Amanda dreamed of, with fancy gowns and…

She was so lost in thought as she planned what she would say to Amanda that she nearly stepped in front of the arriving stagecoach. She jumped back just as the driver pulled the coach to a stop in front of the Wells Fargo station so that both the coach and its team blocked her view of the street. She decided the safer course would be to go behind the stagecoach to cross, and as she did, the coach doors opened and the arriving passengers piled out.

Maria paused when she heard a baby crying. A man in a suit and bowler hat brushed past her muttering, "Finally. One more mile and I was going to throw that kid and its mother out the window." He stalked off.

Maria paused and watched as a woman dressed in a dust coat and holding a squirming child stepped out into the sunlight. But it was the way she held the baby that made Maria look twice. It was as if she had never held an infant in her life.

∽

After ten long, grueling days, Chet and the other cowhands had finally gotten the herd moved to the north range—decent grazing land that was as far from Tipton land as they could get. Horses could be run, but cattle walked at a stroll and moving them took more time. He'd been keeping watch over Trey, even though the boy was now trailing Turnbull and doing the best he could to follow the foreman's orders. Chet knew that Trey thought a lot of Turnbull. He'd jabbered on about the foreman while they rode the fence line together—how when he started to recover from the illness that had kept him housebound for the first several years of his young life, Roger had taught him the basics of roping; how Roger had been the one he could talk to after his pa died and his brother left; how Roger and Maria would likely get hitched one day even though they fought like two dogs with one bone.

But as the days since Maria left wore on, it became obvious that Turnbull was losing patience with Trey, especially when the boy pulled out his sketch pad. "Put that thing away," he'd barked at Trey one night as the men sat around the campfire.

"He's doing my picture," Bunker countered.

Turnbull ignored him and grabbed the sketchbook away from Trey. "You want to be a cowhand or not?" He tossed the pad into the fire.

Trey's eyes went wide with surprise. "But Maria said—"

"*Maria said*," Turnbull mimicked in a high falsetto as he walked away. "You want to be a man? Then stop hanging on to your sister's apron strings."

As soon as Turnbull's back was turned, Chet plucked the book from the fire and stamped out the embers. "Here you go, Snap," he said, blowing on the pages to make sure the fire was completely out. "Best keep this out of sight when he's around."

Bunker leaned over and pointed to the drawing of himself. "Look at that, will you? Right handsome, wouldn't you say?" His comments had the exact effect he wanted. The men snickered, and Trey smiled.

"It's not finished yet," he said shyly.

"Guess I get to be even better looking than I already am then," Bunker replied, earning the outright laughter and ribbing of the other men.

"How about I hold on to that sketchbook for you, Snap?" Chet suggested.

"Good idea," Slim agreed. "That way you don't run the risk that the boss might spot it in your stuff one day."

Trey handed the leather-bound book back to Chet. "Thanks," he said. "There's a drawing of you in there. You can have it if you like it."

The men gathered around Chet. "Let's see, Hunt. See if you're a purty as me," Bunker teased.

Chet flipped through the first couple of pages until he saw his likeness staring back at him. Nobody had ever made a drawing of him before, and he was surprised at this one. The man in the picture wore his hat and his clothes, and carried a coiled whip over one shoulder. But was that the way he looked—those eyes squinted on something in the distance and that mouth a hard, determined line?

"That's you all right," Bunker announced. "Look at the way he got you looking off toward something out there." He gestured toward their surroundings. "Me, I'm looking right at Snap here."

It was true. The drawing of Chet showed a man looking off the page at something only he could see. "Nita says you'll leave one day," Trey explained. "That you've got something you need to do and it ain't here."

Chet tore the drawing from the book, folded it carefully and put it between the pages of his tally book. "It's a good likeness, Snap. Thank you." He placed the sketchbook in his saddlebag and then picked up his saddle and headed for the corral. "Got night watch, gents. Be seeing you in the morning."

As he left, he heard Trey say, "He never said whether he was going or staying."

"Going," Rico replied. "Only question is when."

For once it was a quiet night on the range. Chet and the other night riders had little to do. Some distance away, Chet could hear Happy playing his mouth organ and found himself humming along with the tune. Music soothed the herd and gave the men something to do to pass the time—and some comfort as well. But the music only reminded Chet of that night when he had danced with Maria in the rain. They hadn't needed music that night—the way she'd fit perfectly next to him, the way she had looked up at him, rain drops beading on her perfect lips. If it had just been the two of them, and if that lightning bolt hadn't spooked the horses, he might well have given in to the moment and kissed her. That was sure the thought uppermost in his mind—still was. Kissing Maria Porterfield had become something he thought about a lot.

Cracker let out a low growl.

"Yeah, I know. Bad idea. She's not for me."

The dog yipped in agreement then lay down, still watching the herd but taking whatever chance she could to rest as the hours of the long night wore on. Determined to put Maria out of his mind, Chet turned his attention back to the problem he'd seen with the water flow. Turnbull might not think there was anything out of the ordinary about it and even Bunker had dismissed his concerns, but Chet just had a gut feeling, and he had long ago learned not to ignore such feelings.

"Come on, Crack. Let's ride over to the creek and see how it's running."

As the first light broke on the horizon, he dismounted to refill his canteen and stretch his legs. Turnbull had not asked him about the water flow problem, and he didn't feel it was his place to bring it up again, but that didn't mean he wasn't continuing to check. As he watched the water run slowly into the opening of his canteen, he mentally measured the flow against what it had been a few days earlier. Of course, there had been the downpour that had come so hard and fast that it had added little to the supply, but did that account for the slow trickle? Of course, the only way to find out for sure was to follow the water to its source, and that meant getting on the other side of that barbed-wire fence.

He opened his saddlebag to get some jerky and saw the sketchbook. The sun was still below the horizon but cast enough light that he could make out the drawings. He flipped through the pages and realized that he might not know a single blessed thing about good art, but even he could see that Trey had the gift. He turned the pages slowly, studying drawings of the herd with the ranch hands in the background, one sketch of the fencing with a hole patched up, a couple of the men gathered around the campfire. He turned the page and saw Bunker's mug grinning out at him, then turned the page again and his breath caught.

The drawing of Maria captured everything about her—her beauty, her grit, her smile—especially her smile. Trey had sketched her with her hair pulled back and caught with a ribbon at the nape of her neck. Her curls tumbled down her back and over one shoulder. Trey had caught her at an unguarded moment, though Chet knew that there were few of those. Maria always seemed to be expecting the worst. Her smile was rare and her laughter even more so.

Here, she was grinning out at the world, her eyes focused straight at him. But the way Trey had sketched her eyes made the smile a lie. The expression in her eyes was wary and sad. Chet wondered if the boy would miss the drawing if he were to tear it from the pad and place it with his sketch folded carefully between the pages of his tally book.

"Hunt!"

He looked up and saw Turnbull riding toward him. He quickly closed the sketchbook and returned it to his saddlebag, then turned to wait for the foreman. Dawn was just breaking as Turnbull's horse came straight for him at a full gallop. Cracker let out a low growl of warning and Chet's horse whinnied and sidestepped a little, but Chet steadied him and climbed into the saddle just as the foreman jerked his horse to a stop that sprayed dust in the air—dust that clung to the lather around his steed's breast straps.

"Been looking for you, Hunt."

"I've been out here all night, watching the herd."

"Didn't look to me like you were watching any

herd. Looked to me like you were standing around—reading some letter." His eyes glinted. "You got a woman somewhere we don't know about?"

"A sister," Chet said, taking advantage of the fact that although Turnbull had seen that he was holding some papers, he hadn't been close enough to distinguish the sketchbook from a letter. "I suppose a sister might count as having a woman somewhere."

Turnbull pranced his horse in a tight circle, one that brought the two animals close enough to make each other nervous, but Chet knew that his horse was bulletproof when it came to not letting things rattle her. By contrast, Turnbull's horse was tossing its head and snapping its jaws. Turnbull controlled the animal and then leaned in close enough that Chet could see every hair in his mustache. "You and me, Hunter, need to come to an understanding," he said, his words delivered with such grit that spittle formed in one corner of his mouth.

Chet eased his fingers around the handle of his whip. "I'm listening."

"I run the Clear Springs Ranch. I decide whether or not water flow needs to be looked into. I take care of Maria and her family. I do not need or want your help. Do your job out here, and we'll get along just fine. Keep butting in where you've no business, and we won't."

"Sounds like more of a threat than an understanding."

Turnbull's grin was filled with malice. "*Here's* the threat."

Cracker flattened her ears and growled again.

Chet showed the dog his hand, palm down, all the while never taking his eyes off Turnbull. "I'm listening."

"Keep messing with me and keep sniffing around Maria, and one day you might just be gone."

"Like Joker?"

"Exactly like Joker," Turnbull growled, and he turned his horse and galloped off.

Even though the foreman had as good as admitted that he at least knew the truth about Joker's disappearance, Chet couldn't do anything about it with no proof. What he knew for sure though was that Roger Turnbull was determined to have what he wanted whatever the cost, and that included Maria and her ranch. The thing that troubled him was why—if the man was so set on having it all—he wouldn't be as concerned about all this trouble with the Tiptons as Chet was.

Chet took an extra shift when he heard Slim was down with stomach trouble, and the following night, the sky was alive with lightning strikes that sent their jagged spears from sky to ground, striking anything in their path. The night riders were kept busy putting out small grass fires, and by morning it was clear that the lightning that had finally brought a steady, soft rain that promised to last for hours, if not days, had hit more than the grass. As Chet rode the circuit, he saw half a dozen dead steers killed by the strikes. One cow had fallen onto her calf. He freed the calf as he and the other men worked in the steady rain to salvage what they could in meat and hides from the dead stock and clear the rest away.

Exhausted after nearly twenty-four hours on duty, Chet and the others went down to the stream to wash off the blood and guts of the dead stock. That was when he noticed that in spite of the steady rain that Bunker had now officially declared the monsoon they'd been waiting for, the stream still was not flowing the way it should be. Something—or someone— was messing with the water that supplied the small ranches. Turnbull's threats aside, Chet was determined to find his chance to get onto Tipton land. The only problem was that getting on the other side of that fence was likely to end in bloodshed—his blood.

Eight

ONCE MARIA—WITH ELIZA'S HELP—CONVINCED Amanda that the party would not be a ball but rather the usual and far more casual barn dance, her sister had settled on a less expensive green calico for herself, a solid maroon cotton for their mother, and for Maria, a ready-made dress in shades of blue with full bell sleeves that ended in a wide, lacy border to match the collar trimming the square neckline.

"The neckline is too revealing," Maria had protested after Eliza and Amanda insisted she try the garment on. "And it's so full—there's too much fabric."

"It's light as air, that fabric, and will look wonderful when you dance," Amanda replied as she studied Maria's reflection in the mirror.

"Besides, it's on sale," Eliza had chimed in, being no help at all. "I don't know what possessed me to order that dress in the first place, but it was just so gol-darned pretty."

"Then you wear it," Maria had grumbled, biting her lip as she turned this way and that. But she had to admit that Amanda was right. The way the skirt

swirled was like watching a child's toy top twirl until
the colors ran together. "Not to mention it's too long,
and I'm likely to break my fool neck just trying to
walk from here to there."

"I'll hem it for you," Eliza offered and immediately
went behind the counter where she kept a pincushion
and tape measure. "What shoe will you wear?"

Maria looked at the shopkeeper as if she had suddenly lost her mind. "These shoes," she said, lifting
the skirt to reveal her scuffed and dirt-encrusted boots
she'd brought with her in the wagon and changed into
the minute she'd left the bank.

"No!" Amanda grabbed a pair of soft leather shoes
from the shelf. "These are perfect."

"Amanda, I will either wear new shoes or a new
dress but not both, so take your pick."

Eliza waited, a line of straight pins gripped between
her lips. Maria stood with the boots exposed and
glared at her sister. "Well?"

"The dress." Amanda took pins from the pincushion and knelt to the other side of Maria so she could
help Eliza measure and shorten the dress. "Now stand
still," she ordered.

Maria knew she had won that battle. The dress
would have been her choice as well. The dress would
eventually end up in Amanda's wardrobe, so at least
it would get more than one wearing. Shoes, on the
other hand, were not so easy to share. Her feet were
a full size larger than Amanda's, so buying shoes just
to dance in one night would have been a pure waste
of money. She followed instructions, turning as her
sister and Eliza pinned up the hem. When they had

finished, she hurried off to the room behind the counter that Eliza had designated a changing room now that she carried more ready-made clothing items, changed back into her regular clothes, and finally emerged to find the woman she'd noticed getting off the stagecoach entering the store, the baby now squalling loudly.

"Can y'all help me?" she said without so much as a "howdy" or "please."

Eliza stepped forward, and the woman deposited the child in Eliza's waiting arms and then straightened her form-fitting jacket and touched her hair as if checking for missing hairpins. She was no longer wearing the duster the stagecoach company provided for female customers. Instead, she stood before them dressed in a traveling costume made of a stiff lemon-yellow brocade with the skirt bustled in the back and the tight bodice buttoned all the way to her chin. A fine lace border outlined the top of the gown and the bottom of the sleeves. Her hair was flecked with dust and capped by a feathered flat pancake of a bonnet. Amanda's eyes were wide with envy and admiration. Maria felt as if her Sunday best would be something this woman might wear for a picnic.

"Your child needs changing," Eliza said.

"Oh." The woman blinked as if Eliza were speaking a foreign language. "I sent my—our—valises on to the hotel. Maybe you could…?"

"Of course, Missus…?"

"My name is Loralei Culpepper."

"And the baby's name?" Eliza persisted, gently rocking the child in her arms.

"Chester Lee Hunter the Second," she replied.

"Chet?" Amanda whispered, nudging Maria.

"Yes, Chet," the woman replied, honing in on Amanda. "You wouldn't know where I could find him, would you?"

"Well, sort of. I mean, he works for us." She glanced at Maria, her eyes pleading for help.

But Maria had been struck dumb. So this was the big secret. This was why the drifter was so far from home. He was running away from something all right—responsibility.

"Chet's your husband?" Amanda asked, determined to get the facts.

"Chester is my intended," the woman replied. "We did not make it to the altar before his untimely departure."

"But apparently they sure as tootin' made it to the bedroom," Eliza murmured as she carried the baby to the counter, pulled a length of the brown paper she used for wrapping purchases across the surface and laid the baby on it as she began exchanging his filthy diaper for one she fashioned from a flour sack tea towel.

Loralei removed a lace handkerchief from her sleeve and dabbed at her eyes, although Maria saw no sign of tears. "It is an oversight that I am certain he will be anxious to rectify once he realizes that he is a daddy."

"No doubt," Maria said. "Where are you staying, Miss Culpepper?"

"Well, that remains to be decided. You see, I stopped by the hotel, but the room they showed me is most unsuitable—small and dark, with everything covered in dust." She absently ran one gloved finger along a glass-topped showcase, examined it, and frowned. "It would seem that everything in this town is in a similar state."

"Been awhile since we got any rain," Eliza said, handing the baby back to her.

The child immediately went for the long coil of a curl that hung down from her elaborate hairstyle. She swatted at him as she might a fly. "Stop that," she growled.

Maria fought the urge to snatch the child from her arms.

"I suppose you could come stay with us until Chet gets back," she found herself saying instead.

Loralei's smile lit her entire face, and for the first time since meeting the woman, Maria could see what Chet must have seen—flawless, creamy skin, unblemished by the harsh sun and wind; blue eyes that were like sapphires; and that perfectly bow-shaped mouth. Over Loralei's shoulder, she could also see Amanda and Eliza staring at her as if she had lost her poor weak mind.

"I mean, we have extra room," she continued.

"But not for long," Amanda blurted. "You see, we're planning a party, and there will be folks coming from miles away who will need to stay over and…"

Loralei ignored her as she stepped forward and placed her free hand on Maria's sleeve. "You are too kind, and I accept your hospitality for as long as you can spare the space." She handed Maria the child and headed for the door. "I'll just have the hotel porter bring over my luggage," she said. "You live here in town?"

"Not exactly. My family has a ranch about five miles west."

"My father owns a ranch back in Florida," Loralei

said, as if somehow that made them sisters. "You'll have your man come collect my things?"

"I'm afraid it's just my sister and me," Maria replied.

"You drove yourself?" This idea seemed shocking to the woman.

"We did," Amanda said, moving to the window. "That's our buckboard right there. Plenty of room for your *things*, and you and little Chet can ride in back."

The woman's smile was tight. "Perhaps I have acted in haste here," she said. "Perhaps I should stay here at the hotel, and you would be so kind as to send Chester to fetch me?"

Maria was ready to agree, but Amanda was apparently rethinking her position on the matter. "Chet works for us, miss, and right now is our busy time, so it could be some time before he could get away—weeks, maybe even a couple of months by the time…"

With each word out of Amanda's mouth Maria saw the woman becoming more agitated. "But—"

"On the other hand," Amanda continued, "if you and the baby come with us, think what a lovely surprise that will be for Chet once he comes in from the range."

Loralei frowned. The baby gurgled and grabbed for her hair, the feather in her bonnet, the brooch pinned to the neckline of her dress. Each time she swatted his little fist away, the child gurgled happily and moved on to the next item that caught his attention. "Is there someone—a servant perhaps— who might help with the baby?"

"Oh, I think I can assure you that your child will receive far better care at the Clear Springs Ranch than he ever could at the hotel," Eliza said dryly.

Faced with two untenable choices, Loralei finally pasted on yet another fake smile. "Very well. I accept your kind invitation," she announced.

"Again," Amanda muttered.

Maria looked at the clock behind the counter. "If you could be ready at two o'clock? My sister and I are having lunch at the hotel, and then I have some business to finish at the bank."

At the mention of food, Loralei's eyes brightened. "I would love to join you for lunch."

"I'm afraid that's just not possible," Amanda said. "My sister and I have things we must discuss, and well, you would just be bored to tears. Besides, Little Chet here looks like he could use a nap."

"But it's only now before noon. What am I to do for all that time?"

It did seem cruel to leave the woman—and especially the innocent child—with no place to wait. Maria was about to give in and include them both in lunch when Eliza came to the rescue.

"You could leave the baby with me while you go arrange to collect your things and have them loaded into the buckboard. Then come back here to wait. Would that suit?"

Loralei looked around the store with its supplies of mining equipment and tools in addition to dry goods and a little bit of anything a rancher, miner, or farmer might need. "I suppose I could do some shopping..."

"That's the spirit," Eliza said as she relieved Loralei of the child and shooed all three women out the door.

"He has a son," Amanda whispered as she and Maria crossed the street with Loralei trailing after them, emitting little squeals every time a horse and rider passed by or she had to lift her skirts as she tiptoed around a fresh pile of horse dung.

"So it would seem," Maria replied.

"Have you lost whatever good sense you ever had?" her sister demanded.

"You were the one who insisted she come to the ranch, and the fact is, you're right. The sooner Chet faces his responsibilities, the better." She refused to let herself be hurt by that thought as the hotel waiter led them to a table near the window.

"We could have a wedding as part of the party," Amanda said once they were seated, her dreamy eyes showing that she was already imagining the scene.

Maria hid a flinch.

"What do you think Juanita will say?"

She closed her eyes, imagining the scolding they were both going to endure. "My hope is that once she meets Little Chester, she will forget her irritation and see the need for someone to arrange for his proper care."

"It's certain that his mama is not exactly the doting parent," Amanda said. "I swear, if she had swatted at him one more time…"

"And if Nita refuses, then you and I can help with the baby," Maria blustered, although neither of them knew the first thing about such a task.

By the time they finished lunch, Eliza had their purchases wrapped and ready for them. Together Maria and Amanda walked out to the wagon and watched as Loralei persuaded a man from the hotel to load her belongings—two large trunks and three overstuffed carpetbags. Then she held out her hand to the man as if expecting him to escort her in a dance. Instead, she allowed him to assist her in climbing into the wagon. Not once did she look at the baby that Eliza was holding.

"Good luck," Eliza said as she handed Maria the child and stepped back so Amanda could drive the wagon out of town.

On the ride back to the ranch, Loralei settled herself against the carpetbags and immediately fell asleep, leaving Maria to care for her child as if that were perfectly normal. Within minutes of their leaving town, Little Chester laid his head on Maria's shoulder and was soon sound asleep himself. She was surprised at how solid and heavy he felt in her arms…and how perfectly right.

But then she reminded herself that this child she was mooning over was Chet's child, and the woman in the wagon was someone he had left behind—unmarried and pregnant. How could she have been so wrong about him? Loralei certainly was the last woman she would ever have thought would have traveled such a distance on her own, and yet here she was. How could Maria not believe her story? Why else would Loralei travel more than halfway across the country to find Chet if it wasn't true?

Maria felt her chest fill with a stew of anger and regret and half a dozen other emotions that she did not begin to understand. Were all men not to be trusted, or was she just so gullible when it came to the male of the species that she was an easy mark? Well, as soon as Chet returned to the ranch, she was going to…

"How old do you think he is?" Amanda asked,

then answered her own question. "Certainly not yet a year."

"We can do this," Maria said, lowering her voice but losing none of her resolve. "After all, it's not forever. Chet will see his responsibility and accept it."

"He ran away once," Amanda reminded her. "Nita says he'll take off again, and then where will that baby be?"

For once, her sister was right, and Maria had to accept that perhaps she had permitted her heart to overrule her head when it came to Chet Hunter.

No more, she told herself—and firmly locked away whatever breathless hopes may have been brewing.

❧

The part of his job that Chet enjoyed the most was the roundup in preparation for branding. One cowhand was chosen to separate—or cut—the stock to be branded and earmarked from the larger herd. In Florida, Chet had been well-known as the best cutter around, and he was hoping maybe that might count for something now that he was in Arizona. Of course, if Turnbull had anything to say about it, Chet was pretty sure that he would not be chosen. More than likely Turnbull would send him off to bring in any strays—a solitary job that required following tracks… tracks that wouldn't be easy to find.

Bunker had explained that their outfit was behind on branding mostly because of time lost after Isaac Porterfield's death. "Between the old man dying, young Jess taking off the way he did, and the women and Snap all pretty much lost souls, we probably lost near a month in there. There was a time, truth be told, that me and the others thought maybe there'd be no branding a'tall."

So now the time had come to make up for lost time. First Chet and the other men from the Porterfield outfit would drive the extra horses upstream, to where all the hands from surrounding ranches would come together in one large camp, and the work would begin. The other hands would be there to keep track of their stock as the Clear Springs men set their brand on yearlings and strays they'd rounded up—strays that bore no mark and so belonged to whoever claimed them. As they approached the camp, he saw that Eduardo was back. The chuck wagon was already in place, and a makeshift corral had been set up for the extra horses. After Eduardo had served up the noon meal, the trail boss would hand out assignments and the work would begin.

Chet sat next to Bunker while they ate.

"Turnbull's got a burr under his saddle," Bunker muttered around a mouth filled with food.

"Seems to be a permanent situation with him," Chet replied. "What's he mad about now?"

"The other foremen took a vote and elected Ty Baxter trail boss." He nodded toward a man who was about Chet's age, height, and weight.

"Looks like he could handle the job."

Bunker snorted. "He's the best around."

"Which ranch?"

"None of them. He does this on his own—goes from one roundup to the next, getting the job done. The ranchers finally figured out that if you bring in somebody from the outside, there's not so much strutting around trying to show off by the local boys."

"So if this is the way it works, what's Turnbull's problem?"

"He thought because of the hard times and the fact that Porterfield stock is the only stock in need of branding, the ranchers wouldn't spend the extra money. He's been campaigning for a week or more to have the job. Then Baxter shows up." He snickered. "You shoulda seen Turnbull's face when he realized nothing was gonna change. Wish Snap coulda made a drawing of *that*."

Ty Baxter climbed onto a stump next to a cypress tree. "All right, gents, listen up."

Chet listened as the trail boss doled out the assignments, admittedly a lot different than what he might have given at a regular full roundup. Mostly he laid out some ground rules for how the other outfits were to tend their herds like normal while the Porterfield outfit did their job. When it came to the Porterfield group, Baxter paused and glanced around. "Where's Jar Johnson?"

"He ain't here," Bunker called out. "Went to work for Tipton."

Baxter frowned. "Buffalo Benson?"

"Same story," Slim shouted.

Chet saw Turnbull give both men dirty looks.

Baxter scratched his chin. "Got any suggestions, Turnbull?"

"Hunt could do it," somebody from another ranch shouted, and several other cowboys who Hunt had only met in passing shouted their agreement.

Chet looked at Bunker, who seemed to be focused on his coffee cup and grinning. "What's going on?"

Bunker shrugged and started to walk away. "Turnbull's not the only one in this gang who knows how to work up a groundswell of support for something. Don't let us down, Hunt."

The roundup took a full week. Leaving three of the Porterfield hands to watch over the main herd, Chet and the rest of their crew drove the stock in need of branding back to the ranch. There was quite a bit of good-natured ribbing as Chet and the others left, and Chet was well aware that those men Bunker had recruited weeks before to call out support for him were now men who knew and respected him—as he did them.

After weeks on the range, he was looking forward to getting back, if for no other reason than they would have one of Juanita's home-cooked meals, a cot with a dry mattress, and the chance to bathe and wash out their clothes.

And Maria would be there.

Every night, once the others were sleeping or keeping watch, he had taken out Trey's sketch of her and studied it by the glow of the banked embers of the campfire. He had begun to wonder if there was any chance at all that she held some thought of him. He couldn't seem to stop himself from imagining them together. Of course, he'd have to tell her all about Loralei, but she'd understand. More difficult would be persuading her to come with him to California. He knew there was no chance she would leave as long as her mother was in the state she was in, and besides, who would take over the running of the ranch? Of course, he could stay. But that carried with it a whole other set of problems—Turnbull for one.

Trey rolled over on his side and rested his head on Chet's saddlebag. "Whatcha doin', Hunt?"

Chet quickly folded the drawing and stuffed it inside his shirt pocket. He'd started carrying it there since he'd taken it from the sketchbook. The spot was handier than the tally book, and there was less likelihood it might fall out as he recorded the count of steers and calves. The fact that it lay close to his heart had also occurred to him and been dismissed as sentimental claptrap. "Just thinkin', Snap. How 'bout you? Trouble sleepin'?"

The boy sat up and stretched. "Yep. You think we'll make it home tomorrow?"

"No tellin' for sure. Rain seems to be passing, so I guess it's likely."

"I'll be glad to see Maria and Amanda again— and Ma." His voice dropped to a whisper on this last name.

"Your ma will come out of it, Snap. Can't say when, but knowing you and your sisters tells me she's stronger than this thing that's got her in its grip."

"I sure hope so. Maria says one day I'll be running the ranch, and I'd sure like to make Mama proud."

"I expect your ma is already proud of you," Chet said. "No sickness could change that."

They were quiet for a moment. Chet stirred the fire. Trey reached for his sketchbook and a stick charred by the fire. "You think I'll be up to runnin' the ranch, Hunt?"

"Depends. You're good at the work—kind of a natural. But the question you need to be thinking on is if that's what you want to do with your life."

"I can't imagine livin' nowhere else."

Chet watched as the boy made quick strokes with the stick, glancing up now and then to look at their surroundings. "Ranchin' is more than just someplace you live. You've had a taste of it now. It's long days and nights away from home. It's a love of the land and everything that comes with that—wind, heat, cold, dust, rain, snow. Most of all it's finding a comfort with just yourself for company."

"And your dog." Trey grinned.

"Yep." He realized then that Trey was sketching Cracker, who was stretched out by the fire. "You think you might find that a life you'd want?" he asked as he watched Trey work.

Trey shrugged. "Maybe. How about you? What do you want? I mean, I heard Maria say you'd probably move on one day. So where would you go?"

Chet shrugged. "Maybe California." *Maybe?* Hadn't that been the goal all along? And now he was changing that to "maybe"?

"You got people out there?"

"Nope." The other men started to stir, their inner alarm clocks telling them it was time to get up and get back to work. "Best put that away, Snap," Chet said, nodding toward the sketch pad.

Trey made one more stroke, placed a cover sheet over the drawing to keep it from smudging, and placed the sketchbook back in Chet's saddlebag. "I like talkin' to you, Hunt. You listen like what I've got to say matters."

"A man's thoughts shared with a friend are somethin' to be respected, Snap."

Trey grinned shyly. "I ain't no man yet," he said.

"Gettin' there," Chet told him. "A lot closer now
than you were a few weeks ago." He watched the boy
walk away, his shoulders back with his head held high
and his step the long stride of a cowboy.

∽

Loralei had settled right in to the ranch house. In fact,
she never bothered to dress or leave her room, pleading exhaustion and a "sick headache" that she insisted
kept her from her motherly duties. Of necessity,
Juanita had found Ezma, a wet nurse and widow from
the small cluster of Mexican families that lived nearby,
and Maria had hired the young woman, putting her up
in the room off the main house where Roger usually
slept. She could not see having Loralei and the child
and Ezma in the house just down the hall from her
mother, and once Trey returned, the room next to
Loralei would be occupied as well. Besides, the idea
that Chet might also spend time in the house with
his little family was not something she intended to let
happen. No, the anteroom would work just fine.

Roger would not be pleased to return and find his
dwelling turned into a nursery, but what else was she
to do? The baby had to be fed, and he was not yet old
enough to be able to chew solid food, although Maria
noticed that Juanita had begun to mash up soft foods
like potatoes and applesauce and feed them to little
Chester as he sat playing with a variety of wooden
spoons and crawled around on the tiled kitchen floor.

To Maria's shock, her mother had come down to the kitchen one afternoon, fully dressed and carrying an armful of baby clothes. "These were Trey's," she said, handing them to Ezma. "He's outgrown them, so they may as well be put to use." And then to everyone's astonishment, she lifted little Chester high in the air. "Hello, little man," she crooned as he giggled and flailed about above her. "Just wait until my Isaac meets you."

Maria dreaded the men coming home. Usually she couldn't wait until she saw the cloud of dust in the distance that signaled their arrival. The distant cloud was always followed by the sounds of whistles and shouts from the men and the rumble of hooves moving slowly across the terrain that the recent rains had turned a verdant green. In years past, her father would be the first to come into view and her mother would stand in the courtyard, smiling and waving a red scarf high in the air—their private signal that he was home at last.

But this year it would be Roger leading the way followed by Trey—not Jess—and somewhere in there would be Chet Hunter. In the days that had passed since Loralei's arrival, Maria had used her anger and disappointment in Chet to drive her to work harder to secure the future of the ranch. She'd been a fool to imagine for one minute that there might be something between them. So she had avoided being in the house—or the presence of Chet's child—any more than was absolutely necessary. She'd started taking her meals in the office and returned to her room only after she was sure Amanda would be asleep. Her sister's constant rambling about Chet and how he might react once he returned and found Loralei and the baby waiting for him drove her to distraction. But the truth was that she also spent long hours wondering how he would react when he learned that Loralei had arrived with their son and that his past was no longer a secret. Well, it was hardly her concern. She reminded herself repeatedly that she had misjudged him from the first. Now she just hoped he would stay long enough for them to get the herd to market. After that, he and his little family could take off for wherever he had been headed when he'd first arrived.

She stood in the courtyard waiting, and at the same time wanting desperately to hide somewhere and postpone the moment of Chet's reunion with Loralei. But when she saw her mother come running from the house, the red scarf trailing behind her, she realized that Chet was the least of her problems.

Constance ran to the gate and began waving the scarf. Her husband had always signaled her that he had seen it by leaving the others and galloping toward her. When he reached her, he would scoop her onto his horse, and they would ride together to the outbuilding that served as his office. He would carry her across the threshold and slam the door with his foot. Everyone understood they were not to be disturbed for any reason.

"Not unless the house is on fire or you are bleeding buckets," her father had once told Maria when, as a child, she had dared to march to the door and bang on it with both fists. "This is private time, understood?"

Later she had been the one to explain to Amanda

that their father needed private time with Mama, and Jess had laughed and said, "Yeah, likely as not they're making another baby." And when Trey had been born and Amanda's position as the youngest had been given over to this intruder, Amanda had blanched every time the words "private time" came up.

But there would be no answer to the red scarf today—no private time—and Maria had no idea how she was going to explain her father's absence.

"He's coming," Constance shouted as she stood on the bottom rung of the corral fence to make it easier for her husband to carry her onto the horse.

Sure enough, a single rider was galloping toward them. Maria shielded her eyes and recognized Roger. "Mama, it's Roger," she shouted as she started across the yard toward the fence.

As Roger came closer, Maria saw her mother let the red scarf flutter to the ground. "Where is my husband?" she demanded as soon as Roger had reined his horse to a stop, dismounted, and started across the yard toward Maria.

"Your husband is dead, ma'am," he replied and kept walking.

"How could you be so cruel?" Maria and Roger were now abreast of each other, but she did not wait for an answer—she strode forward as her mother climbed down from the fence and collapsed in tears on the ground.

Roger caught her arm and spun her around. "You've got bigger problems than a crazy old woman who—"

Maria slapped him with all her might. "You work

for that crazy old woman," she shouted. "Now let go of me." She wrenched herself free of him and ran to her hysterical mother.

"Oh, Maria," Constance sobbed. "It's your father. There's terrible news, and I don't know how I will tell the others."

"We'll do it together, Mama. Now let me help you back to the house." *Another lie.* As they staggered past Roger, Maria shot him a look of pure venom. "You'll have to sleep in the bunkhouse for the time being," she said. "The anteroom is in use."

He glanced toward the house, where Juanita was handing the baby to Ezma as she ran to help Maria with Constance.

"You gave my room to—"

"Not another word, Roger, or you can leave. I have as much as I can deal with right now, and unless you have something related to the herd to report—"

"What I have to report is that I think your drifter might be tied up with the Tiptons. He knows too much about what they might be up to for my taste."

Maria made sure Juanita had hold of her mother before she turned back to Roger. "You checked the water flow?"

"There's nothing wrong with the water flow, Maria. There's been a drought that has gone on weeks longer than normal, in case you've forgotten. The water runs slow because we need rain—a lot of rain—days and days of it."

"But Chet said…"

"*But Chet said,*" Roger mimicked her. "Get those stars out of your eyes, Maria. The guy's trouble. I've done some checking, and when I was in town a few weeks ago, I got a wire back from the ranch where he worked in Florida. He ran off, Maria. Something about him and the rancher's daughter from the little that was said."

So that explained Roger's trips to town over the last few weeks. He knew.

"Who's the kid?" he asked, jerking his head toward the courtyard, where Ezma was now playing with the baby.

"Apparently, he is Chet Hunter's son," she said as she turned back toward the house.

"How? Why? When?" Roger was sputtering, but she did not answer him. She was not the one who needed to explain anything. That was a job for Chet Hunter.

Chet was beat, but he couldn't afford sleep yet. Turnbull had as good as admitted that he'd had a hand in Joker's disappearance, and that was news that Chet intended to get to the marshal in Whitman Falls as soon as possible, proof or not. His plan was to wait until the rest of the men were sleeping and then slip into town. He could find the lawman, give him the information, and be back in the bunkhouse before the others were up.

But once the herd was settled and he and the others headed for the bunkhouse, he had a gut feeling that all was not right. In the first place, he would have expected somebody from the family to be out in the courtyard to welcome Trey home and hear about his adventures, but there was no sign of any of the Porterfield women.

Instead, he spotted a young Mexican woman he had never seen before in the courtyard feeding a baby. She turned away as he rode by, shielding her exposed breast and the child from him.

Could be Juanita and Eduardo's daughter, he thought. But Rico had never mentioned having a sister and surely Eduardo would have bragged about his beautiful daughter. He kept riding until he saw Turnbull's horse in the corral. That was odd because the foreman usually left his horse to graze and take water closer to the anteroom off the main house.

He had just pulled the saddle off his horse and placed it on the top rung of the corral fence when he heard a cry of sheer agony from the house. Without any thought for whether or not he should be the one to respond, he took off running.

Apparently, the young woman with the baby had also gone inside to see what was happening, for the courtyard was deserted, as was the kitchen and living room. Chet followed the sound of consoling voices and anguished sobbing drifting from a room at the end of a long hallway. He moved closer. He told himself he only wanted to be sure no one was hurt, but the truth was that he feared that somehow those cries were coming from Maria, and if that was the case, he wanted—no, he *needed*—to make sure that she was all right.

The door was open enough for him to see part of the gathering inside. Constance Porterfield was on the bed, propped up on pillows, fully dressed, and thrashing about. The cries came from her. Juanita kept trying to dab her face with a cloth while Amanda sat on the side of the bed, stroking her mother's hands. Maria stood just inside the door, her back to Chet.

"It's true?" Constance choked out the words even as her eyes pleaded for her daughters to deny whatever she'd been told.

"Yes, Mama, but it did not happen while the men were rounding up the herd. Papa died weeks ago. You've been ill and…"

"But I was with him—twice at the creek. I was with him just before…"

"That was not Papa. You only thought it was. You wanted so much to believe that—"

"Then who was that man? And do not tell me it was Roger Turnbull. I would never mistake my Isaac for Roger."

"No," Maria said. "It was not Roger. It was the new man—the drifter."

"It was the baby's papa," Juanita added as if that explained anything. She motioned someone closer, and Chet watched as the young Mexican woman laid the baby in Constance Porterfield's arms. "Remember?" Juanita said softly. And as if a candle had been blown out, Constance seemed to forget all about her grief as she focused all her attention on the child. "Hello," she crooned. "Hello, little Chester."

Chet's heart skipped at least a couple of beats as he tried to come to grips with a world turned suddenly upside down. The women had talked about him being the man by the creek but also about him being the kid's pa, and now they were calling the infant "Chester." What the devil was going on here?

Behind him another door along the hallway opened,

and he heard a voice he had hoped he would never hear again.

"Could someone please get me some water? This heat is suffocating me and…"

He turned and found himself not ten feet away from Loralei Culpepper. She stepped fully into the hall, dressed in a flowing nightgown and wrapper, staggered toward him and collapsed in his arms. "At last," she whispered just before she fainted.

❧

What now? Maria thought wearily when she heard the commotion in the hallway. She glanced at Juanita, who nodded that she should attend to this latest crisis, and left the room.

When she stepped into the hallway, closing her mother's bedroom door behind her, she saw Chet holding Loralei. Her initial reaction to the sight of him looking up at her like some small boy who had been caught stealing cookies was sympathy, but then she recalled how he had deceived her—and Loralei.

"Well, welcome back, Chet," she said. "As you can see, your little family has arrived, and we've done our best to care for them in your absence."

"We need to talk," he said through gritted teeth as he lifted Loralei and carried her back into the bedroom where he deposited her none too gently on the bed. Maria's instinct was to ignore him and return to her mother's bedside. But she could not seem to keep herself from moving to the doorway and watching as Loralei apparently regained consciousness and murmured his name even as she stroked his unshaven face.

"Stop that," he growled, brushing her hand away. The gesture reminded Maria a little of Loralei's rejection of her child. "What are you doing here, Loralei?" Chet demanded.

Loralei burst into tears and turned onto her side, burying her face in the pillow.

"She has come to bring you your son and to reunite with you," Maria explained. "Isn't that right, Loralei?"

The woman offered a muffled whimper of agreement.

"I do not have a son."

"Really?" Maria clenched her fists. What was it about men that they thought they could get away with blatant lies? Did they truly believe the female of species was that naive? "But you admit you know this woman?"

He ignored the question and came a step closer. Maria held up her hands to stop him. "Just answer the question."

He ran his hand through his tangled hair. "Look, I don't know what she's told you but..."

All of a sudden Loralei sat up and glared at him— once again not a tear was in evidence. "You deserted us, Chester Hunter. Your own child, not to mention me—the woman you professed to love."

"I have never said anything to you about love, and as for the kid..." He turned back to Maria. "On my mother's grave, I swear to you that I have never—"

Again Maria held up her hands—this time to stop his words. "You work for the Clear Springs Ranch, Chet. Your private life is your business and your mess to straighten out, and as long as that does not interfere with your work here, you and your family are welcome to stay on. I have settled your...Loralei and the baby and the wet nurse we found in the anteroom, although Loralei has been unwell, so has been staying here for now. In any event, Roger will move to the bunkhouse. And now I need to attend to my mother, who has suffered a great shock today."

She stalked down the hall, fully prepared to wash her hands of all men. She was reaching for the knob of her mother's bedroom door when Chet called out to her. "Maria—Miss Maria—please wait."

She hesitated, then said firmly, "No." She entered her mother's room and closed the door.

✌

"Chester?"

Loralei's voice was soft and pleading. There had been a time, back in the days when Chet had worked for her family, that Loralei's childlike plea could get to him. Her father had been a hard man—hard to work for and hard on his family. Sometimes Chet had felt sorry for Loralei because it was clear that her father kept her on a tight rein. He'd gone out of his way to be nice to her, even though he and the other hands were fully aware that she was a hopeless flirt who was bound to be headed for trouble one day. And trouble did come— for him.

"Whose baby is it?" he asked, still looking at the door Maria had closed in his face.

"Yours, sugar."

He wheeled around. There was no way. He had *never* lain with her—had never even come close. He moved closer to the bed where Loralei was watching him and saw that she was scared out of her wits.

"What's going on, Loralei? Tell me what's happened to bring you all this way."

She tossed her mane of hair and narrowed her eyes. "When Daddy realized that I was with child, he just wanted to make things right for me, Chet." She nodded her head several times as if trying to convince herself of the lie.

"*This* is why your pa went so crazy that morning?" He'd been startled awake by the barrel of a shotgun pressed to his chest. Loralei's father was standing over him, yelling a list of instructions. He was to get his worthless self cleaned up and be at their table for dinner that noon. He was to ask to speak to him privately and ask for Loralei's hand in marriage. The wedding would be large and lavish, as befitted an only daughter. Chester would be on his best behavior and play the devoted suitor through it all, or he would be killed and his body dumped in the Everglades for the gators to enjoy.

Chet had done the only thing he could. He had agreed, played his part right up until the first chance he had to take off, and then he had run. He wasn't sticking around to see what a man as hard as her father was capable of once he got a crazy idea in his head. But then men had been sent after him—men who tried to hurt him—and Chet had been too scared to go to his own family, afraid of bringing trouble to their door, so he'd left Florida and never looked back.

Loralei had gone quiet, and he saw that she was watching him closely. "I swear I didn't mean for it all to get out of hand, Chet. Daddy just…" she said, reaching for his hand.

He let her take it. "Loralei, I don't know what's

happened, but I know if you are here, then you are in trouble. I will do whatever I can to help you, but we both know that boy is not mine."

Her face crumpled, and her eyes welled with real tears. "Marry me, Chet, and give him your name. Otherwise—"

"I can't do that."

She frowned and glanced toward the door. "It's that woman, isn't it? You've fallen for her."

He stood up and moved toward the door, his mind reeling with this new set of problems. "This has nothing to do with her."

"Oh really. You certainly wouldn't be the first man to set his sights on the rancher's daughter, Chet Hunter." This last was shouted as she picked up a pillow and flung it at him.

"Get some rest, Loralei. We'll figure this out." He picked up the pillow and laid it on the bed and then left the room.

As he passed through the kitchen, the young woman he'd seen handing the baby to Mrs. Porterfield was now washing the child's face and hands. "What's your name?" he asked gently.

"Ezma," she replied.

The kid grinned a toothless grin. "And this is?"

"Chester," she murmured, her thick Spanish accent giving the name a certain beauty.

The kid let out a gurgle of delight and splashed both chubby hands in the pan of water next to where he sat on the table.

"Thank you for caring for him," Chet said, and he started to leave, then turned back. "He's healthy?"

"Oh, *sí*." Ezma smiled and rubbed noses with the child, bringing a fresh burst of gurgles. "He is a good little boy."

"Glad to hear it. *Gracias*, Ezma." This time, he kept walking out into the courtyard. But behind him he heard Ezma whisper to the child, "That was your papa, little one."

Bunker and the other hands pretended to be busy with other things when Chet joined them outside the bunkhouse and started to rid himself of the dirt and grime that resulted from weeks on the trail. Bunker was trimming his beard when Chet pumped fresh water into a wash pan and scooped it up with his hands to wash his face.

"You all right, Hunt?"

"I will be," he grumbled.

Bunker gave another snip of the scissors and then studied his image in the hand mirror. "You thinking of running again?"

"None of your business."

There was a pause, then another snip of the scissors. "Nope. It ain't nobody's business but yours. Just thinking that there comes a time when a man needs to take a stand, and maybe this is your time." Bunker hooked the scissors back onto a nail and laid the hand mirror on the narrow shelf before starting back into the bunkhouse, crossing paths with Turnbull as he did.

"Well, well, well, Hunt," Turnbull said when he saw Chet. "How's your little family doing?"

Chet decided to ignore him. He dumped the dirty water onto the ground and returned the wash pan to its hook. Although the rain had broken the oppression of constant temperatures above a hundred degrees, it was still so hot that his hands and face had dried in the seconds it took to perform this single action. He beat his hat against his thigh to rid it of dust as he started for the bunkhouse door.

Turnbull blocked his way. "I asked you a polite question."

"As I told you once before, a sister back in Florida is all the family I've got, Turnbull, and seeing as how we've been out on the trail for some time, it's been weeks since I've had any news from her. So can't really say. Now if you'll pardon me…"

"There is no pardon for you, Hunter. You are what I told Maria you were when I first set eyes on you—the lowest of the low. A man who won't take responsibility when it's staring him in the face is nothing but scum."

Chet locked eyes with the foreman. "You done?"

"For now."

"Then let me pass."

"Nope. I had Rico move your stuff to the anteroom. You don't belong here, Hunter. Go play house with your whore."

Then Chet did the one thing everything he knew about handling men like Turnbull had taught him never to do—he hauled off and punched the foreman in the jaw.

Nine

THE SOUNDS OF FIGHTING REACHED THE OPEN WINDOW where Maria and her sister had finally gotten their mother settled.

"Oh for heaven's sake," she muttered as she went to the window to see what all the ruckus was about. She might have guessed. The fighters were Roger and Chet—of course. "Stay with Mama," she instructed Amanda as she ran out the door, down the hall, past the room where Loralei was preening in front of a mirror, through the kitchen where Ezma was holding the baby as she and Juanita pretended to ignore the fracas in the yard, and out into the blazing hot sun that matched her temper.

"Stop that," she shouted to no avail, her voice drowned out by the shouts and catcalls of the men encouraging the fight. At least Bunker was restraining Chet's dog. She passed by the saddle that Chet had left thrown across the corral fence. Spying the sand-colored whip that had become his trademark, she grabbed the leather-wrapped handle and kept walking toward the fight, the long rope of the whip trailing on the ground behind her. "Stop now!" she ordered.

A few of the men closest to her grew quiet and stepped aside to let her pass. Others moved well away when they noticed that she was carrying the whip. Chet and Roger continued to wrestle on the ground, rolling around, landing punches, grunting like pigs. She raised the whip and snapped her wrist the way she'd seen Chet do on those occasions when the men gathered in the yard to entertain themselves with various games and stunts. She heard a satisfying *crack* as the tail of the whip arched high in the air and fell to earth again.

The sound of the whip was followed by a dead and absolute silence. Roger, astraddle Chet, his fist poised to strike, froze. Chet looked up at her, blood running down his cheek and one eye already nearly swollen closed. Roger didn't seem to be in any better shape—his lip was puffed up and bleeding, and there were ugly cuts on his face.

"My mother has suffered a great shock today," Maria announced. "We have only just now managed to calm her. If you gentlemen are determined to beat each other to bloody pulps, please have the courtesy to do so somewhere that will not disturb her or the rest of our family." She dropped the whip, turned on her heel, and marched back to the house. She had one more task she was determined to complete.

"Loralei," she said, startling the woman as she entered the room. "I am pleased to see that you appear to have made a full recovery. I have asked Ezma to help move your things to the quarters that you and your—that you and Mr. Hunter will be sharing for the time being."

"But—"

"We are not having a discussion here. My family has done more than what might be expected for you and your child. Please get dressed so you can tend to the baby while Ezma takes care of moving your things."

"But—"

Maria reached for the door and pulled it closed. "Half an hour should give you time to dress and gather your belongings," she called as she continued on down the hall. She was aware of something like a shoe hitting the door, and she was sure the uttered cry of protest might have started with the letter *B* but was not even close to Loralei's usual *but*.

Things did not get any better as the day wore on. Amanda was sure that their mother's relapse meant the party was off, or at least would be moved to another ranch. Trey was beside himself worrying about Chet and whether or not Roger would fire him. He wrestled with his loyalties to both men but was clearly more upset about Chet's future than he was about Roger's dislike of the drifter.

"But how could he not even know he had a son?" he asked that night at supper.

"We are not discussing this, Trey," Maria said, and every word was laced with a warning not to cross her.

"Besides, we've got more important things to worry about," Amanda added. "What if we can't have the party? We already set the date and—"

"And we are also not discussing parties," Maria said.

They ate in silence for several minutes until Trey said, "What are we discussing then?" He glanced from one sister to the other. "Papa always said that food goes down better with good conversation so…"

"So tell us what you drew while you were out on the trail," Maria suggested. To her surprise, Trey frowned. Usually any discussion of his sketching elicited an immediate stream of conversation.

"Roger didn't want me drawing. He threw my sketchbook in the fire, but Hunt rescued it, and he carried it with him so Roger wouldn't see that we had it."

Maria did not want to hear anything good about Chet at the moment. He was a scoundrel—a man who had deserted his family.

"Wanna see?" Trey asked and did not wait for a reply as he ran to his room and returned a moment later with the sketchbook, the edges of the cover indeed scorched and blackened.

In the mood she was in, the evidence of Roger's damage to Trey's beloved sketchbook only made her more upset. But Trey seemed unconcerned. He laid the pad on the table and began turning the pages. Even Amanda was impressed.

"Trey, that looks so real, and look at Chet—that looks just like him. He is so handsome," Amanda said dreamily.

"He is also too old for you, possibly married, and apparently a father," Maria grumbled, not able to resist taking a closer look at Trey's sketch. It was Chet all right, sitting tall and proud astride his horse, his eyes fixed on some distant horizon. "Did you draw Eduardo?" she asked, determined to turn the attention away from the drifter.

Trey turned a couple of pages and pointed to a small drawing of Eduardo. "He's harder to get for some reason."

"I think it looks just like him," Maria assured her brother. "You've really captured his smile."

Trey blushed with pleasure. "Maybe I'll do a bigger sketch and give it to him." He turned more pages and frowned. "I had one of you, Maria. That first night in the tent, remember? But it must have fell out."

"Fallen out," she corrected, curious now to see how her brother had drawn her.

Trey shrugged. "I can do another one."

"Not tonight," Maria replied as she began gathering their supper dishes. "We've had a lot of excitement today, and what you need, young man, is a good night's sleep in your own bed."

Trey grinned. "You sound just like Mama used to…" And then his voice trailed off and the smile disappeared.

Maria rubbed his back. "Mama will come back to us, Trey. She just needs some more time."

"That's what Hunt told me."

Amanda took the rest of the dishes to the dry sink and pumped water into the dishpan. "Well, I for one hope it's sooner rather than later," she announced. "Do you think reminding her about the party might help? After all, it was her idea."

"Give her a day or so," Maria replied.

"I could just throttle Roger Turnbull for telling her about Papa," Amanda continued as she washed the dishes.

"Once Mama is her old self again, she'll realize that we need Roger to help run the ranch." Maria needed to think about everything that had happened, and her sister prattling on about Roger was not helping.

"Maybe he is good for the ranch," Amanda said, "but Mama still won't want him marrying you. She says the only reason to marry at all is for true love like she had with Papa."

It was true. Their mother had drummed that message into all four of her children, even Trey, who had looked mystified by the lecture and reminded her that he was only fourteen and unlikely to get married anytime soon.

"Nobody is getting married, and this conversation is at its end," Maria told Amanda as she picked up the dish towel and began drying the dishes that her sister had washed without being told to do so. "On another topic, you seem to be taking to this housework," she teased.

Amanda groaned. "What I have learned is that if I take on some task—of my choosing—then Nita doesn't pester me."

Maria laughed. "That's very smart."

"Oh, Maria, I am not nearly as dumb as you seem to think I am. For example—"

"I don't think you're dumb at all—just young."

"I am four years younger than you are—and to continue, for example, I can see that this entire business with Chet and that woman has upset you. If you want my opinion, it's that woman you shouldn't trust, and you certainly shouldn't be letting her stay here, and—"

"I did not ask for your opinion, Amanda."

"Well, I'm giving it. Making Chet have to share space with that woman—"

"She has a name," Maria reminded her.

"Oh yes, sweet *Loralei*," Amanda said in a syrupy voice and then shuddered.

"Chet's not staying out there with her and the baby," Trey announced. Both sisters had forgotten he was in the room. He'd been sketching again and so quiet.

"How do you know that?"

"I saw him take his bedroll into the barn, so I asked him what he was doing, and he said he was just setting up camp for the night. He asked if he could borrow one of my books to read."

"And?" Amanda demanded.

Trey shrugged. "I kind of forgot until just now. I'll take one out to him."

"No," Maria said, "you get to bed." She did not miss the way Trey and Amanda exchanged a look and how Amanda motioned for Trey to do as Maria said.

"I could take a book out to him," Amanda offered as she handed Maria the last dish to dry.

"No, that wouldn't look right. I'll have Eduardo take it to him. You go check on Mama."

But Eduardo was sound asleep already, and Maria was reluctant to let Juanita wake him. "It'll keep until morning," she assured the housekeeper, who looked at the book under her arm and frowned.

"What's that?"

"A book."

"Don't be smart with me, *mi hija*. I know Trey said he was taking a book out to the barn. Is that the book?"

Maria nodded.

Juanita held out her hand, and Maria placed the book in it. "You go on to bed. I'll have Javier take it to him. You got enough trouble without having people talking about you visiting that man in the middle of the night."

Maria smiled. "It's hardly the middle of the night," she protested.

"It's dark, and that's as much night as there needs to be for gossip to grow. Now *vamonos*."

Maria knew the housekeeper was right. Besides, what was she thinking? She shouldn't want to be anywhere near Chet these days, and yet all she seemed to think about was when she might see him again. She kissed Juanita's weathered cheek and headed toward the door.

"And don't be sitting up all night with your mama either. I gave her some of that stuff Doc Wilcox left. She'll sleep through the night and likely half the morning."

Maria envied the very thought of a night's rest undisturbed by worry and tension, not to mention the carousel of questions whirling around in her brain. Whatever the matter appeared to be on the surface, there was something about Loralei that just did not fit with Chet. If she had thought at all about what kind of woman might attract him—and she refused to admit to herself that she had—it would not be someone so flighty and dramatic as Loralei. Chet was such a quiet man, soft-spoken and gentle. Of course, Maria's mother had always warned her that people with opposing personalities and traits were often drawn to one another.

"They complete each other," Constance had once said, and then, with a wistful smile added, "as your father and I do."

But as different as they might be, her parents had always had much in common. That did not appear to be the case between Chet and Loralei. Of course, how would she know? She barely knew either of them.

"It is none of your business," she told herself firmly. "As long as Chet does his job, his personal life should be no concern of yours or anyone else's." But oh, how it hurt knowing he had fathered a child—knowing he had loved another woman.

She opened the bedroom door and saw Amanda sitting at the dressing table they shared. "Well?" her sister demanded, her eyebrows arched. "What are you going to do?"

"Nita gave Mama a sedative, so she should sleep through the night."

"I am not asking about Mama and you know it. What about that woman and her child and Chet?"

"As I told you before, that woman has a name, Amanda. Show some respect."

"Don't snap at me when it's Chet you're mad at."

"I have no reason to be upset with Chet. He's done his job, and that is all that matters. If he continues to do his job then—"

"Are you blind?" Amanda held her hairbrush suspended inches from her head. "The man likes you. More than likes you, and frankly, I think the two of you make a far better match than you and Roger do."

"Chet is…" She paused. She had been about to say that he was married, but that seemed to be the one thing that he and Loralei agreed upon. "He has a child."

Amanda resumed brushing her hair. "So she says. He denies it. Who do you believe?"

"It is none of my business—or yours," Maria replied wearily. "Now is there any chance we might get some sleep?"

Amanda put down the brush and plaited her hair into one long braid as she turned to face her sister. "I just want you to be happy, Maria," she said softly.

Embarrassed by Amanda's concern, Maria laughed and cupped her sister's chin. "What makes you think I'm not?"

"Because I'm afraid you'll be willing to settle for someone like Roger Turnbull instead of opening your heart and mind to the possibility of true love."

"What a thing to say. I'm not—"

"The only person Roger Turnbull will ever truly love is himself. Mama sees that even when she's half out of her mind." She got up and climbed into bed. "Think about it, Maria. True love versus second fiddle." She rolled onto her side. "Good night."

By the time Maria had changed into her nightgown and braided her hair, Amanda was breathing evenly, sleeping soundly. Maria pulled back the covers on her bed next to the window. Across the way, she saw the glow of a lantern in the barn and wondered if Chet would get any rest. She was quite certain that she wouldn't.

❧

He should have been straight with the whole Clear Springs crew from the start. He certainly should have confided in someone about the real reason he'd left Florida—perhaps Juanita or Eduardo. If he had, perhaps now he'd have someone on his side. The way things stood, everyone looked at him like he was something lower than the dirt and cow droppings he was cleaning off his boots. There was a second part to a cowboy's code when it came to women. Not only did a man treat them with respect, but he never ever left them to clean up a mess of his making. The worst of it was seeing how Maria avoided even looking at him. If only he had explained things to her. She had a way of bringing everybody around to seeing the truth of a matter. But he hadn't, and so when Loralei arrived toting the kid along with her, what other explanation could there be? Of course Maria believed Loralei—and why wouldn't she?

He unfolded the sketch that Trey had made of his sister and ran his finger over her features. How was he going to prove that Loralei was lying—and whose kid was it anyway? He'd barely glanced at the little tyke but had been aware that the boy was studying him with curiosity and no fear. He was a cute little thing, with big eyes and a toothless grin that would make a stone statue smile. The fact was that every time Chet thought of the kid at all, it just fueled his anger at Loralei. Whatever stunt she was trying to pull here, dragging an innocent child into her scheme was a new low even for her.

He refolded the drawing, placed it back in his shirt pocket, and had just opened the book Javier had brought him when he heard a sound just outside the partially closed barn door. "Who's there?" he called, his fingers inching toward his pistol.

A woman slipped through the opening. She was dressed in nightclothes. In the dark, he couldn't be sure, but he couldn't help but hope. "Maria?" he said softly.

The harsh laugh that answered him told him he was wrong. "Don't you just wish," Loralei said as she moved closer. "Hello, Chester," she murmured.

"Loralei, I…"

"You what?" she said, her voice sultry as she

pulled the dressing gown off her shoulders and let it fall to the floor, leaving her standing there in a thin nightgown. She'd left her hair wild and free and the ribbons at her neckline untied. He could see the roundness of her breasts and the silhouette of her nakedness as she stepped between him and the lantern. "You gonna shoot me, Chet?" she whispered, nodding toward the gun.

He released his hold on it. On the one hand, he felt sorry for her, but trying to seduce him was just not going to work. He stood up and picked up her robe, then placed it around her shoulders. "This isn't right, Loralei. You know that. I said I would help you, but don't read into that any more than there is."

She kicked at him—a kick as ineffectual as her attempts at seduction. "You mean *she* might see me? Is that the problem here? Is that why you've holed up out here pretending there's nothing between us?"

"There is nothing between us, Loralei."

"We have a son."

"You know that's not true. You have a son, but I am not that boy's father." He thought about Maria's mother and her refusal to believe her husband was dead. Was it like that? Did Loralei truly believe that he was the father? "Now tell me what really happened, so we can figure out what to do."

She pulled her robe into place and sat down on a hay bale. He sat across from her on the barn floor. "Start at the beginning," he urged.

She released a long, heavy sigh...and relented. "I don't know what to do, Chet. The night before he came to wake you and force you into that shotgun marriage, Daddy caught me with another man—a friend of his. That man is married, and there's no way that…" She was starting to blubber, and he felt such pity for her. "You were always so kind to me, Chet—to everyone. I know you must hate me, but we were always friends. I could always count on you to see me through the rough times, so I told Daddy I was seeing you as well, and that you might marry me to save my reputation." She grasped his forearm. "Please," she begged.

"Loralei, you need to go home to Florida. Your pa will forgive you, and he'll find a way to explain everything so that you come out fine."

"*No*. You don't understand," she moaned. "After you left and he realized I was with child, I told him it was yours. He got so upset that he and Mama sent me away to have little Chester, and at first it seemed like everything was going to work out—you were gone and everyone thought I had been abandoned. Then Daddy got a letter asking about you, telling him you were here. He was ready to send a bunch of men to hunt you down. He was that mad. I thought for sure he would have you hurt. So I begged him to give us a chance. I said I would come with the baby, and I just knew you would do the right thing by both of us."

Chet had never felt more trapped. His instinct was to run—take Cracker and just keep going. Loralei's father was a powerful man with powerful contacts who could hunt him down—who could have him killed and no one would ever know the truth of it. He had to be told the truth—that Chet had never touched his daughter—or Chet might always be running.

"I'll do what I can, Loralei, but I can't marry you."

Loralei's full mouth tightened into a thin, hard line as she stood up. "If you're thinking you have a chance with that woman, think again, cowboy. Maybe I'll just pay her a call. She's got quite a soft spot for a sad tale, and little Chester has won her heart," she said and headed for the barn door. She slid it open just as he caught up to her, grabbed her arm, and spun her around so that their faces were inches apart.

"Leave her out of this. This is between you and me, and if you want my help, you will treat Maria and the members of her household with the utmost respect, understood? They are not your servants. You will pull your weight around here, caring for that boy as any mother would—should."

She struggled to pull free of him, and he tightened his hold on her. "Say you understand, Loralei, or I'll leave you to this mess you made. I'll go somewhere neither you or your daddy will ever find me."

"You're hurting me," she whimpered.

He loosened his grip. "Promise," he growled.

"All right, but—"

"No but's. These are my terms. Accept them or go home."

Her eyes widened in pure panic. "Daddy will never—"

"You let me worry about your pa. You came here looking for help. I'm offering it but, Loralei, this picture you've made up in your head of you, me, and your son living happily ever after is not real. I can be your friend, but that is all I ever was or will be."

Her eyes filled with genuine tears, and he saw that she was truly scared. He gentled his hold on her, brushed her hair away from her face, and kissed her forehead. She could be selfish and cruel, but there was goodness there too—and she had lived such a hard life under the thumb of a ruthless man. "Get some sleep, Loralei. We'll work this out somehow."

She walked away, still sniffling, and he watched her until a movement in one of the windows toward the back of the main house caught his attention: the room Maria shared with her sister. He couldn't help but wonder if the letter Loralei's father had received had come from Maria, checking up on him. It made sense. He certainly wouldn't have blamed her. After all, she was a woman trying to run a ranch. Why on earth would she take on some drifter all the way from Florida without checking him out? And why on earth had he been foolish enough to think—even for a moment—that she might have feelings for him as he did for her?

Ten

MARIA HAD NO CHOICE. AS ANGRY AS SHE WAS AT
Roger for upsetting her mother, she needed to speak
with him about completing the branding. With Joker
gone, they needed someone who could fill his role as
iron man. So that morning, after she had settled herself
behind her father's desk, she sent Javier to tell the foreman that she needed to see him.

He opened the door to the outbuilding slowly and
stepped inside, his eyes skittering around the room as
if he'd never seen the place before.

"Sit down, Roger. I'm not going to bite." His
right eye was ringed in purple and the scratches on his
cheeks had scabbed over.

He let out an exaggerated breath of relief and sank into
the chair opposite her. "I was worried," he said, grinning
at her. "You were plenty upset yesterday and—"

"This is a business meeting, Roger. We are not
here to discuss anything else, understood?"

"Yes, ma'am."

He was mocking her.

She stared at him until he blinked and the smirk faded.

"Now then, for the branding, who will replace Joker?"

He slouched farther into the chair and scowled. "I suppose you want to have Hunter take the job."

"I am asking you as my foreman—as the man who should know the skills of each man."

"Well, it ain't the drifter."

He seemed determined to pick a fight with her. Maria stood up and placed both palms flat on the surface of the desk as she leaned forward. "Let's get one thing straight here, Roger. I do not know what your problem is with Chet Hunter, but I will tell both of you the same thing. If either of you allows your differences of opinion and personal dislike for each other to interfere with getting these calves branded and our stock to market in a timely manner without further loss, that man will be gone. Do I make myself clear?"

Roger stood as well and placed both his hands on the desk. His face was no more than a breath from her own. "If you don't want trouble, Maria, send Hunter and his whore and bastard kid packing today. Then we can get down to work."

"And if I refuse?"

His mouth twisted into an ugly, mocking smile. "Then, sweetheart, you will have proved me to have been right all along. Ever since that cowboy got here, you've been mooning over him. If you think the other men haven't noticed and aren't mocking you behind your back, think again. You want to be in charge here? Then get some backbone and do what your pa would have done weeks ago."

In a motion so swift she did not see it coming, Roger grasped her chin with one hand, pulled her closer, and kissed her. "Let me do the job I was hired to do by your pa, Maria." Then he released her with such force that she tottered unsteadily as he slammed his hat onto his head and left.

Slowly, she wiped her lips with the back of one hand. She felt as if she needed to rinse her mouth out as well. She shuddered at the way he had forced her mouth open and penetrated it with his tongue. They had kissed before, but never with such brutality. This had not been about desire. This had been an open assault—a conquest—a violation.

She sank back into her father's chair, hearing the familiar squeak of it as she did. She clenched her fists and pounded them on the arms of the chair. "Oh, Papa, I don't know what to do," she whispered. She allowed herself the release of her frustration for just a moment—and then turned back to the pile of papers on the desk—bills that were overdue but could now be paid with the money she had secured through the loan. But nevertheless, there would be more bills coming, and the payroll for the hands, and...

By the time she heard a soft knock at the office door, she had buried herself in the paperwork and regained at least some of her confidence. She was doing her best, and she was running things the way her father would have wanted. The fact that she had hired Chet Hunter was Roger's doing when it came right down to it. If he hadn't stormed off and taken her best hands with him, there would have been no reason—or money—to take on the drifter. By this time, he would have been no more than a memory.

"Come," she called when the knock was repeated.

To her surprise, it was Ricardo who stepped inside. "Miss Maria," he said softly as he approached the desk.

"What can I do for you, Ricardo?" She did not miss the way he kept glancing nervously over his shoulder at the door as if expecting someone.

"Last night I rode over to the Johnson ranch."

Maria smiled. It was well-known that Ricardo had taken a liking for George Johnson's youngest daughter—an attraction that, according to Amanda, the girl returned. "And how is Louisa?"

Rico blushed. "She's fine—everybody's fine."

"Spit it out, Ricardo," she urged when he started edging back toward the door as if he'd changed his mind. "You did not come here to report a midnight visit with Louisa Johnson."

"No, ma'am," he admitted, but his eyes had grown large with anxiety. When he heard Roger yelling at one of the men, he nearly jumped out of his skin. "I heard something that may have to do with Joker," he whispered.

"What?"

"A couple of the hands were talking about a man who been beaten up real bad and how he was just barely hanging on."

"And you thought this might be Joker? Why?"

"I'm probably wrong. It's just that whenever his name came up at night out there on the range, when we'd all be sitting around, a couple of the hands from the Johnson's outfit would look at each other funny like and then turn the talk to something else."

"Thank you, Ricardo. I'll have Mr. Turnbull look into it."

If possible, Rico's eyes went even wider—this time with fear. "Maybe it would be better if you had Hunt check into it. I mean, not that I'm accusing the boss of anything, but he was the one that Joker crossed and—"

"Very well. Ask Chet to come see me." Rico seemed even more nervous and was obviously regretting ever setting foot in her office. "Ricardo, trust me. No one will know that I am speaking with him about this—certainly not Mr. Turnbull."

"Okay then. Thank you, ma'am." He tipped his hat to her and reached for the door.

"Thank you, Ricardo. I know it wasn't easy coming here." Then she had a thought. "By the way, didn't you and Joker work on branding together before my father's accident?"

"Yes, ma'am."

"And how do you think you might do working his job?"

Rico snatched his hat off again. "As iron man?"

"That's the job I need to fill. Are you up to it?"

This time the grin was genuine. "I'd sure appreciate the chance to try," he said.

"Very well then. Ask Mr. Turnbull to call all the hands together, and as soon as I've met with Chet, I'll be out to speak with them."

"Yes, miss. *Gracias*, miss." Rico opened the door, uncaring of who might see him, and gave a whoop of pure joy as he hurried off to share the news with the other hands.

For the first time all morning, Maria smiled.

❦

"Miss Maria wants to see you in her office, Hunt."

Chet realized he'd been expecting this. All morning, he'd been trying to decide what to do about Loralei and her baby once he was sent packing. He was hardly in a position to support them, and as much as Loralei might think getting married would solve everything, Chet knew it would be the worst possible idea.

"She made me iron man," Rico added with a shy smile.

"That's great—really great." He clapped Eduardo's eldest son on the shoulder and headed off toward the office. The door was open, and Maria was seated behind a large desk that looked as if it had been through a storm. There were piles of papers and ledgers everywhere. He stepped inside and removed his hat.

"Rico said you wanted to see me?"

"Yes."

He turned to close the door.

"Leave it," she said. "There are enough tongues wagging around here without adding fuel to that fire." She did not indicate that he should sit, so he remained standing.

She concentrated on a list she was making. He could not help but notice the way she refused to look directly at him. "I have the assignments here," she said.

"Rico's real pleased about you giving him Joker's job."

"It's temporary."

"He'll prove himself. You can be sure of that."

She looked up for the first time since he'd entered the office. "That's not the point. Once Oscar comes back…"

Chet wasn't sure what to say. "Yes, ma'am."

"Oh, stop looking at me as if I've suddenly gone crazy, Chet. There is some evidence that he may be badly hurt but alive. I need someone I can trust—and spare—to investigate. Unfortunately, at the moment I have my doubts about trusting anyone outside my own family and Eduardo's, but you are the most likely candidate. No one will question if I ask George Johnson to take you on at his place and send one of his hands over here…"

"How does that solve anything?"

"Do not question me, Chet. I have come to a decision, and it is not open to debate. My sending you away will calm matters here and—"

"Turnbull's behind you wanting me gone?"

She sighed wearily. "I did not say that, but obviously if I can have the two of you as far apart as possible…"

He glanced at the door she'd insisted he leave open and then took a step closer to her desk. "And what do you want, Maria?"

She was writing the note to the Johnsons, but her hand froze and then she laid down the pen and looked up at him. Her eyes were the color of the ocean on a stormy day. "What do I want?" She shook her head slowly. "Does it matter?"

"It matters a good deal to me."

She smiled for the first time since he'd entered the office, but there was no joy in that smile. "Don't you have enough to worry about without taking me on in the bargain?"

"It's because I want to set things right with you that I'm working on that…other matter. The water?"

"Why do you care? Isn't the plan for you to move

on? Seymour tells me you want to make your home in California."

"Maybe." He took another step closer. "Right now this seems about as much of a home as I might ever need to find."

"Chet, I—"

"That child is not mine, Maria. I can't prove it, but I'm asking you to believe me."

"But why would Loralei come all this way then?"

"She's pretty mixed-up and desperate right now. Her father is a hard man, and she's paid a big price for her mistake."

"No child is a mistake, Chet."

"No, I didn't mean it that way." He wished he had the way with words that she did. Maybe then he could make her understand. "I'm trying to figure out how to do right by her and her baby, but, Maria, I need some time and I need…" He didn't complete the sentence.

"What do you need, Chet?"

"I need to know you trust me and believe that I would never abandon my own child. That boy is innocent in all of this, and to tell you the truth, it eats at me the way Loralei is using him to get what she wants."

Maria studied him for a long moment. "You truly care for little Chester, don't you?"

"My own pa abandoned my sister and me," he said. "That boy is facing a similar life, and that's reason enough for me to care what happens to him."

"You're a good man, Chet—a man who cares for others, sometimes to your own detriment."

"Then you believe me?"

She studied him again for a long, long time as if

making up her mind. "Yes," she said softly. "And right now, I am trusting you to help me find out what's happened to Joker." She finished writing the note, placed it in an envelope, and handed it to him.

He accepted the note but allowed his fingers to stay touching hers. "And if I find Joker?"

She closed her fingers around his. "First get him to a doctor—or a doctor to him—and then do not tell anyone until you have gotten news of his condition to me. After that, I'll decide."

"What makes you think the man's alive?"

Without giving up the name of her informant, she told him what had been overheard at the Johnsons' ranch. It didn't take much to figure out that her informant was Rico, however—something any man on the ranch could have guessed as well.

She released her hold on him. "You should get going once you've said good-bye to—to everyone."

He tucked the envelope into his shirt pocket. "Maria, we can't leave it here. I need you to give me a chance to explain about what happened with Loralei and—"

Her back was to him, but he saw the way her shoulders stiffened at Loralei's name. "Later. I can't right now. I... Just go," she whispered.

He hated leaving her upset, but Chet knew now wasn't the time to push for more. She believed him when he said the baby wasn't his—for now, that would be enough. He quietly turned on his heel and left. Outside, the men were gathering for the meeting. Chet went to the corral and saddled one of the horses.

"What's going on?" Bunker asked, keeping his voice low.

"She'll tell you," Chet said, nodding toward Maria, who was coming across the yard.

"It's pretty obvious, isn't it, Bunker?" Turnbull stepped forward as Chet mounted the horse. "Miss Maria sent him packing and none too soon. You taking your—"

Chet leaned down so that his face was as close as he ever hoped to be again to Roger's mug. "Stop talking, Turnbull, before you look like the fool you are."

To his credit, Turnbull said no more. Instead he turned away from Chet and started yelling at the other men. "All right, gather 'round and listen up. Miss Maria has something she wants to say."

On his way out, Chet rode past the house and courtyard, where he could see Maria's mother playing with the baby while Loralei sat in the shade fanning herself. His instinct was to just keep going, but something about the way Constance Porterfield was laughing as the baby grasped chubby handfuls of her hair made him stop.

"Loralei," he called, and immediately she sat up and turned to him, her eyes filled with a mixture of hope and fear. "Miz Porterfield has not been well. Don't let the baby tire her out."

Now she was on her feet. "Where are you going? Are you leaving me? You can't—"

"I've got a job to do. I'll be back in a week or so. Try to make yourself useful around here."

"You'll be back?"

He nodded as he saw Juanita and Ezma come out into the yard. "I'll be back."

"But…"

Chet tipped his hat to Juanita and Ezma, glanced once more at Maria's mother and the child, and realized neither one of them was paying him any mind at all. The kid would be all right with Juanita, Ezma, and Mrs. Porterfield watching over him. Chet kicked the roan into a gallop. Cracker barked and followed.

⁂

Sending Chet away may well have been a good decision had Roger not found ways to bring it up every time Maria was within earshot.

"Good work there, Rico," he shouted. "Miss Maria had us all scared thinking she was going to give that job to the drifter."

"The man's name is Hunt," she heard Bunker mutter. Of course, even Bunker wasn't brash enough to say those words so that Roger could hear, but she could see that the other men heard and that they—like Bunker—did not find Roger's constant harping on Chet amusing.

Later that same evening, when Maria and the rest of the family were having their supper, Roger stepped inside the house, hat in hand. "Just wanted to let you know we're well ahead of schedule, Miss Maria," he told her. "That cowhand that Mr. Johnson sent over is worth two men like—"

"Thank you, Roger. Please thank the men for their hard work today. Good night."

After they had finished eating and she was in the kitchen helping Juanita wash dishes, the housekeeper kept chewing her lower lip—a sure sign she had something to say and was still working out just how to say it.

"What's bothering you, Juanita?"

The housekeeper washed several more plates before she spoke. "I was thinking about that woman showing up in town like she did. How did she know to come here of all places?"

"She said something about a letter."

"Well, the way Chet reacted to seeing her here, it's certain that letter didn't come from him. And if it didn't come from you…"

"It did not. Although I probably should have investigated a stranger's background more than I did, we were in need of help and—"

Juanita dried her hands on a towel and continued speaking as if Maria had said nothing. "So if Chet didn't write to her and you didn't write a letter asking about Chet, that only leaves one person who could have."

"Roger wrote to her father," Maria said. "He's had a grudge against Chet from the day he came back with the lost stock after the stampede."

"It's more than a grudge, *mi hija*. Roger sees Chet as a threat."

"Well, he has no reason for that."

"He doesn't need a reason, Maria."

Maria finished drying the last of the dishes.

"Sending Chet away was a very smart move," Juanita said softly. "You're allowing time for things to settle down a bit around here. Your papa would be proud."

The housekeeper's praise meant a great deal to Maria, so she did not explain her true reasons for sending Chet away. There was no sense in involving Juanita or any of her family.

"But you still have one problem you need to figure out," Juanita continued. She jerked her head toward the anteroom. "How long are you going to let that woman stay on without earning her keep or at least caring for her own child?"

"I don't think she's capable of caring for the baby, Nita. That's why we need Ezma."

Juanita sucked in her breath. "That's the real reason you sent Chet away, isn't it? You wanted to get him away from her?"

"No. I—"

"You are letting that man get to you, Maria. I'm with your mama when it comes to Roger being a poor match for you, but don't go jumping from that frying pan into the fire by getting mixed up with a man who has a baby by another woman—married or not. It can only lead to heartbreak in the end."

"You have to trust me, Nita. You have to believe me when I tell you that the reason I sent Chet over to work at the Double Bar L has nothing to do with Loralei."

Juanita studied her for a long moment and then shook her head slowly. "That may be part of it, Maria, but I don't for one minute believe that's all of it—and neither do you. Try to get some rest."

Maria stood in the doorway, watching Juanita walk away. Of course, she was right. Maria could not recall a time when Juanita's instincts had not been right. But when she thought about Chet—when she recalled the way she'd felt when he danced with her—she so wanted to believe that the child was not his and that there had never been anything between Loralei and him beyond friendship. But what did she know about him really? What did any of them know?

&

Chet waited until the men who worked for the Johnson family were sleeping and then slipped out of the bunkhouse. After a couple of days on the Johnsons' ranch—days where he had paid close attention to the comings and goings of the men—he had a hunch, and he intended to follow it. He sidled through the partially open door into the barn and stood at the foot of the wooden ladder that led up to the hayloft. "Joker?" he whispered.

Outside, a coyote howled and the horses shifted restlessly. Overhead, Chet heard a movement that had nothing to do with horses. He climbed the ladder. "Joker?" he said again, this time in a low voice.

He waited. All was still and yet he had the sense that someone was there. "It's me—Hunt."

There was a long pause while Chet waited at the top of the ladder. Then very faintly, he heard, "Hunt?"

He followed the sound and found Joker lying on a pallet of blankets near where the barn boards had shrunk, leaving openings that let in light and fresh air. The cowhand smelled of sweat and vomit. "What's going on?" Chet asked as he eased his way past a support rafter.

"It ain't good," Joker whispered before having a coughing fit that sounded like he might be bringing up his guts. "How'd you find me?" he finally managed to ask in a raspy half whisper.

"Long story," Chet said. "The doctor been here to check on you?"

Joker laughed. "The boys are doing the best they can. It ain't as bad as it was." He started coughing again. "Long as I lay here and don't try to talk—the boys check on me when they can."

"Are you eatin'?"

"Can't keep nothin' down. Could you maybe get me some water?"

Chet saw a canteen, its top open. He picked it up. "How long since this was filled?"

"Not sure—this mornin' maybe." He started coughing and gagging.

"Don't talk," Chet ordered.

"Stop askin'..." The rest was lost in a fresh jag of choking sounds.

"I'll be right back." Chet swung down the ladder, taking the canteen with him. He pumped water, uncaring that the squeal of the pump might wake the others. He ran back to the barn and climbed the ladder, spilling water with each step. "The cap's broke on this thing," he said, kneeling next to Joker and forcing some water to his lips. "Take your time."

Ignoring Chet's warning, Joker took the canteen in both hands and gulped down the water.

"You gonna tell me what happened?" Chet asked after they had sat in silence for a few minutes and Joker seemed a little calmer.

"You know what happened, Hunt."

"Turnbull?"

Joker snorted. "He didn't do the beatin', and you'll never prove he was part of it, so don't try. Soon as I can mount up, I'm outta here."

Chet was no doctor, but from what he could tell,

that wasn't likely to happen anytime soon. "Can you walk?"

"Nope. Leg's broke. I been running a fever, so maybe it's got infected."

In the dark Chet couldn't see much, but the odor around Joker told him there was something not right. "Look, Joker, I'm gonna get Miss Maria to send over a doctor to have a look at you."

This news upset Joker so much that Chet was afraid the man might choke to death. "No," he pleaded. "Can't nobody know—not even Mr. Johnson. You're gonna get me killed for sure."

"You're half-dead now," Chet snapped. He found some rags and a bucket. He filled the bucket with water from the trough outside the barn, keeping watch to make sure no one saw him. Back in the loft, he lit a candle he'd found in one of the stalls and did the best he could to clean Joker's leg. It sure didn't look good.

Back down in the barn, he found some iodine and climbed the ladder. "This'll sting some," he warned and gave Joker one of the wet rags to bite down on while he applied the tincture to a deep cut over one eye where the scab had fallen off, leaving the wound open.

"You're gonna have the whole gol-darn family out here, Hunt. Stop that."

"Just a couple more…this one over your eye probably needs closing." He administered the iodine then sat back on his heels. "Wait a minute. Are you saying George Johnson doesn't know you're here?"

"Nobody knows but Dusty and Smiley. I made them promise. Please, Hunt…" He half rose to grab Chet's arm, then sank back exhausted.

"Okay." Chet wasn't sure what he should do. Joker was in bad shape and Chet was pretty sure if he didn't get some help soon, the man would be dead. He went back outside and pumped fresh water into the broken canteen, filling his as well, then took both up to Joker. He wished he had some whiskey. That at least would relieve Joker's suffering some. "Here," he said, placing both canteens within reach. "Try not to drink it all at once. I'll be back to check on you once I can."

There was no answer. At first he thought Joker was dead, but then the cowboy let out a gurgle that told Chet he had just passed out. "I'll be back, old-timer. With the doc," Chet promised. Whether Joker wanted it or not, he needed medical attention. But it was going to be hard to figure out how to get help for Joker without letting anyone know. He couldn't go tonight without being caught, not with such an early morning. He'd have to wait and watch for his chance.

Eleven

THE LAST PERSON MARIA THOUGHT SHE WOULD SEE when she rode into town for the monthly meeting with the cattlemen's association was Jasper Tipton. Furthermore, she was stunned to see the other ranchers treating the man as if he were an old friend, laughing at his jokes and jockeying for position to be in his immediate circle.

"What's going on?" she asked Phil Proctor.

"Can't live without big business, then best figure how to live with 'em," Phil replied.

"I don't understand."

"The Tiptons have made a proposal that the association has decided to consider. Jasper Tipton has come here today to answer questions."

"How come I wasn't told about this?"

Phil looked down at his boots. "I thought Roger would have told you. He was the one who came to us with Tipton's offer." He looked around. "Thought for sure he'd be here today."

"Well, he's not. I am," Maria replied through gritted teeth. She was fighting to hold on to her temper, and as always, she tried to think about what her father would do if faced with such a situation. But the truth was that her father would not be faced with such a situation because he would have had the respect of the others. The respect she, as his daughter, was still fighting tooth and nail for. "Excuse me, Mr. Proctor," she said as she pushed her way through the circle of ranchers until she was standing in front of Jasper Tipton.

"Hello, Mr. Tipton," she said, sticking out her hand for him to shake. "I am—"

"No need for introductions, Miss Porterfield," Tipton interrupted. His smile beneath a full black mustache was tight, his eyes wary. Instead of accepting the handshake she offered, he patted her shoulder. "I knew your father—a fine man. Please accept my condolences."

"Thank you. I understand you have made a proposal to the ranchers in this association, Mr. Tipton."

"Indeed, and may I say that I believe your father would have been most impressed with the details."

"Exactly what are the details?"

He gave her that patronizing look that she'd come to expect when talking business with men. "Well, now, Miss Porterfield—may I call you Maria?"

"May I call you Jasper in return?" she challenged and took a measure of pleasure in seeing him flinch. No one called him anything other than Mr. Tipton.

He decided to ignore the question. "Miss Porterfield, I have had extensive discussions with your foreman, Mr. Turnbull, and he has assured me that—"

"My foreman has no authority to speak for my family, Mr. Tipton. Now if you will be so kind as to explain your offer." She folded her arms and relaxed her stance as if she had all the time in the world. She gave him her sunniest smile.

Around her, the other ranchers moved a little away, as if they did not want Tipton to see them as associated with her. George Johnson stayed put but cleared his throat.

"Now, Maria," he said, "it's almost time for us to get started, and Mr. Tipton is prepared to answer any questions you or anyone else might have, isn't that right, sir?"

Having been rescued, Tipton offered Maria his arm. "Exactly right. Now, Miss Porterfield, if you would do me the honor of allowing me to escort you to—"

Maria exchanged her smile for what Juanita had once called her business face. "Just like every rancher here, I can find my own seat, Mr. Tipton, thank you. I would suggest that you get started, since I plan to ask a good many questions."

The offer that the land and cattle company was making was so one-sided as to be ludicrous. How could her fellow ranchers even be considering such terms? Basically the plan was for Tipton Brothers to buy up the rest of the small ranches with the condition that the current owners and the next generation of their family would be allowed to stay on living in the house and ranching what had been their land with the understanding that the stock now belonged to Tipton Brothers. The ranchers would be paid an annual stipend based on the profits made once the herd was brought to market. They would use this stipend to manage the ranch as they always had—to buy new stock, hire and pay cowhands as needed, and take care of their daily needs.

"There will be opportunities for bonus payments as well," Tipton said.

Maria watched the faces of her fellow ranchers. They were listening to the details, but she was sure that they were hearing exactly what she was hearing. The difference was that, sadly, the fight had gone out of them. She raised her hand.

"Yes, Miss Porterfield?" Tipton gave her another patronizing smile.

"In short, Mr. Tipton, you are offering to make us sharecroppers for your company?"

He smirked. "I'm afraid I don't get your meaning."

"Sure you do, Tipton," a voice called out from the back of the room, setting off a stir of disgruntled murmurs.

"Gentlemen," Tipton shouted above the fray. "Please, if you'll just hear me out." When the grumbling continued and three of the ranchers walked out, he glared at Maria.

She smiled and followed the others from the room.

Outside, George Johnson and the other two ranchers who had left were talking. "She's right," one said.

"She may be right, but she shouldn't have said it," said another. "Now Tipton's gonna make us all pay. He knows he's got the upper hand here. He knows it, and so do we."

George noticed her then. "Maria, that was pretty reckless of you."

"Yeah, you can't be speaking for the rest of us," another rancher said as he joined the group.

"Well, somebody has to stand up to this man and his brother." But the truth was that the more she thought about it, the more she realized that by challenging Tipton, she might have done more harm than good. What was it her mother had always told her father? Something about catching more flies with honey? "He just made me so mad the way he was just assuming we would all fall on our knees and thank him for saving us."

"We have to face facts, Maria," Johnson said. "Things won't get any easier. It's gonna take at least a couple of years for us to recover from this drought, not to mention the falling beef prices and—"

"And whose fault is that? Not the drought—although I wouldn't put that past the Tiptons—but for sure the falling prices."

The other ranchers looked at each other uneasily. Then George said, "Seems like you might have a bigger problem in your own corral, Maria."

"Like what?"

"Not what—who," one of the others replied.

"Turnbull," Johnson told her. "He was the one to first bring us Tipton's offer—said you would be on board with the idea. What does that tell you, Maria?" The three ranchers tipped their hats and walked down the street to the nearest saloon.

Maria stood, watching them go and hearing Tipton's booming voice from inside the meeting hall, where he was still pontificating about the advantages of accepting his offer. She wished she could talk to her father. He would tell her what to do. More to the point, all of this would be his problem—not hers.

If only there was someone she could confide in—
someone who would listen—someone who believed
in her and in her fight for the only way of life she had
ever known. *Someone like Chet.*

⁓

Branding was hot, dirty work under the best of
conditions. Branding in the middle of summer in
Arizona was pretty much what Chet figured hell
must be like. For that reason, he was glad he was
spending his time working the Johnsons' herd. He
wondered how Rico was doing and hoped he was
proving himself to be as good an iron man as Joker
was reported to be. He also couldn't help wondering
if Maria was letting Trey take part in the branding
at the Clear Springs Ranch. The kid had taken to
hanging out with the other hands in the bunkhouse
between supper with his sisters and bedtime. He was
eager to learn everything he could.

"With Snap sick so much, the old man concentrated on teaching Jess—the older boy. He didn't pay
much attention to Snap," Bunker had told him. "Jess
was a quick learner, but you could tell his heart wasn't
in it. He'd put on a good show and all, but whenever
his pa wasn't around, Jess pretty much left the work
to the rest of us."

Hearing that, Chet thought that maybe it was a
good thing that Jess had left. But he still worried about
Trey. The kid would do anything Turnbull asked of
him and never once think about the consequences.
Not that Chet thought Roger would deliberately put
the boy in harm's way. If there was one good thing

Chet could say about Turnbull, it was that he seemed to genuinely care about the members of the Porterfield family—even Maria's mother. In spite of the fact that she had made it abundantly clear that she did not like or trust him, Roger had continued to treat her with respect—at least until that day when they'd returned from the roundup.

Chet smiled as he roped another calf that had wandered too far from the herd and led the little guy back. Maria had been really mad at Turnbull that day. Of course, come to think of it, she'd been just as mad at him—maybe more. And that brought him back to thinking about Loralei and the baby, trying to work out what he would need to do to get them both out of a bad situation. And on top of everything else, there was Joker to worry about.

Other than a quick stop for the noon meal, he hadn't had a break all day, so he'd had no time to get back to the barn to refill Joker's canteen, bring him food, or check to see if the man was still breathing. He hoped maybe one of the two Johnsons' hands who knew about Joker had been able to check on the old man.

"Hunt!"

Chet saw George Johnson waving to him and rode over to meet the rancher. "Yes, sir?"

Johnson handed him a packet of papers. "These need to be at the bank by closing. Think you can get them there in time?"

Chet couldn't believe his luck. Johnson was handing him the opportunity he needed to get a doctor for Joker and maybe even talk to Marshal Tucker. "Yes, sir." He placed the envelope in his saddlebag. Then he noticed that Johnson was studying him closely. "Was there something else, boss?"

"There's no money in that envelope," Johnson said. "Make the delivery and come right back."

Chet couldn't blame the man for letting him know there was nothing worth stealing, but then why choose him at all? "I'll be back as soon as—"

"Bring the doc," Johnson interrupted, speaking in a low almost whisper. "But tell him to stay out of sight, okay? Use the side door for getting in and out of the barn."

So Johnson knew.

"Yes, sir."

"You boys should have said something sooner," he said, keeping his voice low.

"He begged us not to. The man is scared and doesn't know who he can trust."

The rancher nodded, and Chet tipped his fingers to the brim of his hat and took off. It would take an hour or more to reach town, five minutes to deliver the documents to the bank, another quarter hour to find the doctor and persuade him to come, then another hour or so back. It would be dark by the time they reached the ranch. Chet had to believe that Johnson had planned it that way. Was Johnson just as suspicious of the Tiptons as he and Bunker were? Joker had said Roger wasn't directly involved—who had the foreman gotten to do his dirty work and how deep was he in with the Tiptons? There were too many questions and not enough answers.

In spite of the fact that the railroad had bypassed the town of Whitman Falls, the main street was busier than Chet might have expected. A stagecoach pulled in as he was tying his horse and crossing the street to the bank. That put him in mind of Loralei—and the baby. It was that baby that worried him most. Loralei had admitted he wasn't the boy's pa, but even so, he worried. Even if Loralei returned to Florida, Chet knew her father well enough to know that he would never accept the child, would always think of him as his daughter's bastard. The boy would pay a price.

Inside the bank, he waited patiently for a teller to find Clyde Cardwell, whose name was written in bold letters on the envelope. Johnson hadn't said anything about delivering the packet directly to the man, but Chet didn't want there to be any question that he'd done his part.

"You're that fella from Florida that Maria Porterfield took on, aren't you?" Cardwell said as he impatiently signed the receipt that Chet had requested.

"I've done some work for the Porterfields," he replied warily. There was something about Cardwell that put him in mind of Roger Turnbull.

"You planning on sticking around after?" There was no need to explain "after what"—everyone knew that getting the beef to market was the goal.

"Haven't decided," Chet said, accepting the scrap of paper the banker thrust at him and folding it carefully before sticking it in his shirt pocket.

"You heading back to the Johnsons' place?"

"I'm working there for the time being." Before the banker could ask more questions, Chet tipped his hat to the woman working behind the ironwork of the teller's cage and turned to go.

"Give my regards to the Porterfields," the banker called. Chet kept walking.

On his way into town, he had spotted the shingle that identified the doctor's home and office. The sun was low on the horizon and the shadows were beginning to settle over a quieter main street. He passed one saloon and heard the tinny sound of a piano, then another where the low murmur of men's voices drifted out to the street. In a month or so, those saloons would be filled to overflowing with drovers, once they'd rounded up the cattle headed for market and loaded them onto railroad cars in Yuma. But on this night, the town was relatively quiet.

Still, he would not risk using the front entrance to the doctor's office and home. Instead, he rode out of town, headed back toward the Johnsons' ranch, and once he was sure no one had followed him or was observing his actions, he doubled back and approached the doctor's house from the rear.

There was a light glowing in a downstairs window. He peered in and saw a young woman seated at the kitchen table, the remains of her supper pushed aside as she studied a thick book and occasionally made notes on a pad of paper. He waited, but when no one else entered the room, he decided he needed to take action.

He knocked on the back door and was surprised to hear the kitchen chair scrape the floor without hesitation. Then the door opened and the young woman stood before him—wire-rimmed eyeglasses perched on top of a messy bun of hair and an impatient frown on her face. "Yes?"

"I need to speak to the doctor."

"Are you hurt?"

"Not me. No, miss. If I could just—"

"My father is out on a call—along with my mother. A difficult delivery. I don't expect them home for hours if at all tonight."

Chet was inclined to warn her that she was giving far too much information to a stranger knocking on her back door after dark, but he had other problems. "I need help," he said.

She stepped aside and motioned for him to enter and take the chair opposite hers. She poured a cup of coffee and handed it to him. "All right, in three minutes or less, tell me what this is about."

He hesitated.

"Two minutes, thirty seconds," she said, tapping her fingers on the cover of the book she'd been reading.

Chet took a long swallow of the coffee and stood up, handing her the cup. "Look. Is there a vet nearby?"

"Two minutes," she replied. "And yes, but Bugger McFarlane is the biggest gossip in town, and since you seem to need to keep this private…"

Hesitantly, he told her about Joker. With each detail he revealed, her eyes grew wider and her expression more horrified. After a moment, she held up her hand to stop any further explanation, picked up a black leather doctor's bag that looked new, and said, "Let's go."

"You'll take me to your father?"

"No. You will take me to the patient—and do not even think of saying some version of 'But you're just…' I will have you know that I have studied medicine and am preparing to join my father in practice, so let's stop wasting time and get to your friend before he either loses a leg or dies of the infection."

"You got a horse?" Chet asked when they were outside.

"Yes, but we'll attract less attention if I ride double with you, slip off as we approach the Johnsons' place, and make my way to the barn."

He mounted his horse and pulled her up behind him.

"I didn't get your name, miss," he said once they were on their way.

"Addie Wilcox. And you are?"

"Chet Hunter."

"Ah," she said in a tone that rang with amusement, "the drifter. The drifter with the wife and baby from Florida. The drifter——"

"Everybody's gotta be from somewhere, Miss Wilcox," he muttered and spurred the horse into a gallop.

"That's *Doctor* Wilcox," she shouted over rush of the wind and the pounding hooves of the horse.

Twelve

THE DOCTOR'S DAUGHTER DID AN IMPRESSIVE JOB OF cleaning up Joker's wounds, getting him settled in a clean bed in the Johnsons' house, and leaving behind medicines and instructions for using them to help him heal. All of this had been accomplished while the other hands were sleeping. Chet had been assigned the task of keeping watch to be sure no one saw Joker being moved, and the patient was given a knotted rag to bite down on whenever he felt the urge to cry out. Rico's sweetheart, Louisa, volunteered to keep watch until morning. All in all, Joker was in good hands.

"So he'll be all right?" Chet asked as he took Addie Wilcox back to town in the hour just before dawn.

"No. Truth is, he might still lose that leg, and in the best of circumstances, he'll have a pretty bad limp and a lot of pain. I'll have my father come check on him when he can."

They rode in silence for some time, each of them exhausted and lost in thought. Then very quietly, Addie Wilcox said, "It was the Tiptons, wasn't it?"

"Why would you think that?"

"Because Jasper Tipton is determined to own everything—and everyone—within fifty miles of his headquarters. And he's not the worst one. His brother is the real hothead. He thinks he already owns everything. And everyone," she added so softly that Chet wasn't sure he'd heard her right.

"You've had dealings with the Tiptons?"

"You might say that."

"They've threatened your family?"

She snorted a wry laugh. "They've threatened any and every person in this whole area. But they're sly. It never comes out as a threat, and they never do their own dirty work."

Addie was telling Chet more about the Tiptons than he'd been able to learn from the ranch hands or from Maria or anyone else. "They send their hired men?"

"Probably that was what happened with your friend. But don't be fooled—the men on their payroll aren't just working that side of the fence. They've got people on just about every spread around here. Hard to know who to trust these days. That's why Mr. Johnson was being so careful. Guess he must trust you. Probably because you're an outsider. On the other hand, you're not the first stranger to come around and work your way into the good graces of some unsuspecting ranch owner."

"Meaning?"

"Three or four years ago, Roger Turnbull showed up." That was it. It was as if he should be able to fit the pieces together without her having to say another word.

"And?" he asked, impatient now that they had almost reached town and the dawn was breaking, meaning people were starting to be out.

"All I know is that Pa thought he knew Turnbull from somewhere else—couldn't place him, but he was real sure. Then about a year ago, it hit him. One time when he was called to the Tipton home to treat Jasper's wife after a horse threw her, Roger was there. Pa said he seemed to be good friends with both brothers—especially Buck, the younger one. Then Roger started working for the Porterfields. Pa warned Maria's father, and he said he would take care of things."

They had reached a grove of cottonwoods at the back of the doctor's house. Chet reined the horse to a stop and helped her down, handing her the black bag that he'd tied to his saddlebags. "How long ago was that—that Mr. Porterfield said he would handle things?"

She shrugged. "Couple of months before he died. Pa said Mr. Porterfield had had a long talk with Roger and believed the man had made his choice. We all figured that meant he'd decided to stay with the Porterfield outfit and probably hoped to marry Maria, but then Mr. Porterfield had that accident..." She stifled a yawn. "Take care, Chet. Word is that Roger doesn't like you and that's not likely to change."

Chet watched her until she was inside the house. From the looks of things, her parents had still not returned, but he saw her lift the curtain at the kitchen window and wave him off, so he headed back the way he'd come, cutting cross country when he could to save time. On the way, he thought about the idea that

Turnbull hoped to marry Maria—an idea he didn't like one bit. On the other hand, as foreman, Turnbull was somebody her family might approve—not somebody like him. He was just a hired hand—and a drifter to boot.

Why was he thinking about marriage? Didn't he have enough to worry about what with Loralei and her baby?

When he saw a rider coming his way, his instinct was to hide, but the other cowboy had already spotted him.

"Hunt!"

"Rico?" They met at the foot of a mesa. "What are you doing out here?"

"Turnbull sent me out to track strays." He grinned. "Coulda sworn I saw tracks leading right to the Johnsons' place, but Louisa said I must've been mistaken."

"So who's doing the branding at the Porterfield place?"

"Turnbull is—said he didn't want to lose his touch."

"Can you get a message to Miss Maria?"

"Sure. About Joker?"

Chet nodded and pulled out his tally book and the stub of a pencil. While he wrote the note for Maria, he filled Rico in on the details. "I'd keep this to yourself for now, much as you might want to tell Bunker and the others. I've been told from a pretty reliable source that Tipton has men working each ranch—hard to know who to trust."

"How come you trust me?"

Chet shrugged. "The way I figure it, if you did anything to betray the Porterfields, your mama would skin you alive and make you into pulled meat for her burritos."

Rico chuckled, pocketed the folded note, and then

leaned on his saddle horn, studying the horizon where
Tipton Brothers' fencing cut a swath through the land
as far as either of them could see. "You think it'll ever
be the same, Hunt?"

"Nope. The day of open grazing is coming to an
end, that's certain. But there'll always be a need for
ranches, whether they're raising beef or sheep, and
where there's cattle, there will be cowboys. We'll just
have to figure it out as we go, Rico."

Rico nodded. "Guess we don't have no other choice."

The two men parted then. Chet couldn't help
thinking the changes in lifestyle were going to be
tough on Rico. The boy had his heart set on one day
marrying Louisa Johnson, but he had about as much
chance of that happening as Chet did thinking there
might be a future for him with Maria. He rode on,
following the Tipton fence line and realizing he wasn't
seeing any activity. Chances were, like every other
ranch, the Tipton men were busy rounding up the
stock they planned to take to market.

This, he figured, was the perfect opportunity to
figure out the source of the ranch's water problems.

He saw a cluster of trees, hobbled his horse near
the stream, and started following the water. When he
came to the fence, he pulled the strands of wire apart
with his glove-protected hands and climbed through.
Staying close to the brush that lined the banks of
the stream, he worked his way deeper into Tipton
property. Finally, a ways upstream, he saw what was
affecting water flow on the other side of the fence.
The Tiptons had built a dam—one designed to allow
a trickle of water to still make it downstream but

otherwise stopping the natural flow no matter how much rain there was.

The thing of it was, the dam was well inside Tipton's boundaries. The brothers had found a legal way to drive Maria and the other small ranchers out of business, and there probably wasn't a thing they could do about it.

❧

Maria was at her desk when Eduardo knocked and then stepped inside the cluttered room. Chet's dog, who had taken to following Maria everywhere since Chet left for the Johnsons' ranch, looked up and then, apparently satisfied that there was no cause for alarm, went back to dozing.

Eduardo held out a folded paper.

"Rico was hunting strays yesterday over near the Johnsons' place. Hunt asked him to bring this to you. Rico didn't want Turnbull questioning what business he might have with you, so he asked me to deliver it." He bent to rub Cracker's head while Maria read the note.

"It's about Oscar—Joker," she said, lowering her voice in case anyone outside might be inclined to eavesdrop. "Chet says he got Doc Wilcox to come out to the ranch and she..." Maria glanced up at Eduardo.

"She?" he asked.

"Must be a mistake. Anyway the doctor has attended Joker, and he's been moved into the Johnsons' house, but nobody knows that except the family." She turned the paper over, half expecting the words to continue on the other side, but there was no more. "He doesn't say if Oscar will be all right, or why the need for such secrecy, or…"

"Sometimes what's not there tells the tale," Eduardo said.

"Well, maybe you understand, but I do not."

"The sneaking him up into the barn and then into the Johnsons' house tells me he's still in danger, and not from his injuries, although he's probably got a ways to go to be ready for workin' again. No, my thinkin' is that Joker's afraid of somebody—afraid if they know he's alive, they'll come back and *matarlo*." He made a slicing motion across his neck to emphasize his meaning.

"How could Oscar possibly be a threat to anyone?"

"If he knows too much…" Eduardo shrugged.

Suddenly the office door slammed back on its hinges, and Loralei entered the room as if something was chasing her. "You have to do something about that woman," she shouted as she practically threw herself into the chair across from where Maria stood holding Chet's note. Maria noticed that Eduardo had quietly vacated the premises the minute Loralei made her entrance.

"Calm down," Maria ordered, filing Chet's note in a desk drawer and locking it before turning her attention to the distraught woman. "What is it now?"

"She practically ordered me to wash diapers—scrub them with my own hands on that horrid board with that soap that would remove paint from a wall." She held up her hands—her perfectly white hands, unblemished by any hint of housework. Cracker ambled over to take a look, swiped at one of Loralei's hands with her tongue, and then sat patiently, tail wagging, waiting for Loralei to pet her.

"Shoo," she said in disgust, waving her hands at the dog.

Maria bit back a smile. "By 'she' I assume you are referring to Juanita, and I would remind you that while my mother is indisposed and I am charged with managing my father's business, Juanita is in charge of the house. That includes the right to hand out assignments so that the chores get done. If you would perhaps prefer to gather eggs from the chicken coop at dawn each morning and feed the chickens and clean the coop, I could speak with Juanita."

"You are not listening to me," Loralei practically bellowed.

Outside the open door, Maria saw a passing cowhand glance toward the office. She got up, closed the office door, and then said very quietly, "Loralei, my family has taken you and your child into our home. We are providing you with a place to sleep, food to eat, and even a nursemaid for your son. I do not think it is too much to ask that you take responsibility for such normal motherly duties as washing your child's clothing and maintaining the living space that my family has provided."

"But—"

"On the other hand, as I recall, when you first arrived in town you were prepared to take up residence at the hotel. We can certainly see that you and your son are moved there if that is your preference."

For the first time since Maria had met the woman, Loralei burst into genuine tears—sobs that shook her shoulders and sent her into hiccups as she tried to catch her breath. "You…are…horrid," she managed, the flow of tears wetting her cheeks and the front of her dress.

Maria took her seat behind the desk. "No. What I am, Loralei, is tired. Tired of fighting for what's rightfully my family's, tired of worrying about bills and whether or not the rain will be enough and how we can make sure we get our beef to market without losing any more steers along the way."

If she had hoped for some measure of sympathy, she could not have been more wrong. Loralei looked at her as if she had just spouted the same gibberish that came from the baby's lips. "You are surrounded by men who fall all over themselves to do whatever you ask," Loralei said. "If you're so tired of it, then stop trying to be a man and let Roger do his job. He only wants to take care of you and your family, so why on earth don't you stop being so high and mighty and let him?"

"I wasn't aware that you and Mr. Turnbull were on such good terms," Maria said.

Loralei's cheeks flamed an unbecoming blotchy scarlet. "We—that is—he has been kind enough to stop by. After all, you sent Chet away, and Roger is only doing what any gentleman would do." Her expression had turned defiant.

"We are moving away from your purpose in coming here in the first place, Loralei, and I have work to do. So either take responsibility for keeping your son's clothing clean—wear gloves if you must—or you can always move back to town or hire help. But Juanita and my sister and Ezma—as long

as *we* are paying her—have their own duties. Now if
you'll excuse me…" She pulled out a ledger and began
entering figures in the columns.

After a moment of working her mouth into a
tight, angry slit, Loralei stood up, walked to the door,
slammed it open, and left. And the minute she did,
Maria unlocked the desk drawer, took out Chet's
note, and reread it, looking, she realized, for any sign
at all that he might be missing her. But his words
showed no such sign, so she refolded the note and
placed it back in the desk drawer before turning back
to the ledger.

Like the papers on her father's desk, it seemed like
problems just kept piling up for the ranch and Maria.
Knowing there was little she could do to change the
numbers that didn't add up the way she needed them
to, she decided she need to go into town, see Doc
Wilcox, and get the whole story about Oscar.

"I want to talk to Doc," she told Amanda, who
could not understand why she couldn't come along.
"I really need you to stay here with Mama. Nita has
her hands full and…"

"Tell me you aren't planning to cancel the party."

The party had been the last thing on Maria's mind.
"Of course not," she assured her sister. "Why would
I do that?"

"Oh, I don't know. Seems to me you've been
doing all sorts of strange things lately."

"Like what?"

"Sending Chet away for one thing, and then
there's Rico."

"What about Ricardo?"

Amanda heaved a sigh of pure exasperation. "I never saw him set foot in Papa's office before, but the other day, there he was."

"You know what that was about. Ricardo wanted his chance to do the branding. It took a lot of courage for him to come and ask me for that."

"Okay, so then Roger sends him off to track strays, and I heard Slim and Bunker talking, and they were saying that Roger can't do half the job Rico can."

Maria was well aware of the difference. She'd heard the same thing from Eduardo. "Roger just has a lighter touch." The truth was that when Roger wielded the branding iron, the brand was indeed lighter—less clear—than when either Joker or Rico did the work. She didn't want to believe he was deliberately sabotaging the branding, and yet the questions about Roger and his loyalty to her family were beginning to build.

"Seems to me Papa used to fuss about how the Tipton Brothers' brand was so similar to ours. Seems to me—"

"Amanda, you are worrying about things you know nothing about. Roger is an experienced ranch hand. He knows what he's doing."

"Yeah, like stopping in to see sweet Loralei pretty much every night."

"How would you possibly know that?"

"Ezma told Juanita."

Maria closed her eyes. "Look, I'm riding into town because I want to talk to Doc about Mama. I want to be sure we are doing whatever we can to help her, and I think—because Doc sees you as young and fragile…"

Amanda started to protest, and Maria held up her

hand. "I don't think of you that way, but Doc does, so if you were in the room, he might try to protect you by not saying what he really thinks. Just let me do this, Amanda, for Mama."

She had said the magic words. Amanda was devoted to their mother, and of the four children, she had been the most devastated by Constance's ongoing malaise. Tears welled in her younger sister's eyes. "Do you think Doc might be able to help? I mean, all she does is lie there, staring at the ceiling unless Ezma brings little Chester to see her."

"And isn't that a positive sign? The fact that she pulls herself together for the baby?"

"I suppose."

"Amanda, we have to work together here. I rely on you to watch over Mama—you've always been her favorite."

"Next to Trey," Amanda said grudgingly.

"Side by side with Trey." Maria hugged her sister. "I'll be home by suppertime," she promised as she pulled on her riding gloves. "If anyone asks questions, just say I had to go into town to get some medicine for Mama. It's not a lie now, is it?"

Amanda smiled. "Mama would say you are stretching the truth to its limits." She handed Maria their father's hat. "I'm scared for us, Maria. Roger's changed so much. It's like he doesn't much like us anymore, and him hanging around Loralei... I wish Chet were here instead of at the Johnsons' place."

"I know. But one step at a time, okay?" She put on the hat and tightened the rawhide tie that held it in place. "I need to get going."

They walked out together. Across the way, they could hear the noise of the branding—calves bawling, men shouting, horses snorting, and then the telltale scent of burned flesh as the hot branding iron connected with cow hide. Maria paused for a minute then mounted her horse and headed off toward town. Later she planned to compare Rico's work to Roger's. The irrefutable evidence that he had continued to have contact with the Tiptons bothered her. He had once told her that he and Buck Tipton had worked another spread together back in Texas, citing that as the source of their friendship. But he had also pledged his loyalty to her father—and to her. The Clear Springs ranch could not afford to lose any more stock to rustlers or have the Tiptons change the mark and claim the animal belonged to them.

When she got to the Wilcox house, she was relieved to see Doc's carriage gone. The truth was that she wanted to talk to Addie, not her father. Chet's note had said "she," and the more Maria thought about that, the more certain she was that it had been Addie and not her father who had tended to Oscar's injuries. Now she needed to know just how serious those injuries were.

Addie answered the door and invited Maria to sit with her on the porch while they enjoyed a glass of cold lemonade. "Anybody passing by will just assume you're waiting for Pa," she said. "But that's not why you've come, is it?"

"No," Maria admitted. "I want to know about Oscar Crutchfield."

"Well, I can tell you this, if it hadn't been for that

new fella, Joker would be dead. As it is, he might still lose a leg."

"Did he tell you how it happened?"

Addie nearly choked on her lemonade. "We know what happened, Maria. Somebody beat the living stuffing out of him and probably thought they'd left him dead. He's scared, that's for sure, and not saying much, but any mention of the Tiptons and he starts shaking like the last leaf clinging to a cottonwood in December."

"Did you talk to Chet Hunter?"

"I spent a good bit of time riding out to the Johnsons' place and back with the man. Good looking son of a gun, don't you think?"

Maria chose to ignore this. "What did he say?"

"Not much of a talker, that one. Holds his cards real close to his vest. Besides, I understand he's got his own troubles—a woman and a kid?"

"News travels fast."

Addie smiled. "Well, before that woman rolled into town, speculation was that maybe finally a man worthy of Maria Porterfield had shown up. Any truth to that?"

"None," Maria said as she set her glass down and stood. "I should get back. When are you going to see Oscar again?"

"Tonight. Louisa Johnson was in town earlier and made a big deal of inviting me for supper when we crossed paths at the mercantile. Must have been half a dozen people who heard her. Why don't you come along? Then you can see for yourself how Joker's farin'."

And see Chet. Maria shook off that thought. This was about Oscar, not Chet. But the thought of seeing him again—of being near enough to see the laugh lines around his eyes and the way he had of looking at her as if she were the most beautiful woman he'd ever seen—the chance for all of that was more than enough reason for her to consider Addie's suggestion despite the soft voice in her head whispering she was being a fool.

"It's on your way home," Addie added. "George Johnson could send a message to your family, so they don't worry. You could stay the night and that would give you and the Johnsons time to figure out what comes next."

Addie was making a strong case. "I'm not exactly dressed for—"

"You aren't going to a party, Maria, and from what I hear, that drifter can't take his eyes off you no matter what you're wearing. My guess is he'd prefer you not wearing anything at all," she added with a sly smile.

"You are terrible," Maria said, but she was laughing. Addie was a dear friend, and it had been far too long since they'd spent time together. There had been a time when they had both thought that Addie and Jess would end up together, but they'd had a falling out when Addie insisted on finishing her medical training and then Jess had left.

"Okay, let's go to supper at the Johnsons'."

"Thought you might like that idea," Addie said as she gathered their glasses and carried them inside. "Meet me 'round back."

❧

Chet was puzzled when he saw two female riders approach the Johnsons' ranch. He'd been expecting Addie Wilcox, but who was the other woman? He squinted into the harsh, late afternoon sun.

Maria. Had there ever been a woman who could affect him the way this one did? Would there ever be again if he lost any chance he might still have with her? But the closer the riders came, the more his thoughts reverted to the reality and danger of the situation. What was she doing here?

The Johnson family came onto their porch to welcome Addie and express their surprise and delight that Maria had come as well. George Johnson called one of the younger hands over and gave him some instructions. When the cowboy came back to the corral, where Chet was hanging around with some of the other hands, he told them he had to ride over to the Clear Springs and let them know Miss Maria had stopped for supper and would be staying the night.

Chet's heart hammered. Was he nervous for Joker—that she might give away his presence in the house? Or was it that this might be his chance to talk to her and explain once and for all about Loralei and the baby?

And what if he did? What was the point? Did he honestly think a woman like Maria would ever take up with the likes of him? What did he have to offer her? Even if he could get to California and establish himself there and come back for her…

"Hunt!"

He looked up and saw Dusty and the other men staring at him.

"What?"

"I asked you if you wanted to play cards."

The last thing he wanted to do was get trapped inside the bunkhouse, where he wouldn't be able to see what was going on at the house. He grinned. "You boys took the last of my bettin' money last night."

"You still got that stake you been savin' for that place out in Californey," Dusty said. "You might double your money."

"Might lose it all just as likely," Chet replied. "Think I'll head down to the creek and see if there's enough water to cool off."

"Good luck with that—ain't enough water running to wash a baby rabbit, much less a growed-up cowboy," Dusty replied as he and the other hands headed for the bunkhouse.

Chet had located a spot near the creek where he could see into Joker's room. He'd seen Louisa Johnson and her mother tend to the man—feeding him, bathing him, helping him sit up. As he passed by the ranch house on his way down to the creek, he could see the family gathered around the dining room table. Maria was seated between Louisa and Addie, and the young women were laughing about something as they passed dishes heaped with steaming food around the table.

In case one of the other hands had decided to join him at the creek, he continued on down to the bank, stooped down, and dipped his neckerchief in the water. He twisted it and then looped it around his neck. The water—lukewarm as it was—felt good as it leaked down his neck and back, wetting his shirt. He wished there was enough water that he could submerge himself in it—clothes and all. There was little chance he would get close enough to actually speak to Maria, but if he did, it would be nice not to be smelling like cow dung. He ran his hand over the stubble that covered his chin and thought about Maria's skin—how smooth and soft it looked in spite of growing up in the hot sun of the desert.

Thinking about her skin made him picture her eyes—the way she looked at him. A man would give a lot to have somebody look at him the way she did. Early on, it had been like she couldn't quite figure him out, but that had changed. Just before Loralei arrived, when she looked at him, it seemed like she might be feeling the same longing he felt for her. He thought about her lips—the way they fought against a real smile sometimes—maybe because she was afraid if she smiled too much, the men wouldn't take her seriously. But those lips were made to smile—and to be kissed.

"Get a hold on yourself, Hunter," he muttered. But then he heard Maria's voice drifting out through the open dining room window. The gathering was breaking up. He could hear the clink of dishes being stacked, followed by the squeal of a screen door. He edged back toward the house and saw George Johnson take his usual place on the porch in a high-backed wooden chair and light a cigar. Chet took up his position outside Joker's room. A few minutes passed, and then he saw Addie and Maria enter the room. Maria stood by the door while Addie examined Joker's leg. Addie talked to Joker, and then Maria sat on the side of the bed. Chet would give a lot to know what she was saying to the cowhand.

Maria watched Addie examine Joker's leg. "Coming along real nice now that we've got you out of that barn."

"When can he be moved back to the Clear Springs?" Maria asked.

"He can be moved anytime, but I wouldn't recommend it."

"Infection?"

"More like when whoever did this to him finds out he's alive, they might decide they need to finish the job."

Joker winced. "Please, Miss Maria, if the Johnsons have no problem with me staying here for a while longer…"

His fear was obvious. Maria sat on the side of the bed while Addie continued changing the dressing that covered the deep cut over his eye. "Tell me what happened, Oscar."

"Just leave it be, Miss Maria. Nothin' you can do about it, and tryin' will just bring you more trouble."

"Is it Roger? Is that who's got you so scared?"

He tried to deny it, but she still had her suspicions. "Oscar, tell me what you know."

"Just stay out of it, please. Hunt will work it all out."

So was he saying that Chet knew the truth? She patted Joker's hand. "All right. You get some rest now, and we'll talk more later…tomorrow."

"You're stayin' the night?"

Maria nodded.

Joker let out a sigh of relief. "Good. You need to be careful, Miss Maria. Takin' off like you tend to do without a thought for danger out there, that's not wise."

"I'll be careful. You get some rest."

She nodded to Louisa, who was waiting by the door, her knitting in hand, ready to sit with the patient. "I need some fresh air," she said.

"Where's Hunter?" Addie asked Louisa.

"He has this place where he sits at night to keep watch." She indicated a place outside the window. "That's why the window's open so wide, so he can get here if I need him."

Maria nodded, and when Addie started to follow her out, she said, "You see if you can get anything more out of Oscar. I'll talk to Chet."

Addie shrugged and returned to sit with Louisa and their patient. Maria slipped out through the back door and approached the cluster of shrubs and bushes that offered a hiding place with a good view of Oscar's sick room.

"You shouldn't be here, Maria." His voice was low and husky and held no surprise.

Now that she was finally within arm's reach of him, she didn't know what to do or say. She'd been thinking about what he said, about him, since he'd left. She'd had a hard time thinking of anything else at times. And now she felt the strong impulse to run to him, throw her arms around him and press her cheek to his chest. She wanted to feel his warmth and his gentleness. She wanted to take all the times she had imagined—sometimes against her better judgment—what it might be like to kiss him and make that a reality. But because he stayed where he was, so did she.

"This is the one place I should be, Chet. I need to find out what's going on."

"It's between Joker and whoever did this to him."

"And whoever ordered this done to him. What is it he knows, Chet?"

"Stay out of it, Maria, before somebody else gets hurt."

"Oscar works for me, Chet. He worked for my father. He has been loyal to our family, and I intend to see that whoever is behind this is stopped."

Before she knew what was happening, Chet had grabbed her arm and pulled her deep into the bushes with him. With one hand, he covered her mouth, and his lips were close to her ear as he whispered, "Be still. Somebody's comin'."

She felt his arms tighten around her, felt the beat of his heart against her cheek as he cradled her head against his chest. Without realizing it, she wrapped her arms around him and held on, listening as he was for whoever might be nearby.

"'Evening, Mr. Johnson."

She startled as she recognized Roger's voice. She heard his step on the wooden slats of the porch, heard the creak of George Johnson's rocking chair.

"Evenin', Roger. Cigar?"

The scratch of a match, then the scent of tobacco snaked its way around the side of the house to where she and Chet waited.

"I understand Maria's here."

"Yep. Came over with Addie Wilcox. The two girls plan to stay the night, have a nice long visit with Louisa."

"Maria's needed back at the ranch. I came to get her."

Maria's instinct was to run, but Chet tightened his grip.

"Something happen over there, did it?" George asked.

Roger ignored the question. "That Florida cowhand still working for you?"

"Yep. Good man. My guy working out over at Porterfields' place?"

"Fine. Look, George, Hunter might be a good ranch hand, but he's bad news for Maria. It's like he's gotten to her somehow."

"She came here to see Louisa."

"Since when have she and your daughter been so close? Amanda and Louisa, sure, but Maria? Now let her know I'm here so we can get back."

"Afraid you're too late, Turnbull. The girls headed up to bed right after supper. Mrs. Johnson told me not five minutes before you got here that she heard them giggling and whispering together. Do Maria good to have some time like that. She's had a lot on her shoulders since her pa passed. Give her this one night, and she can get back to whatever trouble's brewing first thing tomorrow."

Both men were silent for a long moment, smoking their cigars. Then Maria heard George add, "Course if you ask me, the trouble is that you've got a burr under your saddle about the drifter and Maria— something you've made up in your head and can't seem to be shed of. A word of advice, son. The more you make of this, the more you push her to the man." One of the cigars hit the dirt and glowed weakly. "Now if you'll excuse me, I've got a long day tomorrow, and I'm not as young as I used to be."

The screen door opened with a scraping sound. "Go home, Turnbull. Stop stirring up trouble where there's none in the pot. Maria will be back tomorrow."

She felt a strange sort of hope that perhaps Roger's problem was pure jealousy after all and had nothing to do with being involved with the Tiptons or their plot to take over her ranch. She tried to sit up, but Chet held her firm.

"Stay," he whispered. "He's still there."

He was right of course. What might Roger do if he realized that instead of being in the house with her friends, she was outside—outside and being held in Chet's strong arms?

Thirteen

THE TRUTH WAS THAT HOLDING MARIA, HER FACE pressed to his chest, the scent of her filling his nostrils until he thought he might pass out from the sheer heaven of it, was not something Chet was anxious to put an end to. But when he saw Roger head down to the bunkhouse, he eased Maria to a sitting position. "Stay here until he's inside and then go back into the house."

"No. We have to talk."

She was right. For one thing, he needed to tell her about the dam. He dreaded that, knowing she would see it as one step closer to losing the ranch, but she deserved to know what he'd found out.

"I have to get to the bunkhouse before Turnbull decides to start looking around for me out here."

"Fine. You go and get him to leave and then come back. I am not going back inside until we talk, even if it takes all night."

She had to be the most mulish female God ever put on the face of the earth. "We can do this tomorrow."

"We're doing it tonight. Now go."

"Yes, ma'am." He couldn't help smiling as he walked away. But the minute he entered the bunkhouse, his smile faded. "Evenin', Turnbull." He pulled up a stool and nodded to the dealer to give him cards.

"Where you been, Hunter?"

Chet studied his cards. "That's kind of a personal question, but since you asked, nature called, and I felt inclined to answer that call." He discarded two cards and saw his fellow players smirk.

"Once the branding is done over at our place and Johnson's cowhand returns, you might as well keep on riding west, Hunter."

"Well, now, seems to me that'll be up to·Miss Maria and Mr. Johnson to decide."

"If Johnson is fool enough to keep you on, that's his business, but get one thing straight: *I* do the hiring at the Clear Springs, and I ain't interested in hiring you."

The men around the table played out their hands, none of them so much as glancing Turnbull's way, but all of them well aware of the possibility of a fight.

"Miss Maria hired me, Turnbull, not you. Seems to me that was the day you quit her place and went off to work for Tipton Brothers." He played a card. "How did that work out?"

"He's back at Porterfields', ain't he?" Dusty muttered and all the men snickered.

Turnbull's neck turned a deep red, and as the color climbed to his cheeks, he turned and left the bunkhouse. A minute later, they heard him ride off into the night. "That cowboy has too high an opinion of himself," Smiley said. "Somebody's gonna take him down a notch or two one of these days." He stood up and threw his cards on the table. "That's it for me, gents. Calling it a night."

To Chet's relief, the others took Smiley's cue and turned in their cards as well. Chet sat on the side of his bunk and pulled off his boots as the other cowboys prepared for bed. He laid down, hoping it wouldn't be long before the others were sleeping and he could slip out and find Maria. He had no doubt that she would still be waiting for him to tell her what he'd been able to learn about Joker's injuries. The woman was just that stubborn.

Sure enough, she was still sitting right where he'd left her, huddled under the bushes, her arms wrapped around her knees. "What kept you?" she demanded.

"Had to wait for Turnbull to leave and the others to turn in for the night." He held out his hand to her. "You should stand up and stretch. Come on. We'll walk down to the creek."

She did as he suggested, stumbling a little. He wrapped his arm around her waist to support her, then left it there because it felt right. To his surprise, she didn't push him away. "Maria, you need to back off this thing. Let me handle it."

"And how exactly do you plan to do that?"

"In time, Joker will tell me what I need to know. He's just scared right now."

"And with good reason. Whoever attacked him almost killed him. As it is, Addie isn't sure he'll ever regain full use of that leg. But I don't care. Oscar will always have a job at Clear Springs."

"You're assuming there will always be a Clear Springs Ranch?"

She pulled free of him and turned to face him. "Now understand this, Chet Hunter: I will not lose that ranch. I will do whatever it takes to make sure we never lose our land—our home."

He took hold of her shoulders. "I was right about the water flow, Maria. I got onto Tipton land, and they've built a dam. We can check with the fort, but there's no law I know that'd stop them. I don't think there's anything you and the others can do about it."

She froze. "That's how they plan to ruin us? By driving us to drought?"

"I'm afraid so."

She'd gone so still that he thought maybe she might collapse. Instead, she turned her face to the sky, and in the moonlight he could see tears brimming in her eyes. "Then I've lost it, haven't I? The ranch. It's only a matter of time." Her voice was hollow and defeated. She had so much to deal with, and she was magnificent in handling everything from her mother's illness to keeping the ranch going. It was hard to see her give up.

"We'll figure out a way, Maria."

"I don't see how. If they have the law on their side, then—" She shivered, whether from fear, distress, or the chill of a desert night he couldn't have said, but he pulled her closer and wrapped his arms around her. She settled against him, unresisting.

Once again he inhaled the sweet floral scent of her hair, and this time he kissed the top of her head. "Go inside before Addie comes looking for you."

"I didn't just wait here so I could learn what you know about Oscar. I want you to tell me more about Loralei," she said softly.

"I've told you, Maria. The boy is not mine."

"But she believes that he is."

"No." He told her what Loralei had told him—about the married man, about the letter coming, about her father's threat to hunt Chet down.

"So she came here to save you?"

He chuckled and pulled her back against him. "Loralei is not that noble. Don't get me wrong. She's not a bad person, but she has a lot of trouble seeing beyond her own needs and wants."

"She's a terrible mother," Maria grumbled.

"She's lucky you took her in and that she has Ezma and your mother and Juanita to care for the boy."

"That baby has been like a tonic for Mama. She's more like her old self every day. She's been getting dressed and coming down to the kitchen for meals, and she is always looking for Ezma and the baby. At least I have Loralei to thank for that, I suppose."

He took a step back, establishing some distance between them, wanting instead to hold her closer. "So do you believe me when I tell you there was never anything more than friendship between me and Loralei? Do you believe me when I tell you that boy is not mine?"

She placed her palm on his cheek. "I barely know you, Chet Hunter, and yet there is something about you that tells me I can trust you. So what will you do?"

He leaned into her touch, savoring it. "I don't know yet. What I do know is that I seem to be a guy trouble follows, so best keep your distance."

She ran the backs of her fingers along the line of his jaw. "And what if I don't want to keep my distance?"

Her voice was barely a whisper, and he wondered if she even knew she had spoken the words aloud.

"Maria, I plan on kissing you now, so if that's something you'd rather not have happen, you'd best walk away." He held up his hands so that she was free of his touch. She did not remove her hand from his cheek.

"Fair warning," he said, taking a step closer.

She snaked her hand around to the back of his neck and raised herself onto her toes. "Thanks for asking," she said just before she brushed her lips across his.

And suddenly, all bets were off—his past, her ranch, anything else that might reasonably have kept them apart was scattered to the wind like the dust that constantly blew over the land. He pulled her closer. She pushed his hat off as she buried her fingers in his hair. He grasped the knot of her hair and unraveled it, uncaring of hairpins that fell to the ground around them. As he combed his fingers through the waves and curls, he kept on kissing her. Their lips fit like pieces of a puzzle and nothing in Chet's entire life had ever felt so right.

❧

Maria thought she must be going mad. She had known this man for only a few months and yet instead of pushing him away, she pulled him closer. At the same time, she banished all thoughts of anything or anyone else. Roger, Loralei, the baby, the ranch—they lost all importance. The only thing that mattered was Chet—being in his embrace, matching her breath to his, basking in the feel of his mouth pressed to hers, his fingers combing through her hair. Everything about this moment seemed right—destined. It was as if she'd always been waiting for Chet to come into her life.

She felt the tip of his tongue outline her lips, and it seemed the most normal thing in the world to open to him. When she did, he groaned and tightened his hold on her as he deepened the kiss. Following his lead, she responded, and it was as if he was teaching her a new dance. She had never felt so powerful and vulnerable all at the same time, and she prayed the moment would never end.

"Hey," he finally whispered, his lips trailing kisses along her cheek. "It's late and…"

"Stay," she pleaded. "Can't we just have this one moment?"

He stroked her face with his calloused palm. "Maria, you don't want this, and I don't want you to have regrets come sunup."

"I need you," she whispered.

"You need my help and you have that—you have always had that. We will figure this out together, Maria, but this…" He pointed first to her and then to himself. "This is just crazy and can't come to any good for either one of us."

"Because you'll leave," she said, and this time she did step away from him. She began twisting her hair back into its knot and then, realizing she had no pins to hold it, let it fall over one shoulder.

"I might have to leave. But right now, what you need is someone with a clear head who can help you figure this all out. I can't do that if all I can think about is holding you. Besides, down the road, you'll likely think twice about tonight."

She had been brushing dirt and debris from her clothing, but she stopped and looked up at him. Because it was too dark to see his features, she cupped her hands around his face and ran her thumbs over his mouth and cheeks. "I will think of this night often, Chet, and I will do so with no regrets. I need your help—that's true. And because I know you better than you may think, I know that in time you will decide to do what is best for Loralei and her child—even though they are hardly your responsibility. But not even that can rob me of tonight." Pulling him closer, she lightly kissed each of his cheeks. "Good night, Chet."

❧

Once inside the house, she looked out through the kitchen window and saw that he was still there. He was a good man, this drifter. He was also a man with just as many problems as she had. She smiled as she made her way up the stairs. For the first time since her father's death, she knew for certain that as long as he was with her, she would not face the future alone.

Maria's good mood was short-lived. When she reached Oscar's room, she found Louisa attending a man who had clearly taken a turn for the worse. "What's happened?"

"I don't know. He was sleeping soundly, and then he woke up and asked for some water. The pitcher was empty, so I went down and pumped some in the kitchen. By the time I returned, he was gagging and spiking a fever."

"I'll go wake Addie."

"I'll do it; he's asking for you," Louisa said.

Maria sat on the side of the ranch hand's bed. She took his hand between both of hers. "Just hang on, Oscar," she said. "Doc Wilcox has some—"

"Listen to me, miss." He squeezed her hand with surprising force although his voice was like the rasp of a blacksmith's file on a horse's hoof. "It's about your pa. Shoulda told earlier, but I was too scared. T'weren't no accident. That's why they came for me. I heared something, and they knew it."

Her head reeling from Joker's announcement, Maria leaned in closer. "Who is 'they,' Oscar? And what about my father?"

Sweat poured off the man's face and neck. His breathing came in rattles and gasps. "Do something," Maria begged as Addie rushed in, wearing her night-clothes and carrying her stethoscope. Addie placed her fingers against his neck.

Again the clutch of Joker's hand on hers, pulling her closer. "It was T-t-t…" he stuttered.

"Tipton?" Maria guessed. "Turnbull?"

But the man was gone.

Addie, who had clearly heard everything, frowned. "Louisa, tell your pa that Oscar Crutchfield has expired. And, Maria, you need to get back home. If what I just heard Joker say is true, then you and everyone in your family may be in danger."

Maria looked at Oscar's weathered face. Addie was right. Especially if the name Oscar had been trying to say was Roger's—that was even more reason to get home as quickly as possible.

"Look," Addie said. "There's nothing more I can

do here. I'll head back to town and send the marshal back here to see what he can figure out."

"But he has no jurisdiction outside of town," Maria argued. "Maybe if we go to the fort…Colonel Ashwood might…"

"Mr. Johnson will handle that," Addie said as she pulled Maria to her feet.

"I want Oscar's body brought to Clear Springs," Maria said. "Any cowhand who dies while working for us is buried in the family plot unless they or their family asks for something else." She stared at Oscar and smoothed his damp hair away from his forehead. "I don't even know if he had a family. Maybe Bunker…"

The tears came then, tears for this man who had given his sweat and loyalty to her family and tears for her father who—if Oscar was to be believed—had been murdered in cold blood.

"Maria?" George Johnson stood in the doorway of the small bedroom. "I'll have one of the men drive you…"

"I can ride." She managed to choke out the words.

"Still, somebody should be with you."

She hiccuped as her tears receded. "Then I want Chet Hunter to accompany me, and once I reach our place, I'll send your man back here."

Addie and Johnson exchanged glances. "If you think that best," the rancher said in a tone that indicated he did not think this was wise. He gripped her shoulder.

She stood up and looked around the room as if seeing it for the first time. "If he had to die, I'm glad it was here and that he wasn't alone. Thank you, Addie…Mr. Johnson."

Downstairs while Mr. Johnson went out to find

Chet, Maria gathered her things and thanked Mrs. Johnson and Louisa for caring for Oscar. They walked with her to the corral, where Chet waited with her saddled horse. "I'll send Ricardo with a wagon for Oscar's body," she said as she mounted.

Chet handed her the reins and then mounted his horse. "I can stay till your man gets back," he told Johnson.

"We won't get much done today, Hunt. Take good care of our girl here," he added with a glance toward Maria. "I know she thinks she don't need help, but those are the folks in most need."

Maria's horse danced impatiently. "We should go," she said, her voice still raw from her crying. She did not wait to see if Chet followed as she rode off toward the mesa that was the shortest way home.

The mustang wanted to run, and Maria was more than happy to let it. She felt the rush of hot air against her skin and heard the pounding hooves of Chet's horse gaining on her. It was midmorning and neither of them had eaten or had so much as a sip of coffee. Her stomach growled in protest, but she pushed the horse harder.

"Maria!"

She ignored Chet's call and kept riding.

When they had ridden for several miles, she saw the clouds gathering on the horizon and realized they were clouds of sand and tumbleweed rather than rain. She reined her horse to a halt and looked back at Chet. "Dust storm," she shouted, pointing.

"This way," he yelled and turned his horse so that he was moving parallel to the coming storm. "Come on."

She turned her horse to follow, but the shale rock on the mesa was slippery and loose and the horse stumbled. "Chet!" she screamed as the horse went down. She barely had time to roll free of the animal before the horse panicked and began flailing its legs wildly. She could hear Chet calling her name. His voice was nearer now, but not near enough. She rolled away and into the arroyo next to the narrow trail as she covered her head with her arms and listened to the shrieks of the out-of-control horse.

Then she heard a gunshot and the horse's panicked cries stopped. Slowly, she lowered her arms and waited for the dust to settle as she tried to make sense of what had just happened. But the dust did not settle and the silence did not last. With a roar, the wind carried by the cloud of desert debris surrounded her as it rolled over the landscape like a fog, covering everything in its path and gathering strength as it went.

"Chet!" She choked on the word, realized it was useless to try to cry out, and once again covered her face as best she could as the winds tore away her hat and went to work on trying to rip her hair free of her scalp. She coughed and tried to breathe, but in spite of the neckerchief she'd used as a mask, her throat filled with the orangey-red dust that surrounded her.

She could just make out the now-still silhouette of her horse. In some ways, the animal lying on its side, its back to her, formed a barricade against the worst of the swirling sand, dirt, and debris. But where was Chet, and what did he know of storms like this? The man was from Florida. He might know all about hurricanes and other tropical storms, but this was something foreign. If he tried to get to her—and she was certain that he would—he could easily slip on the trail and injure himself. She wanted to warn him, to try to reach him, but knew both were useless.

So she rested her forehead on her folded arms and swiped at the tears that she felt carving gorges through the dirt that coated her face. The storm coming out of nowhere seemed an omen, and coupled with Oscar's death and the news that maybe her father had been murdered, Maria felt defeated. Yet at the same time, she felt a rage building up inside her that matched the billowing clouds of the sandstorm. She would not let them win. She would find a way, because now more than ever, she was determined that her father's dream would not die—would not be murdered in cold blood.

⚛

Chet spit out the dirt that had instantly coated his tongue when he saw Maria's horse stumble, pulled off his neckerchief, and tried to call out to warn her. The horse went down shrieking in pain, its left front leg hanging at an angle that left no doubt it was broken. He grabbed his rifle from its holder, leaped down, and watched helplessly as her horse continued to fight and his took off. He could no longer see Maria. If she didn't move quickly enough, the frightened horse could easily kill her with one kick, so Chet acted purely on instinct. He took aim, swearing at the granules of sand and the distance that blocked his vision, and fired just as the full force of the storm they'd seen coming their way hit. The abrupt halt to the wounded horse's panicked cries told Chet he had hit his mark.

He couldn't see his hand in front of his face, so it was foolhardy to try to reach Maria, but he did it anyway, inching his way along the trail that zigzagged down the side of the mesa, pausing whenever shale gave way under his feet, praying she was all right. He'd wrapped his neckerchief around his nose and mouth as soon as he'd seen the storm approaching and had shouted to Maria to do the same. Had she? He couldn't remember.

He bumped up against something softer than the boulders. Fear pumping through his veins, he bent to feel the object and released his breath only when he realized he'd stumbled over the corpse of Maria's horse. Blindly, he felt around until he found her canteen and then remembered they had not waited to take water from the Johnsons' place but had planned to stop at the first stream—the stream that ran just on the other side of the mesa.

Using the horse's body to shield him from the blunt force of the storm, he looked around, trying to see through the curtain that surrounded him and blocked out the sun. The howl of the wind made it impossible to hear anything and the force of it tore at him, making it hard to keep his balance. It felt like any minute the rock beneath his feet might give way, sending him plummeting into the valley below. He dropped to his knees and edged his way forward, inch by inch. All the while he prayed he would find her alive and whole. One hand slipped off the trail and into a gully, closing around something hard but pliable—and then that something moved. He swiped at his eyes and saw her huddled below him. He slid down next to her, and she looked up, her eyes slits.

He pressed his back against the wall of the gully and pulled her into his arms. "Hang on," he said. Later, he would reprimand her for not properly covering her face. For now it was enough that she was alive and hopefully uninjured and clinging to him as if she might never let go. And not for the first time, Chet thought that might just be the best idea he'd considered in a very long time.

༄

The storm passed as suddenly as it had come, leaving behind a blizzard of sand granules that stung wherever they touched bare skin, and particles of tumbleweeds that caught on their clothing and hair. Chet continued to shelter her as if they were still caught up in the thick of the gale. She was content to stay there for as long as he wanted to hold her. In his arms, she felt safe and the worries that plagued her day and night did not seem half so frightening.

"I had to shoot your horse," he said finally.

"I know." She was thankful that her father's favorite had been in need of a new shoe, so she had taken one of the stock horses.

"His leg was broke and—"

She touched his cheek. "It's all right, Chet."

"My horse ran off."

"Smart horse."

He chuckled. "Smart lady, finding shelter like you did."

"It's not my first storm. I remember one time when Papa and Jess and I were out on the range and a storm like this one came up. I was maybe ten or eleven. Jess was probably thirteen."

"You both must have been plenty scared." He smoothed back her hair, and she rested her cheek against his shoulder.

"Yeah, but Jess took hold of my horse and used his neckerchief to cover its eyes, then started riding parallel to the storm, pulling me and my horse along behind him."

"Where was your pa?"

"He was trying to catch up to us, and you should have heard the tongue-lashing he gave Jess when he did—I mean, after we were safe and all. But Jess knew about this cave and that's where he headed. It was a big cave—big enough for us and the horses. Papa was amazed in spite of how mad he was at Jess."

"Jess sounds like a smart guy."

"He's close to the smartest man I've ever known. One day Trey might just turn out to be smarter, but Jess just seems to know stuff. He sees things and files them away until he needs them—like that cave. Then all of a sudden, he remembers." She'd been so mad at Jess for leaving that it had been a long time since she'd remembered the good about him. "My brother is a good man."

"Never met the man, so I'm not going to argue with you," Chet replied. "We could probably use some of his smarts right about now." He stood up and looked around. "I'm guessing we're maybe five or six miles from the ranch?"

"More like seven or eight." She sighed wearily and pushed herself to her feet, brushing away what she could of the dirt that clung to her clothes and hair. "We probably should get going. The good thing is that I know the way, so at least we aren't lost." She started to edge past him, but to her surprise, he held her waist to stop her.

"I need to ask you something before we go, Maria."

"Okay."

"Do you believe what I told you last night about Loralei and me? Because if you still have doubts…"

For once she didn't need to consider his question in light of what her father might think or what anyone else might say. Instead, she pulled him closer and, oblivious to the sand and grit that coated them both, she kissed him the way he had taught her the night before. "Does that answer your question?"

He smiled. "Not quite sure. Maybe we could try that again?" He wrapped his arms around her and lowered his face to hers. "In fact, Maria Porterfield, I'm thinking I might need you to repeat that more than once, starting right now."

If this had been Amanda, then Maria would have warned her not to allow such shenanigans no matter how thrilling his kisses might be. But this wasn't Amanda, and this wasn't the front porch of the ranch house, and this was not her first kiss. She was a grown woman, and she was with a man who made her see stars when he kissed her, and she'd be willing to bet that even her mother would tell her that she'd be a fool to say no.

"Promise?" she murmured.

And just before his mouth met hers, she heard him chuckle and answer, "Yes, ma'am."

                              ≈

They walked for an hour or more before they spotted Chet's horse grazing near the creek. Chet set down the saddle and trappings they'd taken from Maria's horse. "Wait here," he said. For once, she didn't argue. Instead, she sat on the saddle and waited, watching as he slowly approached the animal made skittish by the recent storm.

As he expected, the horse moved away from him. So he headed for the creek a few yards away, knelt, filled his hat with water, and held it out in front of him as he approached. The horse whinnied and tossed its head but took a hesitant step toward him, sniffing the air. Chet pulled his neckerchief free and dipped it in the water, and when the horse was close enough, he gently pressed the damp cloth to the animal's snout and wiped dirt away from its eyes.

After a few minutes, he slowly bent and picked up the reins dragging on the ground, then began walking back to where Maria waited, making sure to leave the reins slack enough so the horse didn't panic. Maria had found a dried apple in her saddlebag, and she held it out as they approached.

"You ride and I'll walk," Chet said.

"And carry that extra saddle as well? No. The saddle can ride and we'll both walk."

He tugged her hat further down over her forehead so that the brim protected her face from the hot sun as they struck out across the dust-coated grasslands.

"Couple of hours," he guessed. As they crossed the shallow creek, he took her hand, and once they reached the other side, he did not let go.

Fourteen

REALITY HIT MARIA LIKE A SLAP IN THE FACE THE minute they reached the ranch. As they passed the stream that had all but dried up, she gave a passing thought to the dam the Tiptons had built—more than likely legally. Well, dam or no dam, and whether or not they had had anything to do with her father's death, she would fight them. She would not let them rob his family of the legacy he had worked so hard to build. She would find a way.

Roger saw them coming and rode out to meet them. "You couldn't let the lady ride?" he barked at Chet.

"We had the saddle, Roger, and I am perfectly capable—"

"We could have sent somebody back to pick up the saddle when they buried the animal that I assume this fool decided to shoot." He offered her his hand, his intent to pull her onto his horse with him clear.

"I've walked this far. I think I can make it the rest of the way. Did the storm come here?"

Roger frowned. "No. We saw the cloud, but it was headed east and we thought you were safe at the

Johnsons' place. What the devil were you thinking, Maria, striking out with a dust storm on the horizon?"

"It wasn't on the horizon when we started," she said reasonably.

"You and Hunt rode together?"

Maria released a frustrated growl. "Roger, could we possibly postpone your inquisition until I've had a chance to wash up and get something to eat?" She brushed past him then stopped. "By the way, it might interest you to know we found Oscar—or rather, what was left of him. He died this morning."

She didn't wait to see his reaction, leaving it to Chet to decipher.

She was relieved to see Juanita waiting for her at the house, but on her way there, she passed the anteroom and heard Loralei wailing about how beastly hot it was and how it never seemed so bad in Florida. "It's like living in an oven," Maria heard the woman moan.

"Then go back to your beloved jungle," Maria muttered as the baby began to cry and Loralei turned her fury on Ezma.

Maria stopped and retraced her steps until she stood at the open door of the room. "Loralei," she shouted above the fracas.

Even the baby stopped crying as all went silent, and both Loralei and Ezma looked up, their eyes wide with shock. "If ever again I hear you speak to Ezma that way, I will send you packing. Do you understand?"

"What happened to you?" Loralei asked, ignoring Maria's order. "You look like…" She shuddered. "You look like a ghost."

Maria realized that she must indeed be a strange

sight, her features no doubted coated with layers of dirt, her lips parched and cracked, her hair wild and tangled like a tumbleweed. "Are you afraid of ghosts, Loralei?" She moved into the small room until she was standing over the woman who let out a nervous giggle.

"What a strange question."

Maria leaned in closer. "I ask because as scared as you might be of ghosts, you should be doubly scared of me. I am in no mood to be nice, so apologize to Ezma and stop your complaining or else." She straightened up, crossed her arms, and tapped her foot. "I'm waiting."

Loralei looked from Ezma to Maria and back again. "Oh, very well. Sorry."

"Not good enough. Give it some of that famous Southern charm."

Loralei made a face but then smiled a toothy grin. "Ezma, honey," she began in a syrupy-sweet singsong voice. "This heat just does me in, and I do get a mite cranky. I know you understand, but please don't take it to heart."

"Yes, *senorita*," Ezma murmured and gave Maria a sideways look that begged her to let this be.

"Better?" Loralei growled, now standing and facing Maria directly.

"A little," Maria replied as she turned and left the room. "How's Mama?" she asked when Juanita met her in the courtyard with a glass of cold water. Beyond the courtyard, she saw Chet unsaddling his horse and heading into the barn, his dog dancing circles around him. Roger's horse was tied to the hitching post outside the ranch house, and he was waiting for her by the front door.

"Your Mama has made some big strides toward coming back to us." Juanita handed her a wet towel so she could wipe some of the dirt from her face.

"Thank God. But Nita—Oscar died last night." She hadn't planned to just blurt out the news, but there it was and behind the words came her tears.

Juanita folded her arms around Maria and led her inside the house.

"Someone murdered him. They beat him up so bad and just left him to die." She choked on her sobs, the release of the last several hours of no sleep, grief, and fear.

Juanita tightened her hug. "Let it out, Maria. You need to lay down some of that burden you've been carrying ever since your papa died."

The housekeeper's words only made Maria cry more. How was she going to tell the family that Isaac Porterfield's death might not have been an accident? Should she tell them at all? She had no proof. Maybe if Chet… But now that she was back at the ranch with all of the problems and more, their time together seemed like something she might have dreamed.

Juanita led her past Roger, who had the good sense not to try to ask her any more questions, and on into the kitchen to a chair. "First you eat something, then a bath, and then bed," she ordered.

"I have to—"

"No. Someone else can 'have to' do whatever it is. Not you, Maria. You are making yourself sick." She went to the stove and filled a cup, then brought it to the table. "Drink this down."

"It smells horrible."

"Never you mind how it smells, *mi hija*. It will help you regain your strength. Now, drink."

Maria had always done as she was told. Whatever Juanita or her parents—or even Roger—ordered. But after her father died and Jess left and her mother couldn't function, Maria had stopped taking orders and started handing them out instead. The relief she felt now that Juanita was treating her the way she had when Maria had been a girl was comforting. So she held her nose and downed the beverage.

"Now, a bath," Juanita announced. "Amanda!"

"Right here," Amanda said. "Good heavens, Maria, you look like something that got caught in a stampede." She led the way back down the hall to their bedroom, where the tub had been set up. Trey was filling it with buckets of steaming water.

In a way, she had been caught up in a stampede, Maria thought a few minutes later as she eased herself into the water—Oscar, her father, Chet, constantly having to prove that even though she was a woman, she was capable of managing the ranch. But mostly she was more worried than ever about whom she could trust...and the name that Oscar had tried to utter with his dying breath. She closed her eyes as she soaked in the warm water that Amanda had scented with yucca oil before shooing Trey from the room. Before Amanda allowed her to get into the tub, she had insisted on washing her sister's hair. Now, as she surrendered to the soothing warmth and scent of the water, Maria combed her wet hair with her fingers and thought about Chet—the way his fingers had stroked her hair, the way his calloused hands had touched her face, the way his eyes had been wide with fear for her safety. He cared for her. She had heard it in the thunder of his heart when he held her against his chest. Was this what it felt like to be in love?

She thought about her parents and the love they had shared. She thought about the way her mother looked at her father, the way her eyes lit up whenever she saw him. The way she had smiled that night by the creek when she had thought Chet was her husband. Maria understood that now. For the first time since her father's death, she thought she could begin to appreciate the depths of loss her mother had suffered. No wonder she wanted to live in the past. If Maria couldn't see Chet—if he were to leave—she knew she would never recover from the heartbreak of that. She loved him, but if they were to have any chance for a future together, then she had to deal with everything else.

She wrapped herself in a towel still warm from the sun as she stepped out of the tub. She saw her nightgown spread out on her bed. "Get me my clothes, Amanda."

"But Juanita said…"

"There is work to be done and Oscar's funeral to be planned. I'll sleep tonight." She rubbed her hair to soak up the extra dampness, then plaited it into one long braid. "Oh, and have the men meet me outside Papa's office in half an hour."

"All of them?"

"Yes—except the Johnsons' hand. He should head back home. Chet is back now."

"Even Roger?"

"Of course Roger. He's one of the hands, isn't he?"

Amanda laid out trousers and a shirt that had belonged to Jess and that Maria had taken to wearing once their brother had left. She added clean undergarments for her sister and smiled. "Not sure Roger sees things that way, but looks like you might be about to set him straight."

The men were all waiting for her when she entered the office—even Roger, who leaned against the door frame half-inside and half-outside the room, his arms folded across his chest and a smirk on his face.

"Gentlemen, as you may have heard by now, we have lost one of our own—Oscar Crutchfield has died. After he was brutally beaten, he hid for some time in the Johnsons' barn. Once we found him and moved him into the house, where his injuries could be properly treated, he seemed to be on the mend but apparently his injuries and the fever he developed were too much for him to overcome."

A murmur ran through the room, and she understood that Chet had not given the men details of Joker's death.

"He was murdered?" one of the men asked.

"In a manner of speaking. Colonel Ashwood has been alerted, and Marshal Tucker is probably at the Johnsons' ranch now. It is clear that whoever attacked Oscar is reckless and desperate and has little concern for the lives of anyone who may get in the way."

She heard the name "Tipton" run through the gathering. She held up her hands. "We do not yet know who is responsible. You—and I—may have our suspicions, but we will not become vigilantes, is that understood? We will let the authorities do their job."

"And then we'll take over," Bunker muttered.

"Seymour…" It was a warning, and Maria saw that the older man had the good sense to say no more. She also noticed that Roger had fully entered the room and that he seemed quite interested in what she had to say.

What do you know about this, Roger Turnbull? She couldn't help but remember that the name Oscar had tried to whisper had begun with the letter *T*. Roger had gone into town with her father that day, but had returned alone with some story of how her father had sent him on ahead. Was *he* responsible? Could it be possible?

"Services for Oscar will be tomorrow. His body will be returned later today and he will lie in the house, as have all the hands who have died in the service of this ranch before him. He will join my father and those other men in the family cemetery. Eduardo, if you would be so kind as to recruit two others and prepare the grave while Ricardo takes the wagon to retrieve the body."

Rico and his father both nodded, and she was gratified to see that the hands standing to either side of them immediately volunteered their help.

"What about the branding?" Roger asked. "We're already behind and—"

"I thought you told me things were right on schedule, but either way, this ranch is in mourning. We will resume—and hopefully complete—branding the day after tomorrow. That's all, gentlemen. Thank you."

She picked up her hat and strode from the room, nodding to each man as they made way for her. When she came to Chet, she paused, started to say something… then kept walking.

Later, she told herself. *You can find solace with him later.*

❧

When Chet left the meeting, Loralei was waiting for him. "What's going on?" she asked.

"A man we all worked with died. The funeral will be tomorrow. It'd be a help if you could take care of the boy so Ezma can help Juanita in the kitchen."

"Chet, we have to talk about us."

"There's nothing to discuss. I told you I would help you, but you know how this works—I don't get the bulk of my pay until we get the stock to market. After that, I'll pay your way to any place you want to go, but I'm not coming with you, and before you go, you will write your father and tell him the truth—a letter that I will take care of seeing gets delivered. Those are my conditions."

"You are a horrible man, and I have no idea what it was I ever saw in you that made me—"

"I've got work to do. I'll stop by later." He headed for the barn where Bunker was waiting for him.

The older hand didn't waste time coming to the point. "Tell me everything you know, Hunt."

Chet was tired, and he'd barely had time to wash up and change into a clean shirt before he heard about the meeting. He'd have given anything to just lie on his bunk for half an hour and relive the time with Maria. But clearly that wasn't going to happen. "I don't have much to go on."

He led Bunker over to the corral because at least out in the open they could talk without being overheard and not seem to be plotting anything. He handed Bunker a rag and indicated Maria's saddle. "You do Miss Maria's saddle, and I'll clean mine while we talk. That way nobody will think we're up to no good."

"Just talk to me, Hunt."

So he told the older hand everything he knew, starting with finding Joker in the barn and ending with what Maria had told him about the man saying that her father's death had been no accident. When he finished, he realized that none of this seemed to surprise Bunker.

The cowhand spit out a stream of chewing tobacco, then went back to cleaning the saddle. "Figured as much," he said finally. "Isaac Porterfield had no match when it came to handling horses. Me and Eduardo did some checking after the so-called accident but couldn't find no evidence—at least not that would hold up in court."

"But you found something. What was it?"

"Turnbull sent us out to bury the horse and bring back the old man's saddle and stuff. There were a couple of things that didn't fit right. Like the saddle cinch was awful loose and frayed, but not like it was old and needed replacing. Like somebody had taken a file to it—but not so obviously I could prove anything."

"What else?"

"The animal's shoes had nails loosened or had fallen out altogether. Mr. Porterfield took a lot of pride in his horses, and he took extra good care of his favorites, especially Macho over there. No way he wouldn't have checked these things before starting out."

"Where was he headed?"

"Had a meeting in town with the bank, way I heard it. He was on his way home when it happened. When he wasn't back by suppertime, Mrs. P. had their son, Jess, organize a search. Miss Maria was the one to first spot his body." He shook his head and scratched his beard. "Never saw the likes of her crying, like her heart was just broke in two. Course she rallied after that—had to with her brother taking off the way he did and her mama sick with grief."

Chet was still thinking about the "accident" and one thing didn't make any sense. "Whoever messed with his horse had no way of knowing when or where things might go wrong, and they sure couldn't be sure Maria's pa would die in the process."

"Oh, they made sure all right. They must have trailed him after he left town. Mr. P. had a snakebite on his neck. Thing was, the way the body was lying kind of on top of the horse, that don't make sense. Rattlers don't climb, so how'd the snake get to his neck?"

"Maybe it wasn't a rattlesnake. Maybe it was a copperhead."

Bunker shrugged. "Maybe but not likely around these parts."

"So you think somebody made sure Porterfield's horse fell and then finished the job?"

"I think ol' Isaac knew exactly who put that snake in striking distance." He gave the clean saddle a final slap with the rag. "Trouble is, nobody else knows. And there ain't enough proof to do anything if we did."

They both looked up when they heard the creak of the wagon leaving the barn. "Poor ol' Joker," Bunker muttered.

"Ever built a coffin, Bunker?"

"Yep." He picked up the saddle and started toward the barn. "Come on, Hunt. Might as well get started."

~

Maria heard the sounds of a hand saw scraping its way through wood, then a hammer, two hammers, and knew that someone was building the coffin for Joker. She'd watched from the courtyard as Rico drove the wagon away. In the kitchen, Juanita and Ezma were busy baking and preparing food for the wake that would take place that night. Ezma had reported that Loralei was napping, so Amanda had taken the baby with her to visit her mother. Trey was in the courtyard sketching something, and for once, everything seemed normal—or as normal as things could get given the circumstances.

"Sounds like Seymour has started building the coffin," she said as she passed through the kitchen. "I'm going to ride out and gather some wildflowers for tonight and to put on Oscar's grave tomorrow."

The truth was that ever since she'd learned that her father's death had been no accident, she'd been intent on returning to the site where they had discovered his body. Not that it would do any good. In the months that had passed since that horrid day, there had been dust storms and rain, and no doubt the hooves of hundreds if not thousands of cattle had passed over the spot. But she had to go.

She stepped inside the barn and saw Bunker and Chet working on the coffin. "I'm going to gather some flowers," she said. "Thanks for cleaning my saddle."

"You shouldn't go nowhere alone, Miss Maria," Bunker said. "Hunt, I can finish up here. You go with her."

"I'll be perfectly fine…" Her understanding of her feelings for Chet was too new. If he came with her, she wouldn't be able to think straight, and she needed to have her wits about her.

But already Chet had taken the saddle from her and headed for the corral, his dog at his heels. He slung the saddle over the railing and then chose a horse from those milling around the corral. He saddled it, then turned to her. "Which horse?"

"You really—"

"Which horse, Miss Maria? There's not a man on this spread that would let you go off on your own, so if you don't want me to ride with you, then pick another cowhand."

She entered the corral and placed the bit in the mouth of a dappled-gray horse, then led the animal into the yard closer to where Chet had left her saddle on the fence. "You'll do," she muttered as she slung the saddle into place, cinched the belt, waited for the horse to accept that, then tightened the belt again.

"You talking to the horse or me?" Chet asked.

"You'll both do."

"There're plenty of flowers down by the creek." Chet watched her cinch the saddle and then mount the horse. "But then, you aren't planning to pick flowers, are you?"

"Actually I am, but I have something else I need to do first." She waved to Trey as they passed the house.

"Going to the place where your pa died?" Chet guessed.

"Maybe."

"And exactly what do you hope to find there, Maria?"

"Answers." She urged the horse into a gallop.

❦

When Maria had come to the barn, Bunker had muttered, "Uh-oh." Like Chet, he had known that she would be unable to leave well enough alone once she found out her father's death had been no accident. "Whatever she's up to, you better go along with her," Bunker had said before turning to greet Maria.

Chet hadn't needed to be told twice. Truth was, he wanted to see the place where Maria's father had died. Not that he was any smarter than anybody else who'd seen the place, but maybe there might be something, and Bunker was right. With two men now dead and no one in custody, it was downright foolhardy for her to be out on the range alone.

He caught up to her and followed as she and her horse picked their way over a well-marked trail. She kept her eyes focused on the ground and ignored him. When finally she reined her horse to a halt and slid from the saddle, Chet waited to see what she would do. When she dropped to her knees and began running her gloved hands over the dirt, he climbed down from his horse and approached her.

"Maria?"

"There's got to be something," she said, her voice calm. "Help me look."

He knelt beside her and began running his hands over the ground as well. "What are we looking for?"

"Something. I'll know when we find it."

"You're sure this is the spot?"

"Pretty sure."

Cracker sniffed the ground. "Is that your pa's hat," Chet asked, pointing to the hat she was wearing. He was pretty sure it was, but the mood she was in, he wasn't going to risk making any assumptions.

"Of course," she snapped and kept searching.

"Let me have it a minute."

She sighed, pulled the hat off, and tossed it to him, then continued going over the dirt on the trail.

"Crack," he called and gave the dog a chance to sniff the hat.

"That's not going to work. It's been months, and I've been wearing the hat and…"

Cracker moved along the trail, nose to the ground. She doubled back twice to where Maria waited before continuing to sniff the trail.

"See? She keeps coming back to me because it's me she's smelling on the hat not…"

Cracker barked two sharp yelps and then sat down next to a spot fifty feet from where Maria and Chet waited.

"Worth a look," Chet suggested.

She tightened the rawhide under her chin and walked to where the dog waited. Cracker barked again. "This is ridiculous," she muttered as she dropped to her knees and started a fresh search.

Chet watched while Maria went over the ground inch by inch. After a while, she held up a bedraggled feather that had once been red but was now made maroon by exposure to the elements. She reached over and hugged Cracker. "Good girl," she murmured.

"What is it?"

"Pa wore a feather just like this one in his hat—this hat." She removed the Stetson and stuck the sad-looking feather in the band. "Whatever we're going to find, it's going to be right here."

Seeing that she was more determined than ever to spend the night if necessary searching for clues, Chet squatted down next to her. "Maria, we should go. We can mark the spot and…"

"A few more minutes," she said as she picked up something then discarded it and moved on. An hour later, she had returned to the area where she had found the feather.

"Maria, please." It broke his heart to see her there on her hands and knees, so determined to find something that could not possibly be there—but then she cried out.

"Look," she whispered as she held up two small pieces of turquoise.

"What is it?"

"Not sure but maybe…" She carefully wrapped the stones in a handkerchief and tucked them into her shirt pocket. "Let's go," she said as she whistled for the horses.

They rode side by side without talking. Cracker kept pace, looking up at Maria from time to time. After a while, Chet pointed to a field of wildflowers, and when they reached it, Maria dismounted and began gathering a bouquet. She seemed deep in thought, as if she might be planning something, and that made Chet nervous. "You gonna tell me what you found back there?"

She took a deep breath. "My father once gave Roger a turquoise and silver bolo that he wore for years. It was a sign of trust and appreciation for all Roger had done for us since coming on as foreman." She reached in her pocket and produced two small turquoise stones. "These are from that bolo—I'm sure of it. So why would they be there if Roger wasn't?"

"Maybe he chipped it another time."

"He only wore it on special occasions, and he was wearing it that morning when Papa asked him to accompany him to the bank."

"Still, Maria, it's not proof of anything."

"Well, it's all I've got." She pocketed the stones and walked on, gathering flowers as she did. Finally she turned to him. "Chet, I'll ask you the same thing you once asked me. Do you trust me? I mean do you trust what…has passed between us these last few days?"

"Trust is a funny word for it, Maria."

"Not really. You were betrayed by Loralei, and I would hate to think you might believe me capable of similar tactics."

"What's this about?"

"Over the next days—maybe even weeks—I need to make Roger Turnbull believe that I have had a change of heart where he is concerned—at least until I can find the bolo and make sure I'm right that the pieces fit. Playing up to him obviously means I will have to pretend to ignore you—maybe even appear to be angry with you."

"Don't do this, Maria. You don't know what Turnbull might be capable of."

"Oh, I think I know him well enough."

Chet reached for her, and she did not resist. "Let me handle this for you," he said.

"No. This is something I need to do for my father and my family. Roger holds the key—he may not have had a hand in killing my father himself, but he knows who did."

"Maria, please."

She cradled his face in her hands. "Please don't fight me on this," she said softly, and then she kissed him. "Please, Chet, say you understand why I need to see this through."

Her courage and determination proved to be his undoing. He had never known a woman like Maria. And when he deepened the kiss and she wrapped her arms tightly around him, he lifted her in his arms and carried her to the edge of the field, where the flowers met the shade of a large cottonwood tree. He glanced at Cracker. "Stay," he ordered.

He settled himself on the grass and pulled her into his arms. What he wanted more than anything he'd ever considered was to make love to her. But they were from two different worlds, and he was not the right guy for a woman like Maria.

"Maria," he began.

"Shhh," she whispered. "No more talk, Chet. Just love me."

And, after all, how could he say no?

He removed her hat and eased her down onto the grassy ground, winding a lock of her hair around one finger. He reached over her and picked up one of the flowers she had dropped.

"Kiss me, Chet."

"Where?" he asked, teasing her with the blossom, running it over her cheeks, her eyelids, her lips. "Here? Or here?" He trailed the flower down her throat, to the opening of her shirt. "Here?"

Her eyes widened and he knew she'd never considered being kissed anywhere but on her cheek or lips. She smiled. "Everywhere." She pulled him closer, and he was only too happy to oblige.

"Yes, ma'am," he said as he began kissing her eyelids, then her ears, where he took time to explore with his tongue, feeling more than a little excitement of his own as she squirmed beneath him.

"That tickles," she said.

He moved on to her neck, turning her to find the spot at the nape that he'd thought about a good deal. "How's that?" he whispered.

"Wonderful," she said, her breath starting to quicken.

He pushed open the neckline of her oversized shirt and it fell off, exposing one shoulder and allowing him to taste her collarbone.

He sat back on his haunches and started to unbutton his shirt. "I want you to be very sure about this, Maria."

Her answer was to brush his hands aside while she finished opening his shirt. Then she ran her palms over the planes of his chest. When she raised herself up to feather kisses where her hands had been, he felt a jolt of desire rocket through him.

"Easy there," he managed. If she kept this up, he wouldn't be able to stop himself from having all of her, and even though she had asked him to love her, he wasn't sure a woman like Maria fully understood what that meant to a man like him. More to the point, this wasn't some dance-hall girl he'd met after a cattle drive. This was Maria. His Maria.

"Maria." He cupped the back of her head, his breath coming in short bursts as if he had run miles. His desire for her threatened to make him lose all control. He saw in her eyes that she would not refuse him—that her need for him was just as great. "I... You..." He wanted her more than anything he'd ever wanted in his life.

"Please," she whispered as she reached for him and buried her fingers in his hair, guiding him closer until his mouth was covering one breast.

With each kiss he felt the heat within her growing. His own passion threatened to make him forget anything he might have been thinking about the future and focus only on *now*. This moment. This woman beneath him.

"Touch me, Chet," she pleaded.

"Yes, ma'am," he murmured, and he cupped her breast, massaging it with his thumb until she squirmed beneath him. The way she looked at him, her eyes pleading for more, made him put aside his worries about whether or not they might have a future and feather kisses over her breast, shoulder, and neck until he reached her mouth.

"And stop calling me 'ma'am,'" she said after a searing kiss.

"What would you like me to call you?" he asked as he levered himself above her. His breath caught at the sheer beauty of her lying among the flowers, her eyes roaming over his face and body.

"Yours," she said huskily as she held out her arms to him.

The desire that radiated between them on the sound of that single word made the heat of the day seem more like a cool breeze. He reached between their melded bodies and tried to open the belt she wore. After a few futile attempts, she pushed him aside, sat up, undid the belt and the button front of her trousers and pushed them down, exposing a length of creamy skin that made Chet's blood rush to his brain.

"Well, help me," she said as she tried to push the pant legs over her boots.

He chuckled as he pulled off each boot and the sock underneath and kissed her instep, then teased her ankle with his tongue. As he pulled the pants the rest of the way off, she pulled her shirt over her head and cast it aside. Her hair had come free of the clip she wore to hold it back when she was riding. Strands of it lay over her bare shoulders. He knelt at her feet, taking in the sheer beauty of her—seeing the deep rose of her nipple through the thin fabric of her undergarment, the way her hair caught the sunlight, the way her eyes had darkened to deep pools of desire. "You are so beautiful, Maria."

She smiled. "And you, sir, are overdressed."

He made short work of undressing himself, saw her eyes widen in surprise when he exposed his manhood to her, and knew the moment that shock passed when she smiled and wriggled out of her undergarment.

He was full to bursting with wanting her and not at all sure he could maintain any sense of control. "This could hurt," he warned.

"But not for long," she said, then giggled. "At least when Mama gave Amanda and me the talk, that's what she said."

"Maria, be serious. If I hurt you, you have to let me know and I can…"

She frowned and put on what he had come to think of as her "don't cross me" face. "If you think—"

He shut her up with a kiss and two of his fingers probing her until she raked his back with her nails. Levering himself above her—wanting to see her face this first and maybe only time for them—he eased himself into her.

She startled and then sighed, and it was as if she had willed herself to relax and open to receive him. Her softness surrounded him, and he knew there was no way he could hold out. He felt the build to the explosion he knew was coming, and just before he reached the heights, Maria gave a soft cry. His eyes flew open, and he was ready to withdraw when he saw that instead of the pain or even the regret he might have expected to see, all he saw was ecstasy.

Maria had grown up on a ranch. She had seen animals mate. She had always thought she had a pretty good idea of what it might be like to lie with a man. *Until now.*

She felt as if she had become something other than the woman she thought she was. She had never known such intense need and want. Chet levered himself above her, watching her, his expression soft and—dare she think loving?

She pulled him closer, her hand flattening on his bare back as she felt him tease her with his fingers. She felt a heat and excitement building inside her. She was going to lose all control, and somehow she understood that this would be a relief—a release of all the feelings and longings she had been holding inside. Everything about this moment was absolutely right no matter what the future might bring for either of them.

When he entered her, she gasped and immediately he tried to pull back. But she grasped his hips and urged him to go on, for somehow she understood that the key to her release was him. Quickly she caught on to the movements of this dance of lovemaking— the rise and fall of the beat of it. She cried out as the pleasure peaked inside her. And then it was Chet who cried out and she who held him as shudders racked their bodies like the aftershocks of an earthquake.

After a moment of perfect stillness, he rolled to his back, bringing her with him so that her head rested in the curve of his shoulder. "Are you all right?" he asked, worry lines furrowing across his brow.

She pushed a lock of his hair away from his forehead, then smoothed out the lines with her fingers. "I'm not sure."

He sat up and looked at her. "Not sure how? Did I hurt you?"

"Oh, no." She smiled. "I'm fine—better than fine, in fact."

"Then what?"

"Well, you see, I have nothing to compare what

just happened here to, and I was thinking—purely for purposes of comparison—we might do it again?"

His laughter echoed across the land, so much so that Cracker came running from the creek, where she'd sneaked off to cool down.

Chet saw the dog coming and tried to shelter her. "Crack, no," he yelled.

But it was too late. The dog had reached them and, reassured that everything was all right, took that moment to shake off and drench them both with water.

Now Maria was laughing as well, especially when she saw the dog roll over Chet's clothes to dry herself.

"Talk about throwing a wet blanket on an otherwise great fire," Chet muttered as he stood up and rescued his clothes.

"Cracker is right. We need to head back," Maria said, although leaving this place—this man—was the very last thing she wanted.

The silence that stretched between them as they dressed bordered on uncomfortable. "Chet? I want you to know that I have no regrets. You do understand that?"

He turned to her, hesitant at first, but then he bent and broke off half a single daisy and offered it to her. "I have never met a woman like you, Maria Porterfield. Whatever the future holds for us, I will never forget you."

"You make it sound like you've decided to leave."

"I haven't decided anything, but we both know there's a lot standing between us and anything we might want together. All right?" he asked.

"All right, but I don't have to like it," she grumbled as she pushed away the flower he was now using to tickle her ear.

He wove the stem of the flower into hair and wrapped his arms around her. "We'll find a way, Maria. I promise."

Fifteen

AT JOKER'S FUNERAL, CHET STOOD WITH THE OTHER hands across the open grave from the Porterfield family—and Turnbull, who had taken a position so close to Maria that their arms touched. It had rained all night, just as he'd heard the men mention it had the day they had buried Isaac Porterfield. The men wore their hats, letting the rain splash off the brims while the women stood under black umbrellas. Chet was glad to see that Loralei had apparently had the good sense not to attend the service.

Bunker led them in prayer after Trey read a passage from the Bible, and then Chet and five other men lowered the coffin into the grave and began filling the opening. Maria stepped to the edge just before they threw in the first shovelful of mud and dropped a small bouquet of wildflowers on top of the coffin.

"Thank you, Oscar," she whispered, then stepped back, took Turnbull's arm, and followed her mother and the rest of the family back to the house.

Chet knew the game she was playing with Turnbull, but that did not mean he had to like it.

She was deliberately putting herself in danger. So what if Turnbull let something slip? What could she do about it?

As he joined the others to fill the grave, Chet went over what had happened from the time they'd returned to the ranch the day before. As they rode together and watched the sun sink lower in the Western sky, he had tried again to persuade her to let him handle things for her. But she had insisted that she had to do it her way. On the ride back, he had pulled her onto his horse, so that she was in front of him, her arms around him. Every time he tried talking sense to her, she kissed him, and after awhile, he had given up trying to talk her out of whatever scheme she had worked up. All he could do was watch and wait and pray that when she needed him, he would be there.

When they got within sight of the ranch, she had mounted her horse, then taken off. He'd watched as she rode up to the house, where Turnbull was waiting for her. The two of them had walked inside arm in arm, and Chet had not seen either of them until he and the other men had gone to the house for the wake.

At the wake, she'd been wearing a dress for once—a gray cotton with white trim around the cuffs and neck, her hair pulled back and wound into a tight bun. She had stood between her mother and Turnbull as the men filed by Joker's casket to pay their respects. Afterward, there had been food set out in the courtyard, but then the rain had started up again, so Juanita had sent the men back to the bunkhouse and had Eduardo and Javier deliver the food. The last Chet had seen of Maria, she'd been resting her head on

Turnbull's shoulder and he had been speaking softly to her as they walked into the house together.

Any other man would have been filled with jealousy or would have suspected betrayal, even with Maria's assurances. But he trusted her—and because he had come to respect her more than any woman he'd ever known, he decided to do as she asked. In the meantime, if he and Maria were to have any chance at all at a future, he had to get things settled with Loralei. So after he and the other men finished filling in the grave and marking it with a crude wooden cross, Chet headed for the anteroom.

He knocked and then entered without waiting for permission. Ezma was sitting on the floor, feeding the kid. Loralei was studying her reflection in a hand mirror. Without a word, Ezma gathered the child close, pulled her shawl to cover both of them, and left the room. Chet placed his hat on a peg near the door and sat in the only other chair available.

"You're looking mighty gussied, Loralei. Expecting company?"

She put down the mirror and scowled at him. "I suppose, to get your attention, I need to run around wearing men's trousers and such."

He decided to ignore that. "You look nice. Turnbull should be impressed."

"Roger is a gentleman, Chet. You could learn a thing or two from him."

"I'll keep that in mind."

After a pause that went on just long enough to make Loralei start pacing the small room, she stopped in front of him. "Why are you here?"

He shrugged. "Seemed as good a time as any for me

and you to write that letter to your pa." He noticed
how she kept glancing toward the door.

"This isn't—"

"You see, Turnbull seems to be taking care of the
Porterfield women—especially Miss Maria. I'd say it'll
be a while before he comes calling tonight." He took
out a piece of paper that he'd gotten from Trey and a
pencil. "So let's see—what would be the best way to
say this?" He pushed the writing materials across the
table to where she stood.

"You said you'd buy me a ticket—"

"You and your baby, and I will as soon as we get
the stock to market and I get paid. But surely you
don't want to have to take time for writing this then.
No, best go ahead and put it down now."

She grabbed the paper and pencil and bent over the
table, scrawling words with such abandon that Chet
couldn't help but wonder what she was writing. She
signed her name with a flourish and slammed down
the pencil. "There," she huffed. "Now please leave."

Chet picked up the paper.

> *Dearest Daddy,*
> *Chet is not the baby's father and that is all I will say*
> *until we see each other again. In the meantime, you*
> *must not blame him for any of this. I made a terrible*
> *mistake, but I am well and in a safe place, resting.*
> *Please don't be angry with me. You and Mummy are*
> *everything to me, and I beg your forgiveness.*

> *All my love,*
> *Loralei*

Chet folded the paper, noticing that other than in the first line, she had not mentioned the child. "Do you care at all for the boy?" he asked.

Loralei looked up at him, her eyes filled with confusion. Chet picked up a small wooden toy from the table and offered it to her. "Your son?"

"Well, of course. He is, after all, an innocent in this whole horrid business. But, Chet, I am in no position to raise a child, so I've been thinking that maybe…" She bit her lower lip, then started pacing the confines of the room again.

"Thinking maybe what?"

"Well, I've seen how Mrs. Porterfield takes to the boy. I mean, it's practically the only time she shows any sign of life at all, and I was wondering… Do you think the Porterfields would…"

Chet was so horrified that he could not speak.

"Or maybe Ezma? She seems to truly like him. Of course, she's being paid, but still…"

"Loralei, just stop talking." Chet closed his eyes and tried to come to grips with the realization that getting Loralei out of his life just might be dooming an innocent child to a life Chet wouldn't wish on his worst enemy. "You don't feel anything for the boy?" he asked, unable to let it go.

"That child has ruined my life, Chet. Oh, I know he didn't do it deliberately but—"

"Do you hear yourself, Loralei? We are talking about a baby that you brought into this world. He has no blame in any of this."

She shrugged. "I know. You're right, of course, but sometimes when I think of months and years of being tied down and…" She picked up the mirror and gently touched her cheeks. "Look at me, Chet. Between this constant dry air and the dirt and the sleepless nights when Ezma can't get the child to stop wailing, I am looking so wan and old and—"

"We are talking about a child, Loralei. If you can't bring yourself to find a single motherly feeling, then give the boy to me."

The minute he said it, he knew he was being completely irrational. What was he going to do with a kid? But Loralei was smiling at him.

"You mean it?" She ran to him and threw her arms around his neck. "Oh, Chet, honey, you are such a good man. Thank you. Thank you."

He could hardly go back on his offer, could he? Maybe he'd ride into town and speak to Addie Wilcox. As a doctor, she might know of a good home for the baby. But giving the boy up to be raised by strangers didn't seem much better than letting him take his chances with Loralei. In one simple statement, he had just made his chances of ever being with Maria more complicated.

"For now, he stays right here with you and Ezma," he instructed, his mind racing as he searched for ideas for how he was going to manage this. "Understood?"

"Yes of course, sweetie. You go herd your cows and such, get your money, and I'll be right here waiting—me, Ezma, and the baby." She clapped her hands together as if she were a child herself. "Oh, Chet, things are going to work out after all."

He stood at the door hat in hand, his back to her. "What's his full name?"

"Chester Maxwell Hunter."

Chet nodded, clapped his hat on his head, and stepped outside into the rain. On his way to the bunk-house, he passed by the house and saw Ezma rocking the child as she sat talking to Juanita in the kitchen. He stopped at the kitchen door, and both women looked at him, clearly surprised. "How's he doing?"

"He's fine," Juanita replied.

"That's good. Just wanted you to know he's to be called by his middle name from now on—Max." He couldn't say for sure, but it looked like the kid raised one little fist in approval.

Chet nodded to Juanita and Ezma and headed for the barn.

Max, he thought. It was a good name.

∿

Maria had only the slimmest of evidence that Roger was somehow connected to her father's death. It wasn't anything that was likely to hold up in court— that much she had reasoned out as she and Chet had returned to the ranch. But it was a start. Now what she needed to do was find a way to connect Roger, her father, and the place her father died, and the only way she could figure out how to do that was to renew her relationship with Roger. So the minute she had spotted him pacing the courtyard as she and Chet rode back to the ranch, she kicked her horse to a gallop and took off.

By the time she reached the courtyard, she was breath-less and flushed enough that Roger came to meet her, his expression one of alarm. "Maria? What's happened?"

"I'm all right, Roger," she said but allowed him to hold her for a moment as he helped her down from her horse. "Come inside, will you?" She took his arm. "It's just that Oscar's death has stirred up so many painful memories of Papa, and right now I don't want to upset Mama. And Amanda and Trey are too young to understand all that I am feeling." She had patted his arm. "I need a friend, Roger. Will you be my friend?"

She had expected some sarcastic remark about Chet, but instead Roger had puffed up his chest. He believed that at last he had won, and in victory, he could be benevolent. "You know I am here for you, Maria, I have always been here for you."

"Thank you. I am so very tired."

"Of course you are. Just leave everything to me."

And all through Oscar's funeral and the days that followed, as the men completed the branding and returned that stock to the high ground for grazing, Roger was true to his word. It was Roger who sat at her father's desk, met with the cowhands, gave out assignments. It was Roger who sat at meals with the family, made a fuss over how beautiful Amanda was becoming, and showed an interest in Trey's ideas for the ranch. It was Roger who daily called on Constance Porterfield—flowers or a cup of tea in hand—and won her grudging acceptance by asking her what she thought her late husband might do about this or that problem with the ranch. And to Maria's relief, as Roger's power grew, his animosity toward Chet cooled to a low simmer that he expressed only in smirks and snide remarks.

There was only one potential problem—Loralei.

The woman was not pleased that Roger had no time for her. She made excuses to come to the house when she knew he would be there, and twice Maria had seen her leaving the office in tears. According to Juanita, Ezma had reported that Loralei had taken to muttering to herself about how promises had been made and this time she would not allow a man to simply walk away.

The hardest part of this whole charade was that Maria had to keep her distance from Chet. She longed to sit with him and tell him what was going on. She missed everything about him—his voice, his laughter, his kisses—especially his kisses. But to her delight, it was Chet who found a solution to their separation. One evening Bunker came to the house, hat in hand, just after the family—and Roger—had finished their supper.

"Evenin', ma'am," he said with a shy nod at Constance. "Boss, I wonder if I might have a word with Mrs. Porterfield."

Roger glanced up from his slice of pie and nodded.

"It's about Snap—Trey, ma'am. The boys in the bunkhouse were remembering what a good job he did out there on the range, and we thought maybe if he started staying with us, we could teach him and take him along when we round up the herd to take to market down in Yuma in a week or so."

Trey looked at his mother, his eyes begging her to agree.

"Trey?" Constance glanced at Bunker. "I'm not sure he's up to it, Seymour. You know how ill he was and—"

"Please, Mama. I have to learn some time."

"Well, I suppose. What do you think, Roger?"

Roger had trouble controlling his smile of complete

triumph. For the first time since her husband's death, Maria's mother had turned to him for advice—not to Maria, but to him.

"I think it's a fine idea, ma'am. The boy is certainly outnumbered by you ladies here in the house. Do him good to spend some time with the men." He turned to Bunker. "You'll see that he's always with one of the more experienced hands and never alone, Bunker." As always it was an order, not a request.

"Sure, boss."

"I'll help you gather your things, Trey," Amanda offered.

"Good idea, Snap," Bunker said. "I'll just wait out here on the porch." He glanced at Maria, who was slicing pie for their dessert. "I sure wouldn't refuse a piece of that pie, Miss Maria."

She laughed. "Go on and sit down. I'll bring you your pie—and a cup of coffee?"

"Now that would be mighty nice of you."

"Roger? Another slice?"

Roger smiled. "You know I can't refuse Juanita's pie."

She served Roger first then took the pie and coffee out to Seymour. "What's going on?" she whispered.

He removed his hat and pulled a folded paper from inside and handed it to her. "Best read this later," he instructed. "It's from Hunt."

Just as Trey and the others came outside, she pocketed the note and turned to her brother. "We'll walk you down to the bunkhouse," she said, realizing it might be a chance to see Chet if only from across a room.

"Ah, Sis, it's not that far."

Bunker put his arm around Trey's shoulders. "Bigger distance than you might think, Snap. Besides, you know how the ladies like to make a fuss," he added in a whisper they all heard.

Everyone laughed and headed across to the yard. Bunker walked next to Constance. "Just want to say, ma'am, how well you're looking these days. The boys and me are glad to see it."

Maria's mother smiled, then turned her attention to Trey. "You mind your manners, young man. Just because you're going to the bunkhouse does not mean you are to forget everything you've been taught in my house." She smoothed back her son's hair.

When they all entered the bunkhouse, the men jumped to their feet and snatched off their hats. Maria tried not to be obvious as she searched the room for Chet. She saw him behind the others, standing in the shadows, his eyes on no one but her. She swallowed the urge to run to him. Instead, she hugged Trey. When the women returned to the main house, Roger was waiting on the porch.

"Walk with me, Maria." Again this was not a request.

"Oh, Roger, perhaps tomorrow? Amanda wants to talk to Mama and me about plans for the party, and I promised." She tried to fake a note of disappointment at having to turn him down, but the truth was that it was becoming more difficult by the day to avoid any situation where she and Roger might find themselves alone—where he might assume that his kisses would be welcomed.

He cupped her cheek and leaned closer. "Tomorrow then," he said softly and ran his thumb across her lips.

She repressed a shudder, thinking, *This man may have killed my father.*

She could barely wait to find a moment alone so she could see what was written on the paper that Bunker had slipped to her. Finally, the moment came when Amanda went to help Constance get ready for bed. Maria took the note from her pocket and moved closer to the lamp in her bedroom. The handwriting was small but neat, the words direct and to the point.

Meet me at the creek where we found your mother. C.

How on earth did he think she could possibly get away without raising suspicion? And yet she would find a way. She waited until she heard Amanda coming down the hall, then wrapped a shawl around her shoulders.

"Where are you going at this hour?" Amanda asked.

"The rain has finally stopped, and I thought I would take a walk. It might help me sleep. Do you want to come?"

As she had hoped, her sister made a face. "I'm not having any trouble sleeping. You go ahead."

She was surprised to find Juanita still in the kitchen. "Just going for a walk," she said.

"Sit down, Maria," Juanita said.

"I—"

Juanita pointed to the kitchen chair. "Your mama is in no condition to talk straight to you, so it falls to me."

"And?"

"We all like Chet very much. He has done a good deal for this family—the way he's brought Trey along not being the least of it. But, Maria, he's not for you.

He's a hired hand and a drifter. How will he provide for you should the day come that the two of you—"

"He doesn't have to provide for me. We have the ranch."

"But it's not his ranch, and you have to remember that he came here with the intention of getting some money saved up and moving on to California where he could have a place of his own."

"I know, but—"

"There's no but's about it, Maria. Any fool can see that the two of you can barely keep your hands off each other, but I am telling you that unless something changes, it can't come to good."

"But I love him."

Juanita wrapped her arms around Maria's shoulders. "I know you do, and more's the pity. You have to know when to let him go, Maria, because there will come that day."

Maria hated that she understood that Juanita was probably right. On the other hand, did it have to be that way? After all, who would have thought that she—a woman—could take on the running of one of the largest ranches in Arizona? No, times were changing, and they would find a way.

Gently she pulled away from Juanita's embrace. "I'm still going for that walk," she said stubbornly.

Juanita smiled. "I know. Just keep your head about you."

Outside she kept to the shadows as she made her way to the creek. As she slipped past the bunkhouse, she saw Roger with his hand on Trey's shoulder, lecturing the men about making sure the boy was always with one of them and never off on his own. Knowing Roger, he would feel the need to make his point multiple times.

But just as she passed the open door, she heard Roger ask, "Where's Hunt?"

Maria froze.

"Night shift," Bunker replied. "Him and Happy and Rico." Now that they had completed the branding, those animals had rejoined the rest of the herd for grazing before the final roundup of stock for market. Bunker's explanation seemed to satisfy Roger, and he resumed his lecture. Maria hurried on down the rocky path to the creek.

At her approach, Chet turned, then hesitated for a second before holding his arms out to her. She ran the last few steps. *Is this what true love feels like? This longing for him and feeling I'm only complete when he's with me?* she wondered as he folded his arms around her. She lifted her face to his for the kiss she had been longing for.

"We haven't much time," he said as he kissed her closed eyelids and cheeks, then stepped back, still holding on to her shoulders. "Tell me what's going on."

"I think my plan is working. I told Roger I knew about the dam, and he's beginning to talk more freely about how we might get around that and get the water running again. Of course, that's all just for show, I'm sure. He hasn't let anything slip yet, but in time—"

"You are playing a very dangerous game, Maria. These men are not ones you should try to take down on your own."

"I'm not. I just have to have more proof."

"And then what?"

"I'll go to Marshal Tucker, I promise." She stroked his cheek. "Meanwhile I have some news about Loralei." She told him what Ezma had overheard Loralei say about not allowing a man to simply walk away again. "She was talking about Roger."

"He turned to her because you rejected him, and now that he thinks you've taken him back, he has no need of her."

"My heart goes out to the child," Maria said. "Thankfully he's too young right now to realize what's going on but one day…"

Chet breathed out a sigh and led Maria to a rock. "Sit down, Maria. I need to tell you something."

She could barely believe what she was hearing as he told her of his conversation with Loralei—the letter, the promise to give her his wages, and worst of all, her decision to give up her own child.

"But you aren't the father so why would you…"

"What else was I going to do? Think about it, Maria. Think about the life that boy was being doomed to. So that's what I came to tell you tonight. Once the stock gets to market, I need to figure out what's best for Max. In all of this, he's the one nobody seems to be considering. Maybe going on to California might just be the right thing to do. Ezma has agreed to come with me and care for the kid until I can find a place to buy and—"

"With what? If you give your wages to Loralei, where will the money to buy a place of your own come from? And why on earth would you leave here?" *Why would you leave me?*

For the first time, she began to have doubts about

the depth of Chet's feelings for her. She knew that he cared for her, but loving her?

"If that's what needs to be done, then I was hoping maybe you might consider coming with me."

These were the words she had longed to hear, and yet how could she leave? She had worked so hard to save the ranch—if not for herself, then for Trey. Her brother was far too young to take on the Tiptons, and they were not going to stop trying to take over every acre of land they could.

"I can't," she whispered. "Surely you understand that." He was quiet for far too long. "Chet, tell me you understand."

"I do. It's just that I hoped… You'd best be getting back," he said softly.

She nodded, fighting back the tears that stung her lashes, and turned to go.

But Chet pulled her back, his arms coming around her and his breath soft as rain on her face. "I won't leave until I know you've worked out everything here. Until I know for sure that you and everyone in your family is safe. That's a promise, Maria." He kissed her, and as always, it was as if all her doubts evaporated like a morning mist.

"Chet, when you leave…"

"That's not something we need to be thinking on right now, Maria. We've got this moment. Let's not spoil it by trying to figure out what lies down the road a ways."

He kissed her again—a kiss filled with passion and desire. A kiss she never wanted to end. A kiss that felt like good-bye.

"Now go," he said, releasing her with obvious reluctance.

"I…"

"Shhh," he whispered, touching her lips. "Just go, Maria, and get some rest and promise me you'll be careful."

She nodded, her heart so full that she knew if she tried to speak, she would not be able to hold back her tears. She touched his cheek, and he grasped her hand and kissed her palm, then nodded toward the house. "Go." His voice was husky, and she felt a flash of shared emotion pass between them. Whatever their status in society might be, this man was everything she would ever need or want, and whatever it took, she would find a way to be with him.

Sixteen

"USED TO BE THAT THE BOSS WOULD HIRE EXTRA drovers to take his stock to market," Bunker explained the night before they were to head out for Yuma. "But these last years there's been no money for that, so we'll join up with the other small ranchers and share the work."

Chet understood that beef from Arizona Territory most likely went to California, rather than north and east. "How far?"

"Round about two hundred miles, give or take."

Chet did some figuring. If they could make about ten or maybe fifteen miles a day, it would take around three weeks. Of course, that only figured on there being no problems. Coming back, they could cover more ground, so, all in all, a trip of about four or five weeks.

"Better get some shut-eye, Hunt. Gonna be a long haul."

Any cattle drive meant long days in the saddle, and the drive to Yuma was no different. Chet had plenty of time to wonder what Maria was doing. She had this habit of taking things in hand without much thought for the consequences and that worried him. In addition, Bunker had reported that the number of stock the Porterfield outfit had lost due to rustling, disease, or the ongoing drought was at least twice what Johnson or any of the other small ranchers had suffered.

"Course, Mr. Porterfield always had the largest spread until the Tiptons come along. In those days he could afford to lose stock, but these days…"

The pieces were beginning to come together. The Tiptons had made no secret of their ambition and probably thought that if they got their hands on the Porterfield land, the other smaller ranchers would fall in line. So the Porterfield spread had been targeted. Trouble was, Chet couldn't any more prove that the Tiptons were behind Maria's troubles—other than the dam—than she could prove that Turnbull had something to do with her father's death. He tried to come up with a connection—Turnbull had left the ranch to work for Tipton and then come back, but was that because Turnbull had been mad at Maria or because he was in the process of betraying her?

Bunker reined up alongside Chet as the trail boss called out orders and cowhands up and down the line began herding the stock into grassland to one side of the trail. "Two more down," he reported. "Screwworm. Worst case I ever saw."

"Ours?"

"Yep." Bunker spit tobacco and stared at the horizon. "Don't make no sense."

"Not all that uncommon after branding. Animal has a sore, and they get in."

"Got that part. What don't make sense is how come it's only our stock?"

"So far," Chet said. "Trail boss is apparently stopping the drive so all the stock can be checked. Besides, the other ranches finished branding weeks ago."

"I'll lay you a wager that once we get going again, the only infected cows will belong to Clear Springs."

Bunker would have won that bet when several hours later, Roger came riding up to tell them that from this point on, the Porterfield stock would be separated from the rest and travel alone.

"But cutting our stock from the herd will cost us valuable time," Bunker protested. "By the time we get these animals to market—"

"It's been decided," Turnbull barked, cutting off any further protest. "Now get to work."

They lost nearly a day as the men cut the stock from the larger herd, shot and buried the infected cows who were beyond saving, and finally settled in for a couple hours of sleep. At dawn, they were up and once again on the trail, but even after spending sixteen to eighteen hours a day in the saddle, they had a long way to go before they reached Yuma.

"Hunt, do you think any more bad stuff will happen?" Trey asked Chet as the two of them rode together.

"Hard to say, Snap. You're seeing the tough side of this business now. Lots of stuff like weather and disease can affect the herd."

In the distance, they heard a train whistle telling them they had at least reached the place where the railroad ran parallel to the herd. Eventually the two would meet in Yuma.

"Bunker says we've got nearly a week before we get there," Trey said. "And I heard one of the men say we might even miss the train altogether."

"George Johnson will make sure the train don't leave till we can get there,. Snap. Now, take Crack and go on and get that steer trying to head off on his own. Let's see if you've learned anything."

Trey grinned and took off, waving his hat and hollering until the stray rejoined the march. He looked back at Chet, who gave him a salute. Of course, Chet had no idea if Johnson or any of the other ranchers would stand up for Maria. Somebody was bound to mention the screwworm and that would make the beef buyers nervous. No, any way he turned this business, it came out bad for Maria and the Porterfields.

❧

Maria slipped into the bunkhouse and immediately spotted Roger's bunk. It was the only single bed in the room, the others being double stacked to make room for those times when the bunkhouse was full. She quickly searched the items on the small shelf above Roger's cot and found nothing. Then she searched the bedding, being careful to restore the military precision of the corner tucks and the pristine fold of the blanket once she'd finished. Again there was nothing. Where would he hide the damaged bolo? Of course, he might have gotten rid of it, and then where would she be? The broken bolo was the only shred of evidence she had. No, she had to believe he still had it. She couldn't let herself doubt.

She glanced through the small window when she heard Amanda's voice and saw her sister head for the chicken coop. Ezma followed her, carrying the baby. They were laughing and the baby squealed with delight when Ezma bent to show him the chickens.

Maria waited for them to go around the side of the coop, where Amanda would spread the feed for the chicks. Then she slipped outside and headed for the office. Roger had been spending a lot of time there, though she had removed any ledgers and documents that she didn't want him to see, claiming she had misplaced the ones he needed and would help search for them to buy time.

Inside the office, she sat in her father's chair—the place Roger took nowadays, adjusted to fit his greater height. She placed her hands on the worn wooden arms and swiveled from side to side, surveying the room. Why would Roger risk hiding anything here? *Because he believes that he has won.*

She opened the drawers to the desk—one slender one that held paper and pencils and other supplies. Another larger one that held receipts and files—the history of her father's years building this place from a shack and thirty head of cattle to the showplace it was when he died. Closing that drawer, she looked at the array of items arranged on the desktop. A sepia photograph of her mother and father in a silver frame, an inkwell and pen, an arrowhead Amanda had found when they were adding a room to the house, and a crude sketch of her father that Trey had done when he was around seven and confined to bed most of the time.

Her attention came back to the photograph. She picked it up and carried it to the light. Her father was standing behind her mother with his arms around her. He was wearing the silver ring that her mother had had made for him as an anniversary gift. Maria closed her eyes, then opened them in shock.

Her father had not been wearing that ring the day his body had been found. She had failed to notice and her mother had been too distraught to call the missing ring to anyone's attention. Could it have been taken from his body before they found him? He never would have taken it off. *One thing at a time, Maria.*

She placed the photo back on the desk and looked around the room cluttered with her father's collection of books on ranching and the beef industry, a quiver of arrows he'd been given by a warrior after he'd saved the women and children of that tribe from a stampede, and…

Her gaze stayed on the quiver. There was something not right. She got up and walked over to where it hung. "Backward," she muttered. Both she and her father were left-handed, but whoever had hung the quiver last was right-handed. Roger was right-handed. She took it off the nail and gathered the arrows, pulling them out before peering inside. She turned the quiver upside down and the bolo fell onto the desk. She shook it again and even dug inside with one of the arrows, fully expecting her father's ring to be there as well. But it wasn't. Quickly, she replaced the arrows and hung the quiver back on the nail. Then she took the clips she'd found and fit them to the damaged stone. But why had he kept it? It didn't matter. She'd figure that part of the puzzle out in time.

"Perfect."

Roger Turnbull had some explaining to do, because now, besides the damaged bolo, there was the matter of the missing ring. Whoever had that ring had the answer to the mystery of who had killed her father.

❧

Chet felt as if he'd been in the saddle so long that the leather had become like a second skin. But by morning they would reach Yuma, and that alone was enough to keep everyone in the Porterfield outfit moving forward. Every man among them would happily eat another twelve hours of dirt and dust if it meant they were so close to being paid that they could practically taste that first shot of whiskey. Bunker was planning to buy himself a new pair of boots while Rico had his sights set on a new suit of clothes—one nice enough for courting Louisa Johnson. Every man had given a lot of thought to how he would spend that money, including Chet. In fact, he was so lost in his thoughts of Loralei getting on a stage that he failed to notice the lone rider coming fast across the plain or the lineup of half a dozen more men waiting on the rise they were heading toward.

"What's up?" Trey asked, his voice shaky with fear.

"Trouble, that's what," Rico muttered as they all watched Turnbull approach the stranger.

Bunker translated for Trey. "See the way the boss is gesturing? He's offering him and his boys a steer from the herd in exchange for us passing over their land."

"I thought all the tribes had been moved to the reservation," Trey said.

"There's some that don't hold with being told what to do by a government they don't recognize," Slim said.

The brave shook his head vehemently and held up one finger, then waved his arm over the area where the herd waited and repeated the one finger gesture.

"He's asking for a toll—a dollar a head."

"We can't pay that kind of…"

Turnbull's laugh could be heard all the way back where they waited.

"Get ready, boys," Bunker said. "This ain't looking good." He reached slowly behind him and pulled his Colt revolver from his bedroll.

"Move 'em out!" Turnbull shouted and then whistled and shouted until the herd moved slowly forward. The men spread out, every one of them keeping his eye on the renegade.

To their amazement, the gang backed away and watched as the herd moved slowly toward the rise. Then Chet saw the leader give a signal and suddenly the others came riding down out of the hills, firing their rifles and yelling as they bore down on the herd.

That was all it took to start the stampede, and with a cliff on one side and a rocky ridge rising up on the other, the stock headed straight for the open vista beyond the cliff. The last Chet saw of the Indians as he whipped off his hat, slapped it against his thigh, and whistled loudly as he and the other drovers tried to head off the stampede, the renegades were whooping in victory as they rode over the rise, apparently satisfied that they had exacted a fair price.

By the time the men had managed to turn the herd and the dust settled, it was near sunset and they still had to count the herd and go in search of stray and wounded animals. They'd be lucky to make it to Yuma by week's end.

&

Maria had counted the days—marking them off on a calendar in her father's office—as she waited impatiently for the men to return. She paced the courtyard, thankful that her mother, Amanda, and Ezma had taken the baby down to the creek. She scanned the horizon. The men—certainly Roger—should have been back days ago. A neighboring rancher's wife on her way into town had seen George Johnson outside his house a day earlier. Literally the clock was ticking on settling of the loan she'd gotten from the bank. The deadline for repayment was upon her, and if she did not deliver that payment to Clyde Cardwell by noon the next day, they would lose everything.

On the horizon, she saw a cloud of dust and her heart pounded with anticipation. *Finally*, she thought.

But instead of the men she expected, it was Jasper Tipton and his younger brother, Buck, coming her way.

"Afternoon, Miss Porterfield." Jasper tipped his hat but remained seated on his horse. Maria did not miss the fact that this put her in the uncomfortable position of having to look up at him and into the hot noonday sun. She shaded her eyes.

"Now ain't she looking pretty today, Jasper?" Buck said as he moved his horse around her.

"Mind your manners, Brother," Jasper replied. "Miss Porterfield, I see your men have not yet returned."

"I expect them any time now."

"They ain't comin' till tomorrow earliest—maybe the day after," Buck said.

She wheeled around to face him. "How would you know that?"

The younger Tipton shrugged and just kept grinning at her. She turned her attention back to Jasper. "What is it you want?"

"My brother and I have come to make your family an offer, Miss Porterfield. We will buy you out for twenty-five cents on the dollar. That gives you more than enough money to repay the bank and find someplace you and your mama and sister and brother can settle."

"What about the offer you made at the ranchers' meeting—the one allowing the owners to stay on their place?"

"The one you called 'sharecropping'—yes, well, sadly that offer is no longer on the table."

"How do you know about the loan?" She was blustering, stalling for time so she could think. Of course Tipton knew about the loan. He knew everything that went on in town.

Jasper smiled. "Well, you see, our company just bought the bank, so it's kind of my business to know."

"Tell her the rest," Buck said.

"Not wishing to upset you, Miss Maria, but word has it that your stock didn't make it to market in such good shape. You know how it is on even a short trail drive. I heard there was some screwworm that slowed 'em up and separated 'em from the rest of the herd. Then Turnbull pissed off some renegades, and they retaliated by stampeding your herd. Thing is, by the time your boys got that stock to Yuma, word had spread about the screwworm, and…"

With each word out of the man's mouth, Maria felt her insides cramp until she was sure she would throw up. "Get off this land," she managed, and behind her, she heard Juanita cock the rifle.

"I understand," Jasper replied as he gathered the reins and turned his horse. "You need time to consider. Talk things over with your mama. There's time. My offer is good until eleven o'clock tomorrow morning." He nodded to her, and then he and his brother started across the land, riding slow as if they already owned it. He had set his deadline for one hour before the bank note came due.

So, the men had not been paid—Bunker did not get to order his boots nor Rico his suit. Chet could not buy Loralei a ticket. Unless…

She hurried back to the house. "Nita, have Javier saddle my horse—and put that gun away."

Juanita stuck the rifle back in its place and then followed Maria down the hall. "What are you up to, *mi hija?*"

"I am going into town," she said as she threw off the dress and pulled on a pair of her brother's canvas trousers and a cotton shirt. "It's past time I got Marshal Tucker involved in this."

"You got nothing to show 'cept your word against the Tiptons," Juanita argued. "At least wait till the men get back, then—"

She pulled on her boots and headed back toward the kitchen, where she grabbed her father's hat. "According to the Tiptons, that may be too late."

"You gonna believe those *ratos*? You aren't think-ing straight, Maria. Stop before you…"

Juanita continued her tirade as she followed her to the corral, where Maria saddled a horse and mounted it. "If it gets late, I'll stay in town with Addie. You are not to worry Mama or Amanda with any of this, understood? If they ask, tell them I went to town to see Addie."

"They'll not believe me," Juanita protested, "the way you been pacing around here like a skittish colt these last two days."

"Make them believe you," Maria shouted and took off. As she rode, she mentally calculated how she might juggle the money they'd make from supplying beef, milk, butter, and cheese to the fort for the coming months to cover paying the hands and repaying the loan. She could maybe sell that bull George Johnson kept asking to buy, and maybe some cows to the other small ranchers looking for breeding stock. Maybe that would be enough to get them through the winter. Of course, she'd have to do something about the dam or find another way to get water onto her family's land. Chet would have some ideas.

The two hours it took to ride hard and reach town flew by, and by the time she tied up her horse outside the marshal's office, she was no closer to knowing what she would tell the lawman than she'd been when she'd left the ranch.

Marshal Tucker met her at the door, but instead of inviting her in, he took hold of her arm and led her to a nearby chair. "Why, Miss Porterfield, has something happened out your way?"

Just before he'd closed the door to his office, Maria had noticed someone sitting in that office—someone comfortable enough to have propped his boots on the marshal's desk. She recognized those boots. She'd been eye-to-leather with them just a few hours earlier. They belonged to Jasper Tipton. Her mind turned to a mush of doubts.

"You're busy, Marshal. This can wait. I'll just..." She fingered the bolo that she had tucked inside the pocket of her vest. "I was just worried about my men," she said. It was only a half lie. "They're overdue, and according to Jasper Tipton..."

She did not miss the way the marshal glanced nervously at the window of his office. The Tiptons had not only bought the hotel and saloon and bank in this town. Apparently, they also owned the law.

"Word has it they had some trouble that delayed them. I'm sure they'll be along anytime now," Tucker assured her. "If they don't show up by sunup tomorrow, I'll ride out to the fort and ask them to organize a search party."

His offer sounded halfhearted at best. "I'm sure that won't be necessary," she replied and smiled. "We can't have the marshal running off on wild goose chases because of my silly nerves, can we? After all, it's hardly your problem."

Tucker grinned, and all of a sudden Maria thought about Oscar trying so desperately to tell her the name of her father's killer. "T-T-T," he had managed. Was it possible he had not been trying to say "Tipton" or "Turnbull" but rather "Tucker"?

She had no idea who she could trust.

"I won't keep you any longer, Marshal Tucker," she said. "I need to make a stop at the bank before I stop by to see the Wilcoxes." She edged away from him.

"Nobody sick at your place, I hope? Mrs. Porterfield doing all right, is she?"

"Yes. Everyone is fine. I just want to say hello. Thank you again, Marshal." She practically ran across the street, dodging wagons and potholes as she went.

It came as no surprise to her that Clyde Cardwell was unavailable to see her, and she decided not to argue the point even though she could see the man sitting at his desk. What good would talking to him do? Was she going to beg for more time? Absolutely not.

As she left the bank, she nearly ran into Eliza McNew, who was washing the window of the mercantile.

"Whoa!" Eliza quickly moved the bucket of soapy water before Maria tripped. "Where's the fire?"

Relieved at last to see a friendly face and a person she knew she could trust, Maria poured out the story of how the hands had not yet returned from Yuma.

"Come inside, out of this heat," Eliza instructed. She led Maria to a chair. "Sit. I'll be right back." She returned after a minute, carrying two glasses of lemonade and handed one to Maria. Then she sat in the chair next to her. "Now, the store is empty. There's no one around. Tell me what's got you so upset, and do not say it's that you're worried that your boys haven't come home."

"Well, I am."

"But there's more, so let it out."

With relief, Maria poured out the story of the loan and the visit from the Tipton brothers, and their "offer," and the deadline set by them and the bank that she was going to miss unless she could find a way to come up with the money.

"All right, now let's think about this rationally," Eliza said. "You have until tomorrow at noon, correct?"

"For the bank."

"The bank's deadline is the only one we are considering here, Maria. The Tiptons are just trying to scare you."

"They're doing a pretty good job of it," Maria moaned.

"Yeah, they're good at that all right." Eliza glanced around the store. "I've had some experience with their scare tactics, but just because they own just about everything else in this town, it doesn't mean they need to own every single business."

"So how did you fight back?"

Eliza shrugged. "You have to beat them at their own game. They make threats and set deadlines. You meet or beat those deadlines. For you, that means coming up with the money to repay the bank."

"Whatever money we got for the stock has to first go to pay the men," Maria reminded her. "If what the Tiptons said is true, then—"

"Rule number one when it comes to the Tiptons, honey: do not believe a word that comes out of those two lyin' mouths." She grabbed a pencil and tore off a piece of wrapping paper at the counter and waited. "Okay, so how much do you have in cold, hard cash right now?"

Maria named a figure. "But half of that is the money from the loan and the rest comes from what we made from supplying the fort."

Eliza wrote down the figures separately. "And payroll is what?"

Maria told her and continued to answer her questions as Eliza jotted down figures, added, subtracted, crossed out numbers, and then sighed. "We need to know what you got for the beef at market."

"Yeah. That is, if we got anything at all."

Eliza patted Maria's shoulder. "We'll find a way, honey."

Voices outside caught their attention. "That sounds like Roger," Maria said as both women hurried to the door.

Roger looked exhausted and defeated and somehow much smaller than the man she'd known. He was tying his horse up at a hitching post outside the saloon.

"Roger!" She ran down the boardwalk past the mercantile, the bank, and the saloon. "Where are the others?"

"What are you doing here, Maria?" he asked wearily.

"I was worried, so I came into town to—"

"I sent the others on to the ranch."

She was afraid to ask her next question, but she had to know. "Did you—were you able to get enough to pay them?"

"Yes. Now go home, Maria. I'll be along as soon as I take care of some business here."

"Just tell me how much you got for our stock." She had memorized the number that Eliza figured she needed to repay the loan.

"Don't worry about it, okay? I'm going to work it all out."

"With the Tiptons or the bank?" she challenged,

her temper rising. "Or are they one and the same, Roger?" She pulled the bolo from her vest pocket and showed it to him, fingering the rough edges of the chipped stone then fitting one of the pieces in its place. "Like you handled my father, Roger? I found the pieces where he died, and the bolo where you'd hidden it. How could you? He trusted you, believed in you…"

He took hold of her elbow and steered her to the side of the building. "I know how this looks, but I swear to you, I had nothing to do with that. I've been trying to protect your family by pretending to work with the Tiptons, but they caught on and…" He kept glancing over his shoulder as if at any minute he expected someone to attack him. "Maria, I have to leave—tonight. If I don't get out of here, they're gonna kill me the same as they did Joker."

"And my father?"

"I can't help you, Maria." He started backing away.

"What about the dam?"

His eyes widened. "That wasn't my idea. I tried to talk them out of it, but they started getting suspicious—kept asking me where my true loyalties lie. I always figured I could sabotage the dam once we got back from the cattle drive, but…"

"Why did you hide the bolo, Roger?"

"I couldn't bring myself to get rid of it. Your father believed in me, Maria. He was maybe the first man who did. That bolo meant a great deal to me. I tucked it away one day because I saw you coming to the office, and I…I guess I didn't want you to be hurt when you saw the reminder of your father. I always planned to go back to the office and get it. I swear to you, Maria, I had nothing to do with your father's death."

She was starting to believe him—there was no faking the pain in his voice. "Then who did? If you didn't attack my father, how did the stone get chipped?"

Roger sighed. "Your pa was worried about his meeting with the bank, so on the ride into town, I tried to reassure him. I suggested maybe the bolo would bring him good luck. He laughed and accepted it. He was wearing it when you came across his body. You just didn't notice so that's when I took it."

"Why?"

"I don't know—I just wanted something to remind me that this man had believed in me. Maria, you have got to stop trying to figure this out. If you keep on trying to solve this, you're gonna lose everything." He turned to go. "I can't help you, Maria."

"If you're innocent, you can testify. You can help me find the real killer and defeat the Tiptons."

"No, they won't let me make it that far. You don't know what—"

"Everything all right, Miss Maria?"

She turned to see the marshal coming toward them. His question was directed at her, but his eyes were on Roger.

"Just fine," she said. "No need to trouble yourself." She held out her hand to Roger. "The money please."

He dug in his pocket and produced a small wad of bills—bills she took the time to count, her heart sinking as she did. It wasn't nearly enough. When she looked up, she saw that Roger looked miserable, but Tucker seemed to be struggling to find an expression of concern.

"I'll see you back at the ranch," she said, peeling off a couple of bills and handing them to him. "You look like you could use a bath and decent meal." She walked away.

"Maria, I didn't take any for myself," Roger called.

Maria kept walking.

Seventeen

CHET AND BUNKER RODE ON EITHER SIDE OF TREY AS the men covered the last of the trail that would bring them home to the ranch.

"There's Amanda," Trey said, his voice solemn and raspy. "What are we gonna tell her? She wants this party she's been planning bad."

Bunker sniffed. "We'll let Miss Maria handle the family, Snap. But have to say, I don't think any of us are gonna be in a mood to party."

Chet was only half listening to the conversation. His mind was on the trail drive, the incident with the renegades and Turnbull. The thing was that the foreman seemed pretty upset as things continued to go sour, and when they finally reached Yuma, no man had ever fought harder to sell stock than Turnbull had. On top of that, he'd apologized to the men as he paid them the rest of their wages. Apparently in the past, Porterfield would always sweeten the pot and give the men extra pay, but not this time. According to Bunker, who recorded the entries in the ledger Turnbull would take back to the ranch, the foreman took nothing for himself. On the other hand, if he was in cahoots with the Tiptons, he hardly needed Maria's money. Still, there was something genuine about the way the man had fought hard for every dollar.

Once they'd been paid, only a couple of the hands chose to blow off steam in the local establishments of Yuma. The rest of them had no appetite for new boots, suits, whiskey, or women, and headed back to the ranch. Chet had the money he needed to buy a ticket for Loralei but not enough left over to pay Ezma to care for Max. At least he could finally resolve one problem. On the other hand, the mystery of who had killed Joker—and Maria's father—remained just that. He'd been so certain the culprit was Turnbull. Now he wasn't so sure.

As they came closer to the ranch, Chet saw Amanda standing in the courtyard, and then Juanita came outside, said something to her, and Amanda ran back inside. All of the men except Eduardo headed straight for the corral. Eduardo left his horse tied up outside the courtyard, gave Juanita a peck on her leathered cheek, and followed her inside. There was no sign of Maria.

"You should go on and let your mama know you're home safe, Snap," Bunker was saying.

Trey trudged to the house without a word.

"Might want to work up a smile, Snap," Bunker shouted. "No need to worry her."

Trey nodded and straightened his shoulders a little.

"Can you join us in the bunkhouse, Hunt?"

He'd intended to go find Loralei and get things settled there, but a few more minutes wouldn't make much difference. "Sure."

Once all the men were inside, Bunker closed the door. "This won't take long, boys," he said when the men began grumbling about needing the door open to catch whatever breeze there might be. "Some of us has been thinking."

One of the cowhands cracked a joke about that being something new, and the others snickered.

"I guess we don't need nobody to tell us that Miss Maria is in trouble financially speaking. She's got a loan coming due and the Tiptons breathing down her neck, and well, me and some of the others was thinking maybe we could forego our wages…"

The grumbling about the stifling heat in the crowded room turned to outright shouts of protest. Bunker held up his hands. "We worked out an idea for giving her some help, so hear me out."

Rico let out a sharp whistle through his teeth, and the room went still. "We're talking a freewill offering here. Nobody's to know who gave and who didn't. That's on you. Only you know what you need that money for, so nobody's gonna judge. We're gonna put a box in the privy." He grinned. "Only place we could think of where a man's got real privacy."

Bunker took over. "You decide. You want to make a donation, put the money inside, but you gotta decide today. According to what Snap told me, that loan comes due at noon tomorrow." He reached up to the shelf above his bunk and took down a small wooden box. "Here's the box." He demonstrated opening and closing the hinged lid. "I'll collect the box at nine this evening and deliver whatever's there to Miss Maria."

"How do we know you'll not skim some for yourself?" Slim asked.

"Fine, Slim, you collect the box and take it to her. Don't really matter as long as she knows what she's got before sunup."

Chet was surprised at Slim's challenge. He was a regular in the bunkhouse card games and had always seemed to admire Bunker as much as any of the men did. "Maybe you should both collect the box and take it to her," Chet suggested, watching Slim closely.

The man apparently noticed that several of the men were staring at him so he grinned and then laughed nervously. "I was just joshing with you, Bunker. You know I trust you." He looked around at the others. "Hell, I've played enough poker with this old cowboy to know he don't cheat."

"No hard feelings, Slim," Bunker was saying, then he stretched and grinned and added, "I feel nature calling, boys, so if you'll excuse me." He took the box and headed outside.

Through the rest of the afternoon as he went about his chores, Chet kept an eye out for Maria, but his mind was on that box in the latrine. He wanted more than anything to do what he could to help Maria and her family, but he'd already spent his pay for that ticket for Loralei. He still had his savings, but what if things didn't work out with Maria the way he hoped and he had to move on?

First things first, Hunt. Settle it with Loralei and then figure out the rest.

He headed for the bunkhouse, where some of the men were on their bunks writing letters or napping, taking advantage of the fact that other than normal chores, the hard work of the last several months was over. He pulled the ticket he'd bought for Loralei out of his vest pocket. Before leaving Yuma, he had taken the letter she'd written to her father to the local telegraph office and dictated the contents to be sent to Florida. The clerk had assured him that his message had gone through and would be delivered by the next day. But just to be sure, he had gone to the general store and mailed Loralei's letter as well. If her father saw the words in her own handwriting, he could hardly question the truth of them.

A few minutes later when Chet knocked on the door of the anteroom, it sounded like somebody was ransacking the small room, so he didn't wait to be invited inside. He ducked just in time to miss a shoe sailing toward his head and saw Loralei frantically stuffing her belongings in the carpetbag and small trunk she'd brought with her on the stage.

"Loralei?"

Startled, she wheeled around, then immediately glanced out the small side window. "What do you want?" she asked.

"I came to bring you this." He held up the ticket.

"You owe me two tickets," she countered. "I'll need one for Ezma."

"Ezma and the kid are staying here with me," he reminded her.

"I changed my mind. And do not try to stop me, Chet. That child is my flesh and blood, not yours. You have no say in this." She held out her hand. "And how do you know where I want to go?"

"You should go home to Florida, Loralei. This part of the country is no place for a woman on her own. This ticket will carry you back to Florida. You can change it, I reckon, but I wouldn't recommend it." He picked up the shoe, found its mate, and handed her the pair. "Ezma has agreed to go with you?"

She ignored that and instead snapped her fingers. "The ticket."

He handed it to her. "It's for tomorrow's stage that'll take you to Tucson, where you can get the train east." He picked up a shawl and folded it and in the process noticed that Max's belongings were still neatly stacked on the small shelf next to his crib. Ezma's doing, no doubt.

Loralei was tapping the ticket against her thigh. "I need two tickets, Chet."

"Can't help you there. I've got no more money to give you."

"Oh, that's right—you and the other fools are going to try to pay the Porterfield debt."

"How do you—"

"Never mind how I know. I hear things, and I'm a lot smarter than you ever gave me credit for. Poor little Maria and her family. Have you seen the inside of that house? They have more than enough money to pay off their debts. Handing them your hard-earned pay is just—"

"As opposed to handing it over to you, Loralei?" He glanced around the room. "You have no intention of taking Max, do you? What's really going on?"

She hesitated—and then suddenly broke.

To his surprise, she ran to him and grabbed his shoulders. "You have to help us, Chet."

"I'll do everything I can for your son, Loralei, but—"

She shook him hard. "Will you stop thinking about the kid for five seconds? This is about me—my life, my future. A life is at stake here, Chet."

"I hardly think your life is on the line…"

"Not my life, you idiot. Roger's."

Now he took hold of her shoulders and backed her away. "Turnbull? What's he got to do with any of this?"

She slumped down onto the unmade cot. "He's in trouble, Chet. I know you two have had your differences, but if he doesn't get away from here tonight…"

"You're running away with him? And taking the baby and Ezma as well?"

"No," she admitted softly. "I thought you would give me more money if I said they were going. Roger says we can head east to Kansas City or even St. Louis. He has a friend who runs a riverboat on the Mississippi, and he thinks we could—"

"Where's Turnbull now?"

"I don't know. He was here but left after he told me to be ready as soon as it gets dark." She looked around the room at the overstuffed luggage. "What do you think I should wear?" She sounded like a lost little girl.

"Loralei, I can't let you do this. Turnbull is not the man you think he is. He's using you."

Her nostrils flared as she stood up and faced him once again. "You're a fine one to talk about somebody not being the man I thought he was," she growled as she returned to her packing. "Now get out, and I am warning you, Chester Hunter, if you say one word to that woman about any of this…"

"That woman paid for your ticket out of here, Loralei. And I'd be real careful how you talk about her when you're with Turnbull. My guess is that as much as he's capable of caring for anybody other than himself, he's in love with Maria Porterfield."

"Get out," she screamed, flinging clothes and her hairbrush at him as he left.

"With pleasure," he muttered.

The sun had set over the distant hills, and the shadows made it hard to see what was going on around the ranch. Light spilled into the courtyard from the kitchen, and he saw Juanita standing at the window, but she was focused on kneading dough, not him. From the bunkhouse he heard some of the men reminiscing about the drive, and as he passed by the corral where saddles lined up along the fence, he saw a figure emerge from the latrine set back in a cluster of cottonwoods.

The man's actions were odd, and that made Chet pause and watch. He recognized the man, saw him fumbling with something in his hands when he should have been tucking in his shirt or adjusting his trousers. *The money box.*

Chet closed his hand around the hilt of his whip and eased it free of the saddle horn. Slowly he advanced, circling around until he was behind the cowhand. He hesitated when it occurred to him that maybe Bunker had asked the man to collect the money so they could take it to Maria. But when he saw Slim take a handful of bills and stuff them down the front of his shirt, he had no more doubt about what was happening. He let the tail of his whip uncoil on the ground as he moved closer.

"Evening, Slim," he said, and when the man whirled around, that's when Chet struck.

❧

As soon as Maria rode up to the courtyard and gave Javier her horse to unsaddle and brush down, Amanda came running. "Please tell me we can still have the party. Everything is arranged, and Mama is all excited about it and—"

"Sure, let's have the party," Maria said as she kept walking toward the house. She was so drunk with exhaustion and worry that she would have agreed to anything as long as it did not prevent her from getting a glass of Juanita's lemonade and pulling off her boots. *We can make it a farewell to Clear Springs Ranch party*, she thought and had to swallow hard to keep the tears of bitterness and defeat at bay.

Amanda squealed, gave her a hug, and then ran back inside. Juanita waited for her to sit on one of the benches in the courtyard and pull off her boots, then handed her the lemonade. "You took your own sweet time getting home," she fussed. "We do worry, you know."

Maria drained the glass in a most unladylike way and held it out for more. "Is Roger back?"

"Haven't seen him. The boys came back earlier. Eduardo told me about the sale." She refilled the glass and handed it back to Maria. "What are you going to do?"

"What can I do short of robbing a bank?" She laughed. "I could rob the bank that we owe a good deal of money to that is due at noon tomorrow and then hand the money back to old Clyde." Her laugh turned to a cackle and then to tears. "Oh, Nita, we are going to lose everything, and it's all my fault."

Juanita set the pitcher down and knelt next to Maria. "Now you listen to me, *mi hija*. You have done everything you could to keep this place going. If you lose it, then that's the way life goes sometimes. We will all find another way. Now come inside and clean yourself up and have some supper."

Juanita was giving her what she needed most—she was giving her normalcy. In the worst of times, it had always been easy to believe that everything would be all right once Juanita started giving orders. "Well, come on," the housekeeper said, and when Maria pushed herself to her feet, Juanita linked arms with her and headed back inside.

It was amazing what a plate of tortillas served with Juanita's rice, beans, salsa, and roasted chicken could do to restore a person's energy and outlook. Maria was not beat yet. She had a little money from the sale of the stock and she hadn't used up all of the loan, so she had that to give back as well. She sat at the kitchen table long after she'd finished her supper, juggling the numbers. If she could just…

From out near the bunkhouse, she heard the shouts of angry men and knew a fight was in the making. She was tempted to let them blow off steam by carrying through with the fight. After all, they'd worked so hard, and for what? Though of course, Roger said he'd paid them, so what did they have to be upset about?

Frustrated, she slammed down her pencil and hurried outside. "What's this about?" she shouted, but even as she said the words, she saw Slim with the tail of Chet's whip still wrapped around his arm and a box filled with money on the ground at his feet. In fact, there were bills scattered around that the other men were trying to gather.

"You thievin' little…" Bunker growled as he ran at Slim.

Chet pulled the whip free as the two men collided. Slim couldn't put up much of a fight because he was still nursing his bleeding arm where the whip had struck, not to mention that Bunker was nearly twice his size.

"Stop this right now," Maria demanded, wading into the thick of things just as Bunker reared back to throw a punch. "Seymour, that's enough."

The big man looked down at her and slowly lowered his hand. Then he bent down and picked up the box. "This is for you, Miss Maria." He motioned the men who had been gathering the scattered bills forward. "It's from us," he added as the men stuffed more money into the already-full box.

"I don't… You can't… We couldn't possibly…" She had no words to express the feelings that threatened to overpower her. "Why?" she managed finally.

"Because we don't want the Tiptons to win," Rico said softly. "This place is our home too, Miss Maria."

"But you attacked R. J. here. Why?"

"He was trying to steal the money. Hunt here got suspicious and kept an eye on him. We're pretty sure he's Tipton's man, and I'd be happy to take him in the barn there and get the whole story out of him," Bunker said.

Slim looked first ashamed and then defiant. "I wasn't going to take it all—just enough to leave you short."

"And how would you know what amount that might be?" Maria asked.

"I ain't no squealer. Just sayin' I had my instructions." He folded his arms and then grimaced as a shot of pain apparently ran through him.

And that's when Maria noticed the ring.

"Where did you get that?" she demanded grabbing his hand with no worries for whether or not she might be hurting him. "That ring belongs to my father. He always wore it—he was wearing it the day he died."

Slim started to back away but Chet, Bunker, and the others surrounded him.

"It was given to me," he said. "I swear. All I did that day was fool with the saddle and shoes—nothing more. They said they were just teaching your pa a lesson, miss. He told me—"

"Who? Who is 'he'?"

"Marshal Tucker."

Marshal Tucker. *Marshal Tucker* was responsible for the death of her father.

"What do you want us to do with this varmint, Miss Maria?" Bunker looked as if he might happily string the man up.

"I want you to keep him safe until we can get him to the fort and into Colonel Ashwood's custody."

Two of the cowhands grabbed Slim and hauled him off to the bunkhouse.

"And Tucker?" Bunker asked.

"I'll take care of that," Maria said, and the way she said it, there wasn't a man standing who was going to debate the matter with her.

A single bill fluttered to the ground, and she realized she was still clutching the money box.

"I just hope it'll be enough," Seymour said.

She touched his whiskered face and then stood on tiptoe to kiss his cheek. "Even if the numbers do not add up, it already is more than enough. Thank you." Her voice broke as she looked around the circle of men. "Thank you all." When she turned to head back inside the house, she brushed past Chet and murmured, "I need to see you."

Eighteen

CHET WAITED NEAR THE CREEK UNTIL THE WINDOWS IN the house went dark and nothing stirred except the occasional night bird. Sometime around what he judged to be midnight, he heard the creak of wagon wheels and saw a buckboard slowly roll to a stop some distance from the house. He heard a whistle that could have been mistaken for a birdcall and then saw Loralei, struggling to carry her overloaded carpetbag, make her way to the wagon.

The driver—he assumed it was Turnbull—climbed down to meet her. He had words with Loralei, gesturing angrily toward the anteroom, Turnbull finally taking her bag, throwing it in the back of the buckboard, and then lifting her none too gently onto the seat before taking his own place as the driver. With Loralei still yammering at him, he pulled away. If she'd had any notion Turnbull would go back for her trunk, she was wrong.

Chet was so engrossed in watching them go that Maria was almost beside him before he realized it. She tugged at his sleeve.

"I came as soon as I could," she said. "I wanted to say good-bye to Roger before he left."

"But he—"

"He had nothing to do with my father's death, but he'd gotten so tangled up with the Tiptons that he just kept getting in deeper. He explained everything about the dam and why he kept trying to get me to sell out. He was trying to help, but he just didn't know how to go about it. And now he's gone for good."

He touched her cheek and pushed a strand of hair away from her face. "The men got Slim to the fort, but he's refusing to say anything—he's that scared. Now, come sit and tell me why you asked me to come here."

She did as he suggested and sat on a flat boulder near the bank of the creek. "The money—even with the men giving up their pay—won't be enough."

"I figured as much. So now what?"

She sighed and looked off into the distance. "I hate losing this place, but what I hate even more is somebody getting away with murder."

Chet sat beside her and pulled her close. "There's not a man in that bunkhouse who wouldn't be happy to take care of that for you."

"I don't want revenge, Chet. What I want for my father and for Oscar is justice. I want those responsible arrested and brought to trial."

"That may not work out if Slim doesn't cooperate."

"He as good as told us that it was Tucker who killed my father," she said with a dismissive wave of her hand.

"Tucker is still the law," Chet reminded her.

"In town," she argued. "Neither Papa nor Oscar were murdered there," she added softly.

Chet realized she was not really talking to him. She was just thinking out loud, and the direction her thinking was headed made him mighty nervous. "Listen to me, Maria. You need to stay out of this—if not for yourself, then for your ma and Amanda and Trey."

"Well, I can't just let them get away with murder."

"I get that, but you don't know what these men are capable of."

"Oh, I think it's pretty obvious what they're capable of."

"All right, but let's work out a plan together—one that makes sure you are never alone with Tucker or the Tiptons."

"Well, I have to go into town tomorrow to meet with the bank," she said. "I'm sure that the Tiptons as well as the marshal will be in town as well."

"Okay. Not sure what that accomplishes but…"

"I was thinking you could come with me, and before we go to the bank, we could stop by the Wilcox place and talk to Doc. Doc is not only the town doctor; he's also the mayor, meaning he's the one who appointed Tucker as marshal—and that means he can fire him as well."

"I still don't see how—"

"I was thinking that while we were in town, maybe Bunker and a couple of the other men could ride over to the fort and let Colonel Ashwood know the marshal's been fired and will likely be leaving town."

Chet grinned. "So Tucker walks free in town,

thinking he's won, and the militia picks him up the minute he sets foot outside the town limits. Remind me never to cross you, Miss Maria."

She snuggled closer to him. "I've missed you," she admitted. "Maybe once you've dealt with Loralei, we could—"

"Loralei left with Roger, so whatever you've got in mind, lady, don't be holding back on their account." He bent to her. "So now can I kiss you?"

She tilted her face to his. "Yes, please," she whispered. And when she opened her mouth to meet his, he was lost.

He had dreamed of kissing her every night while they were on the cattle drive—dreamed of kissing her and so much more. Remembering the beauty of their afternoon in the field of flowers, he'd replayed every kiss, every touch, a thousand times over. He had allowed himself to fantasize about what it would be like next time.

She moaned and deepened the kiss they were sharing, threading her fingers into his hair as her tongue sparred with his. And then he felt the dampness on her cheeks and pulled back.

"You're crying."

"Don't leave me, Chet."

"Hey, now." He smoothed back her hair and wiped her tears away with his thumb. "I'm right here, okay?" He held her close. "Remember that first day I got here, and you asked if you could trust me?"

"You said I had to decide that for myself."

"Well, in case you haven't yet decided, the answer is 'yes, ma'am. You can trust me.'"

❧

Maria's plan worked perfectly. The militia had both
Tucker and Slim—who had finally gone on record—in
custody before noon the following morning. She
would have felt victorious were it not for the fact that
any way she looked at it, they were going to lose the
ranch. She had counted the money again and again,
but the total did not change. Still, she was her father's
daughter, and her father had always been an optimist.
"Something will come along, Maria," he had told her
whenever it seemed to her that her world was about
to fall apart.

On the other hand, as she crossed the street with
Chet on one side of her and Doc Wilcox on the other,
she could not help feeling that indeed the world as she
and her family had known it was about to come to an
end. She was wearing the gray dress she had worn for
Oscar's funeral and that seemed appropriate.

"Maybe Clyde will extend the deadline," she said
hopefully. Doc patted her hand, but the expression on
his face told her that an extension was about as likely
as a blizzard in July. "Well, it won't hurt to ask," she
muttered defiantly.

Inside the bank lobby, she was not surprised to see
George Johnson and three of the other small ranchers.
It was hardly unusual for these men to be in town or
in the bank. The confusing thing was that they seemed
to be waiting for her.

"You doing all right, Maria?" George asked.

"I will be once this is over," she replied, glancing
at the large wall clock that pointed to fifteen minutes
before noon.

"Well, if you wouldn't mind stepping over here for just a minute before you see Clyde…"

"But—"

"This will just take a minute," Doc urged and led her to where the other ranchers waited.

"We have a proposal to make, Maria."

She was so focused on the ticking clock that she barely heard the preliminaries until finally George Johnson said, "So in effect, we would all own our combined land—a cooperative arrangement that would be managed by a contract and bylaws drawn up and approved by each member of the cattlemen's association."

"You're buying Clear Springs Ranch?"

"No, we're suggesting you and your family become a part of the Cattlemen's Cooperative. The cooperative will pay off your loan here and give you a new loan for the balance after we pay what you need to give the bank today. That loan would of course be interest free. Once that is paid off, you and your family will be full and equal members of the co-op."

"You're not taking the offer the Tiptons made?"

George grinned. "We took a vote, and that business you said about sharecropping had stuck in our minds. If we're gonna share the land, then we'll choose to share with folks we know—and trust. So, are you in or not?"

Maria hesitated. Was this her decision to make?

"Clock is ticking, Maria," George said softly.

She glanced up and saw that it was indeed seven minutes to noon. "In," she said firmly and then she laughed. "All in," she added as if this were one of her father's poker games and the stakes were high—which in this case, they certainly were.

"Then let's go make this deal." On their way across the bank's lobby, Johnson handed her an envelope. "This covers what you owe," he said.

"But I have…" She gripped the envelope containing the money she'd brought.

"Cleaner this way. You give Cardwell this envelope and give me the one you brought—that money will go into the association's till as your first installment on repaying us. Agreed?"

She looked at the fat brown envelope he handed her. She didn't need to count it to know that the amount was right, covering the loan and the interest in full. These men were her family's friends and neighbors. She had known most of them since she was a tiny child. She made the trade—the association's envelope for hers—and shook hands with each rancher.

Clyde Cardwell stood at his office door, a worried frown adding to the creases of his jowled face, sweat filling each crevice. "Mr. Johnson," he said by way of acknowledging the group now crowding into his office. "Perhaps you could explain what this is about."

"In time, Cardwell, but first this little lady here has some business with you."

The ranchers formed a double row of protection as Maria stepped forward and laid the cash on the banker's desk. From the lobby, she heard the large wall clock tick off the last seconds and then begin chiming twelve bells. She could not seem to stop smiling. Her father's killer was behind bars. Her family's ranch was safe.

She looked around for the one person whose approval meant everything to her, but Chet had quietly slipped away.

⁓

Chet had hung around long enough to understand that with the help of her fellow ranchers, Maria had managed the impossible—she had saved her family's ranch. And because she had risked everything to do that, it was unlikely that she would be willing to leave it—even for him. She would never be happy anyplace but at Clear Springs Ranch. He, on the other hand, had to think about little Max and the promise he'd made to himself to give that boy a far better life than he would ever have had with Loralei or her family—a better life than he and his sister had known growing up. Could he do that by staying in Arizona?

He didn't see that working. Maria would be running the ranch, and either he would stay on as her foreman or maybe pick up work at the Johnsons' place. Either way, she deserved better—a man who was her equal. He could maybe buy a little place right here, but that was a joke since the Tiptons grabbed up every acre of land as soon as it became available. He had no doubt that she was as caught up in the passion they shared as he was. But passion eventually turned to something more settled, and he just couldn't see how he could possibly make Maria happy over the long haul. No, he'd talk to Johnson, and if that didn't work out, he'd pack his gear and head west.

He saw a woman coming his way, midforties with a welcoming smile. "Hello, you must be Chet Hunter." She stuck out her hand. "Eliza McNew. I run the mercantile and I've been friends with the Porterfields since Maria was a baby."

Pleased to meet you, ma'am. Maria—Miss Maria
s spoken highly of you."

"You planning on staying around now that the dust
is starting to settle?"

He was taken aback at her directness. "Well now,
ma'am…" He chuckled and shook his head. "I guess I
don't rightly know how to answer that."

"Yes or no works." She squinted up at him. "Oh,
don't go getting all tense. Word has it Roger Turnbull
has lit out of here like somebody put a firecracker under
him. The Porterfields are gonna need a foreman. Maria's
done more than anybody could have ever imagined, but
the truth is she deserves a life of her own."

"Yes, ma'am."

"So you're planning to stay?"

"I'm considering my options, ma'am." It wasn't a
lie—just not the whole truth.

"Good. I'll see you at the party then?"

"I reckon so."

"Gonna be a real fandango," Eliza promised.
"Amanda Porterfield may not know much about
ranching, but when it comes to planning a party, that
little girl has no equal." She pumped his hand again.
"Good to finally meet you, Chet."

"Yes, ma'am." He watched her return to her shop.
He'd forgotten all about the party. He looked down
at his dirt-encrusted boots, his canvas pants with the
patch covering a split on one knee, and his shirt worn
thin by years of wear. Maybe Miss Eliza McNew had
a shirt she'd be willing to part with for less than full
price. He waited for the women he'd seen entering
the store to leave.

"Got just the thing," Eliza said as she rummaged through a stack of folded shirts and pulled out one dark blue. "Maria's wearing a blue dress, and if you wear this, well, you are going to make one good-looking couple on the dance floor." She held it up to him.

"How much?"

She fingered the price tag then ripped it free. "Look at that. Perfect shirt and on sale for two bits. You wanna pay cash or run a tab?"

"Now, Miss McNew…" Chet began, but she was already wrapping the shirt.

"Look, Chet, sometimes you give by taking if you get my meaning. Everybody knows what you've done for the Porterfields—and what you did for Joker." She pressed the package into his hands. "I'll start that tab because I'm hoping you plan to stay around these parts for a good long time." She squeezed his hand. "We need men like you, Chet."

"Yes, ma'am. Thank you, ma'am."

❧

The first person Maria ran to see once she'd returned to the ranch was her mother. As the days had cooled with the coming of autumn, Constance often sat in the courtyard watching Ezma play with Max. They had all adopted the name Chet had given the boy, preferring it to Loralei's mockery of Chet's name.

"Mama, it's over," Maria told her as they sat together in the courtyard. She explained about the plan for the small ranchers to form a cooperative. Her mother nodded but made no comment beyond, "Your father will…*would* be very proud, Maria."

"I've arranged to repay the men," Maria added. "It puts us further in debt with the co-op, but it seemed only fair."

"Whatever you think, dear."

Maria was near tears, so badly did she want her mother to snap out of her malaise and once again be the strong, opinionated woman she had once been, a woman who freely gave out instructions and reminders of how things were to be done. *The Porterfield way*, she had always said. But maybe Constance Porterfield's enthusiasm for life had died with her husband.

Maria decided to try another topic. "Amanda seems to have everything in hand for the party. It will be a true celebration now."

"I suppose." Constance closed her eyes, and for a moment Maria thought her mother had dozed off. But then she said quietly, "I have been thinking about the child."

"Max?"

"Yes. Juanita tells me that his mother has run off and is unlikely to return for the boy. He's hardly Chet Hunter's responsibility, although according to Nita the man seems determined to provide for him."

"Chet is a good man."

Her mother opened her eyes and, for the first time in months, peered closely at her daughter. "You have feelings for this man?"

"I... Why would you think that?"

"It's there in your voice—the way you say his name." She sat forward, her eyes bright with excitement. "Oh, Maria, have you found love at long last?"

Love? Yes, but did Chet love her?

"I… Mama, really it's…"

"Now you listen to me, young lady, we do n. get a second chance in this world—not at love The one thing your father and I wanted for all you children was that one day you might find what we knew. Is this the man for you? I can't say—only you can know that. But if he is, then let nothing stand in your way."

"He has dreams of his own, Mama. How fair would it be to expect him to give those up? And besides, I know he believes that he has nothing to offer me "

"Then he's a fool, and from what I have observed and heard of this young man, he is no fool."

"We were speaking of the child—of Max."

"Yes, I know. I think we should take him in. Do you think Chet might be all right with that? I quite enjoy having a child in the house once again. It helps me… It. ." Her eyes brimmed with the tears that were never far from spilling.

Maria could hardly believe what she was hearing. If they adopted Max, and they convinced him that he'd be welcome here no matter if he'd started as a hand or not, then Chet would not need to leave after all. It was the perfect solution. She covered her mother's hand with hers. "Let's talk to Doc Wilcox at the party tonight. There may be some legalities involved."

Constance smiled. "Yes, the party. We should go and get ready." She touched Maria's hair. "Wear your hair down, dear. Men love that."

When Maria went to her room, she saw that her sister had hung their dresses on hooks near the door and placed a rainbow of ribbons and other hair

aments on the dresser they shared. Amanda's voice
ifted in through the open window.

"But, Javier, we need more candles. There must
be more somewhere. Did you look in the barn and
the bunkhouse?"

Maria smiled. Amanda was in her element when
it came to planning social gatherings. Maria, on the
other hand, was uncomfortable in such settings. She
fingered the blue dress that Amanda and Eliza had
talked her into buying, recalling how it had felt light
as air when she'd tried it on.

In just a few hours, she would be wearing that dress
and sharing her first real dance with Chet. She closed
her eyes, imagining the scene—the music, the cool
night breeze, the candlelight, his hand spanning her
waist, his breath only a kiss away from her lips.

"Oh good, you're finally back," Amanda said as
she entered the room and plopped down on her bed.
"This party will be the death of me yet," she moaned.

Maria laughed. "You love it and we all know it."
She waited a beat and then added. "Amanda, everything
worked out. We've got every reason to celebrate."

Amanda sat up. "We're not losing the ranch?"

Maria told her all about how the small ranchers had
decided to form their own co-op. "With our combined resources, we can stand toe-to-toe with Jasper
Tipton, and we can beat him at his own game."

Amanda clapped her hands like the delighted child
that she was. "Oh, Maria, I just knew you would find a
way to make everything all right." Then she frowned.
"I'm afraid I have some news that might upset you
though. It's about Roger—and that woman."

"I know all about that. It's all for the best,
you think?"

Amanda grinned. "I do. Now you and Chet can—"

Maria wasn't ready to talk about her feelings for
Chet, so she changed the subject. "Speaking of Chet,
Mama wants to adopt little Max."

The news worked. Amanda immediately began
mentally rearranging the sleeping arrangements in
the house to accommodate the baby. "Of course,
eventually he and Trey can share that room—I mean
now that Jess is gone." She sighed heavily. "It's been
months since Mama had had a letter from Jess, and
Addie Wilcox hasn't heard from him at all."

"Addie may need to move on. Our brother is an
idiot to let a woman like that slip through his fingers,
but you know Jess—he has a mind of his own and will
do what he wants whether or not it's the wisest choice."

"Well, the least he could do is write to Mama. I
sure hope we can make this business with taking in
little Max work. It would take Mama's mind off Papa
dying and Jess leaving and…"

Maria realized that Amanda and Trey—and her
mother for that matter—knew nothing of the arrest
of Marshal Tucker or the fact that Isaac Porterfield's
death had not been the accident they'd all been led
to believe. People were bound to be talking about
Tucker's arrest at the party.

"Amanda, I have some news. It's upsetting, but I
need you to stay calm and help me break it to Mama
and to Trey."

Nineteen

CHET TOOK A GOOD BIT OF RIBBING FROM THE OTHER cowhands once he washed up and dressed for the party in his new blue shirt. "Don't know what you boys are carrying on about," he said with a grin. "Looks to me like I'm not the only one."

"Just the first time me and the others have seen you in anything this fancy," Bunker said. "You're looking more like one of the ranchers than one of us hands."

It was an exaggeration, but Chet took it as the compliment he knew Bunker meant it to be and gave the older man a little bow. Bunker picked up his fiddle while Dusty pulled his harmonica from his vest pocket and played a scale. They would provide the music for the dancing. They heard the creak of wagon wheels outside and the combined chatter of people greeting one another as the guests began to arrive.

"Well, boys," Bunker boomed, "sounds like we got ourselves a party to git started. Let's go."

The barn and yard were crowded with people—some Chet knew but most he didn't. Rico pointed out the other ranchers, then left him the minute he spotted

Louisa Johnson, slicking his dark hair back with both hands as he went to her.

From the minute he'd left the bunkhouse, Chet had kept his eye out for Maria, but there'd been no sign of her. Come to think of it, he hadn't seen Amanda or Mrs. Porterfield either. When he spotted Trey coming out of the house, he worked his way through clusters of guests until he reached the boy.

"Nice party, Snap," he observed.

Trey frowned. "You shoulda told me about my pa, Hunt. I'm not a baby. In fact, right now, I'm the man of this family and I shoulda known. I shoulda…"

Chet could see the kid was close to tears, so he stepped in front of him to shield him from the other guests. "You're right, Snap. But the thing of it is that everything came together so fast, there was no time to bring you in on it. But this thing's not over by a long shot. Your ma and your sisters are gonna need you to be strong for them. There will be a trial and folks are gonna be talking. The way I see it, your job is to set an example."

He sniffed and wiped his nose with his shirtsleeve. "I don't get your meaning."

"I didn't ever have the pleasure of knowing your pa, Snap, but everything I've heard about him tells me he was a fine man, a man folks around these parts looked up to and respected. Maybe you need to ask yourself what he would have done in your shoes."

Trey stared at Chet for a moment. "He always used to tell me most of the time fighting didn't solve anything," he said softly. "When I was sick, he used to come into my room at night and sit with me and talk about the ranch and all the stuff he'd had to think about that day. He used to ask me what I thought—even when I was just a kid."

"That tells me he respected you," Chet said. "And one thing I know for sure—any man would be prouder than he could say of the way you helped out with the herd this season. I expect if there's a heaven and your pa's up there looking down on everything, he's got a big ol' grin on his face and he just nudged God and said, 'That's my boy there.'"

Trey ducked his head, but he was smiling. Chet wrapped his arm around the boy's shoulders. "Now what do you say we go get some of those burritos before they're all gone?"

They started across the yard and Chet saw Juanita with a tray of glasses headed for the tables that had been set up to hold the food. "Here, let me take those for you, ma'am," Chet offered.

Juanita handed him the tray and scowled. "Still trying to wheedle your way onto my good side, I see." But then she grinned. "Stick around, and it might just be starting to work."

"Glad to hear that." He glanced toward the house. "Have you—"

"She'll be along directly. She had some news she had to give her mama and sister and brother. She's getting dressed now, I expect, so just be patient. I see you're looking mighty pretty yourself, cowboy." The woman actually winked at him, and Chet felt his neck heat up.

As he set the tray of glasses on the table, one by one, the clusters of guests stopped talking and turned

their attention to a lone rider coming slowly tow
the ranch.

"Can't be," he heard one woman say.

"But it is, I tell you," replied another.

George Johnson studied the rider and then let out
a low whistle. "Well I'll be jiggered. The prodigal
son returns." And then he started walking toward the
rider. "Jess Porterfield," Johnson shouted, "you are a
sight for sore eyes."

~⁂~

Maria had tried several different ribbons to hold her
hair back from her face. She had followed her mother's advice and left it down, but she'd be helping serve
their guests and dancing—with Chet she hoped—and
she didn't want to be brushing wisps away from her
eyes and cheeks.

"Here, let me," Amanda said, her voice subdued
after hearing the news of the how their father had
died. "Do you think Mama will be all right?"

"Yes."

"She was so quiet after you told her. I was afraid
maybe she would—"

"Mama is strong, Amanda. She just needs to work
this through in her head, and then just like before,
she'll come out of it."

Amanda's fingers worked magic, weaving the
ribbon into a hank of Maria's hair until it formed a
slender braid that, with the ribbons, almost looked like
a crown. "There. You look like a princess. Now let's
go join the party before anything else happens."

But Amanda had spoken too soon. When the two

ers reached the yard, they were surprised to see
ost of their guests gathered around a horse tied up
outside the house. But then they saw a familiar head
of thick, chestnut-colored hair and heard a laugh they
had thought they might never hear again, and they
both took off running.

"Jessie!" Amanda squealed as the crowd parted.
Their older brother scooped Amanda up and swung
her around.

"Look at you," he said. "I go away for five minutes
and you go and grow up into a beauty." He set her
down and his expression sobered. "Hello, Maria."

It was as if everyone around her was holding his
breath. Maria ignored the jumble of emotions assault-
ing her at the sight of her brother and opened her arms
to him. "Welcome home, Jess."

Behind her, she heard a cry, and they all turned
to see Constance Porterfield running across the yard,
her skirts clutched in one hand as she reached for her
eldest son with the other. Jess smiled and went to her.
"Kill the fatted calf, Ma. I've come home to stay."

And suddenly Maria found that she could no longer
ignore the feelings that threatened to overwhelm her.
She was so overcome with emotion that she felt as if
she might faint, but then she felt a hand on her elbow
and the solid presence of Chet Hunter standing next
to her.

"Let the dancing begin," Constance shouted, and
Bunker struck up a tune as everyone stood back and
made room for mother and son to waltz. And as others
joined Constance and Jess, it seemed the most natural
thing in the world for Maria to turn to Chet.

Chet couldn't help but think that just maybe with h[...] brother back, Maria might be more open to the idea o[...] heading to California with him, and he was confused that Maria seemed to be more upset about Jess's return than she was happy.

"Nice surprise, Jess showing up that way," he ventured.

Maria glanced at her mother and brother and then forced a smile. "Yes, isn't it?"

"Talk to me, Maria. You're looking more like somebody who just lost the ranch than a woman who has saved the day and now capped that off with her brother coming home."

"I'm just surprised, that's all." Her tone was defensive, her posture stiff. "I mean, look how happy Mama is."

But when Chet looked over at the other couple, Constance Porterfield was not smiling. She seemed to be deep in conversation with her wayward son, and Jess was looking mighty uncomfortable. All of a sudden, Mrs. Porterfield called out, "Change partners!" and steered Jess to dance with Maria while she waited for Chet to take his cue and dance with her.

It was one thing to dance with Maria. He knew her. This woman now smiling up at him was pretty much a stranger. "We have a good deal of business we need to work out, Mr. Hunter," she said.

He thought he knew what was coming—she didn't want him hanging around Maria, and now that her son had returned, there was no reason for him to hang around at all. He tried to prepare some kind of answer and almost missed what she really had to say.

I admire what you have done in accepting respon-
bility for little Ches…Max. Juanita tells me that the
child is not yours and that Loralei used you, even put
you in a dangerous position with her father, in order
to save face."

"Yes, ma'am."

"I do not know your plans, Mr. Hunter, but I
would like to make a suggestion—several actually."

"Yes, ma'am."

"Max has a home here if you will accept that for
him. His presence was instrumental in bringing me
through the worst of my…illness."

"That's very kind of you, ma'am."

She smiled. "Oh, Mr. Hunter, you will learn in
time that I always have reasons for what I do."

Chet was completely confused now. What possible
value could Max have for her? He frowned. "I don't
guess I'm getting your meaning, ma'am."

"It may have seemed like I was living in the clouds
these last weeks, Chester—may I call you Chester?"

Chet nodded.

"But I am a keen observer of people, and over the
last few weeks, I have observed the effect you have had
on the people living on this ranch—the other hands,
my younger son, and Maria—especially Maria."

Okay, here it came. Cowhands and members of
the rancher's family they worked for did not mix—at
least not romantically speaking. Chet gave her the
only answer he had. "I love your daughter, Mrs.
Porterfield. It wasn't meant to be, but it's there, and
I'll do whatever you think best for her happiness."

"Well, finally, a man not afraid to speak his mind or

his feelings. Good for you, Chester. I had the feel
that you weren't a bit like that mealymouthed, bluste.
ing fool Roger Turnbull."

Now Chet was struck speechless and the expression
on his face must have been pretty comical because Mrs.
Porterfield laughed. "You're a good deal like my late
husband, Chet. He was everything to me, and it has
taken me some time to understand how I might go
on without him. But I see now that making sure our
children find that same true love that he and I shared—
that's my job now. And I plan to start with Maria."

"Well now, ma'am—"

"Maria has finally met her match in you, Chester,
and I aim to see that she doesn't spoil that." She
glanced across the yard to where Maria and her
brother were having a heated conversation near the
refreshment table.

"I'm not sure—"

Mrs. Porterfield tightened her grip on his hand.
"Now you listen to me, Chester Hunter, you say you
love my daughter, and if I am any judge at all of such
things—and I assure you that I am—she is madly in
love with you. Are you truly going to keep drifting
around the country when you have everything you've
been searching for right here?"

Chet could not control the grin that spread across
his face. "Well now, ma'am, when you put it that
way, I don't see how I can refuse."

"Good. Now let's go get some punch and break up
the squabble going on between Maria and her brother.
Those two were always like two dogs fighting over
one bone."

Trey had said the exact same thing. "There is the matter of little Max," Chet ventured.

"Max is part of the package as far as I can see. As long as you choose to have a home here, so does he. And you will always have a home here. Now come along before those two start throwing punches."

"Yes, ma'am."

❧

"You weren't here," Maria hissed. "I did the best I could, Jess."

"Selling out to the other ranchers is your best? Well, it's better than selling out to the Tiptons. I'll give you that much. Maybe it's not too late to fix this."

"Fix what, dear?" Their mother stepped between them, and Maria saw that Chet was standing just behind her.

"Mama, I know Pa's death—"

"Actually you know very little about your father's death, Jess. It was Maria who finally figured it out. Your father was murdered, Jess. The culprit is in custody."

"The Tiptons?" Jess had gone so red in the face that Maria feared he might actually explode.

"No, although I suspect they are behind the whole business, but we have no proof of that. All indications are that your father was murdered by Marshal Tucker. He has been relieved of his duties, of course." She studied her son for a long moment and then smiled. "Perhaps you would like to take on the job of town marshal, Jess. It would certainly give you opportunities for more frequent contact with Addie Wilcox and—"

"Mama." Jess touched her arm and lowered his

voice. "I can't be marshal. I have to run things here. I've come back to—"

"Run the ranch?" Maria challenged. "Not while I'm here."

Jess opened and closed his mouth several times, but no sound came out.

Chet stepped forward and offered Jess his hand. "I don't believe we've met. I'm Chet Hunter—I work for your sister here, and if you'll excuse us, I kind of promised her this dance."

Behind them, Bunker struck up a lively tune and Maria's mother smiled. "A reel—my favorite. Excuse me, I want to dance this one with Trey." She turned to go and then grabbed Jess's sleeve. "Addie Wilcox seems to be tapping her toe, Son. Perhaps her desire to dance will overrule her good sense, and she'll accept your invitation." She gave her son a light shove in Addie's general direction, then winked at Chet as he led Maria to join the other dancers.

The discomfort and shyness Maria felt once she and Chet were left alone—granted, in the middle of a throng of neighbors and friends—reminded her of that first day he had come riding down the trail and into her life.

"You mustn't mind Mama, Chet. She's not been herself since—"

"It seems to me that your mother is quite herself, and I'm beginning to think the apple didn't fall far from the tree when it comes to you and her." He took hold of her hand, but instead of joining the fast-moving square dance, he led her to a cluster of trees just outside the courtyard where Amanda had decorated the branches with candles set in canning jars.

He wrapped his arms around her and tilted her chin so that she was looking up at him.

"And just what did you and my mother talk about?"

"Well, now sometimes you have to read between the lines with a woman like her, but I'm pretty sure she had in mind that maybe I should kiss you, so…"

His lips were full and soft on hers, and the thought occurred to her that if this man were to kiss her a thousand times, she would never grow tired of it.

"You know, your mama also had one other instruction—or maybe it was more of a suggestion."

"What's that?"

"Seems she thinks we make a good match. Seems she thinks one day you and me might just get married. What do you think of that?"

Maria couldn't help it. She laughed and took a step away from him. "Chester Hunter, if that is your idea of a proposal, it needs work."

"I can do better," he protested when she started to back away from him.

"Good," she said, her voice still filled with laughter. "You practice up, and we'll try this again one day. Now…"

He pulled her back into his arms and tightened his hold on her. His lips were so close to her face that every word carried his breath mingled with her own.

"Marry me, Maria, and I promise you I will spend every minute of every day doing my darnedest to give you the life and love that is everything you have ever wanted and more."

They both went absolutely still, surrounded sounds they barely heard—the music, Bunker ca the steps of the reel, people laughing and talking a enjoying themselves…and the rhythm of their breath

"Now that's what I call a proposal—one I will most happily accept," she whispered just before she wrapped her arms around his neck and kissed him.

Last Chance Cowboys: The Lawman

FROM THE AUTHOR...

Sometimes characters I think are minor speak up. (Sometimes they pretty much grab me by the shoulders and shout, "I want to tell my story!") That was the case with Dr. Addie Wilcox. So when her childhood sweetheart and love of her life, Jess Porterfield, returns at the end of *The Drifter*, I knew what the second book in the series would be. In *The Lawman*, Addie has to fight her lifelong attraction to Jess, determined that he won't break her heart again. Trouble is, once he gets appointed to serve as the town marshal and is pretty much living down the street from Addie and her family, avoiding his good looks, charming smile, and determination to win her heart becomes pretty much impossible.

The story of Addie and Jess is all about first love and second chances. Here's an excerpt that I hope sends you running to the store or your computer to read more...

One

Arizona Territory, 1882

THE PRODIGAL SON COMES HOME, JESS THOUGHT, hesitating on the ridge overlooking the Porterfield spread.

Six months gone, and finally he had come home. But he might as well have kept on riding. In the relatively short time that he'd been away, everything about the Clear Springs Ranch, the town of Whitman Falls—indeed, the entire Arizona Territory—seemed foreign. Wrong. As if after his time on the streets of Kansas City, he no longer fit the brush and red mesas of the land he'd always been told was in his blood.

Jess set his jaw and pressed on. As he rode slowly up the trail that led to his family's home, he saw the adobe house that his father had built and added to through the years as the family had grown. He expected to find his mother, two sisters, and younger brother inside gathered round the table in the kitchen. He expected to hear laughter coming from the bunkhouse. Instead, the annual party his parents always hosted after the livestock had been taken to market was in full swing.

The courtyard of the house was packed with people—
some he recognized and some who were strangers.
Everyone seemed to be in the mood to celebrate,
which made no sense given that the ranch had been
about to fail the day he'd left.

Back then, the situation had been dire on all fronts.
His father had just died in what appeared to be a
freak accident. A drought that had gone on for over a
year threatened to send the family and the ranch into
bankruptcy. His mother had been so consumed by her
grief that she refused to believe her husband was truly
gone. And he was ashamed to admit that he had left his
sister, Maria, on her own to fend off the land-grabbing
Tipton brothers who were intent on owning the rest
of the land in the territory.

And yet there were lanterns lighting the courtyard
and bonfires where guests gathered between dances to
warm themselves on this autumn night. He had heard
the music from some distance away, and now that he
was closer, he heard the laughter and excited chatter
of people enjoying themselves. So who was hosting
this fandango? He half expected to see Jasper Tipton
and his much younger wife, Pearl, playing the role
of hosts. Surely Maria had had to surrender and sell
out. Truth was, his father had barely been hanging on
before he died. But it seemed most of the hired hands
were here—including Bunker, who stood along with
a couple of the other cowboys, stomping their feet in
time to the music they produced from a worn fiddle
and guitar and banjo. Just like old times.

"Is that you, Jessie Porterfield?"

Their nearest neighbor, George Johnson, waited for

Jess to dismount and tie up his horse at the hitch post before grabbing him in a bear hug. "Good have you home."

"Looks like there might have been some changes since I left," Jess ventured.

George laughed. "Point is things are pretty much the same only better. That sister of yours is quite the little businesswoman."

"You don't say." Jess felt the bile of his own failure rise in his throat. "So we still own this place?"

"In a manner of speaking. Maria can fill you in, but the short version is that several of the smaller ranchers decided the only way to fight the Tiptons was to beat them at their own game. So we've banded together in a cooperative arrangement. We share the profits—and the debts. We help each other out. 'Course, having just come back from taking the stock to market, we've got a little time to get settled into this new arrangement, but you mark my words, by spring every small ranch in this territory will be holding its own."

So Maria had somehow managed to hold the Tipton brothers at bay and hang on to the ranch. Their father would be really proud—of her.

"You've got a new foreman," George continued. "A Florida boy—came drifting in here not long after you left. Went to work with the others and everyone's pretty sure that him and Maria will be heading down the aisle before too long." Jess was aware that several others had spotted him and a crowd was beginning to form as they pushed forward to listen to George.

"What about Roger?"

"He took off. Some think he might have been

ɔlved in that business with your pa. 'Course, there's
⸱ proof, and he was a good foreman and all. Didn't
ȝet along with the drifter though—not one bit."

"Jessie!" His younger sister, Amanda, squealed as
the crowd parted to let her through. Jess scooped her
up and swung her around.

"Look at you," he said, glad for the diversion. "I go
away for five minutes and you go and grow up into
a real beauty." He set her down and his expression
sobered when he saw his other sister standing at the
edge of the crowd. "Hello, Maria."

He saw Maria hesitate as her expression ran through
a range of emotions that went from anger to confusion
to wariness. After what seemed like an eternity, she
opened her arms to him. "Welcome home, Jess."

As he hugged her—and felt her hesitation even
in her embrace—they all heard a shrill cry, and Jess
looked up to see his mother running across the yard,
her skirts clutched in one hand as she reached out for
her eldest son with the other. Jess smiled and went to
her. "Kill the fatted calf, Ma. I've come home to stay."

"Let the dancing begin," his mother shouted, and
the band struck up a lively tune as she pulled him into
the center of the lanterns that outlined the dance floor.

"You look older, Son," she said, frowning as she
studied his face closely.

"And you're still the prettiest woman around," he
countered, reluctant to get into the last few months.

"Prettier than Addie Wilcox?"

That was the one person he had not allowed himself
to think about. His intent had been first to settle things
with his family and then…

"She waited for you to come to your senses, you know," his mother continued. "Why didn't you at least write to her?"

"I don't want to talk about Addie, Ma. It's you I've come to see. How are you feeling?"

She laughed. "Well, if you're thinking that I'm the batty old woman you left six months ago, stop worrying. I needed some time. I'm still missing your father every minute of every day, but now that the culprit who murdered him is in—"

Jess stumbled. "What are you saying, Ma? He died in an accident and…" Maybe she wasn't better after all. His heart sank.

She heaved a sigh of resignation. "Stop looking at me that way, Jessie. We've all had to face the hard truth of the matter."

Jess thought of what George Johnson had been saying when Amanda interrupted—something about there being no proof that their foreman, Roger Turnbull, had been involved in 'that business with your pa.' "Murdered?" he said, unable to take it all in. The news shook him to his boots. Could it be true that his father's accident had been no accident at all— but cold-blooded murder? He was speechless—first with disbelief, and then growing rage.

"Now you pull yourself together, Jess," his mother ordered as the dance ended. "The culprit—Marshal Tucker—is in custody at Fort Lowell. This is a matter for Colonel Ashwood and his men to handle and you need to stay out of it. Is that clear?"

He slapped at a biting bug that attacked his neck. Some things, he realized—like the bugs and the dust and the underhanded Tipton boys doing whatever they found necessary to control the territory—did not change. "Tucker? But what kind of beef could he have had with Pa?"

His mother looked away and then back at him. She linked her arm through his, but it was less a gesture of consolation than one that felt as if she were trying to make sure he stayed put. "You'll hear it soon enough, so it may as well be from me. At least then you know you're getting the truth of it. Tucker was working with the Tipton brothers. It appears that he decided to take matters into his own hands when your father refused to sell. I suspect he hoped he would endear himself to the Tiptons with his actions."

"You're saying they had nothing to do with this?"

"I'm saying that there is no evidence that points to that. I am saying that Tucker is in custody and Colonel Ashwood assures me that he will be tried and punished to the full extent of the law."

"But what about…"

"Now you listen to me, Jessup Porterfield, I have lost my husband and I will not lose my oldest son in the bargain. So you just contain that temper of yours and let the colonel handle this. If the Tiptons are involved, then they will be arrested."

"*If*? Ma, we both know—"

"No, Son, we don't *know* anything. We suspect, but we do not know, so stay out of it and let the federal authorities do their job. If you're so all-fired interested in taking up the law, talk to Doc. With the arrest of Tucker, Whitman Falls is in need of a new marshal. Now then, speaking of the Wilcox family, they just struck up a *ranchera* and it looks to me like Addie Wilcox is just itching to get out on that dance floor."

She gave him a nudge and went off to dance the reel with his younger brother, Trey, who waved at Jess and grinned as if Jess had just come back from a day on the range, not six months gone with no word.

Disoriented, Jess turned and saw Addie Wilcox tapping her toe in time to the music. He pushed aside the chilling news, his anger, everything, and focused on the one thing he knew he could depend on.

But was that still true?

He studied her. She wanted to dance, all right. Question was would she dance with him? After all, he hadn't just left Whitman Falls and his family's ranch; he had left Addie as well.

Jess crossed the yard, nodding to friends and neighbors as he threaded his way through those watching the dancing. "Welcome home, Jess," he heard more than one of the women say. "Learned your lesson, did you?" He expected he was going to hear that sentiment more than once.

Addie had to be hearing this and she had to be aware that he was making his way toward her, but she refused to acknowledge him. Clearly she hadn't changed a bit in the months since he'd left. She was every bit as stubborn and mule-headed as she'd always been. He ought to just turn right around and ignore her. He ought to ask Sybil Sinclair to dance and see how Addie liked that. He ought to do half a dozen things...but he didn't.

"Evenin'," he muttered, sidling up next to her.

He kept his eyes on the dancers. "Good to see Mama looking better," he added.

"No thanks to you," she replied as she took up clapping her hands in time with the beat.

He bristled. Addie had this way of saying exactly what was needed to get under his skin. "Meaning what?" Of course, he knew what she was saying— knew what probably everybody there was thinking. *The prodigal son.* He'd seen more than one person's lips murmuring those words as they had watched his mother come running to welcome him back—as she had enfolded him in her embrace.

"I asked you a question, Addie."

"Rhetorical, I'm sure." She kept right on clapping and tapping her toes, smiling at the dancers as they passed by.

"Don't you go throwing around those fancy words with me, *Doctor* Wilcox."

"And don't you go playing like you're some uneducated country bumpkin, Jess Porterfield. You owe that much respect to your parents." Her smile tightened. "Besides, I'm not a doctor for real—not yet."

He had to clench his fist to keep from touching her bare forearm below the lace trim of her dress, comforting her as he had in the past whenever she got discouraged. "You wanna dance or not?" he grumbled, holding out his hand to her.

Just then the music finished on a crescendo and everybody applauded. "Looks like, as usual, your timing is perfect," she said. She turned to go but was prevented from moving by the throng of dancers leaving the floor in search of some cider to quench their thirst. Jess decided to try a different tactic and moved a step closer. "Mama thinks I ought to apply for the marshal's job," he said. "Your pa being head of the town council and all, do you think he might…"

She wheeled around and looked directly at him for the first time, her dark brown eyes large with surprise. "Are you serious? Why would Papa trust you? Why would *any* of us trust you not to up and leave again?"

"Addie, I had to…"

Her mouth worked as if finding and then rejecting words before she could spit them out at him. She held up her hands to stop him from saying anything more before she brushed past him, losing herself in the crowd. He glanced around to see others looking at him. Obviously they had witnessed the scene and were now passing judgment. The prodigal son. The disappointment. The failure. Well, he would show them. He would show all of them—even Addie— especially Addie.

The question was *how*. He could hardly take over here at the ranch. From the talk he'd had with George Johnson, it sure seemed like Maria had done a better job than he would have thought—or than he could have done—managing things on the Clear Springs Ranch. Maria had done an impossible job. In spite of the attempts of the Tipton Brothers Cattle and Land Company to buy out all the smaller ranchers in the area including—no, especially—theirs, Maria had found a way to hang on.

So, maybe he should think more seriously about applying for the lawman's job. After all, even though the local marshal had no jurisdiction over crimes that took place outside the town's borders, it would be a way he could look into the matter without raising suspicions. As head of the town council, Addie's father would be the one to hire a new marshal.

That gave Jess pause. No doubt Doc Wilcox would be as down on him as Addie was, so why bother? On the other hand, if he was going to bring the Tipton brothers to justice, he needed this job to give him the time and the cover he needed to track down the *real* killers. With Tucker behind bars at the fort, the town was in need of a new marshal. So if he played his cards right and kept his temper under control—a lesson he'd learned the hard way back in Kansas City—the job could be his. And besides, why *wouldn't* Doc Wilcox hire him? He'd make a fine marshal.

"Hello, Jess."

Jess's scowl changed instantly to a smile when he saw Sybil Sinclair gazing up at him. "I was on my way to get some punch but…"

"Maybe we could enjoy this waltz first?" Jess offered her his arm the way his mother had taught both her boys a gentleman would escort a lady and led her onto the dance floor.

❧

Addie could not for the life of her figure out why she continued to allow that man to get to her. Why couldn't she be more like Jess's younger sister and her good friend, Amanda—calm and sophisticated? She searched the gathering for Amanda, but hesitated when she saw her friend surrounded by the usual trio of admirers. Amanda had been planning this party for weeks now. She certainly deserved to enjoy herself and not have to sympathize with Addie. Besides, Jess was Amanda's brother, newly returned to the fold from his travels following his father's death—a death everyone now knew had not been the accident they'd first thought.

Addie stopped dead in her tracks. Her hand flew to her mouth. *What was she thinking?*

Poor Jess. Did he know? Had anyone told him? Of course not. Jess had a temper, and if he knew what everyone now knew, he'd likely be off trying to track down the killer.

Maybe Jess had overheard some of the talk Maybe that was why he was talking about applying for the marshal's position. After all, Jasper Tipton had built that big house in town to please his bride, Pearl, and his brother, Buck, lived there as well. While the local marshal had no jurisdiction outside the town limits, Jess might just think the fact the Tiptons resided in town opened the door for him to go after them. More than likely he would get himself killed in the bargain. Her head was spinning as she tried to think the issue through from every side.

"This is not one of your medical cases," she muttered to herself. "This is Jess." And when it came to figuring out what Jess Porterfield might be thinking, she fully appreciated that logic was not part of the process. She was still mad at him for leaving all those months ago, but that didn't mean she didn't care about him and, knowing his temper, he was bound to get into trouble. With a sigh, she headed off to find her father. Maybe he could talk some sense into the man—the man she had fallen in love with, planned a future with, and then rejected. But as she moved through the throng of party guests pausing now and then to exchange a greeting, it wasn't her father she saw—it was Jess.

He wasn't spoiling for a fight at all. No, he was laughing and flirting with Sybil Sinclair. Sybil with her blond curls and her bright blue eyes and a cupid's bow of a mouth that made her look like a porcelain doll. Sybil with her tiny waist and her flawless skin and giddy laugh that actually came out as *Tee-hee-hee.*

"My brother is trying to make you jealous," Amanda murmured, coming to stand next to her. "Do not let him know that it's working."

"It's not," Addie insisted, pushing her glasses more firmly onto the bridge of her nose. She straightened to her full height, which was still a good three inches shorter than Sybil's willowy five foot four. She brushed back a lock of hair that had come loose from the practical bun she preferred, and tried not to think about how her stick-straight locks would look worn down like Sybil's long curls. "I really couldn't care less if your brother wants to make an utter fool of himself with that—"

"Good to know you aren't affected," Amanda said wryly. "But two can play this game. Come on. Dance with Harlan Stokes."

Just like Jess, Harlan Stokes had a reputation with the ladies. He had never paid the slightest attention to Addie, but he had definitely set his sights on Amanda. She could get him to do anything—even dance with plain Addie Wilcox. Of course, even as he led Addie to the dance floor, his eyes remained on Amanda, who had accepted another cowboy's invitation to dance. Addie couldn't fault Harlan because her own gaze kept drifting to where Jess was dancing with Sybil. The song was "Sweet Betsy from Pike"—a favorite of Addie's, but she barely heard the tune as Harlan guided her around the floor.

"You think I've got any chance at all with Amanda?" Harlan asked.

Addie glanced up at him. He was only a few inches taller than she was and she knew the other cowhands teased him a lot about his short stature. They even called him Peewee. He looked miserable as he turned her for the sole purpose of keeping his eye on Amanda. Addie knew that her answer called for diplomacy of the highest order.

"Well, you know Amanda is still unsettled in her ways. She's not yet decided on the path she wants to take."

"Not like you, huh? I mean, everybody knows you've been planning on taking over your pa's practice just as soon as you finish your schooling and all."

"Well, not taking over. More like working with him."

Harlan looked surprised. "You've been doing that since you were a kid."

The fact that Harlan's full attention was now focused on her made Addie uncomfortable—so much so that she stumbled and he tightened his hold on her, pulling her closer. "Easy there," he said. "You got your bearings?"

"I'm fine," she said and knew it came out as a rebuff when he loosened his grip. "Thank you," she added. "I'm not very good at dancing."

He frowned. "You're fine, Addie Wilcox. Just fine."

She was surprised to feel a lump in her throat at his kindness. Blessedly the waltz ended just then. "Thank you, Harlan. I know that Amanda asked you to take pity on me and—"

"You shouldn't do that, Addie. Put yourself down that way. You're worth two of most of the females at this party."

This had to stop. Addie could feel the heat rise along her neck up into her cheeks. "There's not a whole lot of competition," she said, looking around at the gathering where men outnumbered the girls and women by a factor of at least three to one.

"You know what I'm saying."

"Why, thank you, Harlan. Does that include Amanda Porterfield?" She was teasing him now.

It was his turn to blush. "Well now, Miss Addie, it would take a lot to measure up to Amanda Porterfield—at least for me."

"You're a good man, Harlan. Thank you for the dance." She punctuated her appreciation with a slight curtsy and laughed when Harlan bowed in return.

"Pleasure was mine, ma'am."

They were both laughing when Addie spotted Jess scowling at her as he carried two cups of punch back to where he had left Sybil waiting.

"Hey, Jess," Harlan called out, "'bout time you got home. The other boys and me have been missing you and your money at the poker games."

Jess kept walking, acknowledging Harlan's greeting only by raising one of the punch cups in a toast. Addie watched him go, drawn in by the familiar, graceful gait.

Stop it, she ordered herself.

Seymour Bunker, the oldest hand on the Porterfield spread and as good with a fiddle as he was with a lariat, struck up a reel. Harlan took Addie's hand and they joined the other dancers. At the same time, she saw Jess set down the cups of punch and lead Sybil into the circle. Addie's pulse raced as she realized there was no way she could avoid taking her turn with him in the change of partners required by the dance.

They came together and then circled away and then came together again, sashaying their way down the line of other dancers. She refused to look at him, her mouth drawn into a tight line and her brow furrowed in concentration as if the steps of the dance were every bit as complex as her study of the thick anatomy text she'd left on the kitchen table back home. Jess tightened his hold on her waist as they made their way down the center of the other dancers. When they reached the end of the line, he let her go without a word and turned back to Sybil, who gave Addie a victorious smile before promenading through the line with Jess.

Addie was aware that everyone was looking at her, feeling sorry for her, and once the dance finally ended, Harlan's cheeks were flushed. "I'm sorry, Addie. I wasn't thinking. I mean, Jess is a durn fool, if you'll pardon me saying so. Leaving a woman like you the way he did…"

"Please don't concern yourself, Harlan. Thank you for the dances. Oh, look, Amanda is looking this way. Maybe she's free for the next waltz."

Harlan gave Addie a little bow and hurried off.

Of course, he wasn't the only one who thought that Jess had all but jilted her. Jess's stupid pride had never allowed him to admit the truth—that he had begged her to go with him and she had refused.

Well, he'd come back. She had no idea why, but she'd be willing to bet that it was because the life he'd been so sure was waiting for him in the city had never materialized. It surprised her to realize that she got no satisfaction from that thought. She watched him drink down his punch in one long gulp while Sybil sipped hers.

The one thing that no amount of irritation at the man could change was that he was undeniably good-looking. He was tall, and his muscular frame gave evidence of his ability to work hard. Tonight he was wearing black trousers, a blue shirt, and a leather vest, as if he'd known he was dressing for a party. And boots, of course—new from the look of them. When he'd first arrived he'd been wearing a black Stetson, but his mother had removed that as soon as she ran to embrace him.

A hank of his straw-colored hair had now fallen over his forehead and Addie saw Sybil reach up to push it back, but Jess stepped away from her touch. He said something to her, smiled, and then walked away. Addie's breath quickened and she closed her eyes, preparing herself for what she might say when Jess came her way.

But when she opened her eyes she saw that he had not only walked away from Sybil…he had also walked away from her.

And she was the fool who had let him.

Please enjoy this excerpt from *USA Today*
bestselling author Rosanne Bittner's

Thunder on the Plains

May 1857

ANNIE WEBSTER FROWNED WHEN SHE OPENED THE
door. "I don't take nobody but gentlemen in my
boardinghouse," she warned defensively, "and only
them that bathes."

The young man standing on her porch removed a
wide-brimmed leather hat, revealing a cascade of thick,
nearly black hair that fell in tumbled layers. "I don't
know much about gentlemen, ma'am, except that I'm
no troublemaker; and I *do* take baths, often as I can."

The woman studied him closely, noticing he was
clean-shaven. Although he wore buckskins, they were
not worn and dirty like those she had seen on so
many other men in Omaha who dressed like this one.
The young man smiled warmly, his teeth straight and
white, too white, she thought. Maybe they looked
that way because his skin was so dark. Whatever the
reason, it was a very handsome, unnerving smile, and
it destroyed her remaining defenses.

She stepped aside, allowing him inside. His lanky
six-foot plus frame towered over her as she closed the
door and folded her arms, a look of authority moving
into her eyes. "Well, what will it be? Money's got to
be paid up front. I've had my share of men comin'

into her eyes. "Well, what will it be? Money's got to be paid up front. I've had my share of men comin' in here and messin' up a room for a couple of nights, then takin' off without payin'."

"I'm not here for a room, ma'am. Name's Colt Travis, and I came here to see a Mister uh—" He stopped and took a folded piece of paper from where it was tucked into his wide leather belt. Mrs. Webster watched warily, for attached to the belt was a beaded sheath that held a huge knife. Around his hips hung a gun belt and revolver. The hands that unfolded the paper looked strong, and were tanned even darker than his face from exposure to the prairie sun, darker than any white man she had ever seen. "A Mr. Stuart Landers," he finished. He looked at her with soft hazel eyes, a gentle gaze that didn't seem to match the rest of his rugged frame. "This poster says I can find him here. He's looking for an experienced scout."

"Experienced? You don't look old enough to have much experience, but then I guess that's for Mr. Landers to decide."

"Is he here then?"

The woman nodded, squinting and eyeing him even more closely. "You an Indian?"

Colt felt the heat coming to his cheeks. It was a question he was sick of hearing every time he met someone new. "I'm just a man looking for a job."

Mrs. Webster straightened. "That's not what I asked."

Colt sighed. "Ma'am, will you please just get Mr. Landers?"

The woman sniffed. "Follow me." She turned and walked over a polished hardwood floor to a

small but neat room with a brick fireplace. Vases and
knickknacks lined the mantel. "Can't blame me for
askin'," she muttered. "Them high cheekbones and
that dark hair and skin, wearin' buckskins and all, what
do you expect? I got a right to know who I'm lettin'
in my door."

Colt said nothing. He glanced around the room,
wondering if the woman scrubbed every item every
day. It was hard to believe that anything in this dusty
town could be kept so clean. The room was decorated
with plants and little tables, stuffed chairs, and a sofa
with flower-patterned upholstery.

"I'm Annie Webster," she said, turning to meet his
eyes. "You can wait here in the parlor, Mr. Travis. I'll
get Mr. Landers."

"Thank you, ma'am."

The woman started out, then stopped and glanced
back at him as though trying to tell him with her eyes he
had better not break or soil anything. Colt just nodded
to her, and she finally left. Colt remained standing,
deciding the furniture looked too fine to sit on. He
wondered if Mrs. Webster was a Mormon. Several
Mormons had chosen to stay in Omaha since they first
settled there for one winter a good ten years before.

The Mormons had a way of making something
out of nothing, and this house was an example. There
were few fine frame buildings in Omaha, more log
and tent structures than anything else, but the place
considered itself a city nonetheless. Even in its young
stage, it was all the city Colt cared to encounter. He
felt closed in in the small parlor, as out of place as a
buffalo might feel inside a house. He looked down at

his boots, hoping he had stamped off enough dust so as not to dirty Mrs. Webster's immaculately polished floor and colorful braided rugs.

"Mr. Travis." Colt turned to see a man of perhaps thirty approaching. He guessed the man's suit was silk, as was the paisley-print vest he wore beneath the perfectly fitting jacket. A gold watch chain hung from the vest pocket. The man looked Colt over appreciatively. "Stuart Landers," he said, putting out his hand. "I am very glad to meet you. Mrs. Webster says you've come in answer to my poster."

Colt took his hand, thinking what a weak grip the man had. Landers's dark hair was already beginning to thin dramatically, his temples and the area just back from his forehead already bald. In spite of the man's obvious wealth, evident by his dress and manner, there was an honesty to his dark eyes that Colt liked right away. "Well, sir, the words *excellent pay* kind of struck my eye."

Landers laughed and motioned for Colt to be seated across from him. Colt reluctantly lowered himself into a stuffed chair, deciding not to lean back. "I am afraid I might have made a mistake putting those words in the ad," Landers told him. "Oh, the pay *will* be excellent, but the ad attracted every sort of man imaginable. Most of those who answered it so far have turned out either not to have near enough experience, or have been so dirty and dangerous-looking that I just felt I couldn't trust them." The man studied Colt intently as he spoke. "Mrs. Webster said you, on the other hand, gave a very good appearance and didn't, uh…well, to put it bluntly, she said 'this one doesn't smell bad.'"

Colt frowned, trying to decide whether or not the remark was a compliment. He rested his elbows on his knees, fingering his hat. "Mr. Landers, I don't know what this is all about or why it matters, but before my folks died, I was raised to be clean and respectful. My father was a missionary, came west with the Cherokee back in the thirties. Fact is, my mother was a Cherokee herself, but she and my pa lived in nice houses and brought me up a Christian. I have to say, though, that whether or not a man is clean and educated doesn't have much to do with how good a scout he is."

"Oh, I am sure of that; but this is a situation that calls for both—an experienced scout who can ensure our safety, but a man presentable and mannerly enough to be around my younger sister. She's never been exposed to this rough frontier life. My father won't allow any nonsense around her—foul language, uncleanliness, that sort of thing. You're half Indian, you say?"

Colt felt the defenses rising again, but he did not detect an insulting ring to the words. "Cherokee. Lived most of my early years down in Texas. My folks were both dead by the time I was fourteen, and I've been kind of a wandering man ever since."

"Well, whether or not you're a half—I mean, being part Indian isn't really so important as long as you were raised by a white, Christian father. You speak well and give a good appearance. I must say, you look young, though, Mr. Travis. May I ask your age?"

"I'm twenty, but I've been on my own and lived a man's life for a lot of years. I've been to Oregon and back four times and to California twice. I've fought

Indians and killed my share, led wagon trains, hunted buffalo, you name it. I even know a little bit about surveying. After my mother died, my father moved to Austin and worked for a surveyor for a few years down in Texas, and I worked right alongside him."

Landers's eyes lit up. "Surveying! Why, that's wonderful! That kind of experience is just what we need! I *knew* if I took my time I'd find the right man."

Colt watched him warily. "I ought to tell you I have a partner, name of Slim Jessup," he said, speaking in a soft Texas drawl. "He's a little less prone to bathing, but I'd make sure he cleaned up. He's quite a bit older, taught me everything I know. He'd be here with me now, but he's over seeing a horse doctor about getting a tooth pulled."

"A *horse* doctor!" Landers grimaced. "For a tooth?"

"Out here you take help wherever you can find it," Colt said. "Slim's in a lot of pain."

Stuart Landers shook his head. "Well, will this Mr. Jessup be willing to come along?"

Colt rose, beginning to feel restless within the four walls. "I can't answer that until you tell me what this is all about, Mr. Landers. I haven't even said I'd do it myself for sure, but even without Slim, I can assure you I can do as good a job as anybody. I have a couple of letters of recommendation from people whose wagon trains I've helped guide west. I hang on to them to help me get new jobs. You want to see them?"

Landers rose. "Well, yes, I suppose I should." He studied Colt more closely as the young man took the letters from a small leather bag that was tied to his belt. He took note of the weapons Colt wore, intuition telling him this young man did indeed know what he was about. Colt handed him the letters, which he had obviously been carrying around for a while. They were worn from being folded and unfolded often, but the writing was still legible.

Colt walked to a window while Landers read the letters. He looked out at the dusty, rutted street in front of the house, again wondering how Mrs. Webster kept the place so clean. It felt strange to be inside a normal home now, even though he had been brought up this way. It had been many years since he had lived in a real house. Since losing his parents, the whole West had become his home, the sky his ceiling, the earth his floor. He had grown to like it that way. Slim said it was the Indian in him.

"Well, these people praise you highly, Mr. Travis," Landers said. He walked over and handed the letters to Colt. "I am impressed and delighted. Time is getting short, and I wasn't sure I would find the right man. You're pretty young, but better qualified than anyone else I've interviewed. It would be good if your partner would accompany you. An extra man never hurts, but as far as protection goes, my father will be bringing along his own little army. What we need is someone who knows the way, at least as far as Fort Laramie; someone who can communicate with the Indians and keep us out of trouble; and a man who knows a little about surveying, well, that's all the better. We want the best, Mr. Travis, since my little sister is coming along." Landers reached into a vest pocket, taking out a little gold case and opening it. "Would you like a smoke, Mr. Travis?"

Colt eyed the five thin cigars inside the case. He nodded, taking one. "Never saw cigars this small before," he commented.

"Oh, they're quite pleasant and very expensive."

Landers closed the case and walked back to sit down. Colt put the thin smoke to his lips and wet the end of it. "I don't understand why your sister has to come along at all," he said then. "The land west of here is no fitting place for a young, pampered girl who's used to a fine house and all the comforts." He moved to the fireplace and took a large flint match from a pewter cup, striking it and lighting the cigar. He puffed on it until the end glowed good and red.

"You don't know Sunny, or my father," Landers answered, smiling almost sadly. "Sunny's got spirit. She'll try anything. And she's the apple of my father's eye. He named her Sunny because he says she brought a new ray of sunshine into his life when she was born. He doesn't go anyplace without her, and she wouldn't let him if he tried." Colt sensed a tiny hint of jealousy in the words, but it vanished in the next sentence. "Sunny's name truly fits her," Landers added, looking away from Colt and out a nearby window. "She has hair as yellow as the sun, eyes as blue as the sky, and a smile that makes it very hard not to love her, at least for me anyway. My older brother, well, I suppose he loves her like any other brother loves a sister, at least a half sister; but he's afraid my father will give her a little too much of the family fortune. Still—"

The man shifted in his chair and looked suddenly embarrassed. "Excuse me, Mr. Travis. I didn't mean to go on like that about personal family matters that are of no interest to you. I never answered your original question—what this job involves." He leaned back, putting his right foot up on the opposite knee. "It's about a railroad, Mr. Travis, a transcontinental railroad—one that will link Chicago with California."

Colt's eyebrows arched, and he could not help grinning. He took another puff on the cigar then, thinking what good tobacco it was. "A railroad clear across the country?" He could not suppress a snicker at the ridiculous idea.

"Go ahead and laugh, Mr. Travis," Landers told him. "You wouldn't be the first man to scoff at the idea. Even I am no exception."

Colt shook his head and took the cigar from his mouth. "To each man his own dream, I guess." He walked back over to the chair but remained standing. "Your *father* intends to build this railroad?"

"He and several other enterprising men who don't know what else to do with their millions. I am perfectly aware there are plenty who think he's crazy, my older brother included. He won't have anything to do with any of this. Fact is, he thinks my father's foolish dreams are going to bankrupt us." The man rubbed at his neck. "Much as I tend to agree he's a little crazy, I personally don't believe my father would let the family business go under because of his dreams. He and his own father and grandfather worked too hard to build what they have, Mr. Travis. They come from rugged stock. My father and grandfather helped settle Chicago when it was just a trading post—Fort Dearborn. They survived the Pottawatomie massacre of 1812, built a trading and shipping empire that's worth millions today. Started out in the fur trade. We own ships that travel the Great Lakes, and we own a good share of stock in the railroads that come into Chicago. More railroads lead into Chicago now than any other city. I'll bet you didn't know that."

"I don't know a whole lot about anyplace east of here," Colt answered, sitting down again and taking another puff on the cigar. "And call me Colt. *Mr. Travis* is too formal for me." He met Stuart's eyes. "Actually, I don't even know much about railroads. Only saw a train once in my life myself, when I went through Iowa and met some people who'd taken a train out of Chicago as far west as it went, then went on with wagons. I have to say, I was pretty impressed with that big locomotive, but I'll tell you, laying rails clear across the plains and over two mountain ranges sounds impossible to me. Hell, it's hard enough to get mules and wagons over those mountains; but then I guess that's not my problem. All I want to know is what my role is in all of this."

Landers pulled at a dark, neatly trimmed mustache. "My father is on his way to Omaha. He'll be here in a few days. He wants an experienced scout who can give him a rough idea of what would be the best route to take in building a railroad west. He just wants to get a feel of the land, to see if it really could be done. He'll need to get a lot of financial backing for this, and before he can get others involved and talk them into investing, he wants to be sure he knows exactly what he's talking about." The man rose and began pacing. "Oh, there has been talk around Washington about such a railroad for a long time now, Mr.—I

mean, Colt. There have even been one or two surveys
done." He ran a hand through his thinning hair. "My
father is convinced that Congress will eventually pass
a bill supporting such a railroad. He wants to get in
on the ground floor—sees the possibilities. If it is a
success, he'll be an even richer man. Of course, if it
fails, he'll be a much poorer one. At any rate, he asked
me to come out here and set things up, find a good
scout." He glanced at Colt and smiled nervously, a
hint of fear in his eyes. "I would have hated to face
him and tell him that after all this time I hadn't come
up with anyone. When my father barks, people jump,
except for my older brother, Vince. They never have
gotten along very well. But my father really is a good
man, Colt. He's just a man who worked hard all his
life and is used to ordering people around, except for
Sunny. She's got him wrapped right around her little
finger, but she doesn't seem to take advantage of it."

Colt felt a little awkward hearing the added personal
comments the man offered, wondering why he was
telling him these things about their private family life.
It mattered little to him, except that this sister the man
kept mentioning did not sound like the type who
should be trekking through dangerous country.

Landers walked closer to Colt, putting his hands in
his vest pockets. "Will you take the job? There will be a
few rules because of Sunny's presence, but I don't think
they will be things you can't live with. I have a feeling
you know how to behave around proper ladies. My
father will pay five hundred dollars, and if something
happens to your horse, he'll replace it. Whatever
supplies you say are needed, he'll provide them."

Colt let out a light whistle. "Five hundred dollars?"

"To each of you, if your partner comes along."

Colt set the cigar in an ashtray and rose, standing a good four inches taller than Landers. "That's a lot of money. A man would be a fool to turn it down, but in a case like this, once we're out there, what I say goes. I can't be spending half my time arguing with your father. I don't care how many millions he's worth, he's got to listen to me once we're out there on the trail."

"My father has great respect for your kind, Colt. Our business was built on traders and trappers. My father did a little wilderness trapping of his own when he was younger. He understands these things. He'll listen to you, especially if it means Sunny's safety."

Colt nodded. "I'll go talk to my friend and come back this evening with an answer."

"Fine." Landers put out his hand again, and Colt took it, trying to envision the "little sister" called Sunny. How little was little? And just how spoiled was she? He had a feeling it was the daughter who could end up being the real headache on this trip, but for five hundred dollars, he could put up with her smart-aleck talk and snooty ways. The girl would probably spend most of her time complaining about the discomforts of life on the trail and whining to go back home, but that was her problem. Besides, he'd spend most of his time scouting well ahead of the actual wagon train. He wouldn't have to listen to most of it.

Colt said his good-byes and donned his leather hat, walking on long legs to the front door, eyeing the lace curtains at the window and vaguely remembering his mother. He had been only five when she died, but he still remembered how lost and lonely he had felt. Every once in a while some little thing would remind him of her. He stepped out into the sunshine then, breathing deeply of the fresh spring air, glad to be out of the stuffy parlor.

&

"Here it comes." Slim Jessup craned his neck to see, then winced with pain, touching his swollen jaw. He had already decided that if he ever had tooth trouble again, he would just shoot himself before he would go through having one pulled. He took a flask of whiskey from inside his buckskin shirt and uncorked it, taking another swallow as he watched the approaching coach and the wagon train behind it.

"Watch that stuff," Colt warned. "We aren't supposed to drink, remember?"

Slim, a nickname applied because his physique was quite the opposite, wiped his lips. "I'm not so sure I'm going to like this job," he told Colt. "This is what I get for lettin' you do the choosin'."

"You find me another wagon train that will pay us five hundred dollars each, and we'll forget about this one."

Both men stood waiting on the porch of Mrs. Webster's boardinghouse. Stuart Landers had ridden out to greet his father in the distance, and the whole train stopped momentarily while a tall, husky man got out of a grand but very dirty coach. Colt and Slim watched the men talk. "That must be the old man," Slim grumbled. "A bastard to work for, I'll bet. And look at all them men with him, all them wagons. Hell, you'd think it was the president of the United States in that coach."

"Or the queen of England," Colt commented. He glanced at Slim, wanting to laugh at the sight of the man in new buckskin pants and shirt, wearing a new hat, his face clean-shaven and his hair cut and combed. Slim Jessup was not a man prone to spruce up for anyone, and that was part of what Colt loved about him—he had done all this for him, respecting his decision to take this job. Slim had been like a father to Colt for years, ever since Colt saved his life.

Colt was only fourteen at the time. Having set out on his own after his father's death, Colt had come upon Slim's camp in the foothills of the Rockies. Slim invited Colt to share his coffee, and before their first conversation was ended, Colt had shot a rattler that had slithered up behind Slim and looked ready to strike. From then on the friendship deepened, and Colt began traveling with the seasoned scout, learning how to track, how to handle Indians, how to find food where it seemed none could be found. Colt had come to be as skilled as his mentor. The two men shared a mutual respect for each other and had traveled together now for six years.

"Somethin' tells me we'll dearly earn the five hundred, and wish we had asked for more," Slim commented.

"Relax. Lord knows we'll probably eat good. Stuart Landers has arranged for one hell of a supply of bacon and dried beef, potatoes, you name it. And he says two men are coming along who will cook for everybody. At least you won't have to eat cold beans out of a can, and we won't have to drink that rot-gut brew you call coffee."

"I make the best damn coffee this side of the Mississippi, and you know it."

"If that's true, I'd hate to taste the rest." Colt moved off the porch as the wagon train began moving again. "Jesus," he muttered. "Would you look at that coach? I've never seen anything like it."

"Special made for Her Royal Highness, I expect," Slim answered. He straightened, trying to pull in his big belly. He removed his hat and smoothed back his graying hair, then scratched at his chest. "All this pretty-smellin' junk you made me put on over at the bathhouse has got me itchin'," he complained. "I need a little dirt and sweat under this shirt."

Colt did not seem to be listening. Slim watched him push his own hat back, exposing a few dark waves that framed his finely chiseled face. Colt had his mother's dark skin and hair, his father's height, and hazel eyes. The young man's handsome looks had cost him run-ins a time or two over young white girls on wagon trains, girls who were quite taken with Colt in spite of his efforts to avoid them. Colt was fully aware that the girls' fathers considered a half-breed not good enough for their "chaste" young daughters.

Colt had learned the pleasures of being a man at the tender age of fifteen, in the arms of a whore in Portland whom Slim had paid to entertain Colt as a birthday present. Slim grinned at the memory. He supposed he loved Colt; felt almost like a father to him. Colt was as close to family as Slim figured he would ever get. It pained him to know that most of his life Colt had wrestled with not knowing to which world he belonged, white or Indian. Slim had tried to teach the young man that he was simply a man, his own man, worthy of being accepted with respect by both races.

The coach drew up beside them then, interrupting Slim's thoughts. Colt stepped back a little. Men shouted at the mules that pulled the following three wagons, and dust rose skyward. Besides the eight men who drove and rode shotgun on the coach and wagons, six more rode on individual horses, all sporting rifles and pistols. Some of them rode behind the wagons, driving a small remuda of horses and mules, apparently extras to be used to switch teams on the coach and wagons so that the animals would not be worked too hard.

The man has thought of everything, Colt thought. He glanced back at Slim, who shook his head in wonder.

Stuart Landers trotted his horse up to Colt and dismounted as the coach door opened and a well-dressed graying man stepped out. He looked even bigger now that he was closer, standing as tall as Colt but much heftier, a man who obviously ate well. "Hello!" he bellowed. "So, this is Omaha. Sure isn't much compared to Chicago." He took a quick look around, then reached inside the coach. "Come on out and have a look, honey."

A small, gloved hand took hold of Landers's hand, and in the next moment there appeared a young woman, certainly not the child Colt had expected. She wore a pink cotton dress that fit her slender waist and developing body enticingly. Although the dress had become wrinkled and dusty from the ride, its poor condition did little to detract from the beauty of the young lady who wore it. She stepped down, looking too warm in the long-sleeved dress. A feathered hat topped her golden hair, and when she looked at Colt, he wondered if anyone possessed eyes quite so blue. He could not help staring, especially when the young lady broke into a brilliant and genuinely sweet smile. "Hello," she said, little hint of shyness in her demeanor. "Are you the scout Stuart told us about?" Before he could answer she turned to her father. "Daddy, he doesn't look like those Indians we saw a few miles back."

"Those were full blood. Mr. Travis here is only *half* Indian." The man let go of his daughter and offered his hand to Colt. "You *are* Colt Travis, I take it. You certainly fit my son's description."

"Yes, Father, this is the one," Stuart put in.

Colt quickly looked away from the daughter, whose age and beauty surprised and intrigued him, but whose remark had left him wondering if it was meant as curiosity or an insult. He took Landers's hand. "I'm Colt Travis," he said. "The man up on the porch there is my partner, Slim Jessup."

Landers nodded to Slim. "I'm Bo Landers," he said loudly, "but then, I guess that's obvious by now." The man let go of Colt's hand and stepped back a little, eyeing him more closely. "Awful young, aren't you?"

"Old enough," Colt answered, feeling the daughter staring at him. It was the first time in his life a young lady had made him feel strangely uncomfortable, made him wonder if he looked presentable. "I've done a lot of scouting and can match anyone else you might pick."

"Stuart has already told me all of that. He says you even know a little bit about surveying."

"Well, I never learned it all, sir, but as far as the land to the west, I can tell you where the solid ground is, where it usually floods, where the ground is always too soft—that kind of thing."

"That's all I need. Pardon my daughter's remark about your Indian looks. It's just curiosity. Makes no difference to me. I've called many an Indian friend in my day. If a man is honest and hardworking and good at what he does, makes no difference to me what runs in his blood."

Slim eyed the conversation closely, grinning to himself. *Yeah*, he thought, *unless that hardworking half Indian man takes an interest in your daughter. What kind of a difference would it make then, Mr. Bo Landers?*

Landers thundered every word, unlike his quieter son. The skin of his face was a ruddy red, and when he removed his silk hat to apply a handkerchief to his sweating brow, the remaining hairs on his balding head were pure white. He replaced his hat and turned to his daughter, putting an arm around her. "This is Sunny, Mr. Travis. She's fifteen. Whatever else we do on this trip, the one thing to remember is that she is to be protected at all costs."

Colt glanced at Sunny, removing his hat. "Miss Landers," he said, nodding his head slightly. She smiled again, a bright, winning smile. Colt thought how her brother's description truly did fit her.

"We're glad to have you guiding us, Mr. Travis," she told him. "I'm so excited about the trip. It's going to be such fun."

Colt suppressed an urge to roll his eyes in exasperation. *Fun?* He looked back at her father. "I have to say, it might be better for your daughter if you left her here in Omaha or sent her back to Chicago, Mr. Landers."

"Oh, no." Sunny spoke up, taking her father's arm. "Wherever Daddy goes, I go. It's always been that way. I'll be just fine, Mr. Travis."

Landers patted her hand. "My daughter goes everywhere with me, Mr. Travis. We have plenty of well-armed men and plenty of supplies. Sunny's personal tutor is also with us, Miss Gloria Putnam. She's still in the coach, not feeling too well, I'm afraid, but she's getting used to the travel. Miss Putnam will help Sunny bathe and dress and do her hair, as well as continue her lessons. I keep my daughter well schooled, Mr. Travis. Sunny will be taking over a good share of my business someday, and by the time she does, she'll be as adept at doing accounting and figures as any man." The man beamed with pride. "Don't you worry about my Sunny. She's looking forward to the adventure. She's got more strength and spunk than you think, and she comes from rugged stock, brave and uncomplaining, loyal to the death." The man scowled then. "Which is more than I can say for my oldest son."

"Oh, Daddy, Vince will come around one day." Sunny tried to soothe him. "He'll see how right you are in this."

Colt allowed himself to look her over once more. *Rugged stock,* he questioned silently. *And she comes out here with her nanny, dressed like she's going to a dance.*

"I do hope the Indians farther west have tamed down some," Stuart Landers put in.

"We shouldn't have too much trouble if we stick to the main trail," Colt answered. "It would be wise to take along plenty of things to trade, like ribbons and tobacco and such."

"Right," Bo Landers agreed. "See to it, Stuart."

"Yes, sir. We'll have all the supplies we need. I already have a lot of things waiting in storage."

Colt took a quick inventory of the wagons and coach, deliberately not allowing himself to look at Sunny again. He had been prepared for a whining little child, but Sunny Landers was certainly no child, nor did she seem prone to complaining. More than that, she was beautiful.

He immediately chastised himself for the thought. Someone like Sunny Landers was as dangerous and wrong for him as a rattlesnake. Besides that, once they got going and she showed her feathers, she would probably prove herself to be spoiled to the point of unbearable.

That sweet smile didn't fool him any.

Acknowledgments

Every novel "takes a village" to come to life. In this case, three people provided me with moral and practical support to see this through. Melody Groves, a real-life Arizonian, kept me honest when it came to ranching details, life in the West in 1882, and the use of Spanish. Editor Mary Altman took what I wrote, added her magic, and made the story better. And my agent and friend, Natasha Kern, just keeps finding ways to make my career dreams come true. Thanks, ladies!

About the Author

Award-winning author Anna Schmidt resides in Wisconsin. She delights in creating stories where her characters must wrestle with the challenges of their times. Critics have consistently praised Schmidt for her ability to seamlessly integrate actual events with her fictional characters to produce strong tales of hope and love in the face of seemingly insurmountable obstacles. Visit her at www.booksbyanna.com.